Birth of the Phoenix

BIRTH OF THE PHOENIX

A Novel

Harriett B. Varney Miller

Copyright © 2010 by Harriett B. Varney Miller.

Library of Congress Control Number: 2009911900
ISBN: Hardcover 978-1-4415-9860-8
Softcover 978-1-4415-9859-2

All rights reserved. No part of this book may be reproduced or transmitted in any form or by any means, electronic or mechanical, including photocopying, recording, or by any information storage and retrieval system, without permission in writing from the copyright owner.

This is a work of fiction. Names, characters, places and incidents either are the product of the author's imagination or are used fictitiously, and any resemblance to any actual persons, living or dead, events, or locales is entirely coincidental.

This book was printed in the United States of America.

To order additional copies of this book, contact:
Xlibris Corporation
1-888-795-4274
www.Xlibris.com
Orders@Xlibris.com

69080

I dedicate this book to my beautiful children.

Author's Note

The characters and events in this book are fictional. Some were inspired by actual people and events, and represent real life situations that many people experience. I hope that I realistically portrayed these situations and apologize for any misrepresentations.

If you or someone you know is a victim of abuse, call the National Domestic Violence Hotline for information on where to get help in your area:

1.800.799.SAFE (7233)
1.800.787.3224 (TTY)

Or visit the National Coalition Against Domestic Violence web-page:

HYPERLINK "http://www.ncadv.org" *www.ncadv.org*

I hope this book inspires people to listen to their inner voices and to become empowered to live their lives to the fullest.

Thank you to my family who provide me with the enormous amount of love and support that enables me to achieve my accomplishments, which includes writing this book.

Thank you to the people who have shared their stories with me, and to those who have made recommendations and suggestions which have contributed to this book.

Part I

Death of the Phoenix

Chapter 1

Her name was Beth. It had always seemed like an average name to her. There were eleven other "Beths" in her high school graduating class of one hundred and eighty nine students. If she did her math correctly, that was 5.8 percent of the population. That made her very ordinary. Like her name, her life always seemed average to her. She grew up in a neighborhood in the suburbs where the kids played kickball in the evenings, and walked to McDonald's for lunch on Saturday afternoon. Every Sunday her family went to church, after which they visited her grandparents or had the parish priest over for Sunday dinner. She and her older brother James spent their evenings watching TV and Beth spent her afternoons walking the dog while eating her daily apple. Maybe it was because it was such a stable house that it became the popular meeting ground for the neighborhood kids. Supper was every night at 5:00 P.M. sharp, baths were on Sunday, Wednesday, and Friday. Her father was always there to figure out her homework and read her bedtime stories, and her mother filled the house with the aroma of home-cooked meals. There was never a reason for the child Beth to doubt there would always be someone around to fulfill her needs and desires. It seemed life would take care of her and she just had to be led through it. The simplicity and stability of her childhood never prepared her for the hardships and challenges that adulthood would present her with.

Twenty years later, Beth looked into the green eyes staring out of the mirror at her. On the surface, her life seemed perfect. For the outside world she had created the illusion of a happy, ordinary life and was able to fool everyone with the façade. But she could not fool the eyes that stared out of the mirror. Beth pulled her long auburn hair into a barrette and prepped herself with the courage to face another day.

There was a loud knock at the door and Beth heard Nancy letting herself in. Beth and Nancy had been best friends since they were babies. One of the first pictures in Beth's photo album was of the two of them sitting in a playpen together. They had remained friends over all of these years. Their friendship almost ended a few times due to the unfortunate interference of men. But soon, the boys moved on leaving the two girls to rekindle their friendship despite the violated trust. Luckily this lifelong friendship was able to survive the adolescent quarrels caused by love triangles and was still in existence now that they were adults. There was a time when Beth told Nancy everything, sharing all of her secrets and dreams with this sister of spirit. But now that Beth was married with a baby and life of her own, they had separate lives and Beth only told Nancy the good things.

"Hello! Beth, are you here? I'm ready to go. Where are you?"

"I'll be right there, I'm just in the bathroom," Beth said as she splashed cold water onto her face so Nancy would not be able to tell she had been crying. The towel was thick and soft and felt good on Beth's face. The marble tiles were spotless, and the chrome around the shower door was shining. Jeff would not have it any other way. He insisted the house always be perfect, but no matter how hard Beth tried Jeff was never satisfied. Beth could not read his mind to determine what his definition of perfect was. Beth entered the living room with a fake smile plastered on her face, ready to greet Nancy and the rest of the world with the lie she had created.

"Hi, I'm ready. Let me get Zack out of his crib and we can go."

"Are you okay?" Nancy had a way of seeing through Beth's false smiles even if she pretended to go along with the facade.

"Yeah, I'm fine. Why?" Beth put on a large smile to deceive Nancy. Nancy smiled and nodded her head, but did not say anything. Zack was crying to get out of his crib.

There was no doubt Zack looked just like his father. He had silky white blond hair and pale blue eyes, a round face with long eyelashes and a stocky build. Beth wished he looked more like her. She always assumed that since her child was formed in her body, he would look like her. But Beth had green eyes, thick auburn hair, and a pale, clear freckled complexion. At least Zack had a pale complexion like her, even if he did not get her freckles. They were the features she hated most about herself when she was growing up. It never seemed fair that she had to pile on the sunscreen while her friends drenched themselves in baby oil that allowed them to walk off the beach with dark lustrous tans.

Beth buttoned Zack's denim coat with the sheep-skin collar. The day looked gray and cloudy, so she put his little red hat on him too. He pulled the hat off and threw it on the floor.

"No! No hat!"

Zack stood firm and adamant that the hat would not go back on. Beth picked it up and attempted to rationalize with Zack that it was cold outside and he had to wear the hat. She told him that since he was two now, he had to act like a big boy and wear his hat without complaining.

"No! Daddy says that I don't have to do what you say!"

Beth looked up at Nancy who smiled at her, "Kids. It's amazing what comes out of the mouth of a two-year-old."

"Yeah," Beth picked up Zack and left with Nancy, the hat still on the floor.

Spending the afternoon with Nancy was always fun. Going food-shopping, getting the car inspected, and dropping off library books did not seem like work when there was a friend to do it with.

The best part of the day was stopping at the little café down town that had a play area to keep Zack occupied. Beth ordered a piece of the vegetable quiche, a chocolate chip cookie, and a mug of Dutch Chocolate Coffee with extra sugar and cream. Beth loved chocolate since it was the one thing that truly made her feel in control. When she ate chocolate no one could tarnish the satisfaction she felt as it seeped into her taste buds, arousing immense satisfaction. The smell of the coffee and the feel of the steam on her face temporarily took her away from the spot she was sitting in. The steam formed little droplets on her eyelashes and the mist cleared her passageways letting the air flow easily into her lungs. Her eyes were closed and for a brief moment everything in the real world went away as she escaped into the aroma of her Dutch Chocolate Coffee. She forgot that Zack was smashing the teddy bear with a hammer, that she did not know what she was going to cook for supper, or that Jeff would later call her a "fat bitch" when the calories from the chocolate went to her thighs.

"Are you listening to me?"

Nancy was looking at Beth with a puzzled look on her face.

"Huh?" Beth was pulled back to reality.

"You didn't hear a word I said, did you?"

"I'm sorry, what were you saying?"

"I was talking about when we were kids and how I used to be so afraid when my father called me in. I knew I would get a swat on my butt."

Nancy laughed.

"Your father hit you? I never knew that."

Suddenly a portion of her childhood was violated as she found out that her best friend kept a secret from her for all of these years. Beth's parents never hit her, and Beth in turn never hit Zack. She did not believe that children should be hit. Beth automatically assumed that the practices that were enforced in her home were the same in Nancy's. To find out otherwise was a realization that she was remembering a lie. What else in her childhood was a lie? Where did the truth stop and the white lies and cover-ups start? She felt guilty and hypocritical with the realization that she was also covering up and lying about her own life. She preached to the world that parents should not hit their kids, yet hid the fact that Jeff hit Zack. And her.

"Well, yeah. It's no big deal. All kids deserve a good spanking once in a while. It keeps them in line, maybe you should think about it with Zack."

"No, I don't believe in spanking kids. What's going on with that guy you went out with?"

"Which one?"

"Listen to you, you have so many men that you can't even remember them all!"

"I can't help it if I meet a lot of men working in an attorney's office."

"The one you went to that play with, what's his name?"

"Oh, you mean the police man, Bob? That's way over. We were out one night and some bimbo came over to him and thanked him for getting her out of her 'situation'. She told him she would be able to repay him *real* soon. Like sure, I wonder what her 'situation' was and how she's planning to repay him? You're so lucky that you don't have to worry about dating. Jeff's such a nice guy and is so great to you. Most women would kill to be able to stay home with their baby and do nothing all day. You have no idea how hard it is being single."

"Yeah, I have a good life."

Beth thought about her life. On the surface she had everything that people expected she would want. She lived in a big house in a quaint neighborhood where the houses were far enough apart so that people could not see or hear what was going on in each other's houses. In her case, that meant the yelling, beating, crying, and silence. Her husband had a good job, which allowed her to stay at home with her baby, keeping her isolated. The appearance was what she always thought she wanted out of life, so it was easy to see why Nancy was envious. If she only knew. Nancy insisted on paying the bill. Perhaps her way of proving that her life was as good as Beth's? Beth wished the rivalry that formed between them in high school was not still present, keeping Beth from confiding in Nancy that her life actually sucked.

Beth wished that the day would go by a little slower, that the lines in the grocery store were a little longer, that the traffic was a little thicker, that the coffee cup would never become empty and the cookie would never disappear. But no day lasts forever, and soon the end of the day came and Nancy was dropping Beth off. Beth could feel her heart racing faster as they approached her house, and pounding harder when she saw Jeff's car in the driveway. Nancy pulled her car up behind Jeff's.

"You get Zack, I'll help you bring in the groceries."

"Yeah, okay"

Beth got out of the car and opened the back door to get Zack, who was sound asleep. This meant he would not go to bed tonight. Jeff would be pissed.

What was she going to make for supper? Beth picked up Zack and carried him into the house. He was getting heavy.

Jeff was standing in the kitchen doorway when Beth entered the house, his fists clenched, legs apart and a mean look on his face with anger jetting out from his eyes. Beth could feel it. It was like his eyes had little invisible lasers extruding out from them and slicing into Beth's heart. Nobody else could see them but her, and no one would believe her since it was all invisible. Did it really exist or was it just her imagination and was she crazy like Jeff said? Beth's heart pounded harder while being sliced up by the razors. They caused her breath to stop at intervals, but she forced it to continue in and out, in and out. She stood staring at him. Afraid to move, she knew she was late and what came next. To her surprise, the razors moved off her, vanishing. The face softened, the fists unclenched. He moved forward, smiling.

"Oh, hi Nancy! What are you doing carrying in all those groceries? Let me help you."

Jeff passed by Beth to help Nancy. He never helped her bring in groceries, but she did not care since she was saved. Beth put Zack down on the couch and went outside to get more groceries.

Nancy was gone and the groceries had to be put away. Beth unpacked the bags, segregating some food for supper. Something quick, a package of kielbasa, a box of rice pilaf, a can of corn. A well-balanced meal with three of the food groups. Milk would complete the fourth. She got out a large frying pan for the kielbasa, a medium pot for the rice pilaf, and a small pot for the corn. It would all be done at the same time; everything would be just right. The smells of the food filled the kitchen as Beth continued putting away the groceries. That done, she set the table. Zack was watching *Barney* on TV as Jeff came into the kitchen. His eyes were glazed, stoned.

"So, did you have fun with Nancy today?"

"Yeah."

"She's looking pretty hot. Those jeans she was wearing show off her tight little ass. Why don't you dress like that? Well, I guess it wouldn't do you any good since you don't have an ass like that!"

Jeff started laughing as he pressed up against Beth, squeezing her ass. Beth pushed him away, trying to get the forks. It never occurred to her to be jealous of Nancy or the other women Jeff lusted over, as it put him in a good mood and diverted his attention away from her.

"What's the matter? Let's do a little quickie right here before supper. Come on, you're such a goodie-goodie. Come on, give it to me."

Jeff grabbed her and tried to kiss her. Beth pulled her head away, looking through the kitchen door into the living room where she could see the back of Zack's head sitting in front of *Barney*. If he turned around to see what the noise was, he would see them. The last thing that Beth wanted was for Zack to be traumatized by the image of his parents having sex in the kitchen with supper cooking.

"Don't! Zack's there! He can see us!"

"He can't see, he's watching TV. I'm really horny. *Come on!*"

Jeff pulled Beth close to him and kissed her hard, biting her. Beth could taste the salt of her blood in her mouth and the pain of his fingers digging into her arm. She tried to push him away, but he turned her around, pinning her against the counter and forced himself into her. The edge of the counter dug into her stomach as her face was pushed onto its cold smooth surface. She tried to support herself so it would not hurt as much while she was being pounded into over and over again from behind. She tried to find something to hold on to, but there was nothing but the smooth, hard, cold counter top sliding under her fingers. He was finally done and walked away, leaving Beth to slide down onto the cold, clean floor. The water in the kielbasa pan boiled dry and was burning. The TV was singing, "I love you, you love me. We're a happy family . . ."

Beth got up off the floor and buttoned her jeans. She rearranged the plates on the table, straightening out the napkins. She cut the kielbasa into neat, even slices and divided them onto the plates—four pieces for Jeff, three for her, and one for Zack. The rice and corn followed, then she called that dinner was ready. Zack came running into the kitchen and jumped into his high chair that had the tray removed.

"Yucky, I don't want to eat this!"

"Zack, stop it. You eat what Mommy cooks for you. This is a yummy supper."

Beth sat in her seat and cut her kielbasa. Zack sat firm with his little arms crossed, looking at his plate. When Jeff entered the room, the tension was too much for Beth and she could not eat her food. Jeff looked at his plate in disgust.

"What's this shit? You call this supper? This is a poor excuse for supper!"

Beth did not respond. She had given up and could not defend the well-balanced dinner she had created. The well balanced meal that Jeff insisted she provided on a daily basis in order to be a good mother and wife. She tried not to think. She tried to just imagine white—a color that had nothing. She tried to think of nothingness. Zack's little face lit up as he saw an opportunity to use his father's disgust to his advantage.

"This is yucky Daddy. I don't want to eat it."

"No Zack, you don't have to eat this shit. Mommy doesn't know how to cook a good supper for her little boy. Mommy's a bad mother, but you're a good boy. You can get something else to eat."

Zack jumped out of his seat, smiled smugly at Beth, and ran from the room. Beth sat in silence while Jeff ate. When he was done, he left the house. She hoped he would be home late, giving her some peace from his constant criticism and abuse. She never questioned where he was when he was out so late since it was a relief to be left alone. Beth scraped the kielbasa, rice, and corn off the plates and into the trash.

Once Zack was in bed and Beth spent two hours cleaning the already spotless house, she went to bed. However, the sleep did not feel like sleep at all as her body was stiff, tense, and tight. It was hard to breathe, her breaths were short and she was unable to get enough air into her lungs. Although her body was in a sleep-state, it was not restful. Her mind was not dreaming or thinking, everything was blank and white. Numb.

The non-sleep got interrupted by a drunken Jeff lifting up her pajama top and biting her nipples. Beth was surprised at first, then startled and confused. When she realized what was happening, any comfort that existed in the non-sleep-state was quickly replaced with repulsion. Her body immediately stiffened as she let herself be bitten, pinched, and eventually used as a tool for Jeff's satisfaction. He collapsed on top of her, she lay under him feeling his sweaty body rise up and down as he breathed. The smell of alcohol and tobacco seeped out of his pours, mixed with his sweat. Beth wanted to push him off, but was afraid to wake him. It was better with him asleep, even if it meant enduring his weight on top of her. She lay awake, her wide eyes staring at the white ceiling that was now gray.

"You fucken' lazy bitch! Why the hell do you fucken' stay in bed all day while I'm out earning money to support you!"

Jeff pulled all of the blankets off Beth so that the cold jolted her body before his kick.

"No wonder why we live in such a dump! You're such a fat, fucken' lazy bitch! You just lay around doing nothing all day! The house is disgusting and filthy! Get your fat lazy ass out of bed and make me some fucken' breakfast!"

Beth rolled off the bed, just missing Jeff's fist coming down upon her. To dodge his blows was a normal part of her life. She silently willed him to stop screaming so that he would not wake Zack. She grabbed a sweatshirt and quickly left the room. She felt like gravity was pulling her to the ground, making it almost impossible to lift her feet and walk to the kitchen. She shuffled slowly down the hall, put toast in the toaster, and melted a slab of butter for the eggs. Zack was crying to get up, Jeff's screaming woke him.

When Beth got back into the kitchen with Zack, the butter in the pan was brown and smoking. Zack crinkled up his little nose.

"Uh, Oh Mommy. Look what you did now. Daddy's going to be really mad. Why can't you cook good so Daddy doesn't have to be mad at you?"

Beth looked down at her little boy and knew these were Jeff's words coming out of this little mouth. She put him down in his seat. He was right, Jeff was going to be bullshit. She quickly poured cold water into the pan, which caused a thick gust of smoke to fill the room.

"Jesus Christ! What the hell are you doing in here? Trying to burn down the house? Maybe I should burn you to show you what it's like! Maybe that will teach you a lesson to be careful with fire!"

Jeff stomped across the kitchen towards Beth, a lit cigarette in his mouth. Beth backed away until she was in the corner, up against the wall and fridge.

"Hold out your arm." Jeff was holding up the lit cigarette. Beth crossed her arms around her body, hugging herself tightly with her hands inside of the sweatshirt sleeves, holding them closed. No sound came from her, but she shook her head vigorously back and forth "no" as her long auburn hair flew around her face. The anger on Jeff's face faded into a sinister smile, and he laughed. His voice dropped to a whisper so that Zack could not hear him.

"Okay, if you won't hold out your arm for me, then maybe you'll do it for Zack. You have two options. Either you let Zack burn you, or I burn Zack. Who's it going to be? You or Zack?"

Based on past experiences, Beth knew Jeff would do it. The thought of Jeff's cigarette burning into Zack's tender baby flesh made her cringe more than the fear of it burning into her own. Jeff smiled triumphantly as Beth slowly unfolded her arms and pushed up the sleeve of the sweatshirt. Her hands were shaking so hard it was difficult to get the sleeve up very far. Jeff was beaming, laughing quietly under his breath.

"Hey Zacky! Daddy has something for you to do for him. I want you to show Mommy what happens to bad Mommies who set the kitchen on fire. Come here Zacky . . . that's it. Here, take Daddy's cigarette."

Zack took the cigarette from Jeff as he was told. He looked up at Beth with his big baby eyes, not knowing what he should do. Beth gently nodded "yes" to him, knowing it would be worse if he did not do what Jeff wanted.

"Here Zack, let me show you how to do it so that you can be just like Daddy."

Jeff put his large hand firmly over Zack's little hand, and lifted it up to Beth's arm. Zack tried to pull his hand back, but Jeff squeezed his hand and pushed the cigarette into the top of Beth's forearm. Slowly at first, then harder until the cigarette burnt out. The smell of singed flesh mixed with that of burning butter. Jeff laughed. Zack cried. Beth did not make a sound.

"You're such a baby. I can't believe your arm actually bled from a harmless cigarette. I guess I'll have to get something to eat on my way to work." Jeff was laughing as he left the house.

Beth lay in her bed hugging Zack as he cried. Beth stroked his silky blond hair while his little body quivered with sobs. She kissed his baby eyes, cheeks, ears, and hands. She said nothing out loud, but promised him silently that she would some how figure out a way to escape and prevent him from growing up to be like his Daddy.

The pain in Beth's arm was getting worse, it was a symbol of the sacrifices mothers make to keep their children safe. Beth knew she had to endure whatever Jeff did to her to keep him from going after Zack. Beth did not know how to leave when to the rest of the world Jeff was a perfect father and husband. Jeff continually told Beth this was the way things were supposed to be, and this was how everyone was. Nancy had kept the fact that she was hit from her, she was keeping it from everyone else. What if this did happen everywhere, only no one talked about it? If this was the case, then it would not matter if she told anyone. They would think she was being ungrateful to Jeff after all he did for her, and his "moods" were just something she should accept. Jeff always told her that she was ungrateful, that any other woman would love to be married to him, and how lucky she was. What if she tried to leave him only to discover people thought she was just crazy, like Jeff said. He had a successful career, while she did not even have a job. He did everything perfect, she was nothing. What if she left and lost everything, and Zack was sent to live with Jeff since he was the responsible, sane one. Regardless, Zack would at least have to spend half of the time with Jeff if they split up. What would happen to Zack when he had to spend time alone with Jeff? Who would protect him from Jeff? Who would let their arm get burnt for him? At least now Beth was there to take the pain, the beatings, and the hate for Zack. Beth held Zack closer and closed her eyes. She was so cold. She wanted to get up and get another blanket, but she did not move. The burnt pan was still in the sink. Beth tried not to think.

Chapter 2

Time went by and as always, Jeff's mood shifted and he was nice to her again. He acted like the perfect husband he portrayed to everyone else. He brought her flowers, laughed and played with Zack. Zack was so happy when Jeff was like this. He beamed excitedly and told Beth as if it was a great secret, "Look Mommy, Daddy turned nice. Won't you play with him?"

Beth lay in bed thinking about the fact that Jeff reinforced Zack's hopes by singing to Beth and trying to dance with her while she cooked supper. But Beth felt nothing. Her face remained emotionless, her mind blank. She waited for the unknown trigger that would send him back into his old self. Maybe his shoe did not go on right, someone pulled out in front of him on his way home from work, or she did not get to the phone in time and the person hung up. Whatever the reason, Beth would not be prepared. She never was. She was always caught off guard. So she lay in bed pretending to be asleep, and tried not to think. Only she felt so sick, she hoped she could hold off from throwing up until after Jeff left. She knew this feeling and hoped she was wrong.

Although Jeff made a good living, Beth never had any money for herself. He provided her with what she needed, but every penny had to be accounted for. Jeff paid the bills and took care of any accounts. Everything was in his name except for a joint credit card and checking account from which Beth had a debit card. Beth used that account to pay for groceries, gas, and other necessities. Jeff kept a close eye on any money that came out of that account so Beth never had any cash. Beth knew she needed money in order to save Zack from what seemed like an inevitable destiny of growing up like Jeff. The idea of Beth getting a job was off limits as Jeff insisted he wanted her home with Zack and taking care of the house. Beth knew she had to build up a savings, so some time ago she started doing things like getting $20 cash back every time she got groceries. Luckily Jeff did not ask for the itemized receipts from the grocery store. She kept an envelope with the money in it in the pocket of a pair of jeans that she never wore. She folded the pants so that the pocket was on the inside, and placed the jeans on the bottom of her fullest drawer.

Beth accumulated a lot of cash on the days she spent with Nancy. Nancy always went to the self-serve gas pumps because they were cheaper. Beth offered to go in and pay while Nancy pumped the gas. Nancy graciously gave Beth $20 to pay. The more gas Nancy needed, the better it was for Beth. Beth put the gas on her credit card, broke the $20, and gave Nancy her change. Beth got to hide away $18, and Jeff saw it as gas on the credit card statement. Going out to lunch would add even more to this amount. When Nancy treated, Beth took money out of the ATM and give the receipt to Jeff with "lunch with Nancy" written on it. Other times when the bill came, Beth told Nancy she did not have any cash and would insist on putting the bill on her credit card, in which case Nancy gave her cash for her own lunch. Another $10-$20 to put in the jeans pocket at the bottom of the drawer. When Jeff saw the statement, Beth told him she brought Zack and Nancy out to lunch. Zack had a little plastic cup with the restaurant logo as proof.

Occasionally, the playgroup that Beth and Zack belonged to went to "Chunky Cheese." Beth took money out of the ATM machine, bought Zack a slice of pizza and a small soda, and ate whatever he did not. Zack was too little to play the arcade games, and he preferred climbing through the tunnels and jumping in the balls to riding on the moving toys. Beth played a few of the arcade games to win some tickets to give Zack a plastic "Chunky Cheese Mouse" to bring home as evidence of what the $20 debit at the ATM was from. Fifteen dollars of it made its way into the envelope. As time went on, the envelope was growing fatter, and Beth was able to change the smaller bills into fifties and then hundreds.

Jeff had been acting indifferent towards her lately, which made existence tolerable. She was able to feel somewhat at peace, and to enjoy the time she had with Zack. Even the rude comments and occasional pushes and slaps that came from Jeff did not seem to bother Beth. She found it easy to block out Jeff's screams when she thought of the envelope getting fatter in her jean pocket at the bottom of the dresser draw. She was never completely at peace though, as she knew there was no predicting when Jeff would snap and have one of his "fits." Besides, Beth had more important things to worry about in this period of temporary calm, like the nausea that came every morning and the bleeding that was not coming at all.

Beth tried not to think about the baby that was inside of her as every time she did, it increased her nausea. Instead she thought about how happy she was when she was pregnant with Zack. She used to fill the shiny porcelain tub with hot water and lilac bath beads, then slowly engulf herself until the water came up to her neck, and only the tip of her round belly emerged from the water like an island surrounded by the steaming water of volcanoes. Engulfed in liquid warmth, she used to feel like she was also in the safety and warmth of a mother's womb. She would rub her belly with oil and whisper softly to the baby inside. She told him that she could not wait to meet him, that she would play and sing to him, and together they would discover the meaning of life. At that time, with the orangey glow of the candle sparkling on the water, she was complete and did not want the moment to end. She wished the feeling of having her baby safe inside of her, which was as close as they would ever be, would never go away. She knew that some day this child would be on his own, and she would not be able to protect him. She knew they would never be as close as they were now, as one person. She felt a spiral of generations before her, engulfed in the warmth of mother's wombs.

That baby who had been safe inside of Beth's womb was now two years old and already Beth could not keep him from continuing the cycle of anger and violence that was passed down through the generations of Jeff's family. Now there was a new baby inside of her, currently safe, but Beth knew it was a matter of time before this child would also be part of a life full of fear. This child inside of her, trusting of her maternal protection, would eventually have its faith violated. All hopes of a loving life with the expectations of innocence, gone. This child would never know the temporary joy that is experienced in childhood when one believes that all is good, and that one's parents are like kings and queens who will raise you in your palace safe from harm. This child would never feel the security of knowing that no matter how much hate, fear, and problems there were outside, everything would be okay once you got home because it was safe there. This child would never know a home full of love with the warmth of homemade chicken soup. This child would never experience the sense of pity at witnessing another child being yelled at or slapped in public, or the sense of joy and pride of knowing that your parent would never do a thing like that. This child would never experience the shame of being yelled at or slapped in public. This child would never know the fear of lying awake at night listening to its father beat its mother, and hoping he would not kill her. This child would never have to choose between burning its mother or being burnt itself. This child would never feel its chest tighten up as its father clenched his fists while screaming, and then released his anger on this child. This child would never experience these things, because this child would never be born.

Beth loved this child inside of her like she had never loved anyone. She loved it because she knew she could save it like she could not save herself and Zack. She loved it because with it there would never be a chance of saving herself and Zack. Beth was saving the baby by not letting it be born. By not being born, the baby was saving Beth and Zack. Beth rubbed her flat belly and thanked the baby for understanding. She promised it that someday, when things were better, it would come back to her.

It was late and Zack was sleeping. Beth did not know or care where Jeff was. When he was out, the house was peaceful. Beth decided to have a bath, just like she used to do when she was pregnant with Zack. She went into the bathroom, turned the water on full blast and poured Zack's Sesame Street bubble bath into the running water. She opened the vanity drawer, found her old package of lilac bath beads, dropped two of the beads into the water and mixed everything together. The smell of the bubble bath and beads, and the swirling steam filled the bathroom. Beth swished the water around, then reached up and turned the faucet to increase the amount of cold water. She went into the dining room to get the tri-wicked candle that she got at Nancy's candle party and when she came back, the water was perfect. She lit the candle, turned off the light, closed the door, and slowly began to undress. She slowly lowered herself deeper and deeper into the water. The water enveloped itself around her, and she could feel it doing its magic as the steamy mist worked its way into her lungs. Her body became completely relaxed and free in this temporary period of bliss. The phone rang suddenly. It startled her for a moment, but then she did not care. She felt so relaxed, and at peace that she did not want to go into the cold to answer it. Whoever it was could call back. She rested her head on the edge of the hard porcelain tub, closed her eyes, and breathed deep in and out, in and out. The phone was still ringing somewhere in another world. In and out, in and out ... The phone finally stopped. In and out, in and out ... Beth focused on the in. She followed the in breath down past her lungs and into her belly. She put her hands onto the spot below her belly to where the mass of cells, which if left alone would mature into a baby, sat. She apologized to the baby for not having chosen a better father and for not providing the safe loving home it deserved. She thanked it for sacrificing its life so she could give Zack the life that every child deserved. She felt the water getting colder, took the stopper out of the drain and turned the hot water on high to let it mix with the cooler water. She swished the water around with her hand and felt the heat surround her body.

"Bang!" The front door slammed open. Stamping feet came down the hall. The bathroom door swung open. Jeff swung his hand against Beth's cheek. She had been so relaxed, that it caught her off guard. Her head hit the shower wall, the water was still running.

"Where the fuck have you been?"

"What do you mean?" Beth whispered. She was mystified. She did not know what he was talking about. Her mind quickly left its mode of relaxation and entered the reality of living with Jeff.

"You know what the hell I mean! Where the fuck were you?"

"I've been here, taking a bath."

"That's bullshit, I called and there was no answer!"

"I didn't want to get out of the tub."

"You just got in the tub, the water's still running. Where the hell were you?" Slap. "With your lover?" Slap. "You trying to wash his smell off you?" Slap. "*Answer me!*"

"No. I was here all the time. The water was getting cold. I was just putting more hot water in." Beth was crouching back as far as she could go, partially covered with water. She noticed that the stopper was still out. "The stopper's out." She held up the stopper. "See? I was here all the time. I was just putting more hot water in."

It was useless, Jeff did not hear what Beth said. His fist came down on her naked body, over and over again. He would teach her. She would pay for being with someone else. He would make it so that no man would ever want to be with her again. She was his and his alone. He would teach her not to lie to him.

The water was still running, but it did not dilute the blood in the tub fast enough to wash it away. Jeff turned off the water and left Beth in the tub. The red water slowly draining away. He was so bullshit. The nerve of her to dare to go out of the house. If he found out who her lover was, he would kill him. He would kill him, then he would kill her. The bitch. It was not bad enough that she went out to meet her lover, but then she had the gumption to lie about it. He considered going back and teaching her another lesson, but he was already wet from her and decided he would rather get a beer. He went outside and got in the car, then noticed there was blood on his clothes. He considered going in to change, but did not want to see *her* again. He started the car and drove down the street to "Jack's Pub." He could hear "American Beauty" blasting as he walked up the sidewalk to the peeling wooden door that opened up to his friends. They would understand him. Maybe they would even know who Beth's lover was, he doubted it though. He walked into the pub and was slightly relieved that the place was almost empty. The loud music was Jack's way of trying to get people in the door. Two other people were sitting at the bar drinking draft beers, Jeff needed something stronger than that.

"Hey Jeff, what happened to you?" Jack put a napkin in front of Jeff. Jeff looked down and realized there was more blood than he thought.

"Ahhh, Shit. My bitch has been out fucken' some asswhole. I taught her though."

"Mmmm. Ya, I guess you did. She won't do that again. What'll it be?" Jack was smiling at Jeff. He had to keep Jeff calm.

"I'll have a JD and coke."

Jeff smiled back, Jeff knew Jack would understand. Jack was such a good guy, always there when you needed someone to talk to. The JD and coke was in front of Jeff before he knew it. God, the service was good here.

"Here ya go, drink up." Jack wiped his hands and smiled at Jeff. "I gotta check on something out back. Can ya keep an eye on the place for me?"

"Ya, sure."

Jack and he had been friends since second grade. Jack always found a way to get alcohol when they were in high school. They would sneak it into the cellar of their buddy Paul's house. The old gang would hang out there: Jack, Paul, Mike, Kevin. God, they had some great times. They used to get so drunk, smoke joints, and play poker. Even back then Jack was making people feel good. Jack really trusted him to have him watch his place like this. Yup, Jack was a good friend.

Jack knew that asking Jeff to keep an eye on the place would keep him from leaving. Even when they were kids Jeff had a temper. He could not count how many times he had to pull Jeff off Paul, Kevin, or one of their other buddies, accusing them of cheating at poker or something stupid like that. Jack hoped that Beth was okay and that he would be able to get help to her before it was too late. If Jeff looked like this, he had no idea what kind of shape Beth was in. He went out the back door to the pay phone on the corner and dialed 911.

"Hello, 911. What's your emergency?"

"Yeah, hi. You better send someone to 18 Maple Street right away. It's a wicked emergency. Break down the door if you have to, but don't say who called you."

"Okay, but who's calling?"

Click. Jack hung up the phone. He knew the pay phone number would show up on the police screen and hoped Jeff would not find out it was him who called.

When the police car pulled up in front of 18 Maple Street, everything looked normal. It was dark and quiet, nothing out of the ordinary. The police officer knocked on the door, there was no response. He rang the bell, knocked a little harder, then opened the storm door to knock on the wooden door, but there was still no response.

"Try opening it, see if it's unlocked."

He did what his partner told him to do. The door was locked, but the doorknob was wet. He held up his hand and saw what looked like blood on it.

"It's locked, but look at this. There's blood on the knob."

"The caller said to break down the door, maybe we should."

They had learned how to break doors down in training, but they never needed to in this quiet community.

"Let's check around the house first to see if there's another way in."

The two policemen walked around the house checking the windows, knocking on them as they went. They could hear a baby crying inside.

"We better get in there."

"Yeah."

They went back to the front door and knocked it in like they had been taught at the police academy. The house was quiet except for the baby crying. They went down the hall towards the crying, opened the door, and saw the baby standing in his crib crying. He was unharmed, so they continued on to find out who else was home. The master bedroom was empty but there was an orange glow coming from the room at the end of the hall. They entered the room expecting to find nothing, instead what they found was worse than they ever imagined. There was a nude woman covered in blood laying in an empty tub. She looked dead.

"Holy Shit! Fuck! Go call for back up. Tell them to get an ambulance here ASAP!"

One police officer ran out to the car to get help, the other one approached Beth and felt her neck for a pulse. She was still alive and her breathing was steady. He was afraid to move her as he did not know what was broken. He went into the bedroom and pulled the quilt off the bed. He brought it into the bathroom and gently laid it over her, wrapping it around her as tenderly as he could. He reached under the quilt and found her hand. He held it and waited. He heard his partner bringing the baby into the living room, the sound of a "Walt Disney" movie filled the silence. When he decided to become a policeman, to dedicate his life to helping to keep the world safe, he never imagined he would have to experience anything like this. He thought he would prevent things like this. What kind of monster could do this to such a beautiful woman? To any woman?

Jeff finished his drink and decided to go back home. Even though Jack knew that Jeff already had too much to drink before he entered the bar, he offered him another drink. Jeff refused. Jack was nervous about letting Jeff leave, but enough time went by that the police should have found Beth.

Driving home, Jeff pulled to the side of the road so an ambulance could pass by him. He slowly followed the ambulance to his street, but stopped the car when he realized the ambulance was joining some police cars at his house. Rage filled inside of him. Beth must have called the police. That bitch! Now he could not even go to his own house. The police would know he had been drinking. The last thing he needed would be to get arrested for driving drunk. He turned his car around and decided to go back to the club he had been at earlier tonight. He remembered Jack's comment about the blood and although Jack was a friend and did not care how he looked, the people at the club may not feel the same way. Jeff's gym bag was in the back seat. He used the shirt he was wearing to wipe himself clean, then put on the tee shirt from the gym bag. He put on his jacket, brushed his hair, and looked at himself in the rearview mirror. He looked fine.

The people at the club did not notice that Jeff had changed, or had even been gone. Jeff hung out at the club for the rest of the night, being one of the last to leave. He stopped at an all night dinner and had the breakfast special with coffee before going home. The front door was wide open, broken. The house was empty. Jeff was exhausted and wanted to get some sleep so he went to his bed, but the quilt was gone. He collapsed under the sheet and fell into a dull, cold sleep.

Beth woke up in a soft bed feeling warm and numb. She was too weak to move, but she felt nothing. She slowly opened her eyes, but they were puffy and did not open all the way. Everything was white, she wondered if this was heaven. She could hear people talking and rushing around and decided that if this was heaven, then she would hear music instead. She closed her eyes and went back to sleep.

She awoke again because someone was sticking a needle in her arm. She opened her eyes to see what was happening. It was a young nurse in a white lab coat, her brown hair was pulled back in a ponytail and she was wearing bright red lipstick. She smiled at Beth.

"It's okay. This will help you to sleep so that you don't feel the pain."

Beth suddenly remembered what had happened and realized where she was. She thought of Zack.

"My baby!"

"He's safe, he was unharmed. Protective services took him to a foster home. Do you know who did this to you?" Beth turned her head away. "Is there anyone we should call? Your husband, maybe? Do you know how we can reach him?" Beth closed her eyes. "It's okay, we can talk later."

Everything was getting foggy, and Beth could feel herself falling asleep. In the background she could hear people talking close by.

"Did she gain consciousness yet?"

"Yes, but only for a minute. She wouldn't talk, she only asked about her baby."

"She's still in shock. Were we able to contact anyone yet?"

"No, one of the neighbors went to the house when the police were there. They said that she has a friend who comes by sometimes, but they weren't sure about family."

"What about her husband?"

"We haven't been able to contact him. He lives with her, but the neighbor said his car had been gone all night. We can try calling the house again."

"Any idea who did this to her?"

"No, she wasn't there that long when the police arrived. There was just that call from a pay phone, anyone could have made it. One more important thing, the x-rays showed that she's about six weeks pregnant."

"When she asked about her baby, I wonder if she meant the one inside of her."

They knew! Beth fought what ever they gave her to sleep and yelled out. "*Noooo!*"

"What, what's the matter?"

The room was quickly filled with the people from the hall. Beth grabbed the lab coat of the nurse with the ponytail.

"Please, please, what ever you do, please don't tell my husband I'm pregnant."

The nurse held Beth's hand.

"Don't worry, we won't tell anyone anything you don't want us to."

Ring ... Ring ... Ring ... Jeff was not sure if the ringing was the phone, or an instrument playing in harmony with the pounding in his head. He realized that it was the phone and slowly reached over to answer it.

"Hello?"

"Hi, I'm looking for Mr. Parker."

"Yeah, this is me."

"This is The Memorial Hospital. Your wife is here, you better get here as soon as you can."

"What about my son?"

"The state has your son, he's safe. It's your wife we're worried about."

"Yeah, okay. I'll be there in a little while."

Jeff looked at the clock, it was 6:45 A.M. He needed at least another ten hours of sleep, but got up to take a shower anyway. He remembered hitting Beth. He remembered her lying limp in the tub like a large porcelain doll. He suddenly felt panic and hoped she was alive. The person on the phone would have told him if she was dead. He suddenly felt an incredible urgency to see her. He went into the bathroom to take a shower and found the quilt lying on the floor. There was still blood in the tub, on the wall, and on the floor. He mashed the quilt down into the hamper, got the "tile cleaner" and scrub brush from under the sink, put the stopper in the tub, turned the faucet on to let some water in the tub, then sprayed and scrubbed every drop of blood off the tiles. He felt an overwhelming urge to wash away any evidence of what he had done. He scrubbed and scrubbed, trying to make everything shiny clean, making it all okay again. Finally satisfied, he took a shower and drove to the hospital.

When Jeff walked into Beth's room, he thought it was the wrong room. He did not recognize this purple, swollen being as his wife. The nurse reassured him that this woman lying in the bed was Beth. He went over to her bed, but was afraid to touch her. He could not believe that he had done this to her. He finally worked up the courage to hold her hand. He reached it up to his mouth and kissed it while he bawled, trying to release all of the remorse that he felt.

Beth opened her eyes and saw Jeff crying next to her bed. She had never seen him cry before, yet she felt nothing. She said nothing. She closed her eyes again and let herself go back to sleep into nothing.

A few days went by, and although Beth was receiving less pain medication, she still felt numb. The physical pain from her injuries did not work its way into her mental being. Physically she was healing, but mentally she was empty. The police, doctors, and nurses all questioned her, but she told them nothing. She kept saying that she wanted to go home to see her baby. There was one woman who came in a lot, her name was Marcia Lowe, and she worked at the local women's center. She kept questioning Beth, but Beth said nothing.

"I know that you're in shock, but it's important to talk about what happened."

"I just want to go home."

"You can go home, probably in the next few days. I'm worried about you going home though. I think it will be dangerous for you and think that you and your son should come to the shelter and stay with us for a while."

"I want to go home."

"Okay. What can you tell me about what happened? Your husband has an alibi for the entire night. The police can't do anything unless you tell us what happened, we want justice for you."

Beth thought of what would happen if she told. It would only infuriate Jeff and he would tell everyone she was crazy. Then, everyone would know that Zack was not safe with Jeff, but they would not give him to her because she was crazy. Zack would be given away, and she would never see him again. She said nothing.

"I know this is hard for you, but I want you to know that I'm here to help. Your husband brought you a bag with some clothes in it. I'm going to put my card in your shoe so that you can call me when you're ready."

Jeff had brought clothes for her? That meant that he went into her dresser! What if he went into her bottom draw? What if he got the pants in the bottom of the draw? What if he felt the lump from the envelope and found her money? All that was for nothing! How would she ever escape?

Marcia saw the look of panic in Beth's face.

"It's okay. You don't have to tell me what happened if you don't want to. I'm here to help. We don't have to do anything. We can just talk if you want to. You don't even have to talk, I can do all the talking. I'm good at that. We can just sit now."

Jeff came to visit Beth often, but he did not talk. He sat in the chair next to her bed and nervously played with his watch. Beth could tell by his nervousness that he did not find the money. Finally the day came for Jeff to bring Beth home. Marcia came to say "good-bye" and when no one was looking, she touched Beth's hand.

"Don't forget what I told you, only you know that my card is in your shoe. Keep it there for when you want to talk."

Beth smiled at her. Jeff was entering the room.

"Ya ready to go?"

Jeff was acting so nice that the nurses were charmed and smiled at him when he came to visit. Marcia did not look at him.

It felt good to be home, everything was clean and neat. Beth was afraid to go into the bathroom. She went into the bedroom instead, and everything was just the way it was supposed to be. Beth could not tell that the quilt had been taken off the bed. She was tempted to lie on the bed and take a nap, but she wanted to see Zack. She opened Zack's door, but it was locked. She proceeded into the kitchen.

"Where's Zack?"

"He's with Nancy. She'll bring him home later."

"I want to see him now."

"We figured it would be better if the house was quiet for you. Nancy said she'll bring him home later."

It was all Beth could do to keep from fainting.

"No, I want him now."

Her voice was on the verge of yelling. She never yelled at Jeff before, she was too afraid of what the result would be. Somehow she was not afraid now, as she had nothing to lose.

"Okay, okay, baby. I'll call Nancy and have her bring him home. It's all right. Just go to bed and lie down, relax. Things are going to be different, they'll be better than before. You'll see. I'll make it up to you."

Jeff put his arm around Beth and gently led her down the hall to the bedroom to lie down. It felt good to be in her own bed, under the soft covers. Jeff was being so nice. Maybe this whole ordeal made him realize how bad he had been and he would change. She could not sleep, so she just closed her eyes and rested, waiting for Zack to come home.

It seemed like forever before Nancy pulled her car up into the driveway.
"*Mommy!*"

Zack squirmed out of Nancy's arms and ran to Beth. Beth hugged him so tight that she could feel him pushing away to loosen her grip.

"Oh, Zack. Mommy missed you sooo much. Did you miss Mommy?"

"Yes, Mommy. I missed you. Why did you leave me? Why were you gone?"

"Oh honey, Mommy didn't leave you. Mommy was hurt and had to get better. I'm better now though, and I'll never leave you again."

Beth hugged Zack, rocking him back and forth. Her cheek rested softly against his fine blond hair. She kissed him, and kissed him. He got impatient and tried to pull away, but Beth would not let him. She just hugged him tighter and would not let him go. She would keep him safe forever. Beth looked up and realized that Nancy was still there.

"Thank you for watching Zack."

"Oh, it was my pleasure. He's a great little guy. We were fine. How about you? How are you feeling?"

"I'm doing good. Much better, thanks."

"What happened to you? Jeff wouldn't tell me anything, he was so worried about you. You look horrible. Do you want to talk about it?"

"No ... no, I'm fine. I don't want to talk."

Beth thought of Jeff listening to them from the kitchen. She wondered what he was telling people. What could he tell people? She wondered what people were thinking. Beth hugged Zack harder and smiled up at Nancy.

"Could you make me a cup of tea?"

"Yeah, I'll go put the water on."

Chapter 3

A week had gone by since Beth came home, and everything seemed back to normal. Although her wounds were healing, her energy was not coming back due to the pregnancy. She knew she had to make plans quick for the baby inside her. It would be too difficult to escape with two children, one a newborn. She rubbed her belly and felt love emerging from it. She thanked the mass of cells inside of her for understanding. Beth knew she was not the first woman who aborted a child to save it from the wrath of its father. There was the fictitious Kay in *The Godfather II* who aborted her child to save it from growing up in a mafia family, surrounded by killing and control of "the family", the child's father being the leader. When the abortion was discovered, Kay was banished from her home and had to sneak to visit her other children.

Beth remembered a newspaper story that her mother read to her when she was a little girl. It was about a queen that lived in a far away county, possibly Africa. The queen was pregnant from a king who was a tyrant and dominated his family and his kingdom with ruthless violence. The queen could not bring herself to bear another daughter who would be tormented, or to bear another son who would be taught to dominate. The queen did the unthinkable—she had an abortion. It was impossible to keep secrets in a kingdom filled with spies, so the king found out about the abortion. His fury was uncontrollable and he vowed to punish all who were responsible for "murdering his child." The doctor was let off easy, he was executed. The queen, however, suffered a much harsher fate. Both of her arms and legs were amputated and then reattached on the opposite sides. Beth was sure that the queen nobly accepted this punishment, willing to sacrifice herself for the sake of protecting her child from being born into hell on earth. Both Kay and the queen suffered horribly for their acts. Was it a woman's duty to sacrifice herself for her children, even if it meant the possibility of spending her afterlife in hell? Beth prayed for some of the queen's strength as she got out the phone book.

Beth looked in the yellow pages, but was afraid to call the number for "family planning." She did not know how to explain her situation to them. She considered asking Nancy for help, but knew that Nancy would not understand as she adored Jeff and would most likely tell him Beth's plans. Finally, she decided to call Marcia; the card was still in her sneaker. Luckily it was a 1-800 number, so it would not show up on her phone bill. She dialed the number three times and hung before she finally gained the courage to let it ring.

Ring, ring . . .

"Hi, this is Marcia."

"Um . . . Hi, this is Beth."

There was a slight silence.

"Beth? Oh my God, I'm so glad you called. I've been worrying about you."

"I need your help."

"Of course. Great, do you want to meet?"

"No, I just want to talk. I need an abortion. I don't have much money, and I don't want Jeff to find out."

"I can bring you to a clinic where they wont ask questions, and they charge on a sliding scale basis. I can help you."

"Thank you. What do I do?"

"We have to make an appointment for a check up first. I can make the appointment and bring you. Is there a time that is better for you?"

"Jeff works everyday, but what about Zack?"

"Is there someone who can watch him?"

"My friend Nancy. But, she'll want to know why and I can't tell her."

"I have a plan. The library is organizing a fundraiser. Why don't you join the committee? We can tell your friend and Jeff that you're going to those meetings and can't take Zack. Sound good?"

"Yeah."

"I'll call you to let you know when the appointment is. If anyone else answers, or if anyone asks who called, just say I'm calling about the library fundraiser. I'll get you some info on the fundraiser, and we can also get you to some of the meetings. It will be good for you to get out of the house and be with people."

"That's great. Thanks. I'll look forward to hearing from you."

Beth hung up the phone; her heart was racing. She felt proud of herself for actually taking the steps needed to protect herself and her children from Jeff. She was terrified to stand up to him in person, but she was amazed at how easy it was to do with out him knowing. Instead of feeling scared inside, she felt joy that she was doing what was right. She was doing what would eventually lead to her independence and safety. There was a surge of excitement, of adventure, in doing this secret planning. She felt like a teenager sneaking out to meet her boyfriend. That sense of knowing she was doing something wrong, but not caring because the end result would outweigh the risks. In her case, the consequences if she got caught would be very significant, even possible death. It was a risk she had to take.

Marcia met Beth at the library, keeping Beth's car in the library parking lot. Nancy had agreed to take care of Zack. It all seemed so easy. Everyone in the clinic waiting room looked nervous. Some women were alone, but most were with their boyfriend or husband. There was a young couple holding hands who looked like they were in high school and scared to death. Beth did not think they were old enough to have sex, maybe they were here to get birth control? Smart kids. Marcia reached out and patted Beth's hand, smiling reassuringly. Beth was used to the routine from when she had Zack. The nurse took a blood and urine sample, and asked a lot of questions to determine exactly how far along she was.

Beth was sent back to the waiting room to wait for a consultation with the "in-house therapist."

When it was finally determined that they could do the abortion, Beth and Marcia peered into the receptionist's window requesting the next available appointment. They scheduled the appointment for the next Thursday at 11:30 A.M. Beth did not think she would be able to handle the anticipation of the next week. The anxiety of wondering if she was doing the right thing, yet eager for the relief of having it be over.

Thursday came sooner than expected. Nancy agreed to watch Zack again since Beth said she had to visit local businesses for donations and it would be impossible to do with Zack. Beth was impressed with herself for being able to lie so easily. Then again, she had lots of practice from all of the times she had covered up for Jeff. Beth waited impatiently for Marcia in the parking lot of the library. She talked silently to the baby she was about to abort, telling him that she loved him and would wait for him to return when the time was right. She told him she was sorry he had to leave her now, but she would think of him everyday. Marcia's red Honda finally pulled into the parking lot and they drove in silence to the clinic. It felt good to have Marcia with her; they did not need to talk.

The waiting room of the clinic seemed exceptionally quiet. Beth felt that everyone was looking at her, knowing what she was about to do. The clock was moving in slow motion, refusing to let time pass. Finally, the nurse came and called Beth's name. Marcia stood up to go with her, but the nurse motioned for her to stay in the waiting room. The nurse led Beth into a small room with an examining table in the middle of it. The room was filled with all sorts of medical equipment that Beth had no idea what it was for. The nurse gave Beth a soft green hospital shirt to wear and said that it tied in the back. The nurse left and Beth got changed. She folded her clothes neatly and placed them on the chair, tucking her panties and bra inside of her pants. She kept her socks on since she hated cold feet. She sat on the examining table, ready to play the waiting game again.

A doctor and two nurses finally came in. The doctor introduced himself and tried to make small talk while he pulled out one of the huge machines that looked like a giant vacuum cleaner with an extra long hose. One of the nurses gently laid Beth on the table, put a blanket on her, and smiled kindly as she held Beth's hand. Beth looked up at the giant silver lamp that hung over the table. It was so bright. On the ceiling above the light someone had taped pictures of far off places. There was one of an orange sunset on a tropical island with palm trees and another with a large sailboat gliding across a deep blue ocean with a deep blue sky that had no clouds. Beth looked at the pictures, wondering how someone would be able to imagine herself in a far off perfect world while she was laying on a cold table about to have her insides vacuumed out. The second nurse gave Beth a shot to numb her while the doctor turned on the machine. The nurse that was holding Beth's hand talked gently to her, telling her to close her eyes, that everything was going to be all right, and that it was going to be over soon. The machine was humming gently and Beth could feel the hose inching its way inside of her, scraping against her insides to make sure it sucked out every cell of that baby along with anything else inside her. Scraping out her soul, leaving her totally empty.

It was finally over and everyone was cleaning up, getting ready to leave. The nurse was still holding Beth's hand.

"Now just lie here and rest until I come and tell you to get dressed. I'll bring you some juice and crackers. You lost a lot of blood and I don't want you fainting on us."

The nurse smiled happily at Beth, as if some great accomplishment had just been achieved. Beth smiled back and nodded "okay."

Beth lay on the table unable to escape from her emptiness. She wanted to get up but there was nothing left in her to give her the energy. She looked over at the "vacuum machine" and noticed that someone had taped a paper jonnie over a large glass jar on the counter next to it. Beth knew that the baby was in there and was tempted to lift the paper and see the mush of blood that was under it. However, she worried about what her reaction would be if there were little chunks of hands or feet, maybe a whole face smiling out at her, thanking her for freeing it from being born into a life of misery. Beth decided not to lift the paper, but instead remember it as the imaginary smiling face. She rolled away from the glass jar and closed her eyes, waiting for the smiling nurse to come back.

About fifteen minutes later the nurse came in with some juice and crackers.

"What are you going to do with it?" Beth asked her.
"Do with what?"
"The baby, what are you going to do with the baby?"
"Oh ... I don't know."
The nurse looked confused. "I'm sure they'll dispose of it respectfully." She put her ever-happy smile back on. "You can get dressed now and come on out when you're ready."

Beth smiled weakly and nibbled on the crackers, hoping they would give her energy. She did not know if she would have the strength to leave Jeff since she believed he would track her down and kill her. If he did not kill her, he would take Zack from her. At least one of her children was free from a life of torment. Beth sipped the red juice, feeling relief. Perhaps she should just give up and accept her life.

"Are you sure you don't want to come back to the crisis center and rest for a while before you go home?"

Marcia was so kind. Always knowing what was best for Beth even when Beth did not. Beth was not used to someone caring about her comfort.

"No, I want to go home. What would happen if someone saw me going in? I can't risk it."

"Okay, but make sure you get some sleep. You need to take care of yourself you know."

"Yeah, I know."

"Are you all right to drive? Do you want me to follow you home?"

"No, I'll be all right. I promise." Beth forced a smile, "Thanks."

Marcia dropped off Beth at the library where she sat in her car for a long time. She felt so weak, yet so free.

Beth considered going home, but needed some time alone so she stopped at the beach. The parking lot was empty as not many people were crazy enough to go to the beach in the beginning of March, which was still considered the middle of winter in New England. Beth seemed to put herself in situations that other people stayed away from. Beth loved the ocean. There was something about the vast wildness of it. It was free and powerful, could not be tamed or controlled, had the power to destroy, and yet was gentle and peaceful. It could be ruthless or healing. It held every quality that she wished to possess; yet she was weak. She had no courage to leave a person who might kill her, no courage to save her son from his father, no courage to have a baby. She was a coward who took the easy way out by denying everything that was important: She denied her baby a chance at life, denied to the world that Jeff hurt her, denied herself the right to the life she deserved, denied Zack a happy childhood. Looking out over the vast blue waves, she felt powerless and insignificant. She felt like one of the tiny grains of sand she was standing on. She felt like she would never be able to escape or make a difference. She felt like a failure.

Beth began walking along the water, but the cramping caused her to sit in the sand instead. It was surreal that the sun could be shining so brightly, the sky and water could be so brilliantly blue, and she should be in such pain sitting on the cold sand. She did not want to get up and wondered how she would drive home and pretend that everything was normal. She laughed at herself. Was that not how she lived her entire life, pretending that everything was fine and perfect when in reality it sucked? She decided it was time to get up and go home to face her fake life. Home? Is that what it was? No, it was a place where she lived until she could find the courage to create a *real* home for herself and Zack. A home where they could laugh and play, leave their stuff lying around, eat peanut butter out of the jar while sitting on the couch, and not have to worry about what was going to happen if they said or did something wrong. Not worrying about doing what was right, when there was no way of knowing what that was. Beth clutched her stomach and walked back to her car, hunched over, praying that Jeff would leave her alone tonight

Beth stopped at Nancy's house to pick up Zack who was sitting in front of the TV watching cartoons. He did not even look up when she came in.

"Hey chick, how was your day?" Nancy peaked out from the kitchen, "Me and the little guy have been having a great time. We went for a walk, played legos, and had hot dogs for lunch. I think that he's pooped out. Huh Zack?"

Zack did not respond; he was mesmerized by the TV. Beth forced a smile and went into the living room to give Zack a hug, but he squirmed away from her. Beth was hurt that Zack turned away from her. He was believing Jeff, becoming Jeff. All little children were supposed to love their mother, but here was Zack not wanting to be with her, even for a hug. Beth sadly sat in the chair across the room knowing she would lose him if she did not do something soon. His sibling just sacrificed his/her life to save Zack. Now it was Beth's turn to make up for what had already happened to him. Beth's mistake was marrying Jeff, providing Zack with a family where he was not safe, and letting him grow up in a home where he learned to hate his mother. Beth closed her eyes and wondered where her life was going to lead her, how she was going to escape from her prisoner, how she was going to save her little boy. Her cramps were horrible and she bent over a little to help them go away. Nancy was in the kitchen rambling about a date that she went on. Every once in a while, Beth managed an "Uh-huh."

Enough time went by so Beth could leave without Nancy feeling insulted, and she was strong enough to face Jeff. Nancy hugged and kissed Zack good-bye, and he did not pull away.

When Beth got home, Jeff was already there. She sat in the car, afraid to go in. She finally got out of the car slowly, unbuckled Zack's car seat. He jumped out of the car and ran into the house yelling, "Daddy, daddy guess what I did today?"

Beth froze, not sure what he would tell Jeff. What highlight of Zack's day was he so excited about? Was it something that would arouse Jeff's suspicions? Beth hung up her coat, scarf, and hat and mustered a meek smile. She carefully emerged forward, trying to determine what kind of mood Jeff was in. He was smiling.

"What did my big boy do today?"

"I went on a date with Nancy!"

"Wow, you're a lucky guy! Nancy's a hot chick!"

"Yeah, and she likes me. She said so. I'm going to marry her someday." Jeff laughed and picked Zack up. He gave him a big kiss on the cheek.

"That's my boy! You're going to end up with a hot wife. Not a bitch like I married."

Zack giggled and hugged Jeff. He hugged Jeff. He would not hug Beth, but he hugged Jeff. Beth's heart hurt more than the cramps. She watched her little boy smugly hug his father, getting approval by having her degraded. Neither of them noticed that she went to her room to lie down.

Exhaustion took over and she fell into a deep sleep and dreamt. There was a bright light with a small figure in front of it. It was a white featureless child that was almost transparent, as if not yet formed. Although the child was silent, it seemed to telepathically let Beth know that everything was going to be okay, that it understood and was letting go. The light got brighter and seemed to surround the small figure until the figure disappeared. The figure was gone and there was nothing left, except for a feeling of peace.

Chapter 4

Marcia called Beth everyday. After one week, Beth felt better physically. After two weeks, Beth decided it was time to take action by not letting her baby have sacrificed his/her life in vain. Beth silently thanked the child everyday and promised it that she would create a life that he/she would be happy and safe in and that she would wait for him/her to be born at that time. The time was not right now, but it would be some day. She would do everything possible so her baby would be born to her in the right situation. She knew she had to act soon, or else a part of her would die and she would not have the courage or strength to leave Jeff. She also knew that if she waited much longer, there would be no helping Zack to learn that this was not the way people lived. It was not the way he had to live. She had to act now if she wanted to save Zack, so she asked Marcia to meet her for coffee on Monday to make a plan.

They met at the McDonalds that had a large play area for Zack. He ran into it and started jumping in the balls, oblivious to anything that was happening around him.

"Do you have any money?" Marcia asked Beth.

"A little bit of cash, but not much. Jeff takes care of all the money and bills, so I don't even know how much money we have."

"Do you have a job?"

"No."

"Have you ever had a job?"

"I waitressed in high school but never went to college because I met Jeff. He was older and so sophisticated, I looked up to him, idolized him. He took me to nice restaurants, brought me flowers, and treated me like I saw in movies, not like I experienced with the high school kids I dated. I was so young that it was like a fairy tale. He told me he would take care of me and I believed him."

"Do you have any family or friends? Is there anywhere you can stay?"

"I have a friend, Nancy, but she doesn't know anything. She wouldn't understand and would probably side with Jeff. I wouldn't be able to stay there."

"What about family? Parents? Siblings? Grandparents?"

"My father's parents died before I was born. I was very close to my mother's parents, but they're dead now. My parents died in a car accident shortly after I graduated from high school, leaving my brother and me orphans. I guess that's why I was so eager to marry Jeff. I looked at him like a savior who would make everything okay. He was my white knight in shining armor rescuing me from a desperate situation. I went from bad to worse. If only I knew then what I know now . . . I should have seen the signs.

"My brother James lives in New Mexico with his wife and three daughters. They have a small house and are just making it. I couldn't expect them to take me in. I also don't want him knowing what I'm going through. We both had such a hard time when our parents died that I want him to think I'm happy."

"Yeah, you couldn't move a minor child out of the state anyway. That would lead to more problems. Do you have enough money to keep your current house or to rent an apartment?"

"No to both."

"Well, the important thing is to get you and Zack out of that house and to somewhere safe. We have an opening at the shelter. Would you want to stay there?"

"What's a shelter?"

"It's a safe home for women like you and their children to stay while they're in the process of leaving unsafe situations and getting themselves on their feet. The first step would be to get you into the emergency shelter, which is a high security home where you can stay with Zack.

"Once things are stable, you can move into a home which is an independent community setting that allows you to live with other women until you get a place of your own. We would relocate you a safe distance away so that you won't have to worry about running into Jeff or anyone you know. We'll try to get you and Zack your own bedroom, but you would share the living room, kitchen, dining room, bathroom, and chores. No one knows where the safe home is except for the people who live there and very few people from the crisis center. You'll be safe, and Jeff won't be able to find you.

"While you're there, you'll get counseling and help getting a place of your own. Before we decide if this is the right choice, I need to ask you some questions. They may seem silly, but I have to ask them."

"Go for it."

"Why do you want to leave Jeff?"

"Are you serious?"

"I told you they'd be stupid."

"You said silly, not stupid. To state the obvious, because he hurts me and I'm afraid of him. I'm afraid that he's going to kill me or Zack, and I want to keep Zack safe."

"There are laws to keep you safe, but in order to use them we'll have to ask the courts for help. Are you willing to do that?"

"I'm scared that Jeff will find out and kill me."

"You'll be safe. The emergency shelter has very high security and no one knows where it is. Jeff won't be able to find or hurt you. The courts will make an order that he can't come near you, and if he does then he'll be breaking the law. It'll be hard, and a lot of work on your part, but you'll be safe. Zack'll be safe. Do you want to do it?"

"Absolutely. What do we do?"

"Are there any preparations that you have to make, or can you leave right away?"

"I can leave right away."

"Will you be safe at home tonight?"

"Yeah."

"Good. Then tomorrow morning pack everything on this list. Try to locate things like birth certificates and social security cards today. Also, if you can find any financial information then bring that too. Only take what you need like clothes, medications, anything sentimental, favorite blankets or toys, you'll know what to take. What time does Jeff leave for work in the morning?"

"Seven"

"Will nine give you enough time to get ready?"

"Yeah."

"All right. Then meet me at the center at 9:15 A.M. There'll be people there to watch Zack. It will be all right. Jeff won't be able to find you and you'll be safe."

"Won't he be able to get Zack? He is his father."

"We're doing everything legally, so it'll be up to the courts to decide."

"Zack loves his daddy, but I'm afraid that Jeff will hurt him."

"The most important thing is to keep Zack safe. Jeff might try to kidnap or hurt Zack to get to you. Most likely the courts will order supervised visits so that Zack will see Jeff in a safe place, but won't be exposed to any more violence. It's very important that you don't tell Zack anything that's happening yet and that you never say anything negative about Jeff to Zack. Zack has to form his own opinion about what's happening. If you start talking bad about Jeff, then Zack may feel the need to defend Jeff and it'll be harder to undo the damage that's been done. Especially since Zack has already started to associate with Jeff."

"Okay."

"I have the form to fill out for the restraining order. What are some examples of why you're afraid of Jeff?"

"Besides beating the shit out of me so that I almost died?"

"That's a great place to start. Let's put that on paper, and discuss the other things. By disclosing that it was Jeff who beat you, the court will press charges for assault and you'll have to answer why you didn't disclose it earlier. The subject of the abortion may also come up. You'll have to be strong."

"I can do it."

Beth felt a surge of power inside of her. She knew she had what it would take to get through this. She had to do it for her baby, she had to do it for Zack. If it were just her, she would probably give in and lose her will until she was dead. She could leave for her children though. She *would* leave for her children.

Beth did not pack much. Jeff had picked out most of their stuff, and she would rather not have anything that reminded her of him. She got the two large suitcases out of the attic and packed everything from the list that Marcia had given her. She found the birth certificates, social security cards, and files marked "house," "investments," "retirement," "life insurance," "car," and "medical." She stuffed clothes for both her and Zack, toys, Zack's snuggly blanket, her makeup and brushes, journal, jewelry, Zack's photo album, pictures, the glass box that her mother had given her on her 16th birthday, and the money that was hidden in her jeans pocket. She gave silent thanks to God for guiding her and helping her to prepare for the escape. She smiled into her mirror and felt good about herself for the first time in years. She was leaving Jeff. She was escaping. She was going to save her child and break the cycle. How could there be anything more empowering? She glanced around, there was nothing else here for her. She wanted to leave this room, this house, and never return or look back. She let out an impulsive laugh, and then quickly stifled it. It was so unlike her to laugh.

Zack sat staring at the TV, not noticing as Beth packed their stuff into the car.

"Okey dokey, Zackey. It's time to go bye bye."

"I don't want to go! My show isn't over!"

"Yeah, but I have a surprise for you. You're going to be really happy. It's better than your TV show."

Zack lit up.

"Really? A surprise? What?"

He got off the couch and started to follow Beth to the door. Beth had his coat waiting for him.

"Well, if I told you, then it wouldn't be a surprise would it?"

"No."

"Okay then, the sooner we leave then the sooner you'll find out what it is."

"I like surprises."

Beth smiled the most sincere smile she had in years.

"Yes, and you're going to like this surprise a lot."

It was 8:30 A.M. Beth would be at the center in plenty of time. Beth was amazed at how quickly she was able to pack everything she needed to leave an old life and start a new one. Zack sat patiently buckled into his car seat while Beth tried to calmly drive to the place that would deliver them from hell.

Marcia was waiting for Beth out front, just like she said she would be. She was with another woman who Beth recognized.

"Beth, I want you to meet Janet. She's one of our most trusted workers and will wait here with Zack until we get back from court."

Beth smiled nervously at Janet. This strange woman was going to take her baby away from her. Beth handed Zack over.

"Hey Zack, this nice lady is Janet. She's going to wait with you so that we can bring you to the surprise. There'll be lots of toys and friends for you to play with here."

"Like a school?"

"Yes, like a school."

Beth smiled and tried to keep Zack from seeing the tears that were welling up in her eyes. Zack had been begging to go to school. Now was his chance. It worried Beth how eager Zack was to walk away with a perfect stranger. Marcia gently touched Beth's shoulder.

"Are you okay?"

"Yeah."

"I have the forms to request an emergency restraining order. Did you find the documents?"

"Yeah, I think I got everything. One advantage of Jeff having OCD is he's anally organized."

Marcia laughed and smiled at her. Beth was glad that she did not have to drive.

The courthouse was a large old building filled with past spirits who never received justice. There were steep slabs of granite for steps, piled high on top of each other so that Beth was out of breath before she reached the large green doors that were heavy to open. There was a white frame of a door that was a metal detector. A solemn young police officer watched them intently as they passed through. Marcia put her keys and cell phone in a small plastic basket so that it would not set off the detector. The police officer silently nodded slightly and they continued down the hall. Once in the courthouse, Beth sat on the bench in the hallway while Marcia passed in the papers. Other than school field trips to the local state house, this was the first time Beth had been in a courthouse. She looked at the people around her and was amazed at how comfortable they looked. Some of them greeted each other happily as if they were old friends catching up while Beth sat quietly, afraid. Marcia sat next to her until they got signaled to move into one of the courtrooms. Everyone sat close together on the benches, like in church, only quieter. There was a guard glaring around making sure that no one spoke or moved. Beth was terrified.

"All rise."

Everyone in the room rose as the judge entered and went to his seat high above. He was wearing long black robes and stared down at them, while paintings of other old men with long robes stared down at him. He sat down and everyone in the room, except for the guards, did the same. Some people were dressed up, some were in casual street clothes, and some were in orange suits and handcuffs. As the guard called people to the bench, they stated their story and the judge issued orders. Beth's name was finally called. The judge read the papers, then looked over his glasses at Beth.

"This man, your husband, beat you so bad that you were unconscious and admitted to the hospital?"

"Yes sir. I have the medical discharge papers here."

"Why wasn't he arrested?"

"I was afraid that he would kill me if I told it was him."

"Then why are you here now?"

"I found out that the court will keep me safe. I'm hoping that you'll protect me by granting a restraining order, and issuing me custody of my son."

"Custody is an issue for probate court, but I can issue temporary custody. You realize that criminal charges will be brought against your husband?"

"Yes sir."

"You will cooperate with the prosecutor?"

"Yes sir."

"Request granted. I issue a restraining order for ten days, temporary custody of the minor child to the plaintiff, and a warrant for the arrest of Jeffrey F. Parker."

The gavel banged on the desk and the judge bent over and wrote something down. Marcia motioned for Beth to come. It was over. Beth was in a daze. It was so easy, why did not she know about this before? All these years of living in hell, and it just took one bang of the gavel to tell her she was free.

Marcia held her hand when they got into the hall.

"Now your journey begins." Marcia smiled at her.

"The judge just said that Jeff can't come near me and that I have custody of Zack."

Marcia laughed a sarcastic laugh.

"Oh, this is just the beginning. You heard the judge. We have to come back in ten days so that Jeff will have an opportunity to have his say, hopefully the order will be extended for a year. The district attorney is going to prosecute Jeff, and you have to testify against him. Also, Jeff will most likely fight for custody of Zack in probate court. He can't hurt you physically any more, but emotionally he's going to use the legal system to continue to get to you."

"How do you know what he's going to do? You never even met him."

"Yes, that's true. But he's an abuser, I've seen it a million times. He wants control, he's not going to let you walk away. It'll become a mission for him to continue hurting you. Since it's the only way that he can have contact with you, he's going to use the legal system. I know this sounds harsh, but I want you to be prepared for what you're up against."

Beth looked firmly into Marcia's eyes.

"I am ready for whatever I have to do."

Despite being so shaken up, Beth wanted to get back to the center as soon as possible to see Zack. Beth was expecting to find Zack playing happily in the playroom, but instead he was curled up on Janet's lap while she rocked him. He looked up at Beth with hurt eyes when she entered the room. He stubbornly stayed away letting her know he felt abandoned.

"Hi Zack, Mommy's back. Are you ready to go to the surprise?"

"I'm telling Daddy that you left me alone. You'll get in big trouble."

Beth looked ashamed at Marcia, who smiled at her and urged her over to Zack.

"We haven't seen the surprise yet, don't you want to go?"

"Okay, but you better not leave me again!"

"I won't, I promise."

Zack angrily got off Janet's lap and followed Beth out. Beth could not help thinking how much Zack resembled Jeff with his clenched fists and heavy steps.

Marcia drove Beth's car so that Beth could sit in the back with Zack. They drove forty-five minutes on the highway, and then took an exit that led through a series of side streets. They eventually came to a large house with a garage under it that Marcia opened with an automatic garage opener from her purse. Once the garage door was safely closed, Marcia unlocked the door to go upstairs and into an entranceway that had a desk and a series of TV's showing the various entrances to the house. The woman sitting at the desk stiffened as if on alert when they came through the door. Marcia showed her a badge and the woman nodded her approval.

"Hi Jane, and this is Beth and her son Zack."

"We've been expecting you. My name is Jane and I'm the security guard. You can bring your stuff upstairs to room six. You'll have it to yourselves for now. I'll send someone to come up to help you out."

Marcia unlocked another door into the house and went upstairs. They carried the luggage to a small bedroom that had two twin beds, two toddler beds, and two dressers. Beth left their stuff on the floor to unpack later so that Marcia could give them a tour.

"Jane is a new security guard, as you can tell they're very strict here. Everything's locked and there are surveillance cameras everywhere. The only people allowed in are the guests and approved employees. This is the most dangerous time for you, so we have to take extreme precautions to make sure you're safe."

Beth did not know whether to feel safe that they were strict, or scared that she was in danger. The rest of the house was homey in a fake sort of way. Everything was set up to be safe, for example the windows did not open and there were help buttons in the bathrooms, yet it had comfortable furniture and pictures. Everything was simple, yet suspicious. Jane was located in a small locked entrance that the front and garage doors opened up to, and there was a hall leading to a back door that locked behind you when you entered it. If the back door opened then an alarm went off. These were the only two ways in or out of the home, making Beth feel like a prisoner.

"I know it must seem weird with all the locks and cameras, but it's for your safety. Once you're out of immediate danger we can move you to a community style apartment, which is like having your own apartment with roommates. It's a great transition to living on your own since you have the support of the other women but live independently. Until then, it's important that you don't leave here unsupervised. This is the TV and game room, here is the dining room and the kitchen. Here is a chart with everyone's assigned jobs to take turns cooking the meals and cleaning. You're not on it yet."

Zack yawned and rubbed his eyes.

"It's nap time. It's been a busy day."

"I'll wait in the living room for you."

Marcia and Beth talked in the living room while Zack napped.

"How are you doing? This is a huge adjustment and can be very confusing. Are you feeling any regrets?

"Absolutely not. I'm so grateful to you for saving me. I would have stayed with Jeff until he killed me."

"You're the one who's doing it. I'm just here to guide you. But this is just the beginning."

"The hard part is over. I can handle anything now."

"Unfortunately, you never had to deal with the courts. The hard part hasn't even started."

"But, the courts are there to protect me."

"That's true, but the courts are a patriarchal power system. At times it seems like they encourage the abuse."

"I'll do whatever I have to, to keep Zack safe."

"Well, that's good because I have some news for you. I called the court while you were upstairs and Jeff was served with the restraining order, so the court date is a week from Thursday."

"How does this work?"

"This morning you were issued a temporary restraining order for ten days. In order to extend it, Jeff has a right to defend himself. From this point on it's going to be tough. By leaving, you took his means of control away so he'll use whatever means necessary to get revenge on you. He'll be more charming than you've ever seen him, he'll try to get Zack by lying about you, your relationship, and anything else to make himself look good and you look bad."

"He would never try to take Zack. He doesn't even take care of him."

"He'll try to get Zack because he knows it'll hurt you. Be prepared. He'll use all of your intimate secrets against you. He'll try to make himself look like the victim, and you the evil woman who was given everything, and in return is trying to take his son away from him."

"So, what can I do?"

"The most important weapon that you have is the truth. Always, always tell the truth so that your story is strong and will remain consistent. Lies get tangled and caught. You need to have faith that the courts will see the truth and make the right decision. In the mean time, we have to prepare you. We both know that Jeff will hire an expensive lawyer. We have a lawyer at the center who can represent you. In order for her to be prepared, you have to write down everything you remember. Start at the beginning when you met Jeff, about your relationship, how and when the abuse started and details about how it continued. Write whatever comes to your mind, it doesn't matter how insignificant or stupid you think it is. Everything helps."

Beth took a bowl of cereal up to her room and propped the pillows behind her head so that she could sit up comfortably. She sat staring at the empty notebook that Marcia gave her for a long time, not knowing where to begin. Her mind wandered back to her life before she met Jeff and how she had so many hopes and dreams. She believed in unrealistic things such as true love and living happily ever after. She remembered all of the sweet things Jeff used to do, and how she mistook them for love. He would constantly call her, having her account for every moment. He idolized her as if she were a goddess and cherished her as if she were priceless. He constantly said how lucky he was to have her, how fabulous she was, how he could not stand to be without her. Beth thought it was very romantic.

When Beth's parents died, Jeff's proposal for marriage saved her from being alone. Then Zack came and everything changed. Jeff was jealous when Beth gave Zack attention and would get angry when Zack cried. It soon became impossible to know what Jeff expected as he would randomly lose his temper. Beth was blamed for all of Jeff's annoyances. It was Beth's fault if she did not get a movie when there was nothing on TV. When Beth cooked chicken, Jeff was angry because they *always* had chicken and he wanted steak. If Beth cooked steak, then Jeff would be angry because steak was expensive, did she think they were made of money? If Jeff burnt something, then it was Beth's fault because she should have turned it off. If Jeff's plans got cancelled because of rain, then Beth should have known it was going to rain and had him reschedule.

Jeff expected the house to be spotless, dinner cooked every night, the baby clean, and happy, and Beth to be thin, dressed nice, made up, and happy at all times. She was to accomplish this even if Jeff was swearing, throwing furniture, or hurting her. If Jeff's expectations were not met then he would call Beth "a lazy bitch" or "stupid cunt." The name calling eventually became a regular part of conversation, and eventually Jeff became destructive. He punched holes in the walls, ripped the cabinet doors off their hinges, and broke furniture. Beth soon felt so bad about herself that she could not understand how anyone would want to be with her. Yet Jeff accused her of having an affair. Then Beth stopped feeling. The words diffused through her like water passing through a screen. They hit a slight barrier, but then continued on through. The screen was left damp for a little while, but quickly dried seemingly unaffected. However, over time the effect of the water on the screen caused the screen to become rusty and deteriorate. Eventually it would get worn away and break. Here at the safe home, the screen was lying in the sun and receiving rust treatment. It would be strong again.

Beth could not stop writing. She wrote about the good times, about the hope that the Jeff who hurt her would leave and the Jeff who loved her would come back. The two Jeff's would rotate over and over again until she stopped believing in the good. When the good Jeff occasionally came back, she knew that it was a temporary condition and she waited with anticipation, never knowing when the mean Jeff would return. Anything could trigger the reappearance; an empty bottle of shampoo in the shower, or not being able to find the socks that he wanted. Eventually, Beth stopped hoping, stopped believing, and stopped feeling. She just existed and became immune. It became normal. It was what Zack believed was normal. Beth wrote it all down, every feeling, every betrayal, every push, punch, burn, gasp for breath. Beth released all the pain that Jeff inflicted on her into the green spiral notebook that was propped up on her folded legs. Here in her small bed in her cozy room where her child slept beside her, and they were safe. She felt the hurt and betrayal leave her and get projected onto the paper. Beth wondered how much of what she wrote would benefit the attorney, and how much of it was benefiting her. She assumed that the benefits for her were greater.

The next morning when Beth woke up, it took her a few minutes to realize where she was. She looked over to Zack's bed, but it was empty. Her heart pounded as she frantically ran downstairs and found Zack happily playing in the living room with a little girl about five years old. Also in the room was the on-staff worker and a woman hugging a small baby. The mother and little girl looked terrified; the small baby was bundled tightly.

"Is everything okay?"

"Yeah, we had an emergency, but are lucky that there's plenty of room here. This is Katie and her daughters Grace and Hanna. They'll be staying in your room with you and Zack."

Beth felt guilty that she was disappointed that her solitude was now gone. How could she feel upset about sharing her room when she was so lucky to have been brought here herself? Shame pushed her negative feelings aside and she gave them all a huge smile.

"It's a pleasure to meet you all. It looks like you already met my son Zack. So, who's Grace and who's Hanna?"

"I'm Grace, and that's my baby sister Hanna."

The little girl spoke up very proudly. The women looked at each other surprised.

"That's the first time Grace spoke since *it* happened."

Beth felt incredible sympathy for this new family. It was obvious that their decision to come to the safe home was not planned like Beth's had been, they were in distress and would need to process what they were going through.

"I'll leave you all alone so you can talk, or whatever. I'll be upstairs if anyone needs me." Beth took Zack's hand and went up to their room.

The bedroom was full but cozy with Katie and Grace in the other two beds, and baby Hanna in a porta crib. Every night after the three children were asleep, Beth and Katie had tea in the kitchen and were becoming close friends. Beth said how grateful she was to be safe after living in fear for so long. Katie did not agree.

"I think it's great here and all, but I miss being home. My husband yells and hits me a lot, but he's a really good father. Grace keeps asking for him, she misses her daddy. Maybe if I tried harder then he wouldn't get so mad at me. I don't know if I'm doing the right thing by leaving him, but I won't take the kids from him. I mean, I'll make sure he gets the kids half time; just like I wouldn't want him to take them away from me. The whole family would be all split up and I'll only see them half time, and how will he be able to take care of them? He wouldn't know what to do."

"Katie, there's no right or wrong way. You have to do what's right for you. Every situation and person is different, we're here to support each other. But please, don't ever think that there's anything you could have done or not done to make your husband not hurt you. That's his choice and I'd make sure things are different before going back."

"He wants us to come back. He said he'll go to counseling and an abusers group. He's really trying and I truly think he can change."

"For your sake I hope so, but please be cautious. Don't let him talk you into anything you don't want to do."

"I wouldn't. He hurt me and I won't forget that, but he's also my husband and the father of my children, and I have to be open to the fact that he's trying to change."

Beth was not sure how to respond to Katie and her thoughts of going back. She wanted to talk to Marcia about it, but did not want to violate Katie's trust.

Beth was never alone. In addition to the front security guard, there was a staff person and the other "guests." They had meetings every morning to discuss how everyone was coping and how their plans were progressing. Marcia checked on Beth daily to see how she was.

"You know, I'm really proud of you. I know it's hard being away from home and many people give up and go back."

"There's nothing impressive about it, its survival. I'm not doing anything that anyone else in the same position wouldn't do."

"Oh, but you're wrong. Many people never get the courage to leave, others give up and go back. But you're pulling through."

"Thanks."

"The most difficult part of this job is seeing women in danger who stay in bad situations until it's too late. Sometimes women plan to leave, but their partner finds out before they're able to escape. Other times they just give up, or they go back. I'm worried that Katie might go back."

"Is it a breech of confidentiality to tell you what she says to me?"

"Not if you think she may be in danger, but I think I already know. It's not your job to support your fellow housemates. Don't forget that you have no control over other people's decisions or outcomes. Not many women are as determined as you. The important thing is to realize what you have to do to keep yourself and Zack safe, and to not get discouraged by other people's decisions. It's my job to try and help Katie, so you focus on taking care of yourself."

"But you're not doing it. What if Katie goes back?"

"Then she goes back. It's her choice and we'll have to pray that nothing happens to her. Hopefully it will give you the strength to do what you have to do. Are you ready for court tomorrow?"

"I don't know. I'm terrified, but I guess that's to be expected."

"Don't worry, just tell the truth and you'll be fine."

Marcia picked up Beth early on Thursday, which came much too quickly. Other than meeting with the attorney to review the materials, Beth tried not to think about going to court and having to face Jeff. She wanted to enjoy the peace while she had it, since she did not know how long it would last. Her and Zack's entire future depended on one person's decision. What if the judge got in a fight with his wife that morning? Beth preferred not to think about it.

Beth felt important in the suit that she got from the local thrift shop. The crisis center referred people with donations to the shop, and in return people from the center could get clothes for free. She felt as if she was in a suit of armor, prepared to do battle with Jeff.

When they entered the courthouse, Attorney Peters' crisp red suit stood out from the blur of blue and gray clothes that blended into the dingy hallway.

"Hey Beth, how are you?"

"I'm scared."

"I'd be surprised if you weren't. I submitted the affidavit we prepared, so we can go into the courtroom and wait until we're called."

"I'm so scared, what if I can't talk?"

Beth's hands were shaking.

"Don't worry, you'll be fine. Just tell the truth and you'll have nothing to hide."

The three of them entered the courtroom, which was crowded with people whispering to each other.

"I thought you said we had to be quiet?"

"The judge isn't here yet so we can talk quietly until he enters."

Suddenly a guard yelled, "All rise."

The room went silent. Attorney Peters smiled at Beth and mouthed, "See, I told you." Beth scanned the room looking for Jeff who was standing in the middle of the room with a well-dressed man that she assumed was his attorney. Everything was very similar to when she was here ten days before, except that this time Jeff was here to defend himself and call her a liar. Beth stared at Jeff and imagined what he would do if they were alone. Panic started building, making her heart race, her chest feeling tight and she was finding it hard to breath. Marcia reached over and held Beth's hand.

"Don't look at him," she whispered.

Beth shifted her gaze to the judge. She could not hear what he said to the numerous people who stood before him as they nodded and walked away, sometimes looking happy or relieved, and sometimes looking angry or scared. The uncertainty of the results was almost too much for Beth to bear. What happened if the restraining order was not renewed? Even if it was renewed, what was stopping him from coming after her anyway? What if Zack had to go to Jeff? How would she bear sending Zack to get abused? Beth felt sick to her stomach, she kept telling herself to relax, to breathe, to stop thinking about "what if's."

"Come on, we were just called."

Attorney Peters gently took Beth's arm and led her up to the judge.

"I've read the affidavit. Mr. Parker, do you have anything to say?"

"Yeah, she's a fucking liar."

"Mr. Parker, that language and tone of voice aren't permitted in a court of law."

Attorney Peters spoke, "Your honor, if I may. There are currently assault and battery charges pending against Mr. Parker for beating Mrs. Parker unconscious. My client is afraid for her life and for that of her child. We ask that the protective order be extended, that the residence of my client and her child be allowed to remain confidential, and that all correspondence is done through me and Mr. Parker's attorney."

Jeff's attorney spoke up.

"Your honor, my client is pleading innocent to these charges and wants his son returned to him as this woman is emotionally unstable and unfit to have the child."

The judge looked at Jeff who was turning bright red, the color he usually turned before he exploded, and then he looked at Beth who was pale white and scared to death.

"I'm renewing the protective order for one year. The child will stay with his mother, and their residence will remain confidential. Whether or not Mr. Parker is guilty of these charges is not the intent of this hearing and if Mr. Parker wants to petition for visitation or custody of the child, he can do so in probate court. You're all dismissed."

Beth could not believe it, a restraining order for a whole year? Did this mean that it was over? Could she finally relax? Her entire body went limp and she felt as if she were going to fall over. She felt a little dizzy and held onto Attorney Peters for support. Jeff and his attorney turned right out the door, so they turned left. Marcia came out a minute later, eagerly looking back and forth at the both of them.

"So, what happened? I couldn't hear from where I sat. It's impossible to tell by looking at you. You look like you are going to faint. Are you okay?"

Attorney Peters smiled calmly.

"Well, this went in the right direction. We got the restraining order for one year, and Beth and Zack can stay with you. We're lucky that Beth's estranged husband is stupid and actually swore at the judge. There's nothing like letting the judge see firsthand what type of person we're dealing with."

"He actually swore at the judge? Well Beth, this is one time that you can be grateful you're married to a man who can't control his anger!"

Beth let out a small laugh.

Marcia smiled.

"Are you two hungry? I am sure that Jeff must be gone. Do you want to get something to eat?"

"Come to think of it, I was too nervous to eat this morning and just realized that I'm starving!"

"I'm afraid that I can't join you, but I'll be in touch soon."

The three women exited the building and departed in separate directions. Marcia and Beth started walking toward a little area about a block from the courthouse that had shops and restaurants. Suddenly Beth froze and grabbed Marcia's arm, squeezing it tight so that her fingernails dug into Marcia's flesh.

"What is the matter?"

"Stop, listen. We can't go on."

Marcia listened, and heard a man yelling from around the corner.

"I paid you good money, and you did nothing. What am I paying you for? My psycho wife ran off with my kid, and I can't do anything about it? That fucking bitch makes me look like I'm the one who did something wrong! Now do you see what I had to live with? I gave her everything, and this is what I get!"

Marcia gently pried Beth's hand off her arm and held it firmly.

"It's okay, he's with his attorney. Luckily he's showing his true personality, so it should only be a matter of time before he'll be looking for another attorney. Let's get away from here and drive to get something to eat."

They turned around and walked towards the parking lot.

It always seems that when something is gained, something else is lost. Beth could not wait to tell Katie the good news. She rushed into the house only to find Katie and her daughters sitting in the living room with their bags packed.

"Where are you going?"

"We're going home. I waited until you got back so that I could say bye in person."

"No Katie, please don't go."

"It's what I have to do. Try to understand."

"Good luck, I'll miss you."

"I'll miss you too."

Beth wanted to shake Katie and beg her not to go, but instead she hugged and kissed her goodbye. Beth knew they would never see each other again.

Part II

Into the Ashes

Chapter 5

After having been in the emergency shelter for two more weeks, there was an opening at a residential home. Beth was nervous about the decrease in security, but it was a good distance from Jeff and would be a homey, community environment. Beth looked forward to being in a home instead of the emergency center.

Marcia drove Beth's car, while Janet followed. They drove for about an hour on the interstate highway, and then trailed off into a long one-lane wooded highway that led to a small city where they crossed over a series of streets. They drove past neat little houses lined up with identical driveways and trees, past two and three family houses with laundry lines connecting them, and eventually came to a big, old house that must have been a prestigious Victorian in its time. Only now the white paint was peeling and the front bushes needed trimming. They pulled into the driveway and Beth's heart skipped a little as she got out of the car, bringing Zack into their new home.

"Here's our new home Zack."

When they entered the house, Zack immediately went into the living room and began playing legos with another little boy. There was a little girl who was playing with some dolls. The furniture was old and worn, but clean.

"Mommy! Look what I made! A house!"

Zack smiled as he held up a red, blue, and yellow box. Tears came to Beth's eyes as she realized that this was the first time in a long time that Zack was happy to address her. She was going to like it here.

Marcia gently put her hand on Beth's shoulder.

"Let me show you your room."

They walked up the stairs to the end of a long hall where they turned into a small blue room with two beds and a chest of draws. The curtains were light blue with little daisies on them and the bedspreads were a pale yellow with little polka dots. There was a poster with a picture of a rainbow arched over a pot with the words "Let your dreams come true." Very small, but very cozy.

"I know it's small, but it's safe. We're supposed to fill up the bigger rooms before we use the little ones, but luckily there's only one empty bed in the other room. So you get some privacy."

"Oh, this is perfect."

Beth could not control herself and started to cry. Marcia held her.

"I'm sorry …"

"Oh no, don't be sorry. You're safe here. No one can hurt you. You don't have to be afraid."

"Thank you for everything."

"It's you who is doing it. You're very brave. Not many people have the courage to do this."

"I'm not brave. I'm a coward running away from my problems."

"No, you're facing your problems. You're addressing and fighting them. If you were hiding, you'd still be in that house pretending to the world that everything's okay. But it's not okay, and you're letting the world know it. You're very, very brave."

"I wish I could believe that."

Beth was still crying.

"Do you need some time alone?"

"No, don't go."

Marcia stayed with Beth for about an hour and then they got her things out of the car and unpacked them. It was all right that the room was small since Beth did not have much stuff. Besides, it made her feel safe like a cub in a cave, or a fetus in a womb. She liked having the walls snug around her, keeping the outside world away.

Zack liked it here too. It was like a combination of an extended sleepover and the preschool that he had been yearning for. Zack had not asked about Jeff or when they were going home, so Beth did not address it. The main thing was that Zack was happy, and Beth was enjoying the peace.

That night, after the children were in bed, the women had a house meeting. This was the time where they did their "house cleaning" and addressed any issues. It was a mandatory meeting that was held every Sunday night and whenever there was a major change such as a new guest. Tonight's meeting was being held in Beth's honor. Marcia decided to stay for the meeting since this was a "special case" and she wanted to make sure that Beth was happy here. Beth wondered what made her a "special case" and felt like a delinquent teenager in the principal's office. A young woman named Lisa was the contact person for the home and ran the meeting.

"In honor of tonight's meeting, I introduce Beth Parker! As always, I'll start the meeting with our confidentiality policy. This is a safe home for victims of domestic violence. Anything that is said or occurs here will never leave this room. You can discuss your own issues among yourselves, but don't discuss anyone else. Most importantly, no one is *ever* allowed to disclose the address or location of the home or the names of any of its guests to *anyone*. Not even your family or best friend. That would put everyone's safety in jeopardy and we would have to move. That wouldn't be fun since we're lucky to have this house. Any correspondence with the outside world must be done through the crisis center.

"The confidentiality policy applies to all meetings and support groups, and everything that goes on here. If you can't discuss something in front of the group, or it can't wait until Sunday, then you can write it down and put it in the suggestion box in the upstairs bathroom. That's the only private place we could think of where people can put in their suggestion without anyone seeing. In addition to the Sunday night 'house cleaning' meeting, we have a Wednesday night support group. That's the time where we get to talk about ourselves and how we're progressing on our journey. There are also support groups at the crisis center, which include women who have successfully created new lives, as well as women who choose to stay with their abusers. It's good to be with people in all stages since each woman is on her own journey and we're here to support each person for the choices they make.

"Now, let's get started. Since this is Beth's first night, we can each tell a little about ourselves."

Beth listened attentively as each woman so openly shared her story. She was amazed that they were all like her. She had always thought that she was the only one in her situation and that no one would understand if she tried to explain what it was like. Now, here were five women with totally different situations but the same story. Regardless of the color of their skin, the neighborhood they came from, their age, looks or weight, they were all connected. Being victims gave them a common ground. They were all beautiful women with the same story of being hurt, degraded, and violated by the person who claimed to love them. The greatest bond of all was that they all left.

Monique was a tiny dark woman with very short black spiked hair that matched her black eyes. She wore no makeup or jewelry and her skin tone was gray and worn, making her look much older than the forty something years that she was. Even her clothes were dark, blending her into her surroundings as if she was a shadow. Was she wishing herself to be invisible?

"I have been here the longest, so I guess I get to go first." She gave a shy smile. "I was with my husband for over twenty years, since I was a teenager, so I spent pretty much my whole life with him. In the beginning it made me feel special that he always wanted to be with me. I didn't realize that I was giving up everything but him. Even myself. When we got married I wasn't allowed to work or have any friends. He claimed that he wanted me home to take care of the house and our child. He would want to know where I was at all times and got very jealous if I even spoke to anyone. It got worse when he started drinking and would get violent to me and my daughter.

"I began to suspect that he was molesting her, but had no proof. She would sit on the toilet for hours crying that she had to pee, but nothing came out. She used globs of toilet paper, wiping herself violently until she was raw. I brought her to the doctor who tested her for a urinary track infection, which came back negative, so he said there was nothing to do. He brushed off my concerns. She would masturbate excessively when she was only three. I didn't know what to do. I was afraid that if I divorced him then he would get split custody and I wouldn't be able to protect her. So, I stayed and did everything that I could to keep her safe. If he was out, then I slept on the couch until he came home. I didn't want to risk him coming home and going into her room. I was sure that I was protecting her from him, but I wasn't. I don't know when he did it to her. My attempts to protect her kept me a prisoner. When he lost his temper and went after her, I would get in the middle. I would let him vent his anger on me instead of her, causing him to change the focus. She grew up hating me. She saw me as weak, and I guess she's right. I am weak for staying with him for so long.

"When she turned eighteen she left. She had nothing to stay for. She hated us both. Him for being a monster and me for being weak. Since I wasn't able to take her away, she got away on her own. I don't know what she's doing now, but I'm happy knowing that she's safe. I haven't heard from her since she left, and I guess I won't now since nobody knows where I am. It is okay though. I'm willing to sacrifice her love for her safety. Once she was gone he got worse and since I had no reason to stay, I came here. I have a job as a cashier at the Super Stop & Shop and should have enough money to get my own apartment soon. Until then, I'm grateful to be here."

The next woman was a very large African American woman who was sitting in the love seat. She sprawled herself on it, taking up the entire thing. She was wearing colorful cloths, large gold hoop earrings, and a beautiful wood beaded necklace. She also had short black hair, only it was curly. She wore blue eye shadow, bright lipstick, and had a spiral tattoo around her wrist. Beth found her very sensual and wished that she had more curves herself. Jeff would never have allowed it; he was always complaining about how fat she was. Beth silently promised herself she could eat whatever she wanted and could gain weight. She could even get fat if she wanted. From now on, it was her life.

"Ohhh, I guess it is my turn." The woman gave a huge smile that made Beth feel warm inside. "My name is Rosie. I hate being alone, I like having a nice man to keep me warm and give me lots of lovin'. Maybe it's me that uses them. I just love the feel of haven' a man around. I got to be more picky though. They just come in and tell me they love me, then leave me with another baby." A hearty laugh. "I have four babies, all by different fathers. The first few were okay, I was sorry to see them go. The second one I even married, but he deserted me anyway. But, the last one was horrible! I don't know how I got mixed up with him! He came home smelling like other women, then demand that I have sex regardless of what I was doing. It didn't matter if I was cooking supper, giving the kids a bath, or putting them to bed. No sir-re. It didn't matter at all. All he cared about was his immediate satisfaction. I had to drop whatever I was doing and go satisfy him. Sometimes I couldn't even get the kids out of the room. They sat there and watched with their big brown eyes, wondering what was going on.

"Then, he'd get mean. Sometimes I woke up from my sleep to find him sticking things in me down there. Ya know what I'm saying, like a bottle or something. And that wasn't all. He screamed and hollered if he wanted something to eat, or punch holes in the wall and through furniture. Once he threw a lamp across the room and one of my babies happened to get in the way. There was blood everywhere, but did he care? No sir-re! All he said was that my baby shouldn't have gotten in the way of that lamp! I was afraid to go to the hospital, afraid they would take my baby away. So, I came here instead. He can't find me here! Who's cooking for him now, I wonder? I'm sure one of his little women is. I'm safe now though. Yes sir. No man will ever use me like that again. Nor any of my babies either. No way. They can play and make all the noise they want. No one's gonna yell and tell them to shut up!"

"You're lucky you have your babies, my ex-husband has mine." A beautiful woman with brown curly hair interrupted. She had big blue eyes and a creamy perfect complexion. She looked like she should be in a fashion catalog even though she was only wearing jeans and a cable knit sweater. Her diamond stud earrings were simple, but brilliant, brightening the dull living room. She pulled her legs up onto the couch, under herself.

"I'm sorry to interrupt. My name's Sheila. I have two kids, a boy and a girl. I miss them so much. My ex-husband Rob is so charming, he can convince anyone of anything. He convinced me that he loved me, that he would take care of me and we would be happy forever. Then, he convinced me that he needed me so much he couldn't share me with anyone or bear to be away from me if I wanted to visit my family or see friends. He convinced me he needed me at home to take care of the house and him, that he needed me there when he got home. Then the children came and he was jealous of them and demanded I give him more attention. He wouldn't let me go to them when they cried. He screamed and called them crybabies even when they were only a few months old. When they got old enough to walk, he threw things at them if they came out of their rooms, telling them to go back to bed.

"I had them fed, bathed, and in bed by the time he came home from work. I cooked two dinners, one for the kids and one for us. It got difficult when the kids got too old to go to bed so early, and had homework and activities that took me away from him. He timed how long it took to go anywhere and tracked the mileage on my car. He flipped out and accused me of having affairs when I went to school meetings. He even accused me of having a female lover. The kids watched as he screamed, accused me of horrible things and repeatedly told me I was stupid, incompetent, crazy and worse. Even though he never touched me physically, I was in constant fear. Every thought and action I performed was based on how he would respond. I felt like my soul was sucked out, transforming me into an empty shell. I was afraid to leave the house since I didn't want to provoke him. I stopped going to school activities, and as a result the kids didn't participate in things like scouts or sports.

"My son's teacher suspected something was wrong, and sent a note home to meet with me. I asked our neighbor to watch the kids after school while I went. The meeting went longer than expected and there was traffic on my way home. Rob came home early and no one was there. He went ballistic. By the time I got home, he had started drinking and was in a rage. He was convinced I had been 'off with my lover.' He threw furniture, punched walls, and called me a slut and a whore."

Beth felt a pang go through her chest. It was as if Sheila was talking about her. She could not believe that someone else had her same story. No wonder Marcia knew what Jeff was going to do before he did it. How many other women were telling this story, only with different variations.

Sheila continued, "He said he was going to kill me, and I believed him. I was so terrified that my heart started racing uncontrollably and I had horrible chest pains. I thought I was having a heart attack, so drove myself to the emergency room. They did many tests, but everything was fine and I was told I had an anxiety attack. I was let out of the hospital later that night to go to my mother's house since they wouldn't release me unless I had somewhere other than home to go to. I wanted to go home and get the kids first, but my mother was afraid. I called the next day to get my stuff and the kids, but there was no answer. When I went to the house, it was empty. I got my stuff and called a lawyer so that I could get the kids.

"I went to court to get custody, but Rob was so charming he convinced the judge that I was crazy, depressed, and incompetent. He said I was incapable of holding a job, never went out of the house, or had any friends. He used the diagnoses of anxiety as proof that I was unstable. He said I neglected the kids and that's why I never went to any of the school functions and why they weren't in activities. He said I abandoned them by going to my mother's house, and I made no effort to see or inquire about them. The judge believed him and granted him temporary custody, and me supervised visits.

"Then he started calling my mother's house and telling me he was sorry, that I should come back and not break up the family. He told me that if I didn't come back, then I wouldn't see the kids again. Despite what he says, he's keeping them not because he loves them, but to punish me for leaving. I tried to get a restraining order to make him stop calling me, but since he was granted custody I didn't have a case. My only way to escape was to come here. I'm in a safe place while I try to get my life in order and fight to get my kids back. I'm hoping that once Rob accepts that I won't come back, he'll get sick of taking care of the kids and let me have them. I miss them so much. My only regret in leaving is that I don't have my children, but I pray that some day we'll be together."

The room was silent. Beth thought of these incredible women. Each one trying to deal with the problems that life handed them, having expectations and dreams of creating a happy family, only to be disillusioned and disappointed. However, they did not give up. They each did what they thought was right to protect themselves and their children. Then, look where it led them. Monique lost her daughter because she stayed, and Sheila lost her children because she left. Beth wondered where her path would lead. She hoped that she would end up like Rosie, abandoned by her abuser and safe with her children. It seemed strange that to her, Rosie was fortunate. Beth knew that to the "normal" person, Rosie's situation would seem like a sad situation worthy of pity and charity. Yet Beth saw it as a story of hope and success.

There was another woman besides Beth who did not tell her story yet. She was sitting next to Sheila on the couch. She was young and plain, her jeans and blue jersey hanging off her. Her long, blond hair was pulled back in a loose ponytail and she wore no makeup to cover her gaunt features and dark circles. Despite her lack of effort to take care of herself, there was an unmistakable beauty that seemed as if it was trying to be hidden or denied. If the hair was brushed, makeup was applied, and the clothes were flattering, this timid young woman would be beautiful.

"I guess it's my turn. I don't have much of a story, just the same story told by a different person. A body trying to survive. Being nourished by food, water, and clothing yet deprived of any meaning. Oh, I guess I should tell my name, it's Stacey. People talk about wanting to be loved, about wanting a man. I've been 'loved' for as long as I can remember. I've always had 'a man' and don't see any joy in it. First it was my father who said that I was special and he loved me more than anyone in the world. He said other people would be mad and jealous if they found out what a special relationship we had, so I could never tell anyone. He said that I would never see him or anyone in my family again if I did. Then my brother played doctor with me, telling me that he was making me ready for when I grew up and had a baby. I guess he bragged to his friends and they didn't believe him, because he brought them over and let them have sex with me. I was about seven years old. He told me that he would kill me if I ever told anyone. So, I grew up silent and used. Just being passed around by men so that they could 'love' me. I had no self. I was just empty and dirty inside. I never deserved to be happy. I was just a thing, an 'it.' I always thought it was that way for everyone, but that no one ever talked about it. Kind of like how everyone shits, but no one talks about it. It was always there, so it never occurred to me that it shouldn't be happening.

"I existed, accepting my fate. I had no choice. Up until recently I was a twenty-three year old woman living at home with her family, not allowed to go to college or work. I was a girl whose place was in the home 'taking care of my family,' mainly by being the family whore. Then one day my father walked in on my brother and me. He went ballistic. One would expect that he would be angry because his daughter was being raped. But instead, he was jealous that someone else was having a piece of what he considered his. He beat the shit out of both of us. The ambulance took me to the hospital and I begged them not to send me home. They told me that I was an adult, of course I didn't have to go home. The doctor realized what was happening and asked the crisis center to help me. They saved me. They took me here where I'm safe and my father and brother can't find me. The police want me to press charges for being raped and beaten, but I'm not strong enough for that. I can't face them or relive what became an almost daily occurrence for most of my life.

"You all have children. I'll never have a child. I'll never create a life, bring a child into this world so that it can live a life of suffering and pain. I'll never understand how people can actually want to have sex, want to be with a man. I only want to be alone. I want to be able to feel."

Beth knew that it was her turn to say something, but her problems seemed so minor compared to Stacey's life. At least Beth had a happy childhood and knew what it was like to be safe and loved. She had a past life to compare her current misery to. What if misery was all she ever knew, and thought that is what life was? Would she have any hope? Or would she just die inside. What about Zack? Their life with Jeff was all that he ever knew, so to him that was how it was supposed to be. Beth prayed silent thanks that they were in this place, safe. She prayed that they would stay safe and together. She tried to smile at the group of women who just shared their stories with her and were waiting patiently for her to do the same.

"My name is Beth. I listen to your stories and can relate to you all. Not because my story is the same, but because I can understand the suffering, the will to get away, and the drive to make it happen. I feel like a coward for running away and hiding, for not standing up to him. I have learned to be silent, to take the pain. I finally got the courage to leave in hopes of saving my son, Zack. He's just a baby, yet I already see him acting like my husband. 'Like father, like son.' I love my son too much to let that happen. I want him to grow up knowing that violence is not acceptable, that it's not how life is supposed to be. I want him to grow up feeling safe and strong in a healthy way, not in a dominant way. So, I ran away from a monster who convinces himself that he's strong by bullying people who are weaker. I'm scared to death of the journey I have ahead of me and what that monster will try to do. But I have hope. I don't know what the world would be like without hope."

"What's hope? I don't know what hope feels like." Stacey spoke very silently.

Sheila answered her, "Hope is what makes you have the will to try even though you know it's useless."

Marcia cut in strong and full of energy. "Will you listen to your selves? You sound like a bunch of prisoners waiting for death row, not the strong powerful women who you are! Each one of you did what many women never find the courage to do. You all stood up for yourself and left! Give yourselves some credit will you? You each have a brand new life waiting for you. You have the power to create it however you want! If that's not the definition of hope, I don't know what is! You're all an inspiration to women everywhere! To people everywhere! Never, ever say that you don't have hope."

Beth felt a warm tingling pass through her body. Although Marcia was talking to everyone, Beth felt as though she were speaking just to her. But then again, they were all the same, so what was true for one was true for all.

It felt good for Beth to climb into the tiny bed in the cozy corner room with Zack sleeping soundly in the bed next to her. Being so far away from Jeff, it was the first time Beth felt safe and she wondered if Zack felt the same way, which was why he was in such a deep sleep. She pulled the worn blankets up over her head and knew she could fall asleep without worrying about being woken up by Jeff and his demands or violence. Jeff. Even the thought of him made her tense up. She wondered what he was doing and how he was reacting to her being gone. The thought terrified her. She reminded herself of the long drive to get here and knew that Jeff would not be able to find her. She thought about the women in the support group tonight and wondered which direction her story would lead. She prayed to God to keep her and Zack safe and to not let Jeff ever hurt them again. Even if he could not hurt her, what about Zack? Would Zack get returned to Jeff like Sheila's children did? If that happened, would she go back to Jeff so that she could keep Zack safe like Monique did? Would she be able to keep Zack safe, or would he end up hating her for giving in? There were so many thoughts racing through her head that Beth thought she would never fall asleep, but she did. She fell asleep and did not wake up until

Zack jumped on her bed the next morning wanting to go downstairs because he smelled bacon. Beth smelled coffee. She could not remember waking up to the smell of coffee since she was a child at her grandparent's house. Usually she was the one who made the coffee.

Beth and Zack went downstairs following the aromas of coffee, bacon and more. They gave her comfort since they reminded her of her grandmother's kitchen, but the sounds scared her. She and Zack were used to being quiet so they would not piss Jeff off. Here, there was lots of noise. There were pans clanging, people laughing and arguing, and music playing. No one was even attempting to be quiet. It made Beth so uneasy, she was expecting Jeff to pop out of nowhere and yell for everyone to shut up. She almost started crying out of fear, but then Zack grabbed her hand and began pulling her towards the kitchen, "Come on Mommy, let's play with everyone." Beth smiled and held back the tears of happiness that almost escaped.
"Thank you Zack," she whispered.
They entered the kitchen together. Beth sharing Zack's childlike enthusiasm about this new environment where people were happy, and laughing, and loud. It triggered an almost forgotten memory about being a child herself, but this was a new experience for Zack. His short existence on this earth had been filled with fear. Had he ever even seen a happy laugh? He had seen Jeff's devious laugh when he hurt Beth, and saw people laugh on TV. But what about a happy, carefree, real laugh? Had Zack ever witnessed that? Had he ever experienced it? Beth suddenly felt her heart swell up in her chest and knew she was doing the right thing. No matter what happened, no matter how hard it was and how dirty Jeff got, she would have the strength and courage to continue. Nothing in her life would ever be as bad as living with Jeff, so there was nothing she would not conquer to get herself and Zack as far away as possible.
Beth suddenly realized that she was standing in the middle of the kitchen crying and everyone was staring at her. Zack was the only one who did not notice. Was it because he was too excited with all of the food and people, or just because he was used to seeing her cry? There was Latin music playing on the radio, and it gave her a longing to dance. She grabbed Rosie's hands and began swinging around the spacious kitchen. For no other reason than that she could. She could do whatever she wanted and no one was going to stop her! Sheila and Stacey joined in and the four children started to jump up and down, clapping their hands in excitement. Zack had a huge grin on his face. Beth could not remember the last time she felt so happy. They were going to like it here.

The happiness that Beth felt earlier was squeezed down by the feelings of fear and anticipation that now filled her thoughts. It was late at night and everyone was asleep but her. Not knowing what to do, she went into the kitchen and began cleaning. Not just regular cleaning like washing the counters and floor, but deep cleaning. She got the urge to clean everything out and make it organized and neat. She started with the canisters. She emptied the contents into bowls lined up in a neat row on the kitchen table. One each for flour, sugar, teas, coffee sweeteners, and condiment packets. She then scrubbed each canister and laid them on a towel to dry. She proceeded to the draws, emptied them all out, washed and sorted their contents. Rubbermaid containers and covers, knives and silver ware, serving spoons and utensils. When she finished washing the contents, she washed the draws, dried everything and put it all back together. She finished by mopping the floor, scrubbing the cabinet doors, counter, kitchen table, and walls. The only thing she did not wash was the inside of the cabinets since she was not sure what food was personal and she did not want to offend anyone. The sky began to turn a light gray when she realized that she had been up all night and was exhausted. She quietly went upstairs to bed where Zack was in a deep sleep beside her. Beth listened to the sound of his tiny breath slowly inhaling and exhaling, lulling her to sleep.

When Beth woke up the sun was bright and the house was quiet, but Zack's bed was empty. She jumped up and ran downstairs looking for him. The first room she came to was the living room, where Zack was sitting on Lisa's lap while she read him a book. They both looked content and happy. Beth could not remember seeing Zack so relaxed. She had always thought of a shelter as a negative place, having pity on its inhabitants, but she was experiencing this as paradise. She was safe with people who understood and cared about her and her child. She felt fortunate to be here.

Lisa and Zack looked up at Beth as she entered the room. Lisa smiled, and Zack proudly announced, "Lisa is reading me a book so that I learn how to read when I go to school! I am going to be smart, smart, smart!"

"You already are smart, smart, smart!" Beth gave Zack a hug and kiss on his forehead.

"By the looks of the kitchen, it looks like you were up half the night." Lisa smiled at Beth.

"Try the whole night. You must think me obsessed!"

"Not at all, cleaning is excellent therapy. We never have any problems with keeping the house clean. It's a safe way for people to get things in order externally, which leads to getting things in order on the big picture. You're moving in the right direction, one small step at a time."

"I'm going to need an awfully lot of small steps. Where's everyone else?"

"The kids are in school. Monique, Rosie, and Stacey are working, and Sheila is sleeping."

"It's late, and she hasn't been up all night cleaning. Is she okay?"

"Yeah, she just sleeps a lot. You know ... depression. It helps her to forget about not being with her kids. It's a means of escape. If she's sleeping, then she doesn't have to think. I'm worried about her, but there's no room in the emergency shelter where she would be supervised. I wish there was somewhere else for her to go where people could take care of her. This is designed as a place where roommates live independently together before being on their own, not a place for people who need the help that Sheila requires. However, there's nowhere else for her to go. We're trying to get her a job, which will keep her occupied and take second step to independence. The first step was making the choice to leave her ex-husband. We're doing the best we can."

"It's never easy, is it?"

"No one ever said that life would be easy."

"I'm going to get something to eat and then go to my room and write in my journal." Beth shifted her gaze and the tone of her voice, "You going to be okay here little man?"

Zack gave Beth a shy smile, "Yeah, I like Lisa."

"Good! Because *I love you*!"

Chapter 6

Beth had been at the safe home for over a week. It was Wednesday night and Beth was looking forward to Support Group. She had gone to two support groups at the Crisis Center during the week, but she was looking forward to the time spent alone with her housemates. Sure, they all talked during the week and at the house-cleaning meeting, but the Wednesday night support group seemed like a special time for them all to be alone together. There was no one out working, no kids or interruptions. They were all here together connected. Beth loved the sense of community that was an extended family she had chosen to be part of.

Every one was hanging around in the living room, casually talking while they waited for the meeting to start. Beth missed having Marcia, but Lisa made a good leader too.

"Okay everyone, welcome. It's good to be together to support each other. There has been a lot of activity this week. Who wants to start?"

Despite her quiet, reserved nature Monique seemed very excited and was eager to be the first to talk.

"I'll go first. There's an opening in the Deli department at work. I asked my manager, and she said that she'd recommend me if I wanted to apply." Monique smiled shyly, everyone hooted and yeah'ed.

"Monique, that's wonderful. I'm so proud of you for taking the step to better yourself. How do you feel?" Lisa asked.

"I'm excited. I don't remember ever looking forward to anything before. I can't believe that my manager actually said she'd recommend me, no one recommend me for anything before."

"Well Monique, that must mean that she thinks that you do a good job and deserve to move up to a better position."

"I've never been good at anything."

"I'm sure that you've been good at many things but didn't realize it. It's difficult to realize your strengths when there's always someone pointing out your weaknesses."

"Yeah, it makes it hard to believe you can do anything."

"But you can do a lot. You know that don't you?"

"I don't believe it. I'm afraid to apply because I don't know if I'll be able to do the job. Part of me wants to stay where I am, and part of me wants to take a chance and try it. I'm so nervous."

Rosie chimed in, "You go girl. I'm proud of ya. It's like I tell my kids, you never know if you can do something unless you try. And if you can't, oh well then. Nothing lost in trying. If you never tried then you would never have known. And who knows? Maybe you'll be the top deli person and end up in management!"

Monique laughed, "Management? Me? Oh God, no. You have a good sense of humor, Rosie!"

Lisa smiled at them both, "Rosie's right, Monique. You're a smart, talented woman. You only need some confidence to get all those years of being told that you were worthless out of your head. How about you, Rosie? How are you doing?"

"Me? I'm doing *fine*. My little babies are doing so good in school. I met with the teacher who said that my oldest should be moved up to the top group! Can you believe that? My lil' child in the top group at school? I do believe that these children of mine are going to grow up to go to college and make fine lives for themselves!"

"Well Rosie, I think you're right. And you know why, don't you?"

"Because they have such great brains!"

Everyone laughed.

"I'm sure that's true, but also because you show them that hard work and determination pay off."

"Me? Huh! I'm not successful. I just work as a receptionist. I talk on the phone all day, it's every teenager's dream job! I get paid for doing what I love to do—talk to people!"

"Yeah, and you're showing your kids that you go to work and better yourself. That you won't let anyone push you around and that you deserve a good life."

"I guess so. I don't know though. I am just doing what I have to do to survive. No more than anyone else."

Sheila spoke up, "Yeah, but you are succeeding. You have your kids, a job, you're working towards getting a place of your own. Look at me. What do I have? I have nothing. I don't have my kids. I don't have the energy or strength to get a job. I have nothing to live for. I'm just existing. If I weren't here, I'd probably be laying dead in an alley somewhere."

Everyone started speaking at once: "Oh Sheila, don't say that!" "You're showing your kids that it's not okay to stay when someone treats you like shit."

"Sheila, you have us." "We love you." "You'll get your kids back, and they'll love you for sticking to your guns."

Lisa knelt on the floor at Sheila's feet and took her hands. "Sheila, listen to me. Don't ever think that your life is nothing. You're setting an example for your kids, and it will work out. You're up against the odds, but you can make it happen. Just keep looking ahead and never stop. Don't ever give up. If you do, then your ex-husband wins. Show your kids that you can do it."

Sheila did not respond. She just sat, staring at nothing. Sheila was going to counseling twice a week and Lisa assured Beth they were giving as much help as Sheila would allow. The more stimulation and attention they could give Sheila, the better. On an impulse, Beth went over to Sheila and gave her a hug.

Sheila smiled at Beth, "Tell us in detail what happened at court last week, Beth."

Beth felt such joy that she was able to make Sheila smile.

"Probate court was different than criminal court. We worked out everything before we went to the judge. I sat in the hall with Marcia while my attorney, Jeff and his attorney met with the probate officer. They used the court guidelines to have Jeff's pay attached for child support, to have him provide us with health insurance, and for me to keep my car. However, he was adamant that he wants split custody and my attorney stood firm that there be no visitation until an investigation is performed at Jeff's expense. The probate officer recommended that Jeff have supervised visitation, and sent us to the judge to decide. Jeff didn't learn his lesson from the last time we were in court and yelled at the judge about having father's rights. The judge declared that there would be no visitation or contact until a Guardian ad Litem, or GAL, evaluation be completed. There is a list of people who can perform the evaluation, Jeff must contact one and pay the fee. Once that's done, I'll be contacted. Now it's a matter of waiting."

"What's a GAL?" Sheila asked.

Lisa answered, "A Guardian ad Litem is a person who's trained to do a detailed impartial investigation concerning family matters and then report their findings to the court. It's usually either a lawyer or a therapist. In my opinion, it is better to have a therapist since a therapist can understand the emotional aspect of everything and can see through the abusive behavior. A GAL's job is not to take sides, but to look at everything and everyone objectively and then make recommendations based on the findings. I think this would be a good situation to use a GAL."

Sheila smiled at Beth, "I'm happy for you, Beth. It makes me proud that you're able to keep your little boy safe."

"It's nothing that I did and you didn't do, Sheila. It's the act of putting your destiny in one person who can sway either direction."

Rosie spoke up, "It's because Beth's husband yells at the judge, and Sheila's husband charms the judge. I don't think it's anything that either of you did, or even the luck of the draw about the judge. I think it's a matter of what kind of abuser you're up against. They all play the game different. It's up to each of you to figure out the best way to play against them. It's like playing chess, each person has their own style, and you have to learn your opponent's strengths and weaknesses so that you can plan your strategy and your next move. Where Beth's husband is stupid and can't even control himself in front of the judge, Beth might be better off playing the game in the courts. For Sheila, she's playing against a cunning serpent, so should play differently. You must learn his weaknesses, Sheila. You lived with him long enough, what makes him lose control?"

"Everything."

Everyone laughed, including Sheila.

Rosie came up with a plan. "Well, it seems to me that even though Beth's husband and your ex-husband act different in court, they're probably like my man in many ways. My man also loses control and gets violent over anything and everything. This seems to be a common trait for all of us."

Everyone shook their heads in agreement.

"However, it's very predictable what makes these men happy. I'm sure your ex-husband is the same way."

"I can't think of anything that makes him happy."

"No? What about when he hurts you? Does he laugh and feel happy then?"

"Yeah."

"What about when he puts you down? He must like that."

"He sure does."

"So, it seems to me that if your misfortune makes him happy, then your success would be the best way to make him suffer. What better way to piss him off than to show him that you can stand on your own two feet and get on with out him."

"Rosie, you never cease to amaze me. How is it that you come up with such wisdom? I think that you must have been a philosopher in a past life." Lisa complimented Rosie.

"Well honey, I don't know what I was in a past life but it sure aint' getten me anywhere in this life!"

"Oh, I don't know about that. I think that you're doing pretty well in this life." Lisa turned to Stacey, "How about you Stacey? You're quiet tonight. What's happening with you?

"I hate to break this to you Lisa, but I'm always quiet. That's who I am. But I do have some good news. I decided to help out in the nursery at church. I figured that since being with a man repulses me, it will be impossible to ever have a child of my own. So, by helping out in the nursery at church I can help take care of the babies."

"That's wonderful, Stacey. But, just because you don't want to be with a man doesn't mean that you'll never have a baby. You could have artificial insemination or adoption."

"I feel too dirty and corrupted to ever let an innocent baby grow inside of me; and no one would ever let a poor, homeless, single mother adopt a baby."

"First of all, you're not homeless. This is your home. Second of all, this is a stepping-stone to a better place. You're taking the necessary steps to improve your life and create a safe home for yourself. You have the power to make your life anything that you want it to be. You just showed us that you're doing that by helping out in the nursery. There's nothing more healing than the innocence of children. I think that they'll give you as much as you'll give them."

Beth remembered how much she enjoyed going to church as a child. It was so sacred and holy. She felt safe and protected, as if all of those statues of Jesus, Mary, and Joseph were looking down and watching over her. She loved the quiet while the priest stood behind the alter and spoke his words of wisdom. Reading from the holy bible and interpreting the meaning to the meager people such as herself. She loved the smell of the incense, the holiness of the singing, the softness of the candles, and the way that the echo of the bell would slowly fade away. She realized that she missed the sacred feeling of being in church.

"Stacey? I don't know if I'm imposing, so please don't feel obligated to say yes, but would it be all right if I went to church with you?"

Stacey seemed excited at Beth's desire to join her, "Oh my God Beth! Of course you can come to church! Zack can come to the nursery with me. I always go everywhere alone. It will be so nice to actually have someone to go with!"

Just the thought of going to church with Stacey made Beth feel at peace.

"This is great, there's so much positive stuff going on in everyone's lives! It's very exciting. I guess it's time to officially close the meeting, but of course anyone is welcome to stay and hang out if you want."

Beth said goodnight and went up to bed. She heard voices in the living room well into the night. She lay in bed and thought of all the conversations they had tonight. She thought of Stacey and the babies at church. Of Rosie and her positive outlook on everything. Beth did not understand how Rosie could have been through so much, yet always had a smile on her face, a laugh waiting to come out, and a positive comment for every situation. Beth thought of Monique trying to get a better position at work and of poor Sheila's feelings of despair. Beth thought about her own situation and Rosie's comments about how the best way to get back at these men, like Jeff, would be to show him that she could succeed. Beth wanted to succeed. She wanted to do it to prove to Jeff that she wasn't worthless, but more so because she wanted to prove to herself that she had a purpose. Beth wanted to create a positive life for herself, just like

Lisa said. Beth thought of the opportunity she had before her. Her life was like an open slate and she had the power to make it anything she wanted it to be. What did she want it to be? What were her dreams? Her goals? What did she want to do with her life?

Beth called Marcia the next morning and asked her if they could get together. Beth knew that it was a long drive for Marcia and that she should call Lisa or go to the crisis center, but she felt she needed Marcia. She looked at Marcia as an almost maternal figure since she was the one who saved her. Marcia said she would come over that afternoon and they could take Zack to the park. Zack was very excited when he found out as a day at the park was a special treat for him. It was a great way for Zack to run around and release his energy while Beth and Marcia sat on the bench and talked. It was still cold out this time of year, but Beth liked to get outdoors. She loved the feel of the fresh air in her lungs. The cold on her face was invigorating.

Marcia showed up around 2:00 P.M. to pick up Beth and Zack. It was a beautiful sunny day with a brilliant blue sky. The sun shone so brightly that it gave the feeling spring was not far off. Apparently the feeling was shared by others because they had a hard time finding a parking space. Beth thought it would be hypocritical to complain about having to walk the distance to the park, when part of why they came was to get some exercise. Beth liked the fact that the play area was fenced in, so Zack could run around and be free. Free. She realized that she was free. Free to not be afraid. Free to not spend her existence trying to please someone. Free to be happy. Zack climbed up on the large wooden castle and ran back and forth across the drawbridge.

"Look Mommy, I'm a knight fighting off the dragon."

"You're a brave boy, Zack!"

Marcia smiled at Beth, "So Beth, how's Zack doing?"

"He seems great. He's happy and relaxed. It's amazing how easily children adjust to change."

"Is he homesick, or miss Jeff?"

"To tell you the truth, he hasn't asked for either of them. He keeps thanking me for bringing him to this 'happy place.' It's like our other life never even existed."

"The younger a child is removed from a negative situation, the easier it is to adjust. He's surrounded by love and happiness. Pretty soon the life he left behind will be nothing more than a bad nightmare."

"That is considering that I'm able to keep him away from Jeff. I don't know how easy that's going to be. I mean, look at Sheila."

"Yeah, and look at Rosie. She doesn't even see the fathers of her children. No one knows how things are going to turn out. It's completely unpredictable. However, I have a feeling you'll end up somewhere in the middle. I don't think that you'll be able to keep Zack from Jeff completely, but I also don't think that Jeff will get custody of Zack. It doesn't seem to me like he even wants it. You're providing a safe, loving environment for Zack. Even if he has to spend time with Jeff, he'll always come home to you and know that being surrounded by love is his real life. He'll grow up knowing the difference between right and wrong because he'll see both sides and know which side he belongs to. No matter what happens, he'll be fine.

"However, I think that you asked me to meet you today to talk about something else. What's up?"

"Well Marcia, I've been thinking about what direction I want to go in. I think I want to get a job."

"Are you sure you're ready for that? Are you ready to leave Zack?"

"I need to feel like I'm accomplishing something. Like I'm contributing. I need to become fully independent. I love being at the safe home, but I know that I can't stay there forever. There are other women who are going to need a safe home to escape to. I need to start thinking of the future."

"You're right that the safe home is a place of transition while you prepare for a life of your own. The transition process has already started, now I see no reason not to speed it along. We have to start thinking of the course you have to take to separate yourself from Jeff. The first step you have already accomplished, by leaving him and getting the restraining order. The next step is to file for divorce and become self-sufficient. I spoke with Attorney Peters, and she thinks you should apply for assistance from the state and let them go after Jeff for child support."

"You mean welfare?"

"Welfare, like the safe home, was developed as a transition for people who are having a hard time and need help until they can get themselves stable. Unfortunately, a lot of people abuse it, which gives it a bad name and makes it more difficult for people who really need it. Once you file for divorce, then you can apply for state assistance. There are a lot of programs available to help you get yourself on your feet. You can get assistance for housing, food stamps, and, most importantly, we can try to get you into a job-training program to help you to get a better job so that you will be able to get ahead instead of just making ends meet. How does this all sound?"

"It sounds too good to be true. I don't understand how I can expect to be given so much when there are so many people who need it more than me."

"You don't understand, do you? These programs were made specifically for people like you. People donate and pay taxes so that people like you can have a chance of making a better life for themselves instead of staying in bad situations, living in poverty, or depending on others. Everyone has the right to be given a chance to be the best that they can be. I believe in you and am willing to recommend to the welfare worker that you be given a chance in the job-training program and that you be put on the list for subsidized housing. I believe you're going to make it, and it's okay to get help when you need it. As human beings, we're all here to help each other out, to take care of each other."

"But I have nothing to give back. How will I be able to repay all of the help that I've been receiving?"

"Believe me when I tell you that there will come a time when you'll be more than able to give back, and I know that you'll end up giving much more than you've received."

"Oh, I don't know about that."

"I do."

On Sunday morning Stacey woke Beth and Zack up at 8:00 A.M. At first, Beth was surprised as she was used to sleeping late on Sundays. It did not take long for Stacey to remind her of her promise to go to church. Stacey seemed so excited that Beth did not dare to back down on their plans. Zack was disoriented in his sleepy state.

"Why are we getting up so early?"

"We're going to church."

"What's church?"

"It's where we go to pray to God to take care of us."

"But you take care of me."

Beth kissed Zack's forehead. It meant a lot to her that Zack depended on her and knew that he could trust her to take care of him. She was glad Stacey was bringing them to church with her.

When Beth and Zack came downstairs, Stacey was sitting at the kitchen table waiting. She had made a pot of coffee and had two bowls, spoons, and Beth's cereal and milk on the table. The kitchen had its own little system that worked out well. It was a smaller reflection of how the house in general worked. Each of them had their own bedroom, which was their private space and no one trespassed into other people's rooms, but there were community rooms they all shared such as the living room, dining room, kitchen, TV room, and bathrooms. Food worked the same way. They each had their own separate cabinet and shelf in the refrigerator where they labeled and kept their own food, but they also had community stuff like coffee, sugar, and paper towels that they all contributed to. Each of them cooked their own food, but they would also unofficially take turns cooking for each other and sharing small treats. It was nice to have breakfast out waiting for her.

Beth offered to drive the short distance to the church so that they would not have to transfer Zack's car seat. The church was a modern brick building that was "seventies" style. It had tall, narrow, stained glass windows that illuminated bright colors into the sanctuary as the sun filtered through them. It was fun entering the building, as everyone seemed to know Stacey. They all smiled and nodded "Hello." Some people asked her who her friend was. It was obvious that although everyone seemed to know Stacey, the knowledge was not mutual. Stacey smiled and said, "This is my friend Beth and her son Zack." She said it smoothly without introducing the other person, who was then obligated to introduce themselves, giving both Stacey and Beth the benefit of finding out their name. Not that Beth would be able to remember all of these new names. She was grateful for the small percentage of people who wore nametags.

"Do you want me to take Zack to the nursery and you can go into the service?"

When Beth was a child, the entire family would go into church together. It was a family-bonding hour. She would sit through the mass, stroking the soft mink fur on the cuff of her mother's coat. It was a time for her mind to wonder. A time to be close to her parents, but to have no expectations put on her. She could feel their presence close to her, but there were no conversations or instructions. She could just be with them.

"Wouldn't it be better if he came into the service too?"

"The church has a nursery so that the adults can enjoy the service without worrying about keeping small children quiet. The service is geared towards adults; children don't understand what's being said. They do age-appropriate lessons in their classes. They learn more that way and can have fun instead of sitting and trying to keep quiet."

"I guess you're right. Thanks for taking him."

Beth felt awkward entering the sanctuary alone. She chose a pew toward the back incase she wanted to go check on Zack, and so she could observe everyone from a distance. It was an interesting variety of people. There were conservative well-dressed people, as well as people in jeans and casual sweaters. There were single people and many couples. It was the couples that Beth kept staring at. She had not seen many couples since she left Jeff, and now they seemed to be everywhere. There were teenagers, middle-aged—and older couples. It seemed that everyone but her had someone, making her feel extremely alone. When Beth was with Jeff she was a couple, always knowing there was someone there for her. But now she had no one. She looked at the older couples and tried to imagine what their lives together had been like. Did they have children? Were they together for years and years, or was this a late-life romance? Beth thought about how nice it would be to grow old with someone. It made her feel angry at Jeff for taking that away from her. Instead she was put down, insulted, hurt. It was not supposed to be like this, and she blamed Jeff for not keeping his end of the bargain. She had done everything she was supposed to as a wife and mother; why couldn't he? There were simple things that were understood. Love your family. Keep them safe. Do not hurt them.

The minister was young and handsome with thick black hair that was slicked back and rested on his shoulders. He had pale skin, freckles, and blue eyes, obviously Irish. He introduced himself as Reverend Josh. Beth was quite surprised by his youth and the personal approach he took. If Beth were in a position to be interested in a man, she would have found him incredibly sexy. However, Beth was too engrossed in her personal thoughts to pay much attention and hardly listened to the sermon. She caught bits and pieces of words such as "It's up to each one of us to set an example of what love means," and "If it weren't for community and taking care of each other, then where would each of us be? Whether it's in the family, the community, on the level of state, country, or world, we are all meant to care for each other."

Each time Beth heard a fragment of the sermon, her mind began to wonder and she started to think about things such as how alone and isolated she was when she was with Jeff. She remembered being a child growing up, being close to her family and feeling safe. She believed the secure existence she had was the way life was supposed to be, the way it was for everyone. Jeff had laughed at her idealistic views. He told her she was naive and stupid, and to wake up to the real world. Since this seemed to be the case with the other women in the safe home, Beth wondered if he was right. Was Jeff correct when he told Beth that it was normal for men to "be in charge of" their families, and for wives to "take care" of their husbands and the house and that it was her duty? She considered if this was matrimony or slavery. She wondered which situation was the norm. How did the rest of America live? Did they have happy families like on TV and like in her childhood? Or was it like the book *The Giver* by Lois Lowry where it appeared to be a perfect society where everyone was happy and safe. But in reality, the people were just pawns being told exactly how to live their lives and were deprived of the simple luxury of feeling. They were told that it was for the best and that they were safe and happy this way. Yet in reality this "utopian" society killed anyone who did not fit into what their idea of how things were supposed to be. Whether it was a baby who would not sleep through the night, a citizen who did not follow the rules of order, or an elder who was no longer useful to society, they would just be murdered. Every aspect of their life was planned and controlled. They were told how to dress, talk, who to marry, and what job they would have. They were even assigned their children. They had no choices, passion, or feelings. It was supposedly for the best because by being told what to do and how to live, they were not given the opportunity to make mistakes. And by not feeling at all, they were not feeling bad. So they lived in a world that they believed was good and "the norm" where in reality they just existed, robbed of experiencing living.

Beth felt like she was a member of this fictional society when she was with Jeff. Every aspect of her life was planning out and controlled. She had no choices of her own. From the outside, her life looked perfect and ideal. But in reality, she was void of feeling and empty inside. She was at risk of being murdered at a moment's notice with no warning, for the simple reason that she did not fit into Jeff's idea of how things were supposed to be.

The handsome minister continued preaching about each person's responsibility to improve society, while Beth linked the examples to her own life and tried to determine what was truth, what was fiction, what were illusions, and what was reality. The service was eventually over, and despite the fact that Beth was sitting in the back of the sanctuary; she waited until everyone else left before she got up. She followed the smiling crowd downstairs and into a large basement/ function room where tables were set up with a variety of baked goods, coffee, and juice. People smiled at Beth and welcomed her to join them. She smiled back politely and excused herself while she searched for Stacey and Zack. She began to panic when she could not find them. Images of Jeff finding them and taking Zack away swarmed through her mind. She frantically pushed through the room full of strangers, her heart racing. Someone asked her what was wrong and she told him that she could not find her son.

"Oh, the kids haven't come downstairs yet. They usually wait a little while before bringing the kids down to give the adults time to socialize first."

Beth looked around the room and did not see any other children. She felt a little relief. "Where's the nursery? I'd like to go up and get him."

"You go back up the stairs to the second floor. The nursery is the first room on your right."

"Thank you."

Beth raced up the stairs and opened the door to find Zack playing happily with the other children. There was a large sand box on the floor and they were taking turns pouring sand through a funnel that led the sand into little cups that each tipped as it poured down to the bottom.

"Hi Mommy, these are my new friends, Mathew and Cindy. We take turns and share, just like good friends should." Zack was smiling proudly at the announcement of his good behavior. He learned quickly that being nice to people gets you much farther than being mean. Beth leaned over and gave him a tight hug and wet kiss on his cheek. Zack squirmed away and wiped his cheek with his sleeve. He rolled his eyes and stated firmly, "No, mommy. Not in front of my friends!"

"Do you want to come downstairs with me?"

"I want to play some more."

Beth felt rejected.

Stacey spoke up, "You're welcome to stay. We're going to bring the kids downstairs in a few minutes anyway."

Stacey was sitting in a rocking chair, rocking a small baby who was snuggled up under her chin. She looked content and happy. Beth did not want to ruin the moment for her. Beth thought of what a loving, wonderful mother Stacey would make. It was too bad that she was intent on never having children.

"Yeah, I'll stay and help bring the kids down when it's time."

A heavy woman with brown wavy hair and glasses got up from playing on the floor with a little girl and shook Beth's hand. "Hi, I'm Gayle. I work here in the nursery and we enjoyed having Zack with us today. I invited Stacey to come to my house for dinner after church. That's my baby Mia that she's rocking. Mia doesn't like very many people, but she loves Stacey. I think there's some truth in letting children judge who should be trusted. Anyone that Mia trusts, I trust. I therefore trust Stacey. To take it a step further, anyone who's a friend of Stacey's is a friend of mine. So, would you like to join us?"

Stacey was smiling shyly, happier than Beth had ever seen her.

"Yeah, we'd love to join you."

Chapter 7

Beth got a call from Attorney Peters on Tuesday afternoon letting her know that she had gone to court and filed the papers for divorce. Jeff should be served the papers by the end of the week, and Lisa could help her apply for state assistance. They had not heard about setting up an appointment with the GAL, which meant that Jeff had not retained one yet. It could be a long wait if Jeff did not move forward, the more time that went by the better. She assured Beth that things were going along fine and as expected.

Later that night the house was quiet. Beth sat by herself in the dark living room, eating Rocky Road ice cream out of the half-gallon carton. For some reason, Beth found filing for divorce very difficult. She knew that she did not want to be with Jeff, and that it would be dangerous for both her and Zack to ever go back. But the thought of filing for divorce seemed so final. Beth had been with Jeff all of her adult life. To separate herself from him completely was like losing a part of herself, even though it was a part she did not want. Beth sat in the dark living room not knowing how to feel.

Beth heard someone come down the stairs and enter the living room. It was Sheila; she quietly sat in the chair opposite Beth. She pulled the blanket off from the back of the chair and wrapped it around herself. Sheila's silence comforted Beth. They sat in the dark, feeling each other's presence. After what seemed a long span of time, Beth broke the silence.

"Do you ever wonder if you made the right decision in leaving?"

"Yeah. I miss my kids so much; I wonder if it would be worth taking the abuse just to be back with them again. I miss being a family."

"Me too. I keep thinking of the happy times we had and I wonder if I did something different then maybe he wouldn't have been the way that he was."

"I think that too. I think to myself, why couldn't it just have stayed okay? Why did he have to ruin the happiness? Why couldn't he just do his part to let the family be a normal family?"

"That's all I wanted too. I tried so hard to do what he wanted, but I never knew what that was. I keep thinking that if I knew, then maybe I could have prevented him from getting so mad. Maybe we could have been the family that I wanted us to be. I keep thinking of the happy times we had, of the times when I knew that he loved me. I miss those times. I wish I could keep those times and let everything else disappear."

"Well, maybe you can keep those times in your memory. The problem I have is that now that I'm away from it and safe, I get this false sense of confidence. I think of all of the happy times and remember the person I fell in love with. I start believing 'that is the person who he is.' But then, *boom!* He does something that pulls me back to reality and reminds me that the true him is an unpredictable crazy person who's miserable and wants the entire world to be miserable along with him."

"That's Jeff too. I guess it's the same with me. Now that I'm away from him, it's easy to remember the nice times and the reason I fell in love. But, I'm all too familiar with how quickly things change. The only sense of predictability was the unpredictability of his moods and what would set him off. But it's hard being alone and scary not knowing what's going to happen next. At least when I was with Jeff, I knew what to expect. I knew what my life was, even if it was constant anxiety."

"Yeah, it's hard to figure out my identity. Being with Rob, I completely lost myself. I tried so hard to be who he wanted me to be, I never thought about me, what I liked or wanted. I was a mother and wife for so long, but who am I now? I'm no longer wife. I'm still mother, but a mother with no children. Where does that leave me?"

"Creating an identity."

"Is an identity something that you create or just something that you are?"

"Maybe it's a little of both."

"Where do I start?"

"When I was with Jeff, everything that I was, was just trying to be who he wanted me to be. I didn't know who I was, or who I wanted to be. My entire existence was trying to be and create what he wanted so that he wouldn't hurt me. Now I have to keep reminding myself that I don't have to be that any more, but I don't know how much of me is me and how much is what I became to please Jeff.

"I'm trying to find out what I want, and to get rid of who I was for Jeff. But I don't know who's who. Sometimes, I'll just finish making my bed in the morning, and then mess it up again and keep it unmade all day, just because I can and no one will care. Even right now, eating this ice cream out of the box. Jeff was always telling me how fat I was, so I watched my weight. But now I can eat as much as I want and get as fat as I want, because there's no one who

I have to be skinny for. I have this unbelievable sense of freedom, but I don't know what to do with it."

Beth scooped a large spoonful of ice cream out of the box and slowly ate it before continuing.

"It's not that I want to be a fat slob, but I don't want to be the other extreme either. I belong somewhere in between. I'm no longer the person I was before I met Jeff; I don't want to be the person I was when I was with Jeff; so who am I now? What do I do with my life?"

"At least you have a choice. I don't have the luxury of trying to figure out who I am. My life is still being controlled by my ex-husband. I have to be who the courts want me to be if I'm going to get my children back. If I get fat, it will be used against me in court. His lawyer will say that I 'let myself go and am unfit to care for children'. The same if I let my guard down for a minute, even to let my bed be unmade. 'They' will find some way to use it against me. I have to go to court again tomorrow for an appeal to try to get split custody, or at least unsupervised visits. It's so scary to think that my entire life, and my children's lives, are being determined by one person. How does one person get to play 'God' to so many people?"

Beth put the spoon into the ice cream box and let it drop to the floor. Suddenly she felt stupid that here she was talking about the freedom to eat ice cream and Sheila was dealing with the much larger issue of trying to be with her kids. They sat in silence for a long while. Finally Beth put the ice cream box back into the freezer and went to bed. She thanked God silently that Zack was sleeping beside her.

The next day showed signs of spring coming. The cloudless sky was a deep, clear blue. The air smelled fresh and clean. Although the trees and vegetation were still winter brown, there were specks of color from the crocuses fighting their way through the frozen ground. It was a beautiful day for a long walk alone. However, there was no one to watch Zack. So Beth found a stroller in the basement to push Zack in. She knew that he would complain since he thought he was too old for a stroller, but she did not care. She wanted to walk fast, not putter along at the speed Zack would take.

Surprisingly, Zack did not complain about riding in the stroller. He seemed to enjoy sitting back and taking in the scenery as Beth pushed him through the park. Being in nature and exercising helped Beth to relax, to feel all of the stress melting off her as she walked faster and faster, pushing Zack. The bare trees made silhouettes of black skeletons against the blue sky. They were eerie and Beth felt a chill circulate through her entire body. She suddenly thought of Sheila who was in court this very moment discovering how her life would be lived. Beth stopped pushing Zack for a moment and closed her eyes. She let herself feel the sudden panic and prayed silently for Sheila and her confrontation with the courts. She felt herself relax, but the uneasy feeling would not leave. She breathed a few deep breaths and continued walking at a much slower pace.

The rest of the day went by very quickly. When Sheila came home, she went directly to her room and did not come out until it was time for support group. Beth asked Lisa how court went, but Lisa would only tell her that it did not go well. She would not reveal any of the details. When it was finally time for support group, Sheila sat solemnly while everyone else took their turn talking. Everyone spoke briefly about themselves, eager to hear how Sheila's day in court went.

Monique was very excited about her advancement to her new position into the deli department at the grocery store. She had to learn how to use all of the meat and cheese cutters, and it got very busy when there was a long line of customers. She loved the fact that she was given responsibility and was trusted. Most of all, it was amazing to her that people would have faith in her when she did not have any faith in herself. Monique was developing a glow that in a different circumstance would resemble the glow of someone who was in love. In Monique's case, it was a result of happiness and pride in herself—two things that she did not remember ever having had.

Rosie had a suspicion that she may have an admirer at work. She was not completely sure, as her suspected admirer also seemed to flirt with the other women in the office. But Rosie did seem to believe that he showed her special attention. She had asked around, and got confirmation that he was not married or dating anyone. She was convinced that he had a kind heart and would not treat her like the last man she got involved with. Rosie's glow was that of someone who was teetering on the possibility of falling in love.

Beth talked about her desire to apply for a work-training program now that she filed for divorce. She did not think that Jeff had been served the divorce papers yet and was anxious about his reaction. Even though she knew that he did not know where she was and could not hurt her, just the knowledge that he would be angry somewhere, scared her. She did not mention the doubts she had the night before.

Stacey seemed happy and told everyone about how excited she was that Beth came to church on Sunday and how much she liked the new friends she was making at church, primarily Gayle. She adored Gayle's baby and was looking forward to going over her house again this Sunday after church. Besides being here at the safe home, she had never felt a sense of family. When she was with Gayle and her baby, she felt the feelings she always imagined about how home was supposed to be like but never thought it was true. Stacey asked Beth if she would come with her to church again this Sunday, and Beth agreed. Stacey was actually looking relaxed instead of her usual meek appearance.

There was positive energy and excitement flowing around the room, as it seemed like everyone's lives were progressing in positive directions. It was finally Sheila's turn to talk. Everyone was silent, giving Sheila her full attention.

"As you all know, I went to court today. It was horrible. Everything bad about me from my entire life came out. Every secret I ever told asshole about my childhood and insecurity during adolescence was brought up against me. He made me sound like a drunk because I drank wine to help cope with him. Because he never hurt me or the kids physically, I didn't have a case on why I was so repressed and terrified of him. I sounded stupid when I tried to explain that I was afraid to get him angry. That it terrified me and the kids when he screamed at us and took out his anger on objects.

"I learned over the years that when I saw that look in his eyes and he was going to go after the kids, then it would be less harmful to them if I stepped in. I would reprimand the kids, or punish them so that he wouldn't do much worse. The problem is that since I was the one who did it, it made me look like the abusive one when I was only trying to protect my kids.

"Then, there was the issue with the school. He said that I was controlling and wouldn't let the kids participate in activities. So, basically, everything he did, I got blamed for. In being a barrier to try to prevent him from exploding, it looks like I was the one being a bad mother. By trying to protect my children, I lost them.

"I get to see them twice a month at the supervision center. It's like I'm a criminal. I have to be monitored while seeing my kids. I don't know what to do."

Nobody said anything. How could anyone respond? It was a solemn few minutes until Stacey broke the silence.

"What about an appeal? Don't give up. It's not over. There must be other options. What about using a GAL like in Beth's case. You know, someone who can see things clearly and tell the truth?"

"Yeah, that's what my attorney suggested. The GAL will recommend to the judge what's best for the kids from a neutral standpoint. She said that it's hard for a judge to see things clearly through highly paid and trained attorneys who represent Rob or me. We're going to request that the kids are assigned their own attorney who will represent their rights."

"I'm sure that once a real investigation is made, the truth will come out and you'll get your kids." Lisa smiled sympathetically.

The rest of the week went by quickly. Beth did not get any information about doing a job-training program, but she did get confirmation that Jeff was served the divorce papers. It was a relief since she had so much anxiety about what would happen when Jeff was served, and now it came and went and nothing happened. Now Beth was eligible to apply for public assistance and a job-training program.

Career Planning. This was something that most people do in high school, but Beth skipped. While other kids were in college getting a BA or BS, she was working on her MRS. Now was her chance to make new choices about how she wanted her life to turn out. She was the one in control of what she wanted. There was no one to stop her, to tell her she could not do it, to put her down. Now she just had to figure out what it was that she wanted. Everywhere she went, she observed people in their jobs and wondered "would I want to do that?" She even took it a step beyond to the jobs that you did not see. She wondered about who programmed the ATM machines, or who thought up the recipes for the "Hamburger Helper"? She thought about the meanings of different jobs, and what satisfaction she would get by doing certain things. Service oriented jobs would give the satisfaction of helping people. Engineering or computer jobs would give the satisfaction of creating something or a high when a problem was solved. She thought about the people who on a daily basis affected her life. It started when her radio alarm clock went off; the radio announcer, the person who designed the clock, the people in the factory who made it, the electricity that gave the clock power, the military people who were responsible for monitoring the exact time that the world followed when going along their daily schedules. Then it continued on and on . . . everything in her room, the house, the food in the kitchen . . . Who was responsible for getting the coffee beans to her? It was overwhelming how many people worked to give her the quality of life she took for granted. Then she remembered being in the hospital and the nurses and doctors who did not know her, but cared about her. She thought about Marcia who reached out and changed her life by putting a phone number into her sneaker. Beth stopped there. She wanted to do something that would help people the way that Marcia helped her. She knew it would be too emotional for her to work with victims of abuse, but she wanted to take care of people who were suffering.

Sunday morning Stacey woke Beth and Zack up to go to church. Zack was excited to see his friends again. Many of the people recognized Beth and told her how happy they were that she came back. It was a wonderful feeling to be included and accepted into a group of good, normal, loving people. She loved the feeling here. It was not like the church that she grew up in with statues of saints looking down and judging her, knowing her every fault and sin. She felt a feeling of peace and acceptance here.

Beth felt inspired as she listened to Reverend Josh's sermon; it was as if he was talking directly to her as he preached about the challenges life gives us. He told about the wisdom of the Native Americans in their practice of achieving balance. He said that life was like a woven Native American blanket where the beauty of the blanket was in the contrast of the colors. If the blanket were one color, it would be boring and dull. It was the mix of dark and light colors that made the design so beautiful. The colors gold, red, blue, white, and black each represent a certain aspect of life: gold was happiness; red was hurt; blue was peace; white was goodness; and black was hardship. Each aspect of life if alone would be dull and meaningless. It is only when woven together that they have meaning, creating the beautiful journey that we call life. Many people want to take out the reds and blacks, but where would that leave us? It would be a dull, ugly blanket. It is the mixture of hurt, love, struggle, and achievement that makes life interesting. Without hurt one would never know love, without struggle one would never know achievement. It is the balance that makes the beauty.

The words of Reverend Josh once again moved Beth as she applied them to her own life. She thought of all the hardships she had been through, but if she had never gotten involved with Jeff then she would not have Zack or an appreciation for the everyday joys that most people took for granted. She would not know that being free was a gift, that being given an opportunity to have a career was a privilege, that knowing if you have food and shelter was something that many people do not know when they wake up in the morning.

After the service, instead of going to the nursery, Beth went to coffee hour to make small talk, drink coffee, and eat strawberries. Eventually she saw Stacey and Zack enter the room, hand in hand. Zack's face lit up when he saw Beth. He pulled away from Stacey and ran to Beth. She kneeled down and gave him a big hug.

"Mommy, we had so much fun! All of my friends were there and we played. Stacey said we're going to visit Gayle and Mia again today! Did you know that Mommy? Did you?"

"Yeah, I know. Is that okay? Do you want to go see Gayle and Mia again?"

"Oh yeah, I like it there. Let's go."

Without Beth knowing, Stacey had baked a cake to bring to Gayle's house.
"Do you mind if we stop and get some ice cream for the cake?"
"Of course not. When did you make this?"
"Yesterday, when you and Zack were at the park. Do you think she'll like it?"
"Of course she'll like it. Why wouldn't she?"
"I don't know. I just want her to like me. I never felt like this before. I usually feel very defensive and don't care what people think. But with Gayle, I want her to like me. I can't explain it."

Beth smiled a knowing smile, "I know what you mean. Gayle will love the cake."

Stacey smiled as they pulled into the parking lot to get ice cream.

Gayle made a roast chicken dinner with all of the fixings. There was mashed potato, stuffing, carrots, gravy, and hot rolls. It was a feast. They all laughed and talked, just like a family. After dinner, Zack sat in the big chair in the living room and held Mia. She was propped up on his lap with pillows, and Zack gently stroked Mia's cheeks. Beth felt a pang of sorrow as she thought of the baby she aborted and felt sad that Zack would never be a big brother to that little baby. She reminded herself that if she had that baby she would still be with Jeff, and Zack would not be in an environment where he could be the loving child he was being to Mia. They all sat around in the living room talking and laughing, Zack being a little man in this family of women. It reminded Beth of the Sunday afternoons she spent with her family as a child. After their dinner settled, they ate Stacey's cake and everyone raved about how delicious it was. Stacey glowed like a woman in love. The afternoon went by quickly, and it was dark when they finally went home.

When they arrived home, the house was quiet. It was an eerie quiet like something bad was waiting to happen.

"Where is everyone?"

"I think that Monique is working and Rosie is probably out with her kids, but where's Sheila? She should be here."

"Maybe she went to the store or something."

"Yeah, I'm going upstairs to the bathroom."

Beth brought Zack into the kitchen to feed him a snack before getting him ready for bed. She reached into the fridge to get the carton of milk, but dropped it when she heard a high-pitched scream. She started to run up the stairs, but Stacey was frantic at the top of the stairs.

"*Stop!* Don't come up. Keep Zack downstairs, *Call 911*. It's Sheila. I think she's dead . . . she's in the bathtub . . . there is blood everywhere. *Hurry!*"

Beth ran back downstairs and tried to focus as she dialed 911. She gave the dispatcher the address and told her to send someone as quick as possible.

"All right, someone is on the way. Stay on the line with me until they get there. What happened?"

"Uh, I don't know. She's upstairs. Let me go up there." Beth looked up and saw Zack standing in the kitchen doorway. He looked terrified. "It's okay Zack. Just stay here and Mommy will be right back. Just stay in the kitchen and wait. Don't leave the kitchen."

Beth ran upstairs with the phone. Stacey was sitting on the floor, hugging her knees and rocking back and forth. Beth ran past her into the bathroom. Stacey was right; there was blood everywhere with Sheila in the middle of it. She was laying naked in the bathtub with her arms hanging over the sides, her wrists cut and the bright red blood covering her white body. "She's in the tub with her wrists slit. There's blood everywhere."

"Is there a pulse?"

Beth put her fingers on the side of Sheila's neck. She felt a pulse.

"Yeah, there's a pulse."

"Okay. The next thing is to stop the bleeding. Are the slits horizontal across the wrist, or vertical down her wrist?"

"They go across, under her hand."

"That's good. Take a bath towel and rip it into strips. Use the razor to get it started."

There was a package of razors on the sink. Beth almost did not want to touch them since the razor that Sheila used was from this box. She pulled herself together, took out a razor, and cut pieces in the towel to rip into strips. Beth put the phone on speaker and did exactly what the dispatcher told her to do. She gently took Sheila's arm, wrapped the towel tightly around the wrist, pulled the towel, and tied it into a knot. She did the same to the other wrist. She pulled the drain stopper out in the tub so that the water drained out, then got a quilt off the first bed she saw and wrapped it around Sheila. She sat on the floor next to the tub and stroked Sheila's hair while she waited for the ambulance.

The fire truck arrived in what seemed a matter of minutes. The large men in their uniforms and equipment took up all the space in the room, pushing Beth into the hallway.

Beth went downstairs to check on Stacey and Zack. Stacey was sitting on the floor hugging Zack, who had given up trying to wiggle away.

"Don't worry. Sheila's going to be okay."

"It's my fault. If I were here then she wouldn't have done it. We left her alone when we knew she was having a hard time. We should have been here and not off having fun."

"Now you're sounding like Jeff. We have a right to go out and have fun. We're not responsible for what other people do. My therapist keeps drilling that into my head. Each person has to live his/her own life without feeling responsible for other's choices. Sheila made the choice to do what she did. It has nothing to do with what you or I did or didn't do. Are you okay to stay with Zack so that I can go to Sheila?"

"I can be strong for Zack. I'll do anything for him."

"I know. Why don't you two watch TV?"

Zack being safe with Stacey, Beth went back to the firemen and Sheila. The ambulance was there, the young clean-cut paramedics securely strapped Sheila onto a stretcher. One of the firemen came to Beth with a clipboard and asked her questions about Sheila. Beth provided him with Sheila's name, address, and that there were no known medical problems. Yes, she was obviously having a hard time as she was going through a nasty divorce. No they were not relatives, just roommates, no there was not a preference as to what hospital she went to.

"Who wrapped her wrists?"

"I did."

"You may have saved her life."

Then they were gone with nothing more than a bloody bathroom to prove that they were ever there.

Beth poured some disinfectant cleaner into the tub, filled it with water, and began scrubbing the bathroom. It was as if she were washing away everything that was wrong. If she washed all the blood away, then maybe she could wash away this entire experience and Sheila would be safe in her room taking a nap or reading in bed. She kept thinking about what the fireman had said, "You just may have saved her life." She had actually done something important that could have saved someone's life. Everything became clear to her and she knew what she wanted to be—a nurse. She suddenly felt a purpose for the greater good, not just for her and Zack.

The phone was ringing and Stacey was not answering it.

"I'm coming!" Beth yelled to the person on the other end of the line even though they could not hear her. She peeled off the yellow rubber gloves and threw them into the sink as she ran to answer the phone.

"Hello."

"Hi, it's Lisa. What's going on there? Someone from the center heard a call over the police radio."

"Oh Lisa, I didn't even think to call the center. It's horrible. You better come over right away. Sheila slit her wrists and almost died."

"Oh my God! What happened? Where is she now? How's everyone else?"

"The ambulance took her to the hospital. They said she'll make it. Neither Monique nor Rosie are here, but Stacey's not doing too good."

"Are you okay?"

"Yeah, I'm just cleaning."

"Cleaning?"

"It was a mess."

"I'll be right over."

"Okay."

Beth hung up the receiver and helped Zack and Stacey upstairs to bed. She waited in the dark living room for Lisa, wanting everything to remain quiet.

Chapter 8

Two weeks went by and no one was allowed to visit Sheila. They were told she did not want to see anyone, but that she was healing well physically. The medical treatment Beth provided combined with the fact that Sheila slit her wrists horizontally saved her life. The problem now was her emotional state of mind; Sheila was not responding and refused visitors. She was in the psychiatric ward at the hospital, but since the insurance would only cover two weeks of psychiatric inpatient care at a traditional hospital, she had to be discharged. It was obvious that she was not in a state to be released; so there was no option but to have her transferred to a psychiatric hospital. She was covered through her ex-husband's insurance to go to a quality care facility. For the sake of the children, Rob offered to pay whatever was not covered by insurance. Lisa believed this was his way of trying to make himself look like the "good guy" and Sheila the "crazy lady," and that by having her committed to a high-end institution he was still keeping her prisoner. Any possibility of getting a GAL was put on hold. Their small group sat silently as Lisa told them these updates during the Wednesday night support group.

"I don't think telling you is a violation of the confidentiality rules as I believe you have a right to know what's happening."

"I don't care what the doctors say, Sheila needs her friends! I say we go and visit her!"

"Rosie, I agree with you that she needs her friends but it's not up to us to make that decision. She's refusing visitors. It's her choice. It's not the doctors who are trying to isolate her. We all knew she needed help, but I don't think anyone, including her therapist, thought anything like this would happen."

"What can we do?"

"Beth and I asked everyone at church to pray for her."

"Prayer can work miracles."

"Amen."

"How's everyone else doing? Does anyone want to share what's happening in their lives?"

"Does it really matter what's going on? Everything else seems so insignificant when Sheila's going through this."

"If there's one thing that we can learn from this entire experience is that life must go on. It's important to continue living and to not give up like Sheila did. Sheila thought that nothing mattered any more. Look where that got her. I don't want to see any of you make that same mistake. You're given one life to live and even though it may not go the way you want it to, you have to keep on going. Don't any of you ever give up because when a person gives up her will, there's nothing left. Sheila's life was saved physically. Now she needs her will back if she's going to live again. You're all living. What's happening in your life?"

Monique, very soft spoken, shyly announced to the group, "I got an award at work."

"Oh Monique, that's great! What kind of award?"

"I got the employee of the month award for 'virtues of determination and dedication' because I 'did an outstanding job of learning and improving myself.' They put my picture and name on a plaque and hung it at the service desk for everyone to see."

Monique was beaming, but Lisa seemed concerned.

"Monique, I'm very proud of you and know that this is a great accomplishment so please don't take this the wrong way. But I don't think it's a good idea to have your name and picture out where everyone can see it. You are, after all, in hiding."

"My husband doesn't live anywhere near here. It's not like he would come into the grocery store and see it. If that was the case, he just as well could come in and see me working. This is the first time in my life that anyone ever told me I was good, that I ever got an award."

Rosie immediately stood up for Monique, "Listen here Lisa. You come in here and tell us to make something out of our selves, that we can accomplish anything. Then you go back to your life that is no part of us. We are all here, trying to follow your advice. And then when we do—*boom!* You say that we shouldn't. I don't see the harm in Monique receiving a little bit of recognition. The Lord knows that she worked hard and deserves it!"

"I know, I just think she should keep a low profile. She worked hard to escape. I don't want to see it all ruined."

Stacey, who had become more withdrawn since the incident with Sheila, also stood up for Monique. "I'm happy for you Monique. I think it's great that you're the employee of the month. You deserve recognition. You've gone too long without being appreciated."

"Thank you so much. It means a lot to me."

Lisa was obviously in the minority about her opinions concerning Monique's public recognition and changed the subject.

"I still don't have a good feeling about this, but I'm happy for you Monique, and wish you the best. Who wants to go next? Stacey?"

"Oh, nothing's different with me. Work is going well. It's pretty boring. I have been spending a lot of time with Gayle and Mia. When I'm not with them, they're all that I can think about. I'm so happy, so high, when I am with Gayle. I feel like I'm on drugs. It is like I'm on ecstasy when I'm with her, and I'm miserable when I'm not. Then, all I do is spend every minute waiting until I can see her again. Is this normal?"

Beth smiled, "It sounds like you're falling in love."

Monique looked confused, "How could Stacey be falling in love with Gayle? They're both women!"

Lisa smiled in agreement with Beth, "Love is a precious gift. You're a beautiful woman who has not been appreciated by men. That doesn't mean that you don't deserve to love, and be loved. If Gayle is the person who makes you feel complete, then go for it! There are all different kinds of love and all different kinds of families. Haven't you been following all the controversy about the gay marriage thing? Beth's right, our Stacey is in love!"

"Me in love with Gayle? I don't understand."

"Everything you describe is the symptom of being hit hard. Just like Monique deserves to be recognized at work, you deserve to be loved by Gayle."

"But what about Mia? How would this be for her?"

"You love children, you love Mia. The more people who love her, the better. She would only benefit from having two moms."

"Two moms? You mean I could be a mom?"

"Haven't you gotten anything out of this group? You can be anything you want!"

"But what about Gayle? How do I know that this is what Gayle wants?"

"Stacey, take it from me. With the way that Gayle looks at and treats you, I have no doubt she feels the same way."

"Should I talk to her about it?"

"If our suspicions are correct, and I'm sure they are, Gayle is probably afraid to talk to you about it. She's probably afraid to scare you away. I bet she'd be relieved and overjoyed if you addressed it."

"Thank you guys so much! I had no idea what was going on, I didn't know what my feelings were. I'm so happy!"

Rosie was the next one to speak.

"This is the most ridiculous thing I ever heard! Two women in love? That's just not right. God made man and woman to go together. You need to get yourself a man, like I do. Remember that man I told you about? His name is Guy, and boy is he a guy! We been going out to lunch almost everyday and boy is he sweet! He talks so nice to me, and gets jealous when the other guys flirt with me. It's so cute how he cares for me. He asked me if I'd go out with him this Saturday night. I would meet him at the restaurant of course, since I couldn't let him come here. So, how about it? Is it okay with you guys to watch my little ones, so I can go out with him?"

"I'll be home with Zack anyway, so it will be fine if you go."

"Oh sweetie, thank you so much. I'm going out to catch me a Guy! Ha ha, get it? Guy. That's his name."

"Yeah, yeah, we get it. You're so funny Rosie. But seriously, you better be careful. It's not a good sign that he's getting jealous and you haven't even gone out yet."

"Oh but honey, we go out all the time. We have such nice lunches."

"Why are you such a pessimist, Lisa? First you're after Monique for getting a promotion and now you're after Rosie for having a date. I'm surprised you're not telling me that I shouldn't go to church!"

"That's not fair Stacey. I've seen many people go from one abuser to another. It's easy to make the same mistake twice. I'm trying to help make sure that you all make a safe transition out on your own. I'm only doing my job. What about you Beth? What's going on with all of the court shit?"

Beth was proud of Stacey for speaking up since she was usually shy and withdrawn. She also noticed that Lisa had a strong habit of changing the subject when the conversation was not going in her direction. Beth was glad that Lisa was saying what she did, because she believed she was right. She remembered feeling flattered by Jeff's jealousy; she thought it meant he loved her. Boy was she wrong. For a moment, she considered backing Lisa and warning Rosie that what seemed like extra attention could actually be the first signs of someone who was controlling and possessive. She thought the better of it and instead decided to talk about herself. Lecturing was Lisa's job.

"Now that I filed for divorce, I can apply for public assistance and get into a job training program to become a nurse's aid. The state will attach Jeff's child support and make sure he provides us with health insurance, so I won't have to deal with him for financial matters. My attorney drafted a divorce agreement asking for nothing but full custody. He cares more about money than us, so hopefully he'll accept it and give me my freedom. There are still the criminal charges against him, so I'll have to see him when I testify for that."

"But you deserve half of everything he has. Half of the house, half of all his money. Don't let him get away with this."

"Why? So I can end up like Sheila? I don't have the money to go against him in a legal battle. Anything I got from him would get eaten up in lawyer's fees. I would walk away with nothing and it would have delayed me from starting my new life. I'm better off stopping it all before it starts. I get more that way."

The afternoon was sunny and Zack was taking a nap while Beth reviewed the applications for public assistance and a job-training program. There was a soft knock on the bedroom door.

"Come in," Beth whispered.

Stacey entered the room and sat on Beth's bed, looking worried.

"What's the matter?"

"I need your help."

"Are you in trouble?"

"No, no. Nothing like that. It's just . . . I want to look pretty. I always felt so ugly inside that I never wanted to look nice. I didn't want to put any effort into my looks just so that it would cause me more pain. But now, it's different. I want Gayle to think I'm pretty when I talk to her about . . . well you know, what we talked about in support group."

Beth was flattered that Stacey came to her for this. It was as if she were the big sister that Stacey never had.

"Of course, I'll help you. You're very beautiful. You just have to learn to highlight your features."

"What do you mean?"

"Well, your hair is thin and fine. I think it would have a lot more body if you wore it shoulder length and blew-dried it with a little gel. Your eyes are sexy. If you put some dark make-up on, it will bring more attention to them. And look at these high cheek-bones, there are people who would spend thousands for what you were born with. Maybe Lisa can get us some vouchers for the consignment store so that you can get some clothes to show off your figure. Don't look so overwhelmed. This will be fun!"

"It's not that I'm overwhelmed. It's just that if I didn't have all of these 'positive features' then maybe my father and brother wouldn't have been attracted to me. Maybe it's my fault."

Beth gave Stacey a big hug.

"Oh Stacey, don't you ever say that. You were a helpless little girl who was supposed to be protected by her family. They were wrong for hurting you and don't ever believe anything different. You're an adult now who can stand up for yourself, and no one can hurt you again. You can make your own decisions and decide for yourself whom to love. No one can force you to do anything you don't want." Beth felt wet on her shoulder and realized that Stacey was crying. Beth held her, rocking her back and forth until she stopped crying.

"Where should we start?"

They both laughed.

"Why don't you take a shower and meet me in the kitchen. I'll find some scissors and a comb so we can start with your hair. Then, we can apply a little make up and the transformation will be under way."

"Should we take before and after pictures?"

"Whatever you want!"

Beth made some tea while she waited for Stacey to come down. Stacey was so beautiful and sweet, she could not imagine anyone hurting her. Some people had such a warped interpretation of love. Jeff being one of them. Beth was impressed that Stacey was willing to overcome what she had been through and take an unconventional chance that held many risks. She prayed that she was correct about Gayle, so Stacey would not get hurt again.

"I'm ready!"

Stacey was beaming with excitement like a little kid on Christmas morning. Beth wondered what kind of Christmas's Stacey had growing up, and was sure this was more exciting than any Christmas morning she had.

"All right, come sit down and let me brush your hair out. I found an actual pair of haircutting scissors. It's amazing the stuff that turns up in this place."

Beth gently brushed out Stacey's long blond hair that went past the middle of her back, almost to her bum. She suddenly got an idea.

"Do you have any hair elastics?"

"Yeah, I have a whole bunch of them upstairs."

"Can you run up and grab me two big ones?"

"Sure."

Beth brushed Stacey's hair into a ponytail, braided it, and put another elastic on the bottom of the braid.

"Okay, are you ready?"

"As ready as I'll ever be."

Stacey held her breath while Beth took the thin-tipped scissors and cut through the hair above the braid. When she got all the way through, she took the braid and handed it to Stacey.

"This braid represents all the hurt and pain that was inflicted on you. In cutting this braid and severing it from your life force, I'm freeing you of any negative ghosts you may carry. You're totally and completely free to pursue life, liberty, and the pursuit of happiness."

Stacey was crying. The wisps of crooked hair framed her face, sticking out in all directions.

"Oh Beth, thank you so much. I'll keep this braid forever as a battle trophy and symbol that I'm separate from my past and it can no longer control me. Thank you for freeing me."

"Stacey?"

"Yeah?"

"Once I clean up this mass of wisps on your head, can you free me?"
"Of course. How short do you want it?"
"Oh, I want it very short, cut it all off if you can. I want to cut off every part of my old self and start over fresh. I don't want to bring anything with me!"
"Beth, I'm the one who's struggling with being a dike! If I cut it all off, then you'll look like a boy. Poor Zack won't recognize his own mother!"
"I think that's what I need right now, to be completely unrecognized as my old self."

Once the braids were cut off, Beth and Stacey trimmed each other's hair to make it neat and even. Beth got daring and cut some angles around Stacey's face. After their hair was blow-dried and the make-up was applied, they looked like they had come out of a salon. Beth turned the dial on the kitchen radio a few notches louder when 'Wonderful Tonight' by Eric Clapton started playing.

"Ohhh, I *love* this song! It reminds me of when I was in high school and all the girls dreamt that someone was singing this song to them."
"I'll sing it to you!"
"And I'll sing it to you!"

They began singing loudly to each other, "And then she asked me, do you feel all right? And I said yes, I feel wonderful tonight . . ."

The longer Beth was away from Jeff, the safer and more confident she felt. She loved living at the safe home, having roommates, and the bonds and friendships that came with it. She felt this was what she missed by not going to college and living in the dorms. However, she also knew it was time to take the next step to achieve the goal of being on her own.

Beth was meeting Lisa for lunch today to review the applications for public assistance and the work-training program so that she would be ready for her appointment on Friday. She did not understand how she would be eligible to receive public assistance since she was still married to Jeff who earned a decent living. Lisa assured her that under the circumstances, she should qualify. Filling out the forms gave Beth a yucky feeling in her stomach. It made her feel ashamed, as if she were a worthless second-class citizen asking for charity. She was relieved that she took the personal and financial documents from home so that she had information like Jeff's social security number and last year's adjusted gross income.

It was exciting to read the college brochure that held unlimited opportunities through the numerous classes and programs. Beth flipped through the departmental classes to the job placement programs and found one for a nurse's assistant; this is where she wanted to be. She read the program description. It consisted of a combination of classroom and work training. The first semester was five classes, and the second semester consisted of three classes and working part-time in a facility. Upon successful completion, she would receive a certificate as nurse's assistant. Beth prayed that she would get accepted into the next session, which started in August.

Beth finished the forms and put them in a folder. Lisa picked her up and they went to the café while Rosie brought Zack and Joey to the center for the "children who witnessed domestic violence" group. Zack seemed to enjoy the program, as it was an opportunity to play with other children. He did not realize that the activities and games they played helped him to learn how to control anger, showed him that violence was wrong, and let him know it was not his fault when people were mean or hurtful. Beth was grateful Zack was participating in this program as it gave her hope that he would escape the fate of his father, and Zack liked the fact that he had his own group.

Going out to lunch with Lisa reminded Beth of the outings she used to have with Nancy. Beth wondered how Nancy was doing and what she thought about Beth leaving Jeff and disappearing without saying bye. She considered asking Lisa to contact Nancy for her, but changed her mind. Beth ordered a chicken wrap, and Lisa ordered a roast beef sandwich.

"So, how are you doing with all this?"

"What do you mean by 'all this'?"

"Well, you know . . . the adjustment, the being-away-from-Jeff, starting a new life, living at the safe home. It's a lot of changes at once. Are you okay?"

"Yeah, I'm okay. I'm scared about going out on my own, as I like the comfort of having everyone around. We're like a family and I don't want to lose that."

"I know it's hard. You're lucky to be in a home with roommates to help you transition to living alone. This is the period when many women feel lonely and return to their abusers. I don't think there's anything that I can say that will make moving out easier. Many people who go through a divorce have these feelings because they don't want to lose the family life, similar to what you have at the Safe Home. This will help you understand what people are referring to when they say they're sorry that you're divorced."

"I don't understand the analogy of leaving Jeff to leaving the Safe Home. The subjects are totally different."

"They are totally different. I'm trying to show you what you'll be facing when you're away from all this and are dealing with people who'll have sympathy when they find out you're divorced."

"Whatever. I'm worried about living on my own and going through the program at the same time."

"I know you can do it. The good part of being sponsored for the program is that it will include childcare for Zack. The fact that you're so excited to get into a program will give your social worker motivation to get more help for you such as low-income housing, food stamps, help with utilities, and other living expenses."

"I feel like a leach getting all this free stuff."

"No, the leaches are the people who have made a living off the system for years and even generations. Let me look at your applications."

Lisa reviewed the applications and smiled as she handed them back to Beth.

"They look great. It's a good example of the type of student you'll be. Do you still want me to come with you on Friday?"

"Of course. Do you think I'd be able to do any of this without you?"

Beth was feeling confident and excited, and was looking forward to sharing her plans at the support group that evening. Zack talked nonstop about the fun he had at the center that day, while they ate macaroni and cheese for supper. She could not imagine being any happier than she was at this moment: she was safe with her son; he was doing well and thriving in an environment free of violence; for now Jeff was leaving them alone; she was taking the steps necessary to establish a home for them and career for herself. It was a wonderful feeling.

The feeling in the house began to change as the time slowly approached 8:00 P.M. Tonight was Wednesday night, the night of the mandatory support group, but Monique was still not home from work. She got out of work at 6:00 P.M. and the grocery store was less than fifteen minutes away by bus, so she should have been home over an hour and a half ago. Lisa called the grocery store to find out when Monique had left work.

"She left at 6:00 P.M. sharp. I spoke to the store manager and he said that she was happy and didn't mention going anywhere after work. He said everything seemed normal."

"What should we do?"

Lisa picked up the receiver for the phone again.

"I'm calling the police. This isn't like Monique, and I'm worried. Why don't you guys go into the living room? I'll be right in."

Rosie, Beth and Stacey waited while Lisa called the police, then they all went into the living room together.

Stacey spoke quietly, "I don't think we should start the group without Monique. The rules are that everyone has to be here on Wednesday night. Since Monique isn't here, we can't start."

Beth and Rosie nodded in agreement.

Lisa did not disagree. "I'm extremely worried and don't think that having a normal group would be beneficial to anyone. However, this is a support group and we need to support each other until we know where Monique is."

"Yeah, there are all types of support and right now the support we need is to pray for Monique to come safely walking through that door."

They sat silently until about 10:00 P.M. When Monique did not come home and the police did not call, Lisa suggested that they go to bed, as there was nothing else to do.

"How can you expect us to sleep when Monique is missing?"

"It won't help Monique if we're exhausted. The police are searching for her and said they'll call me on my cell phone if they find her."

"*If* they find her?"

"I stand corrected, *when* they find her."

"Lisa's right. I'm going to bed. Zack will still get up early in the morning even if I'm tired. Rosie and Stacey, you both have to work in the morning."

"Yeah, right. I'm not going anywhere until I know where Monique is."

"Me neither."

"I have to go home to bed. I'll call as soon as I hear something, I promise. Just keep praying for Monique."

"Good night."

Morning came but Lisa did not call, so Rosie and Stacey called in sick to work. Rosie's three big kids went off to school, and Zack and Joey watched cartoons in the living room while the three women drank coffee in the kitchen. Beth's coffee went cold and they still had not heard anything.

"Why don't we call the police?"

"Because even the police don't know that we're at the safe home. If we call, we could risk the safety of everyone."

"I don't get it, why don't the police know?"

"Do you think police are immune from being abusers? No one can know where we are."

"What about when they came for Sheila?"

"They thought we were women living together as roommates. People do that you know. It's a lot cheaper than living alone."

"I know, but the police are there to help and protect us."

"They do, but if the location of the safe home is known, then it could easily leak out. It's not worth it."

"Why don't we call the center? We can't just sit like this doing nothing. It's really not fair that we don't know what's going on."

"Yeah, all right."

Rosie called while the others watched.

"Yeah ... Uh huh ... All right ... Thank you, bye."

"What did they say?"

"They said that Lisa is meeting with the police and she'll come here after to tell us everything."

"Oh great, more waiting. I wish that someone would tell us something!"

Another two hours went by before Lisa finally showed up. She looked horrible. She had black circles under her eyes, and it looked like she had not combed her hair or put on any make up.

"Come in, sit down."

"Are you okay?"

"What's happening? You look horrible."

Lisa sat down and held her hand up for everyone to be silent.

"Where are the kids?"

"Jerome, Willie, and Ruby are in school and Zack and Joey are watching TV."

"Okay good, I have some really bad news. I've been at the police department all morning."

No one spoke or dared to ask what happened. Beth held her breath, hopelessly trying to make time stop. After a long pause, Lisa continued.

"There's no easy way to say this, but I went to the police department to identify Monique's body. As beaten and swollen as it was, there was no doubt that it was her."

"But who ... why?"

"Her husband, of course. One of his co-workers was in the area visiting his daughter and recognized Monique's picture at the grocery store for being employee of the month. He'd met Monique at various work events such as Christmas parties and summer outings. When he went to work he congratulated her husband and asked why her picture was in a store so far from home? Her husband made some lame excuse and was able to get all the information he needed to find her. He waited outside of the grocery store everyday until he saw her leave. He then followed her, intending to take her home. She obviously refused to go, which enraged him. Someone called the police because of screaming in the park, but by the time the police got there Monique was beaten unconscious and her husband was wandering around not too far away. Monique died on the way to the hospital, they booked her husband, and he broke to pieces admitting everything."

Lisa could have said "I told her so," but she did not. The four women held each other as they cried. How could something so horrible have happened to someone so wonderful? Especially after she had come so far. Monique was proud, but in the end it was her accomplishments that gave her away.

Beth was in a haze when she applied for public assistance. What ordinarily would have been a difficult process for her was nothing more than being led through another activity. She sat numbly in the waiting room that was crowded with people not too different from herself. She reevaluated the prejudiced views she had been conditioned into believing, as she fit in with these people. There were mothers with children, single people with a look of desperation on their faces, people who needed help and hope. Beth thought about Katie who went back to her husband, Sheila lying in the tub with her wrists slit, Monique beaten to death in the park, the desperate faces of the people sitting in this room and her own hopeless situation. She wondered if there really was such a thing as hope, or if this miserable existence was a permanent condition called life.

Beth's name was called, but she did not stir until Lisa took her hand and led her through a dirty hallway and into a small room that had nothing more than a desk with three chairs in it. The desk was empty, there were no pictures, and the walls were dirty. It was a dingy depressing room to match her dingy depressing existence. All the hope and excitement Beth had just two days ago seemed lost as she waited in silence for the social worker to come in and interview her.

A young man finally entered and sat in the remaining chair behind the desk, reviewed her applications, and took a lot of notes. Beth was expecting a woman who would interrogate her and make her feel worthless, but instead here was a kind young man with sincere eyes willing to help her.

"Congratulations for having a plan. I know this is difficult and I'll do everything I can to help. Since you don't need public health insurance, it will make it easier for you to receive some of the other benefits. Starting immediately you can receive checks and food stamps. I'll put you on the list for public housing and hopefully you'll get accepted sooner since you're technically homeless. There is financial aid available for the job training programs, so as long as there's an opening, we can get you accepted. We'll use the center address until you get an apartment, but you should set up a bank account as soon as possible so that we can have your checks directly deposited. Do you have any questions?"

Beth felt so overwhelmed; she did not know what to say.

"Umm, no. Thank you."

"Okay then, that's it. Here's my card, please call me with any questions."

While driving home Beth was able to process what just happened.

"Well, I thought that went great. How do you feel?"

"I don't know what to feel, there's so much going on. I need to think about what he said, like the fact that I'm homeless."

"You have a home, the Safe Home."

"A temporary home."

"Still a home. And we're working towards getting you a permanent home."

"The Safe Home is getting smaller and smaller, but everyone seems to be leaving under horrible circumstances. Death, hospitalization . . ."

"You're going to leave because of a positive reason. You're going to make it. I have faith in you. The difficult part about this job is that everyone doesn't make it, but I keep trying because some succeed, and you will."

"What makes you so sure? What makes you think that I'm any different than Sheila or Monique?"

"Listen to me Beth, there's nothing that makes you different than Sheila or Monique. However, just because bad things happened to them it doesn't mean bad things are going to happen to you. Wait, I stand corrected. Bad things will happen to you, they already have, but it's how you handle them that matters. Always be smart about your decisions, never give up, and you *will* make it."

"I need the name of the hospital that Sheila's staying at. I want to go see her tomorrow."

"She's not accepting visitors."

"I'll go see her anyway. Maybe she'll change her mind."

"All right. I'll call you with it when I get back to the office."

Chapter 9

Beth called the phone number that Lisa gave her for the Jericho Rose Hospital. Beth wondered how it got its strange name. Visiting hours were from 2:00 P.M.-4:00 P.M. daily. Beth asked the receptionist to let Sheila know she would visit the next day. They said they could not guarantee that Sheila would see her, but they would let her know.

On Saturday, Rosie watched Zack. The boys had become such close friends that it was easier to have them both. They told everyone that they were brothers, and no one said anything different. Despite the extreme differences in their appearance, one with a pale complexion, blond hair, and blue eyes and the other with brown skin, hair, and eyes, it was obvious that they had a bond closer than any blood could have given them. They had become inseparable.

Beth drove the hour to the hospital, which was a beautiful ride with the spring flowers in bloom. The trees were alive with their new bright green leaves, the cherry and apple trees were full of blossoms, and there were rhododendron and azalea bushes everywhere she passed. It was a beautiful day to be alive. She was glad she was visiting Sheila at a hospital instead of a graveyard. She came to the hospital sign "The Jericho Rose Hospital" and followed the steep winding driveway up to the grand Victorian style building that resembled a high-end resort from another time, long ago. It was bright yellow with white trim, high gables, and towers that overlooked the landscape of green lawns and immaculate gardens. Beth felt as if she was walking into a fairy tale as she parked her car and proceeded to the large porch that wrapped around the building. Some people rocked in the chairs on the porch, while others walked around the grounds or sat under the trees. Beth entered the spectacular building and was immediately approached by a young, casually dressed nurse who led her to the nurses' station. Her nametag simply said "Jen."

"Hi. My name's Beth Parker and I'm here to visit Sheila Robinson."

"Ahh yes, Sheila's expecting you. Jen, could you please escort this woman to Sheila in the back garden."

Beth felt as if she were here to visit the queen of England as she was led through an elegant formal dining room to a back entrance that opened to a garden area. Sheila was sitting on a bench watching birds splash in a birdbath.

"Hello Miss Sheila, how do you do today?"

"Hey Beth! It's great to see you, I'm glad you came!"

"You look great! You seem to be healing quite well in this fancy resort!"

"Yeah, I'm actually getting help here. My kids have been visiting me and I get to spend time alone with them."

"That's great! How did that happen?"

"It is kind of ironic. Rob wanted me put away to get me out of the picture, but by being here I'm actually getting back into the picture. My doctor is very understanding and thinks that I'm being victimized. Duh, as if it took a PhD to figure that out! He said that emotional abuse is worse than physical abuse because wounds to the soul are more difficult to heal than wounds to the skin. It's also more difficult for a person to know that they're being injured since there's not physical evidence. He told the courts that in order for me to heal, it's vital to my treatment that I have regular visits with the kids. Since the judge didn't want to have my life on his conscience, he agreed. The judge wasn't willing to risk my life in my own hands. I guess I can't be trusted."

"I am sorry you had to do such a horrible thing in order to get help. We were all there for you, we love and care about you."

"I know, but I hated myself and my life, so felt that I had no other choice. I needed more help than you could give and this was the only way to get it."

"That wasn't the only way. You could have gotten help without going to the extreme."

"It was wrong and dangerous, but I couldn't think of any other way out. It must have scared you to find me like that, did I ever thank you for saving me?"

"Sheila, you don't have to thank me."

"Well, thank you any way. I'm grateful that you were there to give me a second chance at life."

"You're welcome. Tell me about this doctor. It sounds like he's just what you need."

"Oh he is. He's smart, cute, and compassionate."

"Cute and compassionate? I usually think of doctors as being old and grumpy."

"Not this one. He's handsome and caring. He believes me and wants to help get my kids back. I really think he can do it."

"Wow. If I didn't know better, I'd think that you're falling for this guy."

"Yeah right! He's my *doctor*, don't forget."

Beth spent the entire afternoon with Sheila at The Jericho Rose Hospital walking in the gardens and talking about life and dreams. Beth felt as if she was on an outing with an old friend. It was wonderful to see Sheila happy and filled with hope for the future. Sheila told Beth the history of the hospital, how initially it was an elegant resort in the twenties, but after the depression became a rehab where the stars came to dry out. Now it was a shadow of what it used to be, but still a wonderful place to heal. There were mostly patients healing from drug or alcohol abuse, but there were also nervous breakdowns and other psychiatric conditions like hers. At one point there was a Native American patient who called the hospital Jericho Rose after the Jericho Roses which tumble over the desert like tumbleweeds and are used for healing. The patient was everyone's favorite at the hospital and people still told stories about him and how he died of an overdose after being released from the hospital, and it is believed that he haunts the grounds. The name stuck and the hospital's name was officially changed in the 70's.

Going to church on Sundays with Stacey had become routine for Beth and Zack. It was something they looked forward to, a time out from the stresses of life and a chance to reconnect with each other. The Sunday afternoons they spent with Gayle and baby Mia were a weekly event that became a routine similar to that of visiting Beth's grandparents on Sunday afternoons when she was a child. Beth chose to sit by herself in church so that she could reflect on the sermon and enjoy the music in solitude.

"This Sunday we're going to talk about forgiveness . . ."

Beth was usually inspired by Reverend Josh's sermons, but cringed at the thought of listening to how she should forgive those who did her wrong; she would never be able to forgive Jeff.

". . . I'm not talking about the traditional inclination to forgive others, but rather to forgive yourself. How many times do we walk around feeling guilty for what we did or didn't do, or feel responsible for the misfortunes of others? These feelings are unavoidable since as humans we all make mistakes. Sometimes we lose our temper, get angry, don't notice a friend in need, fail to complete things, procrastinate, and more. Does this make us a bad person? No, it's human nature. The beauty of being human is the freedom of choice, which will not always be correct. Otherwise, where would life's adventure be, or the joy when things go well?

"As humans, we must realize that we will make mistakes and have to forgive ourselves. We must allow ourselves the freedom to make these mistakes without reprimanding or condemning ourselves. We must realize that on this journey called life, we do what we believe is right at the time. We may realize later that it was not right, but that doesn't change what we did. So, we can only do the best that we can and learn to forgive ourselves for our mistakes. We won't always make correct decisions or act the most appropriate way, but we don't have to live with the regrets. We must stop worrying about past choices so that we can continue on our journey. This includes not feeling responsible for other's decisions, as we can't control other's choices. Don't get stuck living with guilt or regret, forgive yourself and let go. You wont always be right, but you do what you feel is best at the time.

"This is also true for the parent-child relationship as everyone here has parents, and many of you have children. Rather than blame your parents for what they did wrong, realize that they are humans who need forgiveness for their mistakes and thanks for all they gave you. As parents we must not regret our mistakes or feel responsible for our children's choices; but realize we do the best we can and their actions are theirs. We have influenced them, but are not responsible for them."

Once again, Beth felt as though Reverend Josh was talking directly to her. Built up guilt and anger at herself for being with Jeff, her inability to make him happy, and failing Zack brought her to tears. She also failed as a friend by not preventing Sheila from trying to kill herself, or doing something (what?) to save Monique. Beth did not know if she had the ability to forgive herself for the horrendous life she created.

After church Gayle outdid herself in preparing food for a "simple cookout." She had marinated grilled vegetables, pasta salad, rice salad, and grilled chicken and steak tips. When they were all stuffed, she brought out the makings for fresh strawberry shortcake.

"My God Gayle, this is amazing. You'd think this was a special occasion with all of this food!"

Gayle looked over at Stacey, who was beaming happily and answered Beth.

"Well, actually, Beth, this is a special occasion. Gayle and I have an announcement to make, and we wanted you to be the first to know."

Gayle reached over and held Stacey's hand while Stacey continued.

"Gayle asked me to move in with her and Mia, and I accepted. But, it's more than roommates. You were right. Gayle and I love each other. We want to be together as a family and eventually get married."

Stacey and Gayle waited anxiously for Beth's response. She broke into a huge smile and hugged them both.

"I'm so happy for you! You guys are great together. It's awesome that you found each other!"

"Yeah, I never thought that I'd want to be with anyone, but I'm so happy with Gayle, I feel loved, wanted, and safe. I can be myself without worrying about being judged or ridiculed, and it feels good when she touches me, not dirty. I can't imagine anything better than being with her all of the time, and now I will."

"And you'll be a mom," Gayle added.

"Oh yeah, isn't it amazing that I'm going to be a mom? I'll be here to help raise this incredible child. I never thought I'd be part of a family, or that I'd have a child. I feel like the luckiest person in the world."

"We are *both* the luckiest people in the world. I always knew that I wanted to have a baby, but never had any desire to be with a man. Mia's dad is a friend of mine. We agreed that he wouldn't have any financial responsibility or parenting rights. However, he'll always be there if I need help or if Mia wants to meet her dad. I figured I'd do it as a single parent, I never imagined the joy of finding someone to share the experience with. I'm so lucky that I found Stacey and that she wants to be with me. I can't imagine being happier."

"And Beth, we want you to keep coming over on Sundays. We love being with you and Zack, and Mia looks at Zack like a big brother."

"I'd love that."

Another of the Safe Home's occupants would be leaving. However, this one was for a happy reason as Stacey was moving onto her own into a better situation. She was making a positive move in her life, and Beth would continue to see her on Sundays. Beth was happy for Stacey and it gave her hope for herself and Rosie. Rosie seemed to be doing well, but she was not looking into the future. Other residents came and went, only staying for a few days or weeks. Beth thought it was a good sign that there were not many long-term residents as it meant there was no one in need. Lisa had a more pessimistic view that since summer was here and people were not cooped up as much, they did not feel the need to escape, so it was not being addressed. Seeing such a high turnover, Beth felt as if she should start thinking about getting her own home, but Lisa said there was no rush. Even though the long-term residents were not as common, Lisa said she would rather see people stay longer and succeed, than leave too early and not be able to support themselves or end up back in a pattern of abuse.

Rosie was not making plans to get out on her own. Her job was going well and she talked a lot about Guy despite Lisa's warnings. Rosie's kids were enjoying summer vacation by attending the summer camps at the YMCA. Beth thought Zack was too young for the programs, so they enjoyed their summer days at the small beach and park at the town lake. Zack never asked for Jeff or talked about the days before they came to the safe home. It was as if those days never existed. He was not the same child from when they lived with Jeff; now he was affectionate and happy. He loved to cuddle on Beth's lap while she read him books, and he was friendly and outgoing. Beth felt fortunate that Jeff was leaving them alone and not trying to see Zack or contact her. She compared herself to Sheila and was grateful that she did not have to deal with the courts in the same way that Sheila did.

By the end of June Beth began receiving public assistance and was notified that she was put on the waiting list to receive public housing. In mid July she received an acceptance letter into the nurses training program, which included a daycare program for Zack. They would go to school together; Zack was as excited as she was. Beth felt anxious that everything was coming together, as she anticipated the disappointment of having it taken away from her. She had nightmares about being back with Jeff and felt anxious at the smallest reminder of him, such as mention of him at support group, seeing his favorite food or beer in the grocery store, overhearing someone with his name being called. There were a million reminders that haunted her and kept her from being at peace. She checked the restraining order, but there was no clause about contact through dreams as being a violation.

The lazy summer days were very idle, but healing. If the nurses training program were not starting soon, she would be feeling bored and worthless. Instead, she enjoyed this time of peace and relaxation, cherishing the time she spent with Zack. She saw this time as the beginning of a new relationship with him, which was a life created by happiness and positive time together. It was a wonderful feeling that this was the foundation of how their life would be.

Life at the safe home was different now that Monique, Sheila, and Stacey were gone. Beth found herself taking care of the kids while Rosie went out with Guy, leaving the kids home alone. Since Rosie's oldest son Jamole was twelve years old, he was technically old enough to baby sit and Rosie put him in charge. In theory, this was fine, but Jamole would rather play video games or watch TV than be the caregiver for his three younger siblings. So Beth took care of them. Jamole and his eleven-year-old brother Willie played together, and little Joey and Zack were inseparable, so this left little Ruby who followed Beth around copying everything she did. Beth found it flattering the way Ruby would mimic her, and want her to brush her hair and put it into braids. If Beth put on fingernail polish, Ruby would want the same color. Beth did not remember wearing nail polish when she was eight years old, but enjoyed the attention she was receiving from this little girl.

Beth was usually asleep by the time Rosie got home. One night, however, Beth woke up to use the bathroom and heard Rosie laughing downstairs. Beth thought it was strange that Rosie would be laughing to herself, but then she heard a man's voice. Beth could not believe that Rosie brought Guy here to the safe home which was supposed to be a secret place.

Beth did not know what to do. She considered waiting until Guy left before confronting Rosie, but after a half hour of waiting she decided to go downstairs and approach them both. She walked into the living room and turned on the light, feeling like a parent catching a teenager. Guy was lying on top of Rosie on the couch, and they both jumped into the sitting position. Beth smelled alcohol that she had been so used to smelling on Jeff. Although Rosie acted surprised, it was obvious that Guy was more surprised.

"Who are you?"

"The question is, what are *you* doing here?"

"Uhhh . . . Guy, this is my roommate Beth. Beth, this is Guy."

"Okay, now that we've been formally introduced, what's he doing here?"

"You didn't tell me you had a roommate."

"Did she tell you she has four kids?"

"No."

"Sorry Guy, I have a roommate and four kids."

"And she apparently forgot to tell you she's not to bring men home." Beth gave Rosie a fierce glare.

"Okay, Okay. So I forgot a few things, so what. Does that make you like me any less?"

Guy did not answer Rosie's question. "I think that I should just leave as you two obviously have some stuff to work out. Rosie, I'll see you at work."

"No, don't go. It's okay. Beth doesn't care, do you Beth?"

Beth stood firm with her arms crossed, glaring at Rosie. She did not answer.

"Oh well, she's not in the mood to talk. But don't leave. She'll get over it."

Rosie practically pulled Guy back down onto the couch, but he gently gave her a kiss on the head and left.

"Beth, I can't believe you did that! You scared Guy away!"

"*I* scared Guy away? I can't believe that you actually brought him here! You're risking all of our safety and the chance for women after us to have a place to go. How could you do that? If I hadn't gotten up to go to the bathroom I wouldn't have even known. How many times have you had him over? What will Lisa say when she finds out?"

"Oh God, Beth, you wouldn't tell Lisa! She'd make me leave and I have nowhere to go. Oh please, please don't tell Lisa. I promise I'll never do it again!"

"Yeah? And what about the danger you already put us in?"

"This is the first time, I swear. And Guy knows nothing. He thinks we're roommates."

"Rosie, you're drunk and probably high. How can I believe you?"

"I swear Beth. You have to believe me. Please don't tell Lisa. Think about the kids, you don't want them to be homeless, do you?"

Rosie's dark skin turned an auburn color. Her eyes pleaded to Beth.

"Okay, I won't tell Lisa. But you better never bring anyone here again."

"I promise."

Beth and Rosie barely spoke as the days turned into weeks, and soon it was time for Beth to begin the nursing program. Rosie kept her promise and did not have Guy over the house anymore, but she was out almost every night except for when Lisa was scheduled to be there. Beth would lay awake at night waiting for Rosie to come home, until she heard Rosie banging around and laughing to herself. Beth knew that Rosie was drunk and most likely on other substances, but her concern for the kids kept Beth silent. Beth loved Rosie's kids and did not mind spending time with them. But she was concerned about school starting and how she would be able to study and take care of the kids. She finally decided to address the issue with Rosie directly.

"Rosie, I like you and consider you a friend. That's why I need to tell you that I'm worried about you."

"Hey girl, you're worried about me? What in the world for? I couldn't be happier."

"Yeah, well maybe you're happy, but for the wrong reasons. The alcohol and drugs are what's making you happy, and not because things are good. But more importantly, you're neglecting your kids."

"Me? Neglecting my kids? So that's what this is about. You just don't want to be around my kids."

"Rosie, that's not true. I love your kids and that's why I'm worried about you. You're out with Guy almost every night and the kids are left alone. If I wasn't here to take care of them, I don't know what would happen to them."

"Since when have you been taking care of my kids? I never asked you to take care of them and they don't need no taken care of. They do fine by themselves! You'll be happy to know that Guy asked me to move in with him, so you won't have to see me or the kids ever again!"

"Oh Rosie, no! The kids don't even know Guy and you're going to make them move in with a stranger? How can you do that to them?"

"He's not a stranger to me. I love him. I hadn't given him an answer yet, but after this conversation, I'm going to tell him 'yes'."

"Rosie, please don't do this. We can work something out."

"No, it's the right thing to do. Lisa has been putting pressure on me about making a plan to get out on my own, and now you're giving me shit about my kids. So I think it's best that I just leave. Guy makes me happy, and he'll take care of us."

"So, you're just going right back to another man? What about making it on your own and being independent?"

"Who wants to be alone? I want a man to love who'll take care of me."

"Why? So that he can give you another baby and then abuse and leave you? When are you going to stop and make a life for yourself? You're a mother, start thinking about someone other than yourself and look long term. You don't even know those kids upstairs. Jamole and Willie are turning into little men who need someone to show them how to do it. Ruby is truly a precious jewel that needs to be cherished and polished, and Joey is just a little boy who needs you. You talk about needing love, but they all need you. Can't you give your love to these kids instead of passing it out to every man that comes along?"

"Oh, I see what's going on. You been hanging out with Stacey and that bunch of man-hating dykes, and now you're becoming one of them with that short hair. You used to be pretty, but how are you going to get a man when you look like one?"

"Rosie, that's not true and you know it! It's not about hating men, but about learning to be your own woman first. Someday I want to meet a man and have a relationship, but I need to learn who I am first. I need to be able to make it on my own so that I don't end up depending on someone else the way I depended on Jeff. That will only get me trapped again, and I don't want to make the same mistake twice. You have already made that mistake four times. I don't want to see you make it again either."

"My kids aren't mistakes. I'm glad that I have them. I'll live my life how I want, and you can live yours how you want. Don't worry, we'll be out of here before you start school. We wouldn't want to interfere with your career now, would we?"

"Rosie, you're being irrational, just think about what you're doing. Lisa's putting pressure on you because she cares about you and your kids. We all want what's right for you."

"And *you* know what's right for us? It seems like you're having a hard enough time taking care of yourself. Why don't you mind your own business and let me do what's right for me and my kids."

"You're not yourself. I'm worried about you. Just do me a favor and think about what I said."

"Yeah, and you do me a favor and think about what I said. Maybe you never really knew me to begin with."

"No. I know you, I know the *real* you who isn't being influenced by another person, alcohol, or drugs. I hope you can find that person again because I really like her."

"This conversation is over. I'm leaving now."

Rosie left the house and drove away, leaving Beth alone to care for the kids.

Chapter 10

August came quickly and Beth and Zack were counting down the days until school started. The first semester was from August to December and had five classes: Clinical Procedures, Anatomy and Physiology, Medical Terminology, and Communications. The program had a two-week break and then the second semester ran from January to May and had three classes: Computer keyboarding and applications, Pharmacology, Psychology, and the externship where she would receive real-life training in a medical facility. In less than a year she would have a diploma and experience to qualify for an entry-level job in the medical profession. Last year she would never have imagined being free and on her way to independence. It was still hard for her to believe that this was happening to her.

The first day of school was a beautiful sunny August day that was dry with a cool breeze. It was unseasonably cool for this time of year, and Beth was happy to have a break from the sticky humidity. Zack, also eager for his first day of school, woke her up long before her alarm clock went off. It was a relief to Beth that Zack's daycare was on campus run by the early education department. It was a win-win for everyone: the parents had their children nearby, students working at the daycare received credit, and the college benefited by collecting tuition from the students and fees from the children's parents. Zack wanted to wear his "big boy pants," which were elastic waist jeans with lots of pockets in them. He was such a little man.

Beth and Zack drove twenty minutes to the practically empty college campus, as most of the students would not be back for another month. Zack's eyes lit up when he saw the climb-on structures and toys in the fenced-in yard at the campus day care center. There were a few other children playing and Zack ran right over and made himself at home, barely noticing when Beth gave him a good-bye kiss.

"Bye honey, Mommy loves you. You have fun and I'll see you at lunch."

"Uh huh. Bye Mommy, love you too."

Beth closed her eyes tight so that Zack could not see her tears as she hugged him and left him alone for the first time.

Beth followed the campus map to her first class. She had Clinical Procedures and Anatomy and Physiology on Monday and Wednesday; and Medical Terminology and Communications on Tuesday and Thursday. She had time between classes and all day on Friday to study at the library while Zack was in day care. She climbed the stairs to the third floor to room 302 for her first class on Clinical Procedures. She entered the classroom and scanned the fifteen people who watched her. She chose a seat in the middle row, three seats from the front. She felt old in comparison to her classmates, many of whom looked like they were still in high school. The young man in the seat next to her smiled charmingly, reached out, and shook her hand firmly. She felt a jolt of energy illuminate from him and into her through the physical contact. It caught her off guard as the energy expanded into her body, making her shake a little, and landed in a knot in her stomach.

"Hi, my name's Jose. Looks like we're going to be classmates."

"I'm Beth. Nice to meet you."

She smiled politely, jerked her hand back, and stiffly looked forward. She was here to learn, not to flirt with young kids. He reminded her of little Joey with his kinky hair trimmed short and neat, big brown eyes with long eyelashes, and dimples that showed up on either side of his mouth when he smiled at her. Unlike Joey, Beth assumed that Jose used his boyhood charm to seduce quite a few women, and she was not going to be one of them.

A young man entered the room, who Beth thought was another student until he put his books down on the front desk. His brown hair framed his face and almost reached his shoulders. He had five o'clock shadow even though it was 10:00 A.M. He wore faded jeans and tee shirt, and his sneakers looked older than Zack. This certainly did not fit the image of the gray-haired distinguished professor that Beth had imagined. He began pointing to the students and counting out loud to himself.

"Fifteen—Eighteen—Twenty-one. Okay, everyone's here. Take a look around you class. These are the people who you're going to spend the next nine months with, so I suggest that you form study groups and get to know each other well." Jose' gave Beth a huge smile, showing his dimples. Beth felt that knot come back to her stomach and looked away. "Let's see, as you all know this is the Clinical Procedures class and my name is Professor Michael Pransky. Do you all have your textbooks? Yes? Good. Let's get started by reviewing the syllabus for the semester. We'll be on pace to cover one chapter a week, which should be easy to do with two classes. Each Monday we'll have a test on the previous week's chapter, the quizzes will count for one third of your grade.

We'll also have a midterm and a final exam that will each count for a third of your grade."

Professor Pransky continued talking as Beth wrote as fast as she could so that she would not forget anything. A quiz every Monday morning? What a way to start out each week! Beth could see that her Sunday afternoon visits with Stacey and Gayle were going to be shortened. As disappointed as she was that Rosie and the kids left, she was thankful that the house would be quiet.

Beth visited Zack between classes and had lunch with him. She packed them each a bagged lunch and Zack eagerly told Beth about his new friends while he sucked the juice out of his juice-box straw. Beth was feeling overwhelmed with the amount of work she was going to have. Clinical Procedures was going to take hours each week, and she still had three more classes.

At one o'clock all of the same students filed into the Anatomy and Physiology class. Everyone sat in the same seats as this morning. It was interesting how quickly people formed patterns and routine. Jose sat next to her and smiled again, his long black lashes framing his big brown eyes.

"We had a picnic at lunch and missed you."

"I was busy."

"Can you join us for a study group after class?"

"I need to read everything myself first."

"Learning together is more effective."

"No thanks."

The professor entered and everyone was silent. The workload for Anatomy and Physiology seemed greater and more difficult than that of Clinical Procedures, making it impossible for Beth to socialize with her classmates. Especially, not with flirtatious womanizers who would distract her.

Beth and Zack read in bed after supper. Beth read her textbook while Zack flipped through his picture books, seeming to need time to relax after his busy day at school. He soon fell asleep with the book open on his little chest. Beth covered him with his blanket. He looked innocent and angelic with his little hands curled under his chin, and his mouth opened just a crack while he slept.

The rest of the week went by quickly with Beth studying every minute that she was not in class. She felt herself being consumed by the constant desire to read and study so that she would do well in school. Zack enjoyed going to school and was tired after a busy day of playing. But even in the short span of one week, he realized that he did not like competing with books for his mother's attention. Beth's idea of quality time with Zack was to let him read in bed with her. Beth became a hermit in her room and barely spoke to their other housemates. Zack would venture out to play with the other kids and Beth could hear crying at all hours. The only interaction Beth had with the other families was when their meals overlapped.

Beth was surprised at how clean the kitchen had become, but then remembered this had also been her therapy. It was easy to substitute putting other things in order when one seemed to have no control over one's own life. Beth realized that part of the healing process was to begin small projects that are easy to complete, and then to slowly graduate to larger projects like one's life. Beth had graduated from the kitchen and was now working on the very big project of receiving a diploma. In a short time, she had come a long way.

Beth received a lot of encouragement from Lisa pushing her to apply herself to the difficult course work she had immersed herself into. However, she also stressed the importance of nurturing her personal growth and healing by continuing to attend support groups and counseling. Beth felt pressure from all angles: Zack wanted attention, she had to apply herself to her studies, and she had to continue the programs necessary to help her to heal on a personal level. It seemed like there was no time to relax, but she did not mind. Everything she was doing was positive and leading her into a direction where she wanted to be. She was never able to relax when she was with Jeff, but everything she did there was unhealthy and unproductive. She had been at point "A" with Jeff. She was now in point "B" in transition. She wanted to be at point "C," which was independence and freedom. In point "A" she had spent all her energy cleaning and trying to keep Jeff from exploding. In point "B" it was very easy for her to now transfer all of that wasted energy and apply it to completing goals that would lead her to point "C." At "C" she could support herself and Zack and they would be safe, happy, and free from dependence, dominance, and degradation. The strength she acquired as a necessity to fulfill her will to survive now pulsed through her veins and pushed her into determination to overcome any difficulties that would stand in her way to bettering herself and her life. She felt as if destiny held a higher purpose for her and that she would not have been able to complete this destiny if she had not experienced and survived her ordeal with Jeff. She felt as if point "C" included whatever this destiny was and that completing points "A" and "B" were part of the journey necessary for success.

Beth questioned why she had become an abuse victim. Was it a punishment for an evil deed she did in this or a previous life? Was she being punished as part of the larger picture in life relating to karma? Beth doubted herself. She wondered if she was a bad person to have fate hand her such a bad situation. Reverend Josh said that everything happens for a reason, and even bad things are part of an overall plan that leads to the better of all. Was that why this happened to her? Were the experiences she had to endure a requirement that would lead her to a bigger plan? She did not know. Did it matter? She was on the correct path now and miraculously, Jeff was leaving them alone. She constantly feared that at any moment her life at the safe home and enrollment in school would all go away, and she would be back with Jeff, helpless and beaten. But she was here now and she would hold onto this moment. She would take each day as it came and be thankful for all that she had.

It seemed that her readiness to move on was felt by fate and dealt her the hand she wished for. The next day Lisa delivered a letter to her from the State Housing Authority. Lisa laughed as she waved it in front of Beth.

"Hummm, I wonder what's in this letter? Lets see ... It's addressed to Beth Parker. It's from the State Housing Authority. Could it be that an apartment is available for Ms. Parker? Could she get a home of her very own?"

"Give it to me!"

Beth had to practically wrestle Lisa to the ground before she could get the letter from her. She tore it open and could barely hold it still while she read.

"I'm in! They have an opening for Section 8 housing at the housing complex at Pond View Estates! It says that I can move in on October first. That's a month away! How am I going to be able to wait an entire month?"

"You'll be so busy with school that October will be here before you know it. I'm so happy for you! It will be much easier to concentrate on school and you'll have privacy."

"I know. This is the first time that I'll have a place of my own. After my parent's death, I was devastated, and living on my own never entered my mind. I went straight from living with my family to living with Jeff, never having my own space. I'm so excited!"

The month of September went by quickly. The college kids came back and the campus was full of learning and hormones. Beth visited Zack everyday to eat lunch, but spent the rest of the day studying. On the nice days she put a blanket under a tree by the pond to study, otherwise she would go to the library. She studied until her brain felt full of cotton and she could no longer think; she even dreamed about vocabulary words and concepts. Her classmates formed study groups, but Beth preferred to study alone as they spent much time laughing and socializing. Beth had no time to waste. She had to take this seriously and get as much done during the day so that she could spend her nights with Zack. Jose persistently invited her to participate in the study groups or to let him quiz her, but Beth politely declined. She knew that most women would be flattered by his charm and sex appeal, but she had been seduced in the past and was too mature to be deceived by a young Casanova.

Beth tried to prepare Zack by telling him they would have their own apartment soon.

"But I like it here."

"I know that you like it here. I like it here too, but it's time for us to get our own home just like Joey did. This is where people stay until they get their own home, and it's other people's turn now."

"We can stay with them."

"Yes, we've been staying with them and it's been fun. We made lots of new friends and always have people to play with. We'll still be friends with everyone, just like we're friends with Stacy, Gayle, and Mia."

"And Nancy?"

"What do you mean?"

"We don't see Nancy any more."

"You're right. We haven't seen Nancy in a long time because we live far away from her now."

"Call her."

"You know Zack, some times when people move or make new friends, they don't see their old friends as much."

"We'll still see Nancy, right?"

"Yeah, we'll see Nancy someday."

Beth had not thought about Nancy, as she was part of that other life with Jeff, which she did not think about. It seemed interesting that Zack asked about Nancy, but not Jeff. Beth had been warned not to talk negatively about Jeff, and as a result they did not talk about him at all.

Once Zack was asleep Beth called Nancy despite the warnings not to contact anyone from her "old" life. Beth did not see the harm in a quick phone call since there was a block on the line and it was untraceable. Beth slowly pressed the buttons on the phone to dial Nancy's phone number.

"Hello?"

"Hi Nancy? It's me, Beth."

"Oh my God. So you decided to call an old friend? I thought you wrote me off."

"I'm sorry Nancy, I didn't mean to not call you."

"Or tell me that you were going to disappear."

"Yeah, that too."

"Or say 'Goodbye'."

"Or say 'Goodbye'."

"I'm glad you called because a lot's happened. I don't know how you could walk away from a perfect life."

"Nancy, there's so much you don't know."

"Let me finish."

"Sorry."

"Jeff is an amazing guy who gave you everything and you threw it away. He was a mess, but I was there for him and now he's happy. It was *you* who was making him miserable. We're together now that you're gone."

"Nancy, *no*. You *can't* be with him!"

"So, you realize what you're missing? We were always attracted to each other, but he was married. The problem with your marriage was that he's in love with me. You lost your chance, so don't come back."

"You don't know what you're doing! You don't know what he's like!"

"Yeah, I know what he's like. He's a loving wonderful man who wasn't appreciated. I satisfy and keep him happy. But there is the issue of Zack who we both love and can give a better life to than you, but we would have to be in contact with you. We decided to let him go and have our own baby. But if you come around or call again then we'll take Zack away from you."

"Nancy, you wouldn't do that!"

"Yes, I would. So here's the good-bye that I never gave you: good-bye from me and Jeff."

Beth hung up without responding. Nothing she imagined prepared her for this. She felt the numbness and knot in her stomach that she used to feel with Jeff. She should be angry at Nancy, but instead she was scared. Nancy was her best friend and this hurt tremendously. She understood how easy it was to be charmed into believing you were the entire reason for Jeff's existence. That was until he realized that you are human and not a stone goddess, and began chipping away until you become as cold and emotionless as the stone he thought you were. Beth curled up on the couch and cried uncontrollably into a pillow so no one would hear her. This explained why Jeff was not fighting for Zack and why he just let her go. She had been quickly replaced. Did it even matter to him that they were gone or had been with him? Part of her was relieved that Jeff was occupied and would leave her alone, but another part was terrified of Nancy. The feelings of panic and worry for Nancy were too strong to be angry. She felt helpless at not being able to stop Nancy from endeavoring into this situation that would ultimately bring her pain, and it broke her heart.

With mixed feelings, Beth realized that since she was healing from Jeff's abuse, the stone skin that had sealed her soul was now pealing away and allowing her to feel. In one sense it was nice to feel again and experience the emotions of contentment and awe as the fall colors turned. Her soul was opening up and feeling the peacefulness of taking a walk by the pond, loving Zack, preparing and eating a good meal, being loved and cared for by Lisa, Stacey, Gayle, and her other friends. But her emotions also felt the anxiety of worrying about her exams, how she was going to manage on her own, and what would happen to Nancy. All of the hurt, pain, and fear that she had repressed while with Jeff was now surfacing and she could feel the physical tingling in her skin as it surfaced. She felt shaky, anxious, had nightmares or lay awake sleepless during the night, and felt her heart racing and got panicky during the day. She had a constant urge to cry, but was glad the tears never came, as she knew that if they started then they may never stop and she had to hold things together for Zack. She was not in a position to release her emotions; there was too much responsibility and advancement that she had to accomplish first. Instead, she channeled her energy into studying which was a productive diversion that kept her occupied.

Beth studied under the tree by the campus pond and tried to focus on the vocabulary for her Medical Terminology test. But remembering her conversation with Nancy prevented her from concentrating. Jose appeared out of nowhere and lay on her blanket. Beth was annoyed at his arrogance, but felt too worn out to become angry.

"What are you doing?"

"I'm lying on a blanket next to a beautiful woman. What are you doing?"

"I'm studying, and this is my blanket. You have no right to lie on it uninvited."

"Oh, but I do. This is my spot and you inadvertently placed your blanket on it. So it's you who's trespassing. I'll forgive your rudeness and let you share the spot, if you share your blanket."

Beth was about to defend herself, but saw a twinkle in his eyes and dimples at the tip of his smile, and in her current state of emotional weakness gave in and smiled.

"Okay, fine. You can share my blanket as long as you're quiet and don't interrupt my studying."

"It's a deal!" Jose smiled as he shook Beth's hand. The connection as he looked into her eyes sent tingles through her body. His shake was very firm and confident, yet did not hurt, as it was also gentle and soft. Beth could feel kindness and love being emitted through him and smiled sincerely as she moved a little closer.

Part III

The Rebirth

Chapter 11

October came quickly and since the first was on a Wednesday, Beth would move into their apartment on the following weekend. Beth was not sure how they would fill an entire apartment with their few belongings. Lisa assured her there were donations she could have. Beth felt so helpless knowing that she was completely dependent on other people's generosity to furnish her new home.

Beth could hardly sleep on Friday night. She lay awake thinking about all that happened in the past seven months. Was it only seven months ago that she was preparing to leave her last home with little belongings or expectations about where the future would lead her? At that time she had no goals or plan; she only knew that she had to get out if she was going to survive. Now she was moving once again. Only this time, she had a plan, goals, friends, and was on the road to a career and her independence. Seven months ago she walked out of her home onto an unknown path; now, she was walking into a home that held a future and promise.

Beth woke up early on Saturday morning and took her last shower at the safe home. She stripped and remade her bed so it would be ready for the next person who needed shelter and protection. She packed her makeup, pajamas, brush, and blow dryer; everything else had already been packed. Zack was still sleeping, so she went to the kitchen and had coffee with one of the residents.

"So, today's the big day. You're moving into your own place."

"Yeah, I'm so excited. I've been here longer than I should have been."

"Mmm. Me too."

"Your time will come to get a place of your own."

"I don't want a place of my own. I want to go home to my husband and my life."

"I know it's hard, but you were in a very dangerous situation and it isn't safe for you there."

"It wasn't that bad. I think that if I tried harder, then maybe we could make it work and be a family again. I feel lost and alone here."

"It's hard at first, but I know you can make it."

"But I'm sick of things being hard and although I'm not supposed to, I've been calling my husband and he really misses us. He wants us to come home and I want this all to end."

"It would be harder going back."

"I made up my mind."

"Did you tell Lisa?"

"No, I don't know how to tell her. She's done so much that I'm afraid to disappoint her."

"You should talk to her before you make any decisions."

"My decision is made."

"When are you going to leave?"

"I don't know. I guess tomorrow, so I don't ruin the excitement of you getting your own place. I'll have Lisa bring me and the kids to the main office so that I can take a cab home."

"I hope you'll keep going to the support group."

"I'll try but I'll have to lie to my husband about it."

"Is that a good way to live?"

"You're right. Maybe I shouldn't go."

"That's not what I meant."

Lisa's car pulled into the driveway.

"I wasn't expecting her here so early."

"Promise you won't tell her."

"I promise."

Lisa came into the house with a big smile that Beth would have matched ten minutes ago.

"Hey, you're up! I was going to wake you up with breakfast in bed!"

She held up a Dunkin Donuts bag and pulled out two bagel, egg, and sausage sandwiches. They opened the wrappers and ate the sandwiches. Beth forced hers down with the coffee.

"You won't believe what surprises there are for you! Where's Zack? He's part of this too!"

"He's still sleeping. I'll wake him up."

Zack reluctantly got up, not sure if he was excited or disappointed that they would be leaving this cozy room and secure house for the unknown. It would be lonely with no other children to play with, and he did not want to rush his last morning at the happiest place he ever knew. He complained about having to wear the red corduroy overalls Beth put on him and was upset that his other clothes were not in the bureau where they belonged. This was his room and he wanted to stay.

Beth eventually accomplished the struggle of getting Zack dressed and ready to leave after bribing him with a chocolate frosted donut with colored sprinkles. Beth sat in the back seat with Zack while they drove the short distance to Pond View Estates, through the large sign at the entrance and along the one-way street that circled around the apartments and back to the entrance. The apartment buildings were lined up on either side of the circular road with parking spaces in front of them. Each building had two entrances with four units at each entrance, two on the bottom floor and two on the top floor, and storage and laundry in the basements. There was grass surrounding the buildings with some children playing on the playground and pool in the center while others road their bikes around the circle, which sparked Zack's attention. Beth saw a U-Haul-It moving truck, which she assumed was someone else's, as she did not have enough to fill a truck. As they pulled closer, she noticed that the truck was empty and one of the center volunteers, Janet, was sitting on the front steps.

"What's Janet doing here?"

"She drove the truck and opened the apartment so that everyone could bring in your stuff."

"What stuff? I don't have any stuff."

"Oh Beth, just stop it. You know we have donations. Let's go see what they brought."

Beth was overwhelmed that complete strangers were so generous to someone they never met. They parked the car and walked up to the apartment, Zack holding Beth's hand, finding it completely furnished. The living-kitchen-dining room had a small round wooden table with four chairs surrounding it, a burgundy velvet couch that was very worn yet inviting, a low wooden coffee table, and a wooden rocking chair with plaid cushions on it. There were a pile of cardboard boxes stacked up against the wall that were labeled pots/pans, dishes, sheets, towels and more. Zack led Beth into his small bedroom and pulled his hand out of hers so he could jump on the child-sized bed that was shaped like a race car. There was also a small bureau with a lamp on it, a bouncy horse, and a cardboard box marked "boy's toys and books." Beth left Zack and went across the hall to her room, which had a full-sized bed and bureau, where she sat on the bed and let herself cry. Lisa came into the room, and put her arm around Beth.

"When did this all happen?"

"Janet and some volunteers came early this morning so that you would have the entire day to settle in. Come, look in the boxes. There's all sorts of stuff."

Lisa opened the first box that was labeled "sheets, blankets, towels" and pulled out the bath, hand and face towels, colored sheets, fuzzy blankets, small Jungle Book comforter, and large comforter with lavender roses. It was obvious that the worn and frayed items were second hand, but it did not matter to Beth as they were a 100 percent improvement from what she had. The next box contained pots, pans, cookie sheets, a baking pan, and utensils, with which Beth hoped she would create good meals. The bottom box had four sets of plates, bowls, mugs, and cups wrapped in newspaper, a plastic bag filled with silverware and a sharp knife. They put the linens away and the kitchen supplies next to the sink to be washed. There were no sponges, dish detergent or cleaning supplies, none of which would be covered by food stamps.

Janet returned to the U-Haul-It truck, Lisa stayed with Zack who was napping in his new bed, and Beth went grocery shopping. Zack's resistance about moving seemed to have disappeared.

Once everyone was gone, Beth sat in her new living room alone. It was very bare with no pictures on the wall, curtains on the windows, nick-knacks, TV, or radio. She unpacked the groceries so that the kitchen cabinets now had minimal items: a box of cocoa puffs (store brand = $2); a jar of spaghetti sauce ($2.50); two boxes of elbow pasta (two for $1); a box of macaroni and cheese (store brand = $0.89); a jar of instant coffee ($3); a jar of peanut butter (free, thanks to WIC); a box of graham crackers ($0.99); a box of ginger snap cookies ($0.99). The refrigerator was slightly better thanks to WIC: a dozen eggs, a cube of cheese, a gallon of whole milk, a carton of fruit drink (the real thing was much too expensive), a tub of margarine, a bag of apples and a bag of oranges. There was one bar of soap, three rolls of toilet paper, a bottle of baby shampoo, and a bottle of dish detergent, but she had no money for cleaning supplies. She took one of the facecloths and hand towels from the bathroom and washed the dishes. Despite the empty shelves, walls and rooms, Beth felt an immense wave of gratefulness that she had her own apartment, and horrible guilt that she was a recipient of charity. She felt worthless and vowed to become self-sufficient and give back to others like herself.

Zack woke up from his nap and entered the living room looking confused and disoriented, rubbing his eyes. His little lips were puffy as he climbed onto Beth's lap. She hugged him while they sat together in silence. Zack gradually woke up and was curious about his surroundings.

"Will you play with me?"

Beth smiled and hugged him a little longer, more tightly this time.

"Of course, I'll play with you. I bet there are all sorts of fun things in that big box in your room!"

Zack's face lit up with joy as he jumped off the couch and ran into his room, dragging Beth behind him. Beth slowly removed the box's contents: a brown floppy stuffed dog, and a small green little-tykes dump truck, and a box of tiny cars. Zack carefully examined each toy, beaming as if each were the only toy in the world despite the fact that not long ago he had a room full of toys. Beth realized that his preference of having three toys and safety was more important in a two-year-old's eyes, in any eyes. Beth removed the books stacked on the bottom of the box and handed them to Zack. There were a few *Curious George* books, *Mike Mulligan and Mary Ann*, a giant book of fairy tales, *The Bernstein Bears*, *Thomas the Tank Engine*, and some *Little Golden Books*. Zack picked up the *Curious George* book about when George got a paper route and folded all of the newspapers into boats that floated down the river. He hugged the book and looked up at Beth, his blue eyes had never looked so blue or innocent, his light lashes curled up above his eyes and his cheeks were slightly flushed.

"Read to me?"

"Of course."

Zack climbed onto Beth's lap as she wrapped her arms around him and read *Curious George*. Alone in their new home, Beth realized that from now on it was just the two of them, on their own with nothing but each other. Material things, places of residence, even friends would come and go out of their lives, but through it all they would have each other. These two bodies, flesh and blood, he who came from her, she who was willing to die for him, connected. They were all that mattered in this huge vast world filled with outside forces that could not reach them at this moment. Mother and child, the strongest bond in existence, was the only bond that mattered. There was a force surrounding them, bonding them in love, protecting them from harm.

Beth would have liked to spend the entire weekend in their new apartment alone, but since she had no phone, there was no way to let Stacey and Gayle know that they would not come to church and dinner. It was nice to have an hour alone listening to service and a homemade meal afterwards. Zack was fussy getting ready for church. It may have been that he did not sleep well in his new bed, or that he was getting adjusted in his new routine. He seemed relieved to arrive in the familiar setting of church.

"I'm going upstairs to tell my friends about our new house!"

"Okay. Give me a big hug and kiss, and then I'll bring you up."

Zack hugged Beth and gave her a quick kiss on the cheek before running ahead up the stairs to the nursery. He was so excited to tell his friends all about the new apartment, car bed, toys, and books that he did not notice Beth leaving to go to the service. She loved the solitude of sitting alone and enjoying the service. She did not have to concentrate like when in class or studying. The rituals of the service went by quickly, then when Beth felt at peace listening to the chorus sing their hymn, it was time for the sermon. Reverend Josh stood quietly for a moment before he began speaking.

"The title of today's sermon is 'We are all lepers.' I can tell by the shuffling and looking around at each other that some of you are uncomfortable with the title, but I'm going to continue anyway. We all know the story of Jesus and his great love for everyone, even the lepers who the rest of society shunned and rejected, sending them off on their own to live and die in seclusion. Jesus, however, had compassion for the lepers. He spoke to them, treated them with respect, and even healed them. He saw and treated them as people who deserved to be loved and who should not be judged. Let us take a trip back in time and think of what exactly a leper was two thousand years ago. Leprosy is a very serious health condition which was very contagious and for which there was no cure, presenting many risks to society. In addition to the obvious health risk of contamination and thus becoming a leper yourself, there was the social risk. People with Leprosy were not attractive as their skin literally was being eaten away and deteriorating off their body. This made them different from the rest of the citizens, and we all know how much people fear those who are different from us. It presents the risk of change. A very scary thought.

"Okay now, lets fast forward two thousand years to the present day. Leprosy is not a major health risk any more, but there are many other health threats that people fear such as AIDS. There are many who are prejudiced towards people with AIDS because of fear of contamination and of the unknown. Entire groups of high-risk classes are discriminated against because of people's fear of the dreaded disease. Some of these classes include homosexuals, drug addicts, Hispanics, and people of color.

"Just a few generations ago, and in many places today, most people lived in the same countries, cities, or neighborhoods as those who were of the same nationality or ethnic background as themselves. Now, with modern transportation moving people all over the globe, families are separated and nationalities are intermarrying. In a progressive sense this is good as cultures are being shared, people are marrying for love, and the world is becoming a smaller place. However, there are people who do not want change. They fear those who are different and are prejudiced against anyone who threatens their lifestyle. Some people fear or hate people of different ethnic background, social class, religion, or sexual preference. The blacks are afraid of the whites because of years of repression, while the whites are afraid of the blacks because they fear being violated. The poor hate the rich out of desperation, while the rich are afraid of being robbed by and have no respect for the poor. The republicans do not agree with the democrats, and the democrats do not agree with the republicans. Some people believe that their religion is the true religion and thus all other religions are wrong. Some people do not want immigrants in *their* country; other people do not want homosexuals contaminating their children; there are people who are afraid of anyone who is even the slightest bit different than themselves. The list goes on and on. Although none of us want to admit it, each of us fits into one of the categories on the list. We may not be in the groups who are discriminating, but we are a member of a group who is discriminated against. Somewhere out there, there is someone who hates each one of us for who we are and what we represent. Heck, as Americans we are hated by half of the world! So, there it is. We are all lepers.

"The solution? Why not follow Jesus's example and love everyone. Do not judge. To quote Jane Adams in her lecture to Ethical Culture Societies in the summer of 1892 on the subject of The Subjective Necessity for Social Settlements: 'They did not yet denounce, nor tear down temples, nor preach the end of the world. They grew to a mighty number, but it never occurred to them, either in their weakness or in their strength, to regard other men for an instant as their foes or as aliens. The spectacle of the Christians loving all men was the most astounding Rome had ever seen. They were eager to sacrifice themselves for the weak, for children and the aged. They identified themselves with slaves and did not avoid the plague. They longed to share the common lot that they might receive the constant revelation. It was a new treasure which the early Christians added to the sum of all treasures, a joy hitherto unknown in the world—the joy of finding the Christ which liveth in each man, but which no man can unfold save in fellowship. A happiness ranging from the heroic to the pastoral enveloped them. They were to possess a revelation as long as life had new meaning to unfold, new action to propose . . . There must be the overmastering belief that all that is noblest in life is common to men as men, in order to accentuate the likenesses and ignore the differences which are found among the people whom the Settlement constantly brings into juxtaposition.'

"So, yes we are all lepers. There is something in all of us that someone else fears and hates because we are different from them. However, we all also have the power to change the world. We all have the power to love unconditionally and to not judge others. We all have the power to let the love of Jesus live through us. May there be peace on earth, and let it begin here, with us. Amen."

Beth sat and contemplated the sermon while the music played and the chorus sang. At first she felt offended by it. She felt it was pessimistic to assume that everyone was hated by someone. It seemed contradictory to talk about how everyone hates each other, and then to talk about how everyone should spread love. Which was it? Love or hate? She found herself ignoring all of the hate and violence in the world. She did not watch the news or any TV shows that might be emotional or upsetting. She was relieved that she had no TV at her new apartment, as she did not have to be exposed to the problems that were going on in the world. She tried not to think about Jeff and was having a hard time dealing with listening to the stories of abuse at support group. She would lie awake at night and worry about the women who were with their abusers, or were trying to get away (including herself). She would even get upset and a little paranoid if people were not nice to her in public. She would take it personally instead of rationalizing that they were probably just having a bad day. She could not handle any more negativity; she just wanted everything to be okay. She wanted the world to stop being so horrible. Church was the place where she came to find peace, and even here she was told that every single one of us is hated. Where could she go to find peace? Was there no sanctuary that was sacred? She felt helpless and wanted to give up in despair.

But was that the message? Was the message about giving up and accepting that the world was filled with hate and prejudice? No. It was about not giving up. It was about being the one to stop the hate and to spread love. Just like how she broke out of the cycle of violence by leaving Jeff. She thought about herself, Zack, and all of her friends. They were all like the misfits on the island of misfit toys in the Christmas movie *Rudolph, the Red-Nosed Reindeer*. Before she knew what domestic violence was or realized that she was a victim, she thought that women who were in abusive relationships were weak and stupid. She did not understand why they did not just leave, or even how they got into a relationship like that in the first place. She was sure that people were prejudiced and judgmental against her and Zack for being a single mom family, for being homeless up until yesterday, for being in an abusive relationship, and for being on welfare. She knew that there were many negative stereotypes geared towards her and her friends. Would people treat Sheila differently if they found out that she was in a psychiatric hospital and had attempted suicide? Would Mia be made to feel different in school because she has two moms? How did people treat Stacey and Gayle when they discovered that they were lesbians? Did people treat Jose differently since he was Hispanic? Beth continued sorting through her friends and acquaintances in both this and her previous life (which is what she considered her life before leaving Jeff). She could not think of a single person who would not be judged or hated by someone, somewhere. Reverend Josh was correct—we are all lepers.

Beth never heard of Jane Adams, but it made sense what she said. If everyone could live as Christ lived instead of preaching and trying to convert others, then the world would be a much better place. Her mother always told her "show me, don't tell me," "live by Jesus' word, don't preach it". A place where people "were eager to sacrifice themselves for the weak, for children and the aged" instead of casting them away to live off public assistance and wither away alone in nursing homes. If each of us could find Christ in each other, there would be joy and love in the world instead of hate and prejudice. How wonderful the world would be if everyone could look for the good in each other and find the positive qualities that we share instead of focusing on the qualities that make us different. Imagine the power in the world if all people could become united based on our similarities instead of separated by our differences. On a micro level, Beth had the power to leave an abusive relationship and raise her son with love and safety. On a macro level, did she have the power to extend the creation of positive change to the world? Perhaps, if we all spread peace then it would engulf the world, one person at a time.

Beth was very quiet at Stacey and Gayle's house. She was exhausted from the changes this weekend, and was worried about her lack of studying. It was enjoyable for her to watch how happy Stacey and Gayle were together, especially Stacey who had been so unhappy and was convinced that she would be alone forever. Here she was with a loving partner and child, part of a family. They were in sync with each other as they prepared the meal and set the table. It was like watching a married couple who had spent their lives growing old together. Gayle chopped vegetables and Stacey put them in the casserole dish, sprinkling them with spices. Stacey added milk, parsley, butter, pepper and sour cream to the mashed potatoes while Gayle whipped them with the mixer. Gayle handed Stacey the hot mitts just as Stacey reached for the oven door to check on the roast. They moved around each other as one unit preparing, cleaning, and setting the table. It was as if they were one body and mind in two people. Beth was perfectly contented sitting and watching them. Just to be surrounded by such love and happiness was like a drug for Beth. The effect was calming for Zack also. He played on the floor putting together a puzzle while Mia sat in her baby seat watching him with adoring eyes.

The dinner was finally done and the food was placed on the table, surrounded by four pairs of eager eyes. In addition to being grateful for the great company, Beth and Zack were appreciative to have a complete home-cooked meal. The food at home was cheap and fast, nothing like the slow cooked feast of fresh meat and vegetables. Gayle filled the wine glasses from a bottle of red wine that she had opened before placing the food on the table. Gayle and Stacey smiled at each other and held up their glasses. Stacey nodded at Gayle who began a toast.

"We are happy and blessed to be surrounded by friends and fortunate to have this meal to share—"

"I'll toast to that! You have no idea how much me and Zack love coming here!"

"In addition to this feast, we have some great news to share."

"Oh?"

"We decided to get married, and want you to be the first to know! After all, if it weren't for you then we may never have gotten together!"

"Oh my God! I am so happy for you guys! Congratulations!"

Instead of toasting their glasses, Beth got out of her chair and went in between Gayle and Stacey and grabbed them both, pulling them into a huge hug. Zack climbed off his booster seat and squeezed in between them all.

"Me too, me too! I want hugs too!"

Beth started to cry, but once the tears started they would not stop. They just kept on coming. Zack was worried, wondering what was wrong. Gayle picked up Zack, telling him that everything was okay, while Stacey hugged Beth and tried to comfort her.

"It's okay. Don't cry. It's not bad that we're getting married is it?"

"I'm sorry, I don't mean to be crying. I'm happy, really. I'm crying because I'm so happy!"

"Wow, you have a funny way of showing it. Most people laugh when they're happy and cry when they are sad!"

Beth started to laugh through her sobs.

"There, see! Now you're laughing. That's more like it!"

"Okay, I'm better now. Let's complete this toast and eat this fabulous meal before it gets cold!"

They all laughed and got back in their seats to eat. Zack was relieved to see that Beth stopped crying and soon shifted his focus to his plate of mashed potatoes and gravy. He gently pushed his fork into the pile of mashed potatoes so that the gravy made little rivers in the fork lines. He would then scrape off those potatoes, eat them, and start over again. He was keeping himself very entertained while the women discussed wedding plans.

"I know it's quick, but we want to get married as soon as possible."

"We're thinking we'll have the wedding in December, with a winter solstice theme."

"Most importantly, we both want you to be our maid of honor and Zack to be our ring bearer."

"Unfortunately Mia is too young to be the flower girl, but we decided to have her be the flower baby, kind of like a little fairy. So, will you be our maid of honor and ring bearer?"

"I, we, would be honored! Are you sure there isn't someone else you would rather have?"

"You're our best friend. We want you!"

Beth started to cry again, but this time Zack paid no attention to it. He seemed more worried that his pile of mashed potatoes was getting too small to make very good gravy rivers.

Monday, in school, Beth was having a difficult time concentrating on her work. She kept thinking about Stacey and Gayle getting married, and about her new apartment. It was rainy and damp out, so Beth found a quiet corner in the library where she could be alone. She read the same paragraph for the third time and she still did not comprehend what it said. She was beginning it for the fourth time when she felt that someone was watching her. She looked up and sure enough, there was Jose leaning against the bookshelf with his arms crossed, smiling at her. She could not help but to smile back at him. Her resistance towards him was fading as she let herself feel the warmth that he emitted.

"How long have you been watching me?"

"Long enough to see that you're not getting any studying done. Do you want me to help you or do you just need a diversion?"

"I would love to have a diversion, but I really need to study. I didn't get any studying done this weekend, and I'm afraid that I'm going to get behind. You know what happens if you get behind. It's a downward spiral that doesn't stop until you crash. Then it's impossible to work your way out and all your hard work goes to waste."

"Oh God! We *must* do *something* to prevent that from happening!"

"Yeah, but what?"

"Let me pull up a chair and we can study together. Don't worry, I'm really tough and won't let you get sidetracked. If you even try to daydream then you'll have to deal with me!" His dimples were showing as he smiled at her.

"Oh no, not that! Anything but that! I promise that I'll study hard!"

Beth found that she retained more by studying with Jose, as talking about the information and being quizzed by him helped her to understand and remember it better. They studied together everyday after that and in addition to studying better, Beth enjoyed Jose's company and was generally happier. She felt very light and free when she was with him, and floaty and dazed when she was not. She would lay awake at night thinking over every conversation they had and expressions he made during the day, eventually drifting off to sleep. She liked the fact that he never asked her out or wanted to see her outside of school. It felt safe. She was not being hit on and nothing was expected from her. If this was a different time in her life, she might have been suspicious wondering if he had a girlfriend or was ashamed to introduce her to his friends. However, anything more at this point would have scared her and pushed her away.

Chapter 12

Zack was excited about Halloween coming and was determined to be "Spiderman." Beth dreaded his disappointment since she could not afford a costume, and hated his being deprived as a result of their situation. Last Halloween she thought nothing of buying his clown costume, plastic pumpkin pail, decorations, and bags of candy to give out. Now before buying anything she considered how that purchase would affect buying food, gas, clothes, or utilities. She had not known the stress that millions of people face everyday being in a constant state of crisis just to survive.

The closer Halloween came, the more anxious Beth became. Lisa stopped by the apartment with an invitation to a party for the center the Saturday afternoon before Halloween that a local restaurant was sponsoring. Beth declined, telling her that Zack already got invited to a party from one of the kids at the day care. When Lisa asked if Zack needed a costume, Beth told her that he already had one. She did not want to depend on the center for everything. They needed their independence even if it meant going without.

Jose could tell that something was bothering Beth. She kept dazing and was very preoccupied when she was supposed to be studying.

"What's the matter?"

"Nothing."

"Why do women always say that nothing's the matter when it's obvious that there is something eating away at their insides?"

Beth laughed at Jose's extraordinary way of seeing the truth and making his observation a visual analogy. Most guys would know that something was wrong, but just shrug it off.

"Ahh, see? I made you laugh! You were not laughing just a minute ago, there was a shadow of sadness hanging over you. Please tell me what's wrong."

"Halloween is next week."

"Are you afraid of the ghosts and goblins? I'll protect you."

Jose flexed his muscles, making Beth laugh again.

"No, it's just that I don't have any Halloween stuff."

"Halloween stuff?"

"Yeah, you know, candy, decorations, a Spiderman costume."

"A Spiderman costume?"

"Yeah, my little boy wants to be Spiderman for Halloween, but I don't have a costume. That means no Halloween party or trick-or-treating, and he's not going to understand why."

"Beautiful Beth, will you please let me get your little boy his Spiderman costume? I realize that I may be imposing, and I don't want you to be offended, but I consider it an honor to do this. Is that okay?"

Beth tried not to, but she started to cry and nodded her head "yes." She cried because he was sincere in his offer. She did not feel that she was a recipient of charity but rather a recipient of a strong human connection. Jose put his arm around Beth and held her against his chest, gently stroking her head and wiping her tears away with his thumb.

"Don't cry, beautiful Beth. Everything will be okay, it will be fine."

Beth let him hold her, let him give her support instead of carrying it all herself. She let Jose release her from the burden of depriving Zack of celebrating Halloween. Jose made her feel good about accepting his offer. He was being a friend that she could count on, but not yet trust.

The next day Jose gave Beth the Spiderman costume, Spiderman gloves that squirt out "silly string," some fake purple spider webs, two bags of miniature "Snickers bars," and a pumpkin. They put the stuff in the trunk of Beth's car so that she could give them to Zack when they got home. Beth wanted Jose to give Zack the costume, but Jose insisted that it would mean more coming from Beth. When Zack saw the costume, he tore open the package and put it on, refusing to take it off even to sleep. Beth was concerned that the costume would not make it to Halloween after being worn twenty-four hours a day, and convinced Zack to take it off for bed. He hugged the costume and smiled while he slept.

Beth surprised Zack by taking him to the crisis center Halloween party. Lisa was surprised to see them, so Beth told her that they decided to come to this party instead. Zack was happy to wear his costume officially for the first time. He was overwhelmed at the sight of the black strobe lights, the screeching music, the haunted ghosts, and green witches. There was a long table covered with spooky foods such as hospital gloves filled with popcorn, witch's fingers (short bread cookies with almond fingernails), a chocolate cake with gravestones, mud pudding with worms, blood punch and much more. The room was decorated with bunches of orange and black balloons, spider webs, cray paper, and scarecrows. There were stations with different games set up: dunking for apples, eating donuts off strings, coloring black velvet cards with pictures on them, having a Polaroid picture taken with a giant spider. Beth thought that Zack would leave her to run around the room playing with all of the kids and activities, but instead he hugged her leg and held her hand while they stood observing the festivities, being her little baby among the goblins and ghouls. Out of nowhere, little Joey ran up to them and gave Zack a hug.

"Zacky, where you been? I been missing ya."

"Joey! My big brother!"

"There's a haunted house over behind those hanging sheets. Ya want to come through it with me?"

"Only if Mommy comes. Will you come, Mommy?"

Beth shook her head "yes" and let Joey lead them to the haunted house. Zack held her hand so tight that there was no chance of losing him. There was a short line for the haunted house and then they crawled through an entrance covered with a sheet and onto a dark narrow tunnel of pillows. The fear was in the unknown of not knowing where they were being led. Finally, there was a light at the end of the tunnel opening up to a small room with red lighting and a witch sitting on a rocking chair. Beth thought the witch had a strong resemblance to Marcia. The witch smiled and spoke to Zack in a screechy voice.

"Hello, little boy. Welcome to my home. Would you like to have something to eat? Help your self to some eye balls, guts, or frog's brains."

There was a small table set up with a bowl of skinned grapes, a bowl of cold spaghetti, a bowl of chopped walnuts and plate settings for four.

"No. I want to go."

Beth picked up Zack and brought him out of the haunted house. She offered to have him eat a donut off a string, but he just wanted to sit and watch everyone. Joey tried to convince him to play some games, but he would not.

"So Joey, how've you guys been doing? Are your brothers and sister here?"

"Oh, we're doing good. Jamole and Willie didn't want to come, but Ruby is a princess. She's here somewhere."

"What about your mom? How's she doing?"

"She's fine. I don't like it when she cries though."

"Does she cry a lot?"

"Only when she and Guy fight."

"Why do they fight?"

"He gets mad at her and says that she shouldn't drink. She tells him to mind his own business and that she can drink if she wants to."

"Does he drink too?"

"Sometimes, but not usually. He just gets mad and leaves, so then she cries. Jamole takes us kids upstairs to his room and tells us that everything's going to be okay."

"Where's your mom now?"

"Oh, she's over there hanging out with her friends."

Beth looked where Joey nodded his head and saw Rosie laughing while she talked to two women.

"I'm going to go say 'Hi' to her."

"Okay."

Joey shrugged his shoulders and went to play some of the games that were set up. Zack still had not let go of Beth's hand.

"Hey, look whose here! It's my old friends Beth and Zack!"

Rosie seemed genuinely happy to see them despite the bad words and hostile feelings that they shared the last time they were together.

"Look at you Zack, I think that you grew since the last time I saw you. You're turning into a little man! Are you three yet?"

Zack shook his head "no."

"He'll be three in February. How about you? How's everything with you, Guy, and the kids?"

"Oh, we're great. Guy loves the kids and they love him. We're one big, happy family!" Rosie smiled and laughed her hearty laugh.

"That's great, Rosie. I'm happy for you."

"So, you out on your own now?"

"Yeah. Me and Zack have an apartment at Pond View Estates."

"Ya still in school?"

"Yeah."

"Any men in your life?"

"No."

Beth did not mention Jose.

"You still seeing Stacey and her dyke friend? Is she here?"

"Stacey and Gayle. I see them, but Stacey's not here. They're engaged, they're getting married in December."

"What? Two women getting married? That just ain't natural."

"Well, they love each other and they're happy."

"Yeah well, there's happy and there's *happy*. There are plenty of my girlfriends that I love and am happy with, but that don't mean I go marrying them. Marrying is for a man and a woman. That's the natural order of things, the way God meant for them to be."

"How do you know what God meant?"

"I'm a good Christian woman. It says it right in the bible, 'Thou shalt not lie with mankind as with womankind: it is abomination.'"

"Yeah, I'm familiar with Leviticus. First of all, it's talking about men, not women. Second of all, if you read on it states that 'A woman shall not wear anything that pertains to a man, nor shall a man put on a woman's garment',

'Do not eat any meat with blood still in it', 'Do not cut hair at the sides of your head or clip off the edges of your beard', 'Do not cut your bodies for the dead or put tattoo marks on yourselves', 'If a man commits adultery with another man's wife—with the wife of his neighbor—both the adulterer and the adulteress must be put to death'. However, you wear pants which are men's clothes, I've seen you eating rare hamburger, you cut your hair and Guy shaves his beard, you have a tattoo, and neither you nor Guy are being put to death even though you're still married and are thus committing adultery. It seems convenient for you to pick and choose what portions of the bible you use to judge other people, but you don't want to be judged yourself."

"Since when did you become a bible freak? That's the most ridiculous thing I ever heard! Not wearing pants and being put to death for loving Guy! Anyway, I came here to have fun, not to argue about God's word. You're crazy, you should be in the nut house instead of Sheila! Speaking of Sheila, I ran into her a few weeks ago. She was in the coffee shop with that doctor of hers. Now that's a happy ending. Who would have thought that Sheila would end up with her doctor? Maybe I should try to kill myself so that I can hook up with a sexy doctor!"

"What do you mean Sheila ended up with her doctor?"

"You didn't know? Here I thought the two of you were such good friends. She and her doctor are together. She says it's purely professional, but it seems like there's something more than that doctor-patient relationship going on. How many people do you know that go out for coffee with their doctor on a Saturday afternoon? I'm no fool when it comes to matters of the heart. It's pretty clear by the glow they were emitting that they're a couple. Maybe they don't even know it themselves yet, but mark my words, them two are *in love!*"

"Oh Rosie, you're just imagining things. He's not just an ordinary doctor. Maybe it's part of her therapy that they go out."

"Yep, it's therapy all right. There ain't no better therapy than a little horizontal bob!"

"You don't know that. Don't go spreading rumors."

"At least they're good rumors. Besides, I don't think it's a rumor. I wasn't imagining the vibes they were giving off!"

"Yeah, whatever. I'm going to bring Zack around to play the games."

Beth led Zack away toward the games. Zack held on tight to Beth's hand, having no interest in throwing the beanbags through the large wooden Jack-o-lantern's eyes, nose, or mouth, coloring the pictures of Halloween characters, or beading plastic candy corns into a necklace. He was perfectly content standing by Beth's side and watching the other children. Beth smiled down at Zack whenever he looked up at her, but her mind was elsewhere. She was trying to figure out if Rosie was correct about Sheila and her doctor. Would it be ethical for Sheila to be having an affair with her doctor? Did that not violate the doctor-patient relationship? If it was true, why had Sheila not told her about it? She thought she was one of Sheila's best friends. It didn't seem fair that Rosie should know about this before her. On the other hand, would Sheila know how to get in touch with Beth since she was no longer at the safe home and did not have a phone? She decided that she would call The Jericho Rose Hospital and find out herself from Sheila what was going on.

On the way home, Beth stopped at a pay phone at the plaza to call Sheila.

"Hello, Jericho Rose Hospital."

"Hi, my name is Beth Parker. I'm calling for Sheila Robinson."

"I'm sorry, Sheila Robinson is no longer a patient here."

"Could I have her new phone number?"

"I'm sorry, that information is confidential."

"Thank you any way. Bye."

Beth hung up the phone receiver with her finger and then lifted it back up again and called the crisis center. She got the answering machine, so dialed Lisa's extension.

"Hi Lisa, it's Beth. Do you have Sheila's new number? She's not at the hospital anymore. Oh, and it was good to see you at the party, it was fun. Thanks, bye."

Zack watched Beth from his car seat. She got back in the car and they drove home. Zack took a nap in his Spiderman suit while Beth studied.

Zack was so excited to go trick-or-treating, he could hardly wait until 5:00 P.M. Beth put the purple spider webs around the front door and the pumpkin out on their deck. She was not sure what to do with the bags of candy as there was obviously no one in the apartment to give it out, and if she put it in a bowl in the hallway then the first kid who came along would dump the entire bag. Even though she had lived here for almost a month, she still had not met any neighbors. She took a chance and knocked on the door across the hall where a woman and her daughter of about twelve years old lived. Maybe the daughter was old enough to go out and the woman could give out Beth's candy. The woman answered the door.

"Can I help you?" She had long black hair and eyes that penetrated into Beth. She was about five feet, one hundred and ten pounds and was of Italian or Mediterranean decent.

"Yeah hi, my name's Beth. I live across the hall and was wondering if you could give out our candy?" Beth smiled and held out the bowl.

"My name's Maria. Yeah, that's fine. My daughter's going trick-or-treating at her father's house." She smiled back and took Beth's bowl of candy.

"Thanks."

That was easy, but trick-or-treating was another story. Zack held on tight to Beth with one hand, and his plastic pumpkin with the other. He would not let go to knock on the doors, so Beth had to knock. Zack would just hold up his pumpkin to the person who opened the door and wouldn't even say "trick or treat" or "thank you." Zack hid behind his mask, waited for the candy to drop in and then pulled Beth away to go to the next door. They went through three of the complexes when Zack wanted to go home. He seemed very sad for a child celebrating one of the major holidays in the American culture. When they got home he placed his plastic pumpkin full of candy on the counter and announced to Beth that he wanted to go to bed. She helped him brush his teeth and let him go to bed with his costume on.

"Did you have a nice Halloween?"

"Yeah."

"You got lots of candy."

"Yeah."

"You seem sad. Are you sad about something?"

"No. Just scared."

"What are you scared of?"

"All of the monsters."

"Oh Zack, they're just people dressed up. They're not real monsters. Just like you were dressed up like Spiderman, but you're not really Spiderman. It's all just costumes. Just pretend."

"I know, but it's scary. It makes me have bad dreams about a bad man who yells and hurts me, who hurts you."

Beth realized that all the scary costumes and images of Halloween were triggering the bad memories of Jeff's violence. Did this mean that he was forgetting that the violence with Jeff was real and that it was becoming nothing more than a bad dream?

"Oh honey, you don't have to be afraid. You're safe now. No one will hurt you anymore. Let me hug you until you fall asleep."

Beth crawled onto the little bed and wrapped herself around Zack until he fell asleep. Then she quietly slid off the bed and went into the living room, where she eventually fell asleep studying.

The next day at school she and Jose studied in the library in between classes. She was exhausted from staying up so late and from all of the stress of Halloween. She tried to focus on the material, but her mind kept wandering.

"You're not studying. You keep looking off into space."

"No, I'm studying. I'm just looking off so that I can tell myself what I just read."

"That makes absolutely no sense. What's going on? How was your Halloween? Didn't your little boy like his Spiderman costume?"

"Oh Jose, he loved the Spiderman costume. Thank you so much for doing that."

"Not enough decorations?"

"No, the decorations were great."

"The wrong candy?"

"No, no. It's none of that. Everything you did was great. Having you care about us and making us happy was the best part of Halloween."

"Then what is it?"

"It's hard that Zack has bad memories of his father. Scary memories. Halloween was difficult for him, as it brought back scary thoughts. I don't know what to do."

"Maybe there's nothing you can do. When I lived in the Dominican, it was a different life style. Things that are wrong here were okay there. We didn't know they were wrong until we were away from it. Do you understand what I'm saying?"

"I have absolutely no idea."

"Okay. Let me try again. When we were in the Dominican it was a different culture, even different than the Dominican culture here. The neighbors, the police, no one interfered with your family. Each person's family was their own business, to do with as they saw fit. If a kid was bad, or a wife didn't cook supper right or looked at another man wrong, then it was okay for the man to teach them a lesson, to put them in place. It was his family and it was up to him to do what he wanted. That's just the way it was. Then we came here and there are laws about what goes on even in your own home. The police come and say that it's wrong, that no one has a right to hurt someone else. Then you start getting used to this new lifestyle and you start feeling safe. Not worried if you're going to get hit or watch your mom get beaten. But it still happens. Tempers get heated, jealous, drunk. But now when it happens it's not something that you just learn to live with, like the cold in the winter. Now it's something that's not supposed to be there and it makes you mad. Mad and scared. Now little things start making you scared when you see them. Things that you never thought about before. Hearing sirens at night. Watching people fight. Seeing people hungry."

"You understand."

"Yeah, I understand."

"I never met a man that understood. I thought it was just women who lived through this."

"Women have sons. You have a son. I understand how your son feels."

"But it doesn't make sense, look at you."

"Yeah, look at me. And?"

"And you're nice."

"Your point being?"

"I thought people learned what they lived. I thought that boys who grew up in abusive homes grew up to be abusive men, and girls who grew up in abusive homes grew up to be victims."

"You're kind of right, and I guess that can be true. But it's also a matter of a person's inner self and how they react to what's going on. Everyone has a choice."

"Are you an exception?"

"Most people are sensitive, and become what they become because they're trying to justify or cope with the madness they're living. Let's take the example of a couple of young, sensitive kids who are learning about life, love and the world they live in. They grow up in a home where there is constant fighting and yelling. They learn that this is the world, right? The little boy learns that men control, and the little girl learns that women are controlled. This is what they believe, right?"

"Yeah, I guess so."

"Now think deeper. This little boy feels hurt each time he hears the yelling. He feels pain each time his mother, sister, brother or himself are physically hurt. He's filled with frustration because he's not big enough to protect himself or the people he loves. This frustration and sensitivity can go in a number of directions. It can turn into anger and hate at the world and he can lash out at the world through violence and anger, blaming everyone for the injustice he experienced. He can become hardened and emotionless in an attempt to not feel the pain. He can justify the love that he has for his father by convincing himself that this is how life is supposed to be. However, he can also vow never to become what his father is. He can take his sensitivity and hold onto it, put himself between his father and his sister, brother or mother. If this little boy is taken out of the scary place, then he can promise himself that he wants a life that is opposite from where he came from. He can dedicate his life to trying to help people instead of hurting them."

"That's you?"

"Yeah, that's me."

"And the little girl?"

"Oh, the little girl. She can grow up in many directions also. She can justify her love for her father by believing that he is strong and powerful, and that her mother is weak and the cause of his anger. She can lose her sense of self-worth by believing that because she is a girl she has no power, thus leading her to be pushed around and taken advantage of by other men. Or, in an attempt for self-preservation, she can want to be like her father and grow up bossy and manipulative, insensitive to those who are suffering just as she became insensitive to her mother who she believed allowed herself or deserved to be in her situation.

However, she can also gain strength from her sensitivity, determined to stop the injustices occurring in the world. So you see, Beth, you can't stereotype people and think that they're going to be a certain way."

"So you think we should feel bad for people who hurt others because they're actually sensitive individuals who are trying to justify the injustices that were done to them?"

"Oh Beth, you know that's not what I'm saying. But, saying that every child who grows up in an abusive home will become abusive is the same as saying that every kid who grows up with no violence becomes a model citizen. Good parents sometimes produce bad kids, just like kids who grow up in bad situations can turn out okay. When someone does something wrong or has problems, there's usually a reason why they're that way. You can look into a person's past and discover the hurt that made them the way they are, but each person is responsible for there own actions. Even though a person's bad actions can be understood, it doesn't mean that they're justified. Everyone is responsible to overcome their hardships, not use them as an excuse to hate the world."

Beth felt frozen in her chair, staring blankly at the open textbook. She felt close to Jose at this moment, who provided insight as to why Jeff was the way he was. She understood that it was her compassion for those who suffered that caused her to become involved with Jeff. Compassion and sympathy towards the injustices he experienced in his childhood, and the hurt and pain he blamed the world for instead of taking responsibility and changing his life. Beth looked up at Jose and for a moment felt afraid, knowing that he also had the same past. Then she looked into his kind brown eyes and knew that she could trust him. The tears that were constantly on the brink of being released suddenly exploded out of her and she started crying uncontrollably.

Jose put his arm around her and led her out of the library, paying no attention to the people who stared at them on the way out. They crossed the lawn to the parking lot and went into Jose's car. Jose put his arms around Beth and held her to his chest. He stroked her stubbly hair and kept kissing her head, ears, eyes, cheeks. He whispered while he kissed.

"Oh my beautiful Beth. It's okay. Everything's going to be okay. I'm sorry. You don't have to cry. You are so beautiful. Don't be sad. Shhhh. I'm sorry, my beautiful Beth."

In addition to crying uncontrollably, Beth started shaking so that her entire body was in convulsions. The warmth of Jose holding her was more than she could handle. She never thought that she would want to be with a man again, but all she wanted right now was Jose. He made her feel so safe and unthreatened. He kissed her so gently and soft, just brushing her skin and not going near her lips. Suddenly she wanted her lips to be kissed. She wanted her lips to feel the soft love of his kisses, so she tilted her head back and let her mouth meet his. He paused for a moment, then opened his mouth onto hers. Her body was still shaking, she was still crying hysterically yet was able to kiss him through the tears. His lips kept meeting hers through the sobs, the kisses in rhythm with the sobs. He held her so firmly, the sobs and kisses together getting softer and slower until it gradually all stopped. Their lips were barely touching, Beth opened her eyes and they met Jose's eyes. She smiled slightly and then snuggled her head under his chin. His arms stayed wrapped around her while his fingers played with her hair. They stayed in that position for over an hour. Jose finally broke the silence.

"Beth?"

"Mmmmm?"

"We're going to be late for class."

"Oh, I'm sorry. Let's go."

"Are you okay?"

"Yeah."

"Are you sure? I'll stay with you if you want."

"Where did you come from? Are you my guardian angel? It's important to both of us to get through this program. I would never expect you to miss class for me, but thank you for offering."

"If you needed it, it would be worth it."

"Thank you."

Beth felt like they had just had sex, yet it was just a kiss. This one kiss made her feel more loved than she had ever felt after having sex with Jeff.

"Let's go. Where's my bag?"

"In the library."

"Jose! You left our bags, books, and everything in the library? Someone might steal our stuff!"

"It's all a matter of priorities. Being here with you is more important than worrying about some books. They can be replaced."

"But those books are worth a lot of money."

"You're worth more."

Beth had nothing to say in response. They went to the library, got their books that were untouched, and went to class.

There was a time when Beth was relieved that Jose did not suggest they meet outside of school, but things were changing. The leaves had fallen off the trees and the season was changing all around her. Nature seemed to be going to sleep, gathering its strength, and preparing itself to rejuvenate. Shedding and letting go of all existing life so that it could come back strong and new with a fresh start. Like a phoenix being destroyed, only to come alive out of the ashes more powerful and beautiful than ever. Beth felt as if this was her period of change, the winter replenishing, and the ashes cindering, so that she would be able to come back to life refreshed, strong, beautiful, and whole. Just as the plants under the ground need nourishment to make them strong, Beth needed love. She was no longer satisfied with just seeing Jose in school; she wanted to be part of his life. She asked him to come over and study in the evening or on the weekend, but he always declined. He insisted that she needed to spend time with Zack and that he had to work.

Another month went by and Thanksgiving break was a week away. Stacey and Gayle invited Beth and Zack to have dinner with them. This was the first major holiday that Beth was spending away from home. She had to remind herself that her past life with Jeff was no longer home, that her apartment was her home and her friends were her family. Thanksgiving was a holiday for family and traditions. She wondered how Jeff and Nancy were spending their Thanksgiving. Would they go to Jeff's parents' home like she and Jeff had done for so many years? Would they go to Nancy's parents' home? Or would they start a tradition of their own by having it at their house or with friends? It was no longer her house, Jeff was no longer her family, and Nancy was no longer her friend. It was a time for her to make her own traditions in her new home, with her surrogate family and new friends. Beth wanted Jose to be part of that tradition.

Now that it was cold outside, Beth and Jose studied everyday in an empty classroom. It was quiet, and gave them privacy so that they could talk, joke, and physically lean on each other while studying. Jose would put his arm around Beth, or Beth would lie between Jose's legs using his chest as a pillow. They would be intertwined with each other, but not do anything more sexual than light kissing. There was incredible electricity connecting them. Jose looked at Beth with lust in his big brown eyes, so Beth did not understand why Jose never made an attempt to do anything more physical. Maybe it was the same reason why he would not see her outside of school? Did she dare ask him? The old Beth would never have dared, but the new Beth was empowered and determined to face all challenges head on and never keep a secret inside of herself again.

Beth loved watching Jose's serious face as he studied. Instead of dancing, his eyes looked stern with a little crease between them. His mouth opened slightly and ever so often he would brush his hand over his forehead as if he had hair there to wipe away.

"Why are you staring at me? You're supposed to be studying. You're always distracting me."

"Why don't you ever kiss me?"

"I kiss you all the time." He seemed annoyed.

"No, I mean *really* kiss me. You know, like you *love* me." Beth felt that she sounded a little like Zack when he got into a whiney mood. Jose put his book down and looked seriously at Beth, straight into her eyes.

"Okay, you want to know why I don't kiss you?"

"Yeah."

"I don't kiss you for the same reason that I don't go out with you. Because you are too distracting and I can't jeopardize dropping out of this program. This is the only chance I have to make something of my life."

"I don't get it."

"No, of course you don't get it. You never get anything. I need to stay focused so that I can make it through this program. If we still want to be together when the program is over, then we can go out then. But right now the time is wrong, I need to study."

"So you're telling me that I should just sit here and wait for another six months before you decide to take a look at me?" Beth was mad. It was a good thing that they were alone because she could not help but to yell at him.

"Wait six months to look at you? I can't stop looking at you! You're all that I see when I try to study! Your face, breaking my concentration, ruining my focus! How am I supposed to get through this program when you're sitting on me pushing my will power to the max because I just keep thinking about my dick instead of my books? *No!* I won't give it up! I need to keep my focus!"

"So that's why you won't come over to my house to study?"

"How would I be able to study when there's a bed in the next room waiting for me to take you into?"

"How about dinner? Thanksgiving Dinner at my friends' house? There will be no temptation, and it's kind of like an unwritten law that you have to have dinner on Thanksgiving. Maybe then, if you're with me, you wont miss me and you'll be able to study with me."

Jose was silent for a moment, then his familiar smile and dimple lit up his face. He hugged Beth, "Yeah. I'll have Thanksgiving Dinner with you."

He leaned his head down and kissed her passionately. Beth's entire body felt the kiss, was part of the kiss. Her entire soul was sucked into him. Everything in her mind was dark and calm with the motion of the kiss rippling through her. He finally separated his mouth from hers and smiled down at her. "How was that?"

"Mmm, Yeah."

"Yeah?"

"Yeah."

"Okay, so you'll let me study now?"

"Yeah."

On Tuesday when Beth and Zack came home after school, there was a cardboard box filled with food at the top of the stairs in front of their door. Beth stopped for a moment, not knowing what to do. Was it for her? She told Lisa that she was spending dinner with Stacey and Gayle and did not need a dinner. Then she realized that it must be for Maria from across the hall. She knocked on Maria's door. She had not seen her since Halloween.

"Yes?" Maria was in her bathrobe and opened the door a crack.

"There's some food out here. I think it might be for you."

"No, that was left for you. A woman came by about an hour ago. You better get it in the refrigerator before it goes bad." Maria smiled a polite smile and closed her door, but not before Beth noticed a look of hunger in her eyes as she looked at the box of food.

Beth felt a sense of gratitude and shame mixed together as she carried the box into the apartment and placed it on the kitchen table. With a heavy heart she put the turkey, boxed pie, bag of apples, jug of cider, carton of eggnog, box of butter and fresh vegetables in the refrigerator. She put the canned goods and bag of potatoes in the cabinet. She was grateful for the food, but felt a sense of shame that she was the recipient of a food drive. She was constantly being told about the "open hand pantries" at various churches and that there was a free dinner every night at a different location in the city. However, her pride kept her from attending any of these programs. She thought of the giant cardboard box at the library that she used to drop cans of food into when she brought Zack to story hour. That was another life. It was bad enough trying to go to the grocery store at the least crowded times so that people would not see her using food stamps. Now her neighbor saw food being dropped off at her door. She was so grateful for this food that would provide over a week of meals for her and Zack, but she went into her room, closed the door and cried in shame for having to be in a situation where she needed charity.

Beth insisted on making a pie to bring to Thanksgiving Dinner. She used the bag of apples and bought a box of pre-made piecrust, a bag of brown sugar and a 99 cent container of cinnamon. There was only a half day of classes on Wednesday, so she was able to go home and peel the apples, coat them with sugar and cinnamon and put them in the refrigerator so she could bake the pie in the morning. She wanted the pie to be fresh and warm when she brought it to Stacey and Gayle's house.

In the morning Beth put the pie in the oven to bake while she took a shower. She took extra care in shaving her legs and washing her hair. She had some melon lotion that was donated, which she had been saving for something special, and spread it over her entire body. She slowly put on her nylons to make sure she did not snag them. She wore the skirt and blouse that she got to go to court last spring. She felt very conservative, but she wanted to look nice. In addition to this being a holiday where she was going to dinner at her friends' house, this was the closest thing to a date that she had for years and she wanted to look her best for Jose. She unwrapped the towel from her head and rubbed some gel in her hair before brushing and blow-drying it. Her hair had grown since it was cut at the safe home, and blow-drying it gave it volume and a nice wave. It was growing in choppy and framed her face with uneven angles. She twisted some of the gel on the angles so that they looked a little spiky. She applied some make-up to highlight her features.

She had barely finished when Jose knocked on the door. He was also dressed up; instead of his usual jeans, he was wearing kaki pants and a polo sweater. He smiled so that his dimples showed and although she had just seen him the day before, she was so happy to see him that she greeted him with a tight hug. He held her tight while she nestled her head into his shoulder. The smell of his cologne sent tingles through her body. They hugged until he pulled away, putting his hands on her shoulders and holding her in front of him.

"You look absolutely beautiful."

She could not talk for a moment, and then asked him to come in.

"It smells incredible. Can we stay here and eat pie?" His eyes were dancing as he spoke. Zack ran over to him and grabbed him by the hand.

"Come, see my room!" Zack led him into his room and showed him all of the toys.

They eventually emerged from the room, hand in hand, smiling. Beth did not want to interrupt them, Zack looked so happy with this kind man. The contrast in their color and size complemented each other made them each complete. Beth used a towel to carry the pie to the car and they drove over to Stacey and Gayle's house.

Beth was impressed that Jose did not seem uncomfortable or nervous going to dinner at a strange house. If it had been Jeff, he would have been angry and anxious the entire morning and drive to the house. Beth would have been a wreck and Zack would have been irritable by the time they got there. This would have made Jeff angrier, but then he would be charming when they arrived at their destination as if nothing had happened. Instead, they were with Jose who smiled and talked about his sister's baby, making them laugh and happy when they arrived. Jose brought a bottle of wine that was graciously received by Stacey.

Beth introduced everyone as they sat around the living room waiting for something to happen. Everyone silently smiled happily at each other, waiting for someone else to start the conversation. Finally Gayle broke the ice.

"So, how do you like school?"

"Oh, it's fine. A lot of work, but it will be worth it."

"What made you choose this program?"

This was turning out like an interrogation.

"Well, I want to be a doctor so I figured this was a good introduction into the medical field. Most hospitals pay for their employees to go to college, so I can start low and work my way up."

Beth never knew that Jose wanted to be a doctor.

"A doctor? What kind of doctor do you want to be?"

"If I stay in the States, then I want to work at an inner city clinic. There are so many poor people who can't afford proper medical care."

"Where would you go if you don't stay in the States?"

"I would go back home, to the Dominican. It's very poor, and many people need help. I could set up clinics in the villages."

"That sounds like a lot of work."

"Most things that are worthwhile are a lot of work. I want to do something worthwhile with my life."

"Good luck."

"Thank you."

Stacey came out of the kitchen and handed everyone a glass of the wine that Jose brought.

"I would like to propose a toast."

Every one held up their glasses and waited for her to continue.

"A toast to good friends being together."

"And to Jose becoming a doctor," Gayle added in.

Every one clanked their glasses together and sipped the wine. The ice was broken and they continued talking and laughing until Stacey called them in to dinner. It was peaceful being with Jose, Stacey, and Gayle. The wine gave Beth a warm glowing feeling as she sat contently, surrounded by friends who made her feel happy and safe. Zack and baby Mia played on the floor. Mia sat in her seat laughing as Zack squeezed and shook different toys at her.

It was a very traditional Thanksgiving meal with gravy, mashed potatoes, squash, peas, cranberry sauce, warm dinner rolls, and a turkey that was over eighteen pounds. No one acted shy when it came to taking seconds or thirds as they stuffed themselves. Beth worried that no one would have room left for her pie. After the table was cleared and the dishes were washed, there was plenty of room for Beth's apple and Stacey's pumpkin pie. They lingered, talked, drank coffee, and had more pie. The day turned into evening, the evening into night. Both Mia and Zack fell asleep in the living room. Beth finally told Jose that it was time to go home. She liked the way that it sounded, telling him that *they* had to go *home* as if they were a couple going home together. He smiled at her and got up. They drove silently on the way back to Beth's apartment.

As they drove, Beth went over in her mind different ways to ask Jose to come upstairs. She did not want to sound forward or set herself up for rejection, but she also wanted his company a little longer. Not to have sex, which may be implied if she asked him up, but just to have him with her. She did not want the day to stop; she wanted it to last a little bit longer. When they drove into the parking lot, Jose pulled into a parking spot instead of parking in front of the walkway for Beth and Zack to get out.

"I'll carry Zack upstairs. He's sleeping."

Problem solved. Jose was coming upstairs without needing an excuse or made up reason. Beth smiled and got out of the car. She unlocked the front door and held it open while Jose carried Zack in and up to the apartment. She unlocked the apartment door, and Jose laid Zack in his bed and covered him with the blankets. Beth put her arm around Jose and hugged him as they stood over Zack. He looked so angelic sleeping peacefully as though he did not have a care in the world. Beth felt as though she did not have a care in the world either. Zack was adjusting well and was recovering from his experiences with Jeff. She was on her way to becoming independent, and with Jose standing over Zack with her arm around her she felt as if they had a protector who would keep them safe.

Jose started leading Beth out of Zack's room.

"Did you want to study?" Beth whispered.

"We have all day tomorrow to study. There's no school, remember?"

"What should we do? I have no TV or anything."

"That's okay. I have something else in mind." Instead of leading Beth into the living room like she expected, he led her into the bedroom and gently laid her on her back where she stared at the ceiling, her entire body frozen. Part of her was tingling and ecstatic that he was actually here with her, completing her fantasy; another part of her was terrified. She was scared since despite her body's craving for Jose, her only sexual experiences had been with Jeff who hurt her. There was a swarm of mixed feelings and emotions overwhelming her. On one sense she was breathing heavy, her heart was racing and the tingles that she felt whenever she was around Jose were shooting through her body. On the other sense she was feeling panic about letting Jose touch her, feeling guilty, worthless, and afraid. Did she deserve to be loved? She felt ugly, dirty, and ashamed. She did not want Jose to see her body. She could hear Jeff's voice telling her how repulsive, fat, ugly, and unattractive she was. She did not want Jose to see how horrible she actually was and as a result not want her any more. Her body froze up and she started to cry.

Jose held her close. She could feel his heart beating against her ear. She could hear his breathing as he apologized to her.

"It's okay, I'm sorry. I should have asked before I came up. I didn't mean to make you cry. I won't do anything you don't want me to do, I'll leave."

"No, no, please don't leave. I want you here with me. It's just that it's been a while and I'm scared. I'm not used to being with some one."

"Shhhhh. Don't cry, don't be scared."

"Just hold me."

"Okay. I'm here. I won't leave you, I'll just hold you."
"Thank you."
"Shhh. Don't talk. Don't cry."

Beth kept crying though. She cried because she felt safe. She cried because she felt scared. She cried because she had so much hurt inside of her that wanted to come out, and here was a person who she loved holding her and letting all of that hurt come out and leave her body. She cried because Jose loved her.

Jose held her until she stopped crying. Then he began caressing her back, arms, stomach, chest. She felt safe and it was okay. She felt relaxed and released, it felt good to be loved. Once her entire upper body had been gently massaged, Jose lifted off her shirt and undid her bra. He then kissed, sucked, and licked her upper body while she lay limp and lifeless. She felt as if she was in a dream where everything was foggy and in a daze. She was able to let her mind empty while her body was brought back to life through the power of human touch. Jose took off his own shirt and held Beth close to him so that their bare chests molded together, stuck together with sweat. Beth could feel their hearts beating together, and she became increasingly aware of the parts of their bodies that were separated by clothing. Beth pulled down her skirt, underpants and nylons and pushed them onto the floor. She then undid Jose's belt, pants button and zipper and pulled off his pants, underwear and socks and threw them onto the floor. She lifted her blankets so that they could crawl underneath the weight of them. It was warm and cozy. The warmth of their bodies under the weight of the blankets made Beth feel safe and alive. She wrapped her arms and legs around Jose, closed her eyes and gently began kissing him. The kisses became longer, wetter, and more passionate. Beth could feel the hardness of Jose's penis against her leg. She could feel the softness of his body hair against her skin. His hands made their way down her back, over her ass, gently caressed her outer thigh and eventually began to separate the softness between her legs. She could feel her body responding to his touch, opening up and becoming warm and wet. He played with her, but did not enter. She sucked on his shoulder, gently biting his skin. He pulled away from her. She panicked.

"No, don't go."
"It's okay. I just need to get a condom. Where are my pants?"
"Oh? Were you expecting this?"

He stopped and kissed her forehead. He sensed the defensiveness in her voice and did not want her to feel used.

"Beth, I'm so happy to be here with you. I was not expecting it, but did wish for it. I have a condom because it's better to be prepared and not need it than to want it and not have it."

"Why are you with me?"

"I'm with you because you're a beautiful woman who I'm very proud to be with."

"But why me? There are lots of women you could be with who don't have the problems that I have."

"I'm a healer, and you need healing. I'm here because we need each other."

"Is this how you heal all your patients?"

"This is how I show you that I love you as a woman, not as a patient. There are no other women, only you."

"Do you promise?"

"I promise that you're the only woman in my life right now."

"Right now? Does that mean you're planning on leaving me? On having other women?"

"Oh Beth, why don't you want me to love you? Please don't try to fight with me. I'm trying to be honest with you. Do you want me to tell you lies so that you'll fuck me? I can get that down at the local bar. You mean more to me than that."

"Don't swear at me! I'm not trying to fight with you! Don't make me sound so horrible!"

"You're not horrible. I just don't want to lie to you. Whatever happens will happen. If it's meant to be that you and I are together then we are. If not, then we'll separate. Let's not ruin this beautiful moment that we're having."

His voice and eyes showed his hurt.

"I'm sorry. Your pants are on the floor."

"No, tonight's not the night. You aren't ready, you don't trust me enough."

"Don't blame this on me!"

"Shhhh. Don't fight. When the time's right, we'll know. For now, come here and let me feel you next to me. Let me smell your sweet scent."

Beth felt she had ruined the moment that she waited for and fantasized about so many times. It was so much better than she had ever imagined, but now it was gone. She and Jose were wrapped around each other, their skin sweaty and hot. Beth closed her eyes and thought about everything that Jose had just said. It did not seem fair that he always made so much sense when she wanted to be angry and blame him for things. If it had been Jeff, he would have insulted and degraded her making her feel small and worthless. With Jose, she felt small and worthless because he respected and loved her and she did not feel that she deserved it. She did not feel that she deserved to be loved, yet here was this man lying next to her, holding her, loving her any way. He loved her enough to lie naked next to her and not fuck her. It scared the shit out of her.

When she woke up in the morning, Beth lay as still as she could so that she would not wake up Jose. It felt so good to have him here holding her. She did not want him to go away. She was afraid that he would not come back. Part of her wanted to tell him to leave so that Zack would not see that he spent the night, but a stronger part did not care. Zack was too young to know about morals and to think anything of the fact that Jose was here. She could hear Zack waking up in the next room and suddenly realized that even though she did not care if he knew that Jose spent the night, she did not want him to walk in on them naked. She pulled herself away from Jose, covering him back up. It was difficult for her to cover up his smooth body and firm muscles. He was so beautiful when he slept. His mouth opened a crack and it would occasionally lift into a small smile. Beth wondered what he was dreaming about. She was tempted to wrap herself back around him, but instead got out of bed and got dressed.

Zack was awake and playing on the floor with his trucks when Beth went into his room. She sat down and started to push one of the trucks around on the floor in an attempt to play with him.

"That's not how you do it mommy! You do it like *this!*" Zack grabbed the truck from her and pushed it under the bed. "That one goes into the garage."

Beth sat silently and watched him arrange the trucks in an orderly manner. Zack was very particular about how he played with his toys. Everything had to be a certain way and he got upset if anything was not how it should be. Beth heard Jose getting up in the next room.

"I'll be right back, Zack."

"Okay." He barely noticed her leave.

Jose was finishing getting dressed when Beth entered the room.

"Hey, I should get going."

"Stay. We can study."

Jose gave a slight laugh and his smile showed off his dimple.

"I would love to stay, but I have a lot to do today."

"I thought you were going to study today?" Beth felt a pang go through her chest. For some reason, she was terrified of him leaving her. She felt a desperate need for him to stay with her. "Please don't go."

Jose stopped and looked intently at Beth.

"If you want me to, I'll stay. But I really need to study. How will we be able to study with Zack here?"

Beth felt offended and defensive about Zack.

"Zack's fine. Why wouldn't we be able to study with Zack here?"

"Zack's a great kid, but he's just a little boy. He shouldn't have to be quiet. Little boys should be able to play and be loud. That's the fun of being a kid."

Again, Jose was right. Beth thought of Maria and Vickie across the hall and wondered if they were home. It was still early, she would wait until Zack got tired of playing in his room and then see if Vickie could bring him outside to play. It was unseasonably warm for late November and Zack loved going out to play. Jose went into the kitchen.

"Where's your coffee pot?"

"I don't have one."

Jose opened the refrigerator.

"You don't have much to eat."

"I have a turkey."

"Yeah, but it will take about five hours to cook. Do you plan on eating anything in the mean time?"

"There's cereal in the cabinet and milk in the fridge."

"I'll go out and get some coffee and bagels. I'll be right back."

"Why don't you take Zack with you. It'll give him something to do."

"Hey, Zack buddy. Do you want to come to the store with me?"

Zack came shuffling out of his room, still in his pajamas. There was something about his eager yet sleepy expression that made Beth laugh.

"Come on Zack, mommy will help you get dressed so that you can go with Jose."

Beth took a shower while Zack and Jose were gone. She felt fresh and clean. She was on a high from spending the night with Jose. She felt like jumping up so high that she would just fly around and watch every one below her. Her entire body felt light and free as if it had been released. She felt like Jose was a drug that gave her an intense high when she was with him and which she craved when he was gone.

Beth opened the refrigerator to see what it looked like through Jose's eyes. The turkey took up most of it but there was other food too, mostly from the box of food that was dropped off. She felt offended that Jose did not think she had food; it was not like they were starving. She suddenly got an idea. She remembered the look of hunger in Maria's eyes when the food was dropped off at her door. She would invite Maria and Vickie to have the turkey dinner with her and Zack. Jose worked as a bartender on Friday and Saturday nights, so either night would be okay. It would be just the girls, and Zack of course. Beth got a blanket and sat on the couch to study while she waited for Zack and Jose to come back.

The day ended up being quite productive. Jose bought so many bagels that they stuffed themselves. Beth and Jose had large coffees, and Zack had his own bottle of chocolate milk. Zack felt like part of the group and brought his storybooks into the living room to pretend reading like Beth and Jose. He was still sleepy from the long Thanksgiving Day, and took a long late morning nap. Even though they did not talk, it was comforting having Jose at her apartment studying next to her. Somehow it made it easier to concentrate.

In the afternoon Beth heard Maria coming up the stairs, so she went out to meet her. Vickie was at her father's house so she could not take Zack outside to play, but they could to come to dinner on Saturday evening. Beth felt sad when Jose left, but she tried not to show it. She did not want him to think she was being neurotic or possessive. He hugged her for a long time before leaving.

"I'll see you Monday at school."
"Okay."
"Have fun with your friend tomorrow."
"She's not my friend."
"Yet?"
"Yet."
"I wish I could call you."
"I know. It's hard not having a phone."
"Maybe Santa will bring you one for Christmas."
"Yeah right, and will Santa pay the monthly bill for me too?"
"Maybe . . . If you're a good girl."
"I don't want to put conditions on getting things. I'll just wait and get my own phone when I can afford it."
"Ya know, you don't have to be so defensive all the time."
"I'm not defensive."

Jose gave her one last hug before going to work. Beth did not like the feelings of jealousy that she was having. Even though he was working, she did not like that Jose was at a bar while she was sitting at home. It made her remember when Jeff went out to the bars and came home drunk. She felt panicky and tight inside. She kept reminding herself that Jose was not Jeff; that Jose was working, not drinking; that Jose was filled with happiness and love, while Jeff was filled with anger and hate.

Chapter 13

Beth stayed up late studying on Friday night. She knew that she would not have much time to study on Saturday between cooking and having Maria and Vickie over, and Sunday was church and their weekly dinner at Stacey and Gayle's house. It had been a while since Beth cooked a full meal, never mind an entire turkey dinner. She got up early on Saturday to make sure she had enough time to do all the preparations. She melted a stick of butter, sautéed the onions and celery, added the bag of breadcrumbs and a quarter cup of boiling water. She washed the turkey, rubbed the insides with sage and mushed the stuffing mixture into it. Judging by the table on the turkey tab, it would take about five hours for the turkey to cook. She put the stuffed turkey back in the refrigerator to wait until noon when it would be transferred into the oven. Her mother had always cooked turkeys upside down so that all of the juices and flavor would seep into the breast of the turkey keeping it tender and flavorful. It was tricky flipping the turkey over to cook right side up for the last half hour to let it brown, but when done correctly it was absolutely delicious.

The next step was peeling the vegetables. She peeled the potatoes, cut them into cubes and placed them into a pot of water on the stove to be boiled and mashed later. She did the same to the carrots and sweet potatoes. There were three pots of peeled, cut vegetables sitting in water on her stove, waiting to be cooked. With the food preparations complete, her next mission was to clean the house. Luckily three rooms and a bathroom was not a huge challenge. Within an hour they were picked up, swept, and cleaned with disinfectant spray. She now had time to take a shower, play with Zack, and then study while everything cooked and Zack napped.

At 5:30 P.M. sharp there was a knock on the door. The table was set, the white potatoes were mashed with butter and milk, the sweet potatoes were roasting in the oven with brown sugar and butter melting on them (they had already been boiled), the carrots were sitting on the stove with a butter and brown sugar mixture glazed over them, the dinner rolls were browning in the oven, the gravy was slowly simmering on the stove and the turkey was right side up, perfectly browned, on a large cookie sheet since Beth did not have a serving plate large enough. Everything was prepared and perfect. Beth opened the door and let Maria and Vickie in. Maria handed Beth a bottle of white wine and a cork opener, which was good since Beth did not have one.

"Oh my God, it smells amazing in here. I could smell the aroma across the hall in my apartment, but as soon as you opened the door a gush of warm air and delicious smells came pouring out. We must be the envy of the building."

Beth smiled shyly. It felt good to be complimented; it did not happen very often. She used to study cookbooks and try every recipe in an attempt to satisfy Jeff. No matter what she did, he had something bad to say about it. He would call her creations "shit," or say that they were too inedible to eat. Beth was proud that Maria was impressed by her preparations. Hopefully she would still feel that way after she ate it! She suddenly remembered her manners.

"Come in, sit down. Would you like something to drink?"

"Sure. What do you have? We can save the wine for dinner."

"Good idea. Apple cider, milk, or water?"

"Apple cider would be great."

"And you Vickie, what would you like?"

"Cider, please."

Everyone was being overly polite and formal, but instead of being uncomfortable it was fun. It was like being a little kid and pretending that you were having a formal tea party and everyone had to be on their best behavior. It made Beth feel special and in a weird way grown up. It was as if she had finally reached the point in her life where she was in a position to entertain. Here she was for the first time having guests in her own home. Not Jeff's house, not a guest in someone else's home, but being a hostess on her own. Independent.

"Please, won't you have some cheese and crackers while I finish getting dinner ready?" Although Beth did not think much of the cheese and crackers when she received them in the box of food, she was grateful that she had an appetizer to serve to her guests.

"That would be great, thanks. Is there anything I can do to help?"

"No, no. You just sit and relax. Everything is just about ready."

Beth transferred the potatoes and carrots into mixing bowls, scooped the stuffing out of the turkey and heaped it into two cereal bowls, placed the hot pan of sweet potatoes onto a folded face cloth on the table and placed the cookie sheet with the turkey in the center of the table. She poured the gravy into two coffee mugs since she had no gravy boats and hoped that they would not spill. She remembered past Thanksgiving Dinners with fancy china where all of the dishes and serving plates matched. It seemed like everything on the table had been taken for granted. Looking at this Thanksgiving Dinner with the mismatched place settings and lack of serving plates, she felt a sense of gratitude and pride that she never felt before on any previous Thanksgivings. She closed her eyes and said a silent prayer of thanks to the people who had generously donated the food that made this dinner possible. She opened her eyes and smiled at the feast.

"Dinner is served!"

Maria, Vickie, and Zack came over to the table.

"Where do you want us to sit?"

Beth was about to tell them to sit anywhere, but Zack quickly took charge and answered. He was already becoming the little man of the family. Beth was not sure how she felt about that.

"Well, this is my seat, and Mommy sits there. So, you can sit in that chair next to Mommy and Vickie can sit here next to me!"

"That's great Zack. What a good job." Beth smiled at Zack and gave him a kiss on the top of his head. He smiled back proudly and climbed onto his booster seat.

The dinner was absolutely delicious. Beth was sure it was the best meal she had ever cooked. It seemed like a meal prepared with the intention of pleasing friends was superior to a meal prepared with the threat of criticism. For the second time in a week, they stuffed themselves to the point of not being able to get up from the table. The combination of good food and two glasses of wine made Beth feel happy and satisfied. She sat contently and listened to Zack tell Vickie all about his "school," and Vickie tell Zack about her "real school." The subject turned to TV shows, but Zack had not watched TV since they lived at the safe home, which was almost two months ago. He eagerly asked Vickie about all of his favorite shows like a prisoner who awaits news from the outside world. Although it was peaceful not having a TV, Beth felt like she was somehow depriving Zack of this vital means of communication in today's society. Vickie came up with a solution.

"Mom, can I bring Zack over to our apartment to watch TV?"

"Is that okay with you, Beth?"

"Yeah. That's fine. Zack would like that. Thank you, Vickie."

Maria went across the hall to unlock the door and get the kids settled, and then came back.

"Ahhh, some quality adult time."

"Yeah. I haven't had that for a while." Beth took another sip of her wine. Except for when Beth was in class or support group, she was always with Zack. It did not bother her though. She liked the fact that her friends accepted them as a pair and welcomed Zack. Beth did not understand Maria referring to adult quality time as if it was something she did not get much since she only had Vickie part time. Beth loved the fact that Zack was with her all the time, and could not imagine having Wednesday nights and every other weekend alone. Both Maria and Vickie seemed happy with Vickie going to her father's house, and it would make it easier to spend the night with a boyfriend without worrying about a twelve-year-old in the next room. Beth never saw any men come to Maria's apartment despite the fact that she was very attractive, so Beth wondered what the situation was. The effects of the wine prompted Beth to be forward with Maria and ask her personal questions that she would not ask otherwise.

"Vickie seems like a great kid."

"Yeah, I'm so lucky. I see so many kids her age who get into trouble, but she's so sweet. She does have a temper though. I guess it's the Mediterranean in her!"

"So, you're of Mediterranean decent?"

"Yeah, my parents are from Italy. That makes me first generation American."

"There must have been some heavy cultural conflicts in your house."

"Oh, yeah."

"What nationality is Vickie's father?"

"He's from Italy, straight off the boat."

"Really? How did you meet?"

"Me and Dominic were born in the same year. His family and my family were close friends when they lived in Italy, so when we were babies they decided that we would get married when we grew up."

"Really? Like an arranged marriage? That's fucked. I didn't think they still did that in this country. Why didn't you just say no?"

"Well, it's not really an arranged marriage in the sense that one day my parents said 'Hey, we're going to find you a husband.' For my entire life, I was told that I was going to marry Dominic when I grew up, so I never thought anything about it. It was just something I had to do, like go to school or learn to cook."

"And that was it? You just grew up and married this person that you never met before?"

"Yeah, well we used to write to each other a lot and our families sent pictures back and forth. There was just one problem."

"What do you mean a problem?"

"Well, my younger sister, Josephine, was bigger than me when we were little."

"That's a problem?"

"The understanding was that he would marry the oldest daughter. You know, the oldest son marries the oldest daughter. It would tie the two families together."

"Makes sense to me . . . Just kidding. What is this, the mafia?"

"No, it's not the mafia. Anyway, when my parents sent them pictures of our family they thought Josephine was me since she was bigger. So Dominic spent his life thinking he was going to marry the wrong sister. He actually fell in love with Josephine's picture. Then, he came here and was introduced to me."

"Oh, that's horrible. So what happened? Why didn't he marry her instead of you?"

"No, he was too worried to tell anyone. Besides, it would go against the family tradition. So, Dominic married me like a good son to please his parents. He kept it a secret for a long time."

"He kept it a secret? How did you find out?"

"Let's just say that my images of what marriage was supposed to be like didn't match what real life turned out to be."

"I know how that is."

"Yeah, I'm sure it's a common problem. Anyway, all Dominic ever did was compare me to Josephine. He was always trying to make me be like her. If Josephine cut her hair, Dominic would want me to cut my hair. If Josephine wore a black dress, Dominic would go out and buy me a black dress. Dominic made us buy a house across the street from Josephine and her husband. Then we had to decorate our house like hers. The grand finale was when Josephine got pregnant. Then, the pressure was on for me to get pregnant even though we hardly ever had sex up to that point."

"You were married and never had sex?"

"I said 'hardly ever,' not 'never had' sex. Dominic would want to have sex whenever we saw Josephine. I think he would pretend that I was her when we had sex. So, three months after Josephine's baby boy was born, I disappointed him with Vickie. Since Josephine was able to produce a healthy boy and I was only able to produce a girl it added to the belief that Josephine was perfect and I was only second best. It reinforced the fact that I would never be able to compare to Josephine."

"That's horrible!"

"Yeah. It sucks, but what sucks more is that I actually loved him. You see, just like Dominic grew to love Josephine, because his entire life he was told that he would be united with his true love when he grew up. I also fell in love with the idea of Dominic before I ever met him. So, I put up with his obsession and let him love me for whatever there was in me that reminded him of Josephine."

"How could you love him after he did that to you? He's an asshole!"

"Once a person falls in love, they can't just turn it off. Just like he couldn't turn off the fact that he was in love with Josephine."

"But what about Vickie? Doesn't he love his own child? Vickie seems close to him now."

"He didn't pay much attention to her when she was a tiny baby, but as she grew older she looked more and more like Josephine. It was like Vickie was a little miniature Josephine that Dominic was allowed to have. He adored her. Still does."

"Maria, this is the most fucked up story I've ever heard. And believe me, with all of the support groups that I go to, I've heard a lot of fucked up stories."

"Thanks for reminding me how fucked up my life is."

"No, I didn't mean it like that. I just never heard anything like this before."

"Thanks."

"I'm sorry, but this is like a movie or something."

"Sometimes truth is stranger than fiction. Unfortunately it happens to be my life that we're talking about."

"So what happened? Why aren't you together?"

"It's very sad actually."

"This whole story is sad."

"No, really. My sister, Josephine, got breast cancer."

"She got breast cancer? That's horrible! This story just keeps getting worse and worse. Is she okay?"

"No, she died."

"No, seriously, how is she?"

"I am serious. She's dead."

"Oh my God, I'm so sorry to hear that."

"Yeah and it gets worse."

"Your sister died of breast cancer. How can it get worse than that?"

"Well, now that Josephine's dead and he has Vickie, Dominic doesn't need me any more. You see, the first reason Dominic was with me was to be closer to Josephine, but now Josephine is dead. The second reason Dominic was with me was because of the pieces in me that reminded him of Josephine. However, now he has Vickie who is the splitting image of Josephine. There is no reason for him to be with me any more, so he left."

"You love him and he is gone."

"You got it honey. The only way that I still have him is through Vickie. I love the fact that they are together since I can peek in on the life that I wanted, only I'm just a spectator."

"You lost your sister and the man that you love."

"Yep."

"Maria, I am so sorry. I can't imagine what it must be like for you."

"I just live my life in the background watching Vickie grow more and more like Josephine everyday. Josephine was so beautiful, it is understandable why Dominic loved her."

"You're beautiful too."

"Thanks, but nothing compared to Josephine."
"I don't believe that."
"Once a person is dead, all of their humanly flaws disappear."
Beth had nothing to say in response. The two of them sat in silence for a long time. Beth took another sip of her wine. The room was a little fuzzy and she did not think she should attempt standing up. It had been a long time since she was drunk.

It was difficult getting up to go to church in the morning. Beth felt sick, the room had a surreal feel to it, everything was spinning, and Zack was up and ready to go. Beth pushed herself to get ready so that she would not disappoint Zack. The kitchen was a mess. Luckily she had the commonsense to put the leftovers into the refrigerator the night before, but the dirty dishes were still on the table with food caked onto them, and the sink was filled with dirty pots and pans. This was something she would have to deal with later. She was glad that she had studied a lot Friday and Saturday because it did not seem like she would get any studying done today. She looked into the refrigerator to get something that would quench the incredible dry mouth she was experiencing, it felt as if her mouth were full of cotton. Her spirits lifted when she saw that the gallon of apple cider was still about a quarter full. She took the jug out of the refrigerator and started gulping the cider straight from the jug. When she lowered the jug, Zack was standing in front of her staring with wide eyes.
"Mommy, you're not supposed to drink out of the bottle. That will spread germs, you know that."
"I know honey, I'm sorry. I figured that I would finish the rest of it, so I didn't want to dirty another cup."
Beth looked around the messy kitchen and laughed to herself at the thought of how Jeff would react to such a disaster. She felt a sense of happiness and relief knowing that it did not matter; she could have a dirty kitchen and drink cider out of the jug if she wanted to.
"Oh. There are no more cups, are there? They're all dirty."
"You're right, they're all dirty."
"You have a lot of dishes to wash."
"You're a smart little boy."
"I know."
"I love you."
"I know."
Zack had a big smile on his face. Beth picked him up, flew him over to the couch, and started to blow on his belly. Zack laughed hysterically. Beth felt like she was going to throw up from the motion.

It felt good to be in church. Beth's body felt so sick that it was a relief to have an excuse to sit silent and motionless. She was tempted to close her eyes while she listened to the sermon, but luckily Reverend Josh's good looks kept Beth's visual attention.

"This weekend we celebrate the traditional holiday of the American Thanksgiving. There are many different directions that I could take today's sermon. I could be realistic and talk about the first Thanksgiving and the fact that the pilgrims and Indians didn't eat turkey like we do today, but ate clams and corn. I could talk about how the pilgrims would never have survived the harsh New England winter if it had not been for the Indian's selfless help. In return, the Indians were driven out of their homes and many of them were murdered by the introduction of foreign disease and violence. However, I won't talk about those issues today. I will be positive and talk about the symbolism of Thanksgiving. As with most holidays and rituals, the history is usually inaccurate, as the culture has retold the stories to symbolize a message. The message of Thanksgiving is to be grateful and thankful for what we have. Ultimately, no matter how little or much we have there is always someone who has less or more than us, it's all relative. So we should be thankful for what we have without comparing ourselves to others.

"I'm going to tell a story about when I was a young boy. I come from a very poor stereotypical Irish Catholic family. There were many kids, but not much food. I don't know how my mother kept us all fed and clothed. When I was about eight years old my school was having a food drive for the 'poor' people. In reality, we were in desperate need of the charity from this event. I was very excited and asked my mother what I could contribute. My aunt happened to be visiting that day after school and offered me a small can of beans. My mother took the can of beans from me. I thought she was going to tell me that we couldn't afford to give food to others when we needed it ourselves. Instead, she took a jar of strawberry preserves from the cabinet and gave it to me to bring to school. She told me that instead of giving the poor people the food that we didn't want, we should give them something that they would really like. I was so happy and proud that I would be bringing the jar of preserves to school. It was like my mother had given me a jar of gold. When I went to my room, my mother and aunt thought that I was out of earshot. My aunt asked my mother why she gave me the jar of strawberry preserves when we were poor and needed the food ourselves. My mother told her that as long as a person had something to give to others, they are not poor.

"My mother was a very wise woman. I didn't know that we were poor since I contributed something special to the food drive. I had a warm safe home to live in, three meals a day, and much love. To a child it is these things, and not money, that establishes his sense of worth. It's too bad that when we grow up, it's the final numbers on the bottom of an excel spreadsheet that determines our net worth. Regardless of how much or little a person has, the joy of doing something for someone else is priceless. It reminds me of the story in the New Testament where an old woman gave her only coins to the collection plate and Jesus said that this woman was giving more than the rich man who gave ten times more money. In giving everything she had, she gave of her heart. The act that this woman performed is much stronger than that of a person who just gives the excess that is not needed or wanted. More than the amount that was given, this woman believed that despite her poverty and desperate situation, there was someone worse off than her who would benefit. In her mind, that made her rich in comparison to another. One does not have to give away all of their worldly goods in order to feel valuable. The act of giving your self, of doing a good deed, babysitting for a neighbor, stopping in traffic to let another car go, helping a stranger put their groceries in their car. These are all actions that make a person rich. Humanity depends on the generosity of other to survive. This generosity comes in many forms; it comes in the form of a smile, a hug, a positive attitude. When one appreciates what they have, they can be thankful for their very existence and that of their loved ones. It is this thankfulness that is the meaning of the holiday that we celebrate this weekend. Let us all close our eyes and be thankful for being here together and for all that we have. Amen."

Beth felt grateful for the opportunity to sit quietly and contemplate with her eyes closed. She thought about the box of food that was left on her doorstep and wondered about the people who contributed to it. What made them stop in the grocery store and buy the pie, potatoes, and other items that were so much more than the can of vegetables or box of macaroni and cheese that is traditionally dropped in the donation box. Did they think about who their donation was going to? Did they picture her as an actual person or just a charity that was their obligation? Were they actually much worse off than her? Should she be donating food for the people who did not even have a home, but had to eat in a shelter? Perhaps she could volunteer to help to cook the meals for them? Like the majority of people with good intentions, she thought of all of her current obligations and decided that she would wait until she finished school before adding another item to her already busy schedule.

Beth was very quiet at Gayle and Stacey's house that after noon. She was relieved that instead of having a big dinner, they were serving turkey soup and homemade bread from their bread maker. Beth played with Mia on the living room floor while Gayle set the table. Stacey read the Sunday paper and Zack played trucks. They were all quietly doing their own thing. It was a comfortable feeling to know someone well enough that you could entertain yourself in their home. Beth felt content. During dinner Gayle and Stacey reviewed the plans for their wedding with Beth. The date was set for Sunday, December 21, which was the winter solstice. Since neither of them had any family and Beth was their only friend, the wedding was going to be very small. Besides the five of them (including Mia and Zack), there would be Reverend Josh and a few friends from church and each of their jobs. The service would be in the sanctuary with a reception following in the main hall at the church. They would play CD's through the church sound system, and for flowers they would have poinsettias and holly. The theme would be the winter solstice celebrated in the tradition of the pagans bringing forward the coming of the sun. They picked this theme because their marriage celebrated the coming of light through the acceptance for two women to wed. Beth listened to the details with a smile on her face, nodding and confirming how great it was. She was in a daze observing through a veil what they were planning, until Stacey casually listed some of the tasks that Jose would be doing. Beth knew Jose would come, but did not think he would want to be part of a pagan wedding since he was a devout Christian. She was worried about how he would feel about such an untraditional ceremony. Would he consider the pagan theme sacrilegious? Would he be willing to participate in a ceremony that went so strongly against his beliefs?

"Oh, I don't know. I don't think Jose should participate."

"Why not?"

"Well, let's just say that he might not be open to such an untraditional wedding."

Stacey looked hurt and angry, "I thought that you, of all people, accepted us getting married. You're the one who brought us together!"

"No, no. I don't mean untraditional in that you two are getting married! Oh my God. I never even considered that as not being anything but right! I mean that Jose is like *wicked* Christian and might not be open to the whole pagan thing."

Every one laughed.

Chapter 14

December went by very quickly. The semester was coming to an end in school, so there was a lot of material to cover. Jose came over to study some evenings and on Saturdays. Now that Zack knew that Maria and Vickie had a TV, he wanted to go over there whenever possible. Beth worried that she was imposing by letting him go over so much, but Maria insisted that he was always welcome. She said that it helped her not to feel so lonely when Vickie was with Dominic. Letting Zack go across the hall gave Beth time to study. She looked forward to the two-week holiday break.

Beth wished she could do more to help plan Stacey and Gayle's wedding, but she knew it would be impossible since the wedding was three days after her last final exam. She worried that she should not have accepted the role as maid-of-honor since she could not afford to give a shower or help with the planning. They both assured her that they were enjoying the planning since neither of them thought they would ever get married. They said that two brides made the planning process easier as a groom never did any of the work anyway, and especially since it was such a small wedding. Beth had no idea how she would be able to afford a wedding present and finally decided to give them a gift certificate for a week of babysitting so they could go on a honeymoon.

For the first time in Beth's life, the month of December was going to be a horrible month. Like so many millions of families in America, she had no idea how she was going to provide Christmas for her child. To spend $25 on a Christmas tree was way outside of her budget, never mind all of the decorations, tree stand, lights, and ornaments. Then there would be Christmas morning with no presents. Zack was old enough that he understood the concept of Christmas, Santa and presents. He read Christmas stories and made Christmas crafts in day care, he watched Christmas specials on TV, he was being carried away with the spirit and magic of the holiday. This left Beth loosing sleep at night wondering how she was going to create the illusion of Christmas. She wished that she were able to qualify for a credit card so that she could 'charge Christmas' and pay it back later, which was the American trend. She remembered all of the applications for credit cards that used to come in the mail when she lived with Jeff and how she thought it was stupid that that people would actually fall for the gimmicks of 'buy now, pay later'. Now she wished more than anything that one of those credit card companies would be willing to give credit to an unemployed, single mother on welfare.

Beth wanted to stop going to support group during December so that she could prepare for finals. She was having a hard time keeping up with the studying and really needed that time. As opposed to the house Wednesday night support groups, the Tuesday evening support group was open for anyone, including many women who were currently in abusive relationships. Emotionally, it became increasingly difficult and frustrating for Beth to witness women stay with or return to their abusive partners. Many women left one abuser and went straight into a relationship with another. It was very disturbing and Beth did not believe she belonged there since she was making a safe life for herself and Zack. Besides, she was going to counseling, and while Zack was in his kid's group she was participating in a program on how to help kids heal and how to rebuild your life. Lisa emphasized that part of the reason Beth qualified for so many services was because she was participating in all the programs that were recommended, and that included going to support group. Lisa thought it was good that Beth was disturbed by the women who stayed with their abusers because it would help Beth to understand and forgive herself for staying with Jeff for so long. It would also help Beth to become aware of any unsafe situations she may encounter in the future and be able to stop herself from becoming involved early on.

After support group one night Lisa asked Beth if she could talk to her in private.

"I have a few things that I have to talk to you about. First, and most important, I have this for you."

Lisa handed Beth a small folded piece of paper. "It's Sheila's phone number. I'm sorry it took so long for me to get it to you. I had to check with her. Since you don't have a phone, she asked me to have you call her."

Beth took the paper and stuffed it in her wallet. She was not sure what she wanted to do about calling Sheila.

"Thanks."

"Next, I need to talk to you about Christmas."

"What about it? This is a horrible time of year, now I know why the suicide rate is so high in December."

"Beth, don't talk like that. There are a lot of people who want to help you."

"I am sick of getting help from people! I feel like a fucking charity case! I can't even afford a fucking Christmas tree!"

"Beth, calm down. There are donated Christmas trees. I can have one delivered!"

"No! I don't want another hand out! All I do is take handouts from people! 'Yes, let's donate to the poor needy people who don't have anything.' That's *me* they're talking about. *I'm* the poor desperate person that people feel bad for! *My life* is so pathetic that I have to live off other people! I'm sick of it!"

Lisa grabbed Beth's shoulders and shook her.

"*Stop it, now!* Think about what you're saying! Look at how far you've come. You're becoming independent. Stop thinking about your own pride, and think about Zack. Don't you think he deserves to have Christmas? It's not his fault that Jeff's an asshole. Don't you think he suffered enough? Take the Christmas tree and make a Christmas list for Zack. He's who Christmas is for. Think of him, not you."

Beth stood silent. She did not know what to say, Lisa was right. It was not fair to Zack. She would accept what Lisa offered her for Zack's sake since Christmas was for children.

"Now, sit down and make out a Christmas list for Zack. Make sure that you include his and your clothes and shoe sizes. Put down a few options for Zack so that there are choices for people to get."

Beth sat down and began making out the list. She thought about what Zack might have said he wanted from watching the commercials on TV and from being in daycare. She finished the list and gave it to Lisa.

"I'm sorry."

"I know. You're going to do fine."

"Thank you."

"You're welcome."

Beth was depressed the rest of the week. She felt worn out and exhausted. The stress of the upcoming exams on top of the stress of Christmas was wearing her out. Jose kept asking her what was the matter, but she did not have an answer to give him. She just felt like giving up. She felt ashamed that she could not give anything to her little boy for Christmas.

On Saturday morning there was a knocking on Beth's door. She opened it up and there was Lisa holding the scrawniest Christmas tree she had ever seen. No wonder it was donated, there was no way that anyone would have bought it. Seeing its horrible condition, Beth felt better about accepting it as she was the one performing an act of charity by taking it in. She could not help but to laugh. It was a true 'Charlie Brown Christmas Tree'.

"That has got to be the *ugliest* Christmas tree that I have ever seen!"

Lisa looked hurt.

"You don't like it?"

"No, I *Love* it! Bring it in!"

Lisa smiled as she dragged in the tree and then went back into the hall to get a flimsy stand. It was difficult to get the stand to hold the tree, but they finally managed. They stood back and admired the tree, Zack sitting on the couch watching the entire escapade. Beth did not dare mention to Lisa that she had no ornaments.

"This is great, thank you."

"You're welcome. As you know, there's a Christmas party at the Crisis Center this afternoon. Since you have to study and can't go, I was wondering if I could bring Zack?"

Zack's face lit up.

"Oh pleeeaze Mommy, can I go?"

"Santa will be there."

"Santa? Oh Mommy, I haven't seen Santa! Can I go? Please?"

Beth felt put on the spot. She could not say no if she wanted to. But she did not want to. Jose would be coming over to study, and they would be alone.

"Of course you can go, you silly goose!"

Beth hugged Zack.

"Great, I'll pick Zack up at about 1:30."

"That's fine."

"All right. Well, I have to go. I'll see you in a few hours."

"Thanks for the tree."

"You're welcome."

Beth looked at the tree and tried to think about how she could decorate it. She turned back to Zack.

"Do you want to string some popcorn?"

"Yeah!"

Beth went into the cabinet and took out the bag of popcorn kernels. She popped them in the big pot on the stove and went into her room to get her little sewing kit. She took out two spools of thread and two needles. She put the thread from each spool through the needles and handed one of them to Zack. He looked scared as he took it.

"It's okay Zack. You're a big boy now. You're almost three. You can do big boy things, just be careful. Make sure that you point the needle away from you and your fingers. Push it carefully through the soft part of the popcorn like this."

Beth gently pushed the needle through the large part of the popcorn and it smoothly came out the other side.

"See how easy that is? Now you try."

Zack cautiously took the other needle and copied what Beth had done. He did it very slowly and carefully so that the needle would not prick his tiny fingers. He smiled proudly as he held the needle up with the piece of popcorn dangling on the string.

"I did it!"

"That's great! I knew you could. Now just keep pushing them down the string so that you can add more."

The two of them sat and strung the popcorn for over an hour until the entire bowl was gone. When a string started getting long, Beth would tie it in a knot and start a new one. Zack placed the strings of popcorn on the lower branches and Beth put them on the higher ones. When they were done, Zack colored in his coloring book while Beth studied. At around 12:00 P.M. Beth boiled some macaroni with melted margarine for lunch. Both Jose and Lisa would be coming soon.

Beth was getting used to not planning her schedule the way she used to when she had a phone. With the absence of a phone she was at the liberty just to accept events as they occurred rather than calling people to set up specific times. In one sense the lack of structure was frustrating, but in another sense the spontaneity was a relief. It made her more aware of each moment as it occurred instead of planning her day. Lisa would be coming over to pick up Zack at 1:30 P.M., but Jose had no way to tell her what time he would be coming over. If there was an emergency, Beth could be contacted through Maria's phone. Beth had the cell phone from the crisis center that connected to 911, so although she had no phone for communication purposes she at least would be able to call for help if needed.

Jose still had not come over when Lisa picked up Zack. Beth's first instinct was to be concerned that he was so late. Rationally she knew that everything was fine and that he would call her if he had to. Once Lisa and Zack left she took a deep breath to center herself and sat down to study until he came. He finally showed up.

"Hey, where's Zack?"

"Lisa took him to a Christmas party. What did you do all day?" Beth tried not to sound annoyed.

"I studied at home for a while, and then did some errands. How about you, how's your studying going?"

"I actually got a lot done today. Do you like our Christmas tree?"

"Yeah, I love it. The popcorn looks great."

"Thanks."

"I think I need a study break. How about you? Do you want to go out for a little while? Maybe hit the mall like the rest of America."

"I don't have any money."

"You don't have to buy anything. You can just look. Besides, I need help picking out something."

"What?"

"I'll show you when we get there. It's a surprise."

"Okay."

Beth's mind was feeling foggy anyway and she needed a mental break. It would be fun going to the mall to watch the people and see the decorations. Maybe it would help get her into the Christmas spirit.

The mall was jam packed, they drove around for twenty minutes before they even found a parking space at the far end of the lot, then they froze walking all the way back to the mall. Once in the mall, there were so many people it was difficult even to see what was on sale. Beth started feeling dizzy and claustrophobic from the masses of bright lights and from being pushed by the crowd. She grabbed onto Jose's hand and held tight, feeling like Zack when he was scared.

"Come this way, what I want is on sale in here."

Jose led Beth through the security detectors into the large electronic store. They wandered through the isles, but Jose seemed to be leading them in a specific direction. It was obvious that he had a destination in mind. They finally came to the back of the store where all of the TV's were set to the same channel, showing mountains with a deer running through a large field. The camera then focused on a yellow flower, zooming in so that the entire display section exploded with the micro image of the yellow petals. Jose led Beth past the large flat screen plasma TV's until they came to piles of small cardboard boxes with TV's in them. These TV's weren't large enough to earn a spot in the display section where they could show the nature clips. There was a bright orange sign on top of the stack that read 'Sale: $89 for TV/VCR/DVD combo'.

"This is what I want." Jose picked up one of the boxes.

"Do you want me to find a carriage?"

"No there aren't any around. Besides, this is small enough for me to carry. Do you like it?"

"Yeah, who's it for?"

"It's for you and Zack for Christmas. Do you like this one, or do you see another one that you'd like better?"

Beth was about to insist that Jose should not buy it, but she saw a look of desperation and need in his eyes. He needed her to accept this. She smiled at him. Beth knew that this was the least expensive one, still being more than Jose could afford.

"It's perfect."

"Let's go look at the videos and see if we can find any that Zack would like."

They walked past the rows of new release videos, costing about $20 each, a look of disappointment on Jose's face. Beth spotted a bin of videos with a sign on top reading '$5 each'.

"There might be some in here that he would like."

The smile came back to Jose's face. Beth searched through the bin and pulled out two movies, *Robin Hood* and *King Arthur*, both of which were animated by a film company that she had never heard of.

"How do these look? I think he'll like them."

"Those look great, I think *I'll* like those!"

"Well, I know what we'll be doing on Christmas day!"

"Speaking of Christmas day, I was wondering if you want to come to my family's house with me."

"Really? Jose, are you sure you want me to come to your house for Christmas?"

"I wouldn't ask you if I wasn't sure. My whole family is going to be there, I want them to meet you and Zack. Of course, that means that we would have to watch the movies another day."

"I don't think Zack would mind. Thank you Jose, we would love to come."

"Great, let's go buy this stuff. My arms are getting tired."

They went to the cashier and Jose paid for the TV and videos with two crisp one hundred dollar bills. The cashier took the bills and looked suspiciously at Jose. She glanced over to the service desk, caught the eye of a man in a suit, and gave a slight nod. She printed out the receipt, put a bright green sticker with the store's name on it on the box, and put the videos in a small bag that she handed back to Beth. The way the cashier looked at Jose made Beth feel nauseous. It was a look of disgust like looking down upon someone who was a disgrace or even subhuman. Beth looked up at Jose who also must have noticed, as he seemed very upset. He shifted his eyes down, picked up the box, and started walking towards the door.

"Let's get out of here."

Beth silently walked beside him. As they approached the entrance of the store the man in the suit that the cashier nodded at placed himself between Jose, Beth and the door. Jose and Beth had no choice but to stop. Again, Jose looked down at the floor avoiding eye contact as he spoke to the man.

"Excuse me."

"Excuse you for what."

"You're blocking our way. Could you please move?"

"I think you need to come with me first."

"Why, I did nothing wrong."

"Let's not make a scene. Just come quietly so that I don't have to call security."

"You have no right to ask me to come. I paid for this and have a receipt. What grounds do you have for keeping me from leaving the store?"

"If you resist my request then you're leaving me no choice but to call security."

"You don't have to do that, I'm coming."

Beth followed Jose as he walked beside the man past the service area and into a little room. The man stopped Beth from entering the room.

"You don't have to come in. It's him that we're interested in."

"I'm with him. If he goes in, then I go in too."

"Suite yourself."

There was a cafeteria-style table with chairs around it in the center of the room and a few posters about the current labor laws hanging on the walls. Jose put the TV on the table and took a seat. Beth sat next to him and held his hand. The man sat in the chair across from Jose.

"So, that's a nice TV you got."

"I have a receipt. Is it a crime to buy a TV? I thought that's what you did here, sell electronics. Or do you only sell electronics to non-Hispanic people?"

"Very funny, no we're not prejudice."

"You could have fooled me."

"So, you paid with cash."

"The last time I checked, cash was a legal currency in the United States."

"How did you get so much cash? Do you always carry large bills?"

"I took them out of the bank to go Christmas shopping. Get to your point. What are you accusing me of? If you're accusing me of something, then I have a right to a lawyer. Otherwise, you have no right to keep me here."

"You're not being accused of anything. We've been having problems with counterfeit $100 bills. I know that things can get tight around the holidays and there's a lot of temptation for people to pass counterfeits to get Christmas gifts for their families."

The man patted the top of the TV box. Jose half stood in his seat.

"Are you accusing me of paying for this with counterfeit money?"

"I told you, I am not accusing you of anything."

"Then you have no right to keep me here and I'm leaving."

"If you go to leave, then I'll call the police and will accuse you of something."

"Of what?"

"I'll think of something."

The three of them sat in silence for a long time. Jose's handsome face looked haggard and beaten. Beth wanted to hold him close to her, but instead she held his hand under the table. A knock on the door finally broke the silence. Beth could hear voices outside the door.

"These fucking spicks. Why don't they go back to where they came from?"

"Yeah, too bad there wasn't a hole in their boat and they all drowned. They're contaminating our country!"

Two security guards came in.

"We checked the bills and they're real. You can let them go."

"Did you hear that? It was all just a big misunderstanding. I apologize for the inconvenience. You can go."

Jose picked up the box and started to walk out the door, Beth beside him.

"You'll hear from my lawyer."

"On what grounds?"

"I'll think of something."

When Beth and Jose got back to Beth's apartment neither of them spoke. Although it seemed like forever since they had left, not much time actually elapsed. It was amazing that their energy and mood could become so changed in such a short period of time. Jose sat on the couch and stared into space. Beth wanted to do something, but she did not know what she could do. Even though it was Jose who they were targeting, she felt as though she had also been violated. Again. She sat on the couch next to Jose, leaving a bit of distance between them to give Jose some personal space. They sat in silence for what seemed like hours. Outdoors the day turned into night very quickly. It seemed ironic that the season of joy and light was the same time of year that the days were the shortest. Beth did not dare to disrupt the silence by getting up to turn on the light or close the shade, so they sat in the dark.

Jose finally looked over at Beth and gave her a faint smile. He reached over, pulled her to him, and held her tight. Beth could feel the desperation in his embrace. After a while she felt wet on her cheek, then felt Jose trembling and realized that he was crying. She could not remember ever seeing a man cry and it scared her. It made her feel helpless and angry. What right did those people have to intimidate and accuse Jose? Would they have questioned him if he were white or well dressed? She stroked the back of his head until he stopped crying. She finally broke the silence.

"Jose, I'm so sorry. That was horrible. Those assholes had no right to do that."

"I'm used to it, I live it everyday. I have to accomplish twice as much as a white person just to be equal. I'm automatically fifty feet behind the start line in everything that I do."

"That's not true Jose. Look at how well you do in school. Every one likes you. You're one of the smartest in the class."

"I do well in school because I worked my ass off and studied on my own while struggling through a school system with no textbooks and education standards that allowed half the class to graduate even though they missed most of the classes and were unable to read. You say that people like me, but I had to earn that by working twice as hard to get people to accept me. Even you wouldn't talk to me. I had to be constantly persistent before you finally gave in."

"Jose! That's not fair! You know that my reluctance to open up to you was the same that I had towards everyone in the class! It was about my fear and lack of trust in people, not about race!"

"Beth, you don't know what it's like to constantly be different, to constantly be judged. I leave the house in the morning never knowing when I'm going to be targeted or despised, just because of my nationality. Usually it shows up when I least expect it, like today. You don't know what it's like to never know when you're going to be hated."

"Yes I do, at least you only get it on the outside and know that you're loved in your home. You have a place where you're accepted. For years I lived in constant fear, never knowing when I was going to get hit or ridiculed. I was hated most of the time in the place where I was supposed to be loved."

"So you do know. What you experienced in one house I experience in the whole world. Well, except in my neighborhood with my family and friends. But even then, you never know when the police are going to show up and think of something that we're doing wrong, some reason to give us a hard time or bring us in, even if it's just for looking a certain way. There are places where I know that I can't go, and that I can't even drive through. If I do go there, even if it's for a legitimate reason, I'll get pulled over, given a ticket, questioned for no reason other than the way I look. I used to work for a furniture store doing deliveries. Once we went into a neighborhood to deliver a couch and the neighbors called the police because they thought we were actually under disguise and were trying to rob the houses. My boss had to come down to the police station to prove that we were supposed to be there. Just being in a particular place is reason to have the police called on you when you're different. You'll never have to experience that."

Beth remembered when she was a little girl and her family would drive up to central Maine to visit her grandparents. On the ride to their house the local people either drove very slow in front of them, or tail gated behind them. One time when her father pulled over to let the car behind them pass, the other car sped ahead very fast and yelled "Masshole" out the window as they drove by. When Beth asked her father what a Masshole was, he told her it was the local's name for people from Massachusetts. She asked him if she was a Masshole, and he told her "no". He said it was a bad name that people used because they were afraid of anyone who was not like them. He told her that she needed to forgive these people for their ignorance in not accepting others, and that it was important for her to set a good example and be nice to everyone. On those trips her father never went over the speed limit and was overly polite to everyone. He told Beth that he did not want to give the locals any reason to use against him.

Once Beth's family arrived at her grandparent's home, everything was different. Beth would wake up in the small upstairs bedroom to the smell of strong coffee that was perking in a tin coffee pot on the gas stove, and the sound of country music playing over the old fashioned radio in the kitchen. The radio always seemed to be the center of the activity. Beth would walk bare foot down the steep cold stairs into the large kitchen with its specked linoleum floor and lime green icebox (it was really a refrigerator, but Beth's grandparents called it an icebox), and gas stove. There was an oversized sink for washing dishes or giving her and her brother baths in when they were very small. When they were done with their bath, Beth's grandmother wrapped them up in big fluffy towels that smelled like Downy. Beth would sit huddled in the soft towel until the warmth wore off and she was cold. She would then get changed and shift to the couch and cuddle under the hand-crocheted afghan that had the same Downy smell.

Beth would sit at the fifties style kitchen table and watch her grandmother cook breakfast. The bacon was started before Beth woke up and was sitting in the large cast iron pan over the low gas for at least forty-five minutes. Beth's grandmother would put the cooked bacon on a plate covered with paper towels to allow the fat to absorb, and poured the fat from the pan into a tin can which would later be used to make soap. She would use some of the fat to fry the eggs in it. While the eggs were frying, the homemade blueberry, raspberry, or strawberry muffins (depending on the season) would cool on the little wooden table next to the window. These were the best breakfasts in the world. Sometimes when Beth went to an old-fashioned dinner she would be reminded of her grandmother's cooking. But, not really.

Beth's grandmother would proudly parade Beth and her brother around the small town they lived in, showing them off to all her friends. The old ladies would invite them in for cookies and homemade berry muffins. The men in their flannel shirts and navy blue work pants stained with grease would smile and pat them on the head. Beth loved going to the library in its old brick building that smelled of old books and time gone by. Beth and her brother would stand still, afraid to breathe. Hence it would break the silence of this sacred building. The atmosphere in the small town bookshop was much more welcoming. There was a kid's section with pillows on the floor where she could sit and read the children's books while her grandmother read though the flaps of all the books in the 'bargain' section at the back of the store. There were posters of book covers and books about fairy tales, Native American myths, and stories about Buddha. Sometimes they would spend the entire afternoon there.

There was always the comfort of knowing that everything would be the same year after year, and that nothing ever changed. Even the big black phone in her grandparent's living room was the old-fashioned kind that weighed a ton and had to be dialed instead of the push buttons that the rest of America was using. Beth had to be taught how to dial it. Even as an adult, every time Beth heard the operator on a recorded line instruct the caller to stay on the line if they did not have a push button phone, Beth would smile because she knew that this voice was talking to her grandparents.

Everything was simple and easy at her grandparent's house. Any problem could easily be fixed by a trip to 'Leny's', the local discount store that carried everything from clothes, to dish detergent and kitchen supplies, to hunting and yard equipment, to canned food and medical supplies. The building looked like it was about one hundred years old and everything was stacked on tall shelves that tilted sideways on a warped floor so that when you walked through the narrow isles you were not sure if the items or the shelves would fall on you.

Beth wondered if the little town that she remembered so vividly was still as timeless as it had been throughout her childhood. Beth would be proud to be part of this community, but she always felt like an intruder. The only reason she had been accepted was because of her grandparents, but they died years ago. She would love to visit the town, but without her grandparents she was an outsider, a "Masshole." Therefor, she was different, suspicious, mistrusted. She longed more than anything to be accepted into that community and to be part of it herself. To feel like she could walk around the town and into the shops, and people would welcome her without looking at her like an outsider. She thought that this might be how Jose felt on a day-to-day basis in this country that he considered his home.

"Obviously, you've never been to Central Maine."

"Why? What's Maine like?"

"Well, they're afraid of anyone different. Even me. You wouldn't have a chance. Let's just say that you went there for a family vacation with your old grandmother, your sister, and her baby for a nice vacation as innocent and harmless as possible. You probably wouldn't even have your bags unpacked into the little cabin you rented when the sheriff would show up thinking that you were a bunch of outlaws coming up to hide out in the mountains. The neighbors would be terrified to leave their houses."

"You're exaggerating."

"Actually, I'm not."

"I don't get it. Why are people so afraid of anyone who's different?"

"I don't know. Maybe it's fear of the unknown. Or maybe it's just to make themselves feel better?"

"Yeah, people can feel like they're better than everyone else when it's convenient for them. But when it's in their best interest they want these same people around."

"What do you mean?"

"Who do you think does the majority of yard work, kitchen help, house cleaning, and low income labor? Basically, all of the jobs that no one else wants to do?"

"I don't know."

"The illegal immigrants, the minorities. We're the cheap labor that supports this country. People can get away with it since we have no rights. If an illegal immigrant went on strike because of low wages and poor work conditions, then they would just be replaced and deported. If they got hurt on the job then they wouldn't get workman's comp or a paid leave. They would have to either not work, hence not eat, or work injured so that they could get paid. But hopefully they wouldn't get injured so bad that they needed medical attention because the employers would, of course, not have to provide them with medical insurance or other benefits."

"Well, if they are here illegally, then they're taking the jobs away from the Americans. They shouldn't be here."

"And how are they supposed to live if they don't work?"

"They should go back to their own country. They come here, take our jobs, and then send money back to their families, taking money out of our economy."

"Think about where these people are coming from. They're coming from such bad conditions that they're forced to leave their families and country, risking their lives to work for next to nothing just so that they can send a little bit of money back home to feed their kids. Think of how hard it was for you to move from where ever you came from, but you're in the same country and culture. Think of these people who are so desperate that they give up everything they have in hopes for a better life. Then, they're treated like shit for being here and they live in constant fear of being deported. The politicians come up with ways to deport illegal immigrants as campaign topics, but then they use these same people to clean their houses and do their gardening because it's convenient for them to have the cheap labor. They're all hypocrites."

"When I was a little boy living in the Dominican Republic the tourists would come to our village. We little kids would run after the trucks begging the tourists to toss us coins. The tour guide would tell the tourists not to toss us anything because it taught us to beg. He told them to give donations to the schools instead so that we would learn that getting an education and a job was what was important. Then, we kids grew up and wanted to work. Yet instead of being given jobs, there are fund-raisers to send charity to the 'underprivileged'. We don't want to be the underprivileged poor people who receive charity, we want to work and support our families with honor."

"I know I'm sounding like a jerk, but why do they come here? Why don't they get jobs in their own countries?"

"They would if they could, but there are no jobs. This is one world. What gives people a right to think that because they have the luck of being born in a certain country that they are the only ones to benefit from what that country has to offer? Why does everyone else have to be poor? Doesn't every person have a right to work and have the opportunity to succeed? Isn't that the concept that this country was built on?"

"I'm sorry. I never thought about it that way. When my ancestors came over from Ireland they lived in poverty and many people died of starvation. No one would hire them, there were signs that read 'Irish need not apply'. This was all before it was against the law to discriminate because of race or nationality. Then there was an Irish president, President Kennedy, and now the Irish are an important part of this country. Some people even say that the Kennedys are America's royal family. Look at the Italians, the Polish, the Jewish and so many others who were isolated and discriminated against when they were new or different, but eventually became part of the norm. Even the Native Americans, who are the only true Americans, were slaughtered and almost wiped out of existence. When I was at the Halloween party, I was discussing a portion of the bible, Leviticus, with a friend of mine. In one section it states 'When an alien lives with you in your land, do not mistreat him. The alien living with you must be treated as one of your native-born. Love him as yourself, for you were aliens in Egypt. I am the LORD your God.' Despite this, people have been fighting and resisting people from other countries through out time. Maybe it's just human nature to resist any one different from them, even though change is inevitable and eventually succeeds."

"Maybe human nature will change."

"Let's hope so, but there are also the people who come to this country to reap the rewards without working."

"You mean the people who just 'live off the system'."

"Exactly."

"Unfortunately there are immigrants as well as generations of Americans that 'live off the system' and take benefits from those who are just looking for a little help until they can make it on their own."

"Yeah."

"Those people give us all a bad name."

Beth knew that they both suffered because of those who took advantage of the 'system'. She heard the downstairs door close and the scampering of soft footsteps followed by slow loud footsteps coming up the stairway. There was a soft tapping on the door. Beth got up to open it and Zack came running in the room, hugging a huge teddy bear that was almost as big as him.

"Look what I got from Santa Claus!"

"Oh Zacky, it's so cute and cuddly! Can I hug it?"

"Okay Mommy, but don't squish him."

"What's his name?"

"Monty."

"Monty? That's such a funny name!"
"It's not a funny name, Mommy. You'll hurt his feelings."
"I'm sorry, Monty is a nice name. He looks like a Monty."
Beth gave the bear a big hug and then handed him back to Zack who hugged him tight. Lisa came in the apartment carrying a tray with cookies on it.
"Oh, I see that you met Monty!"
"Yeah, He's a cool bear."
"Him and Zack became fast friends."
"I can see that."
Zack was smiling up at Lisa and Beth while they discussed Monty as if he were a 'real' friend for Zack.
"Look Mommy, we got cookies!"
"Yum, yum. Can I have one?"
"Sure. Can Jose have one too?"
"Uh huh."
Lisa left and Beth boiled some water for macaroni and poured a can of tomato sauce in a pan for supper. Jose did not talk much while Zack showed him Monty and a coloring book that he got at the party. After supper Zack colored on the floor in his new coloring book while Beth and Jose studied.

Chapter 15

Finals week was very stressful. Beth barely slept as she stayed up most nights studying. She read the same material over and over again, afraid that she might forget something. It was difficult focusing and giving attention to Zack, so Maria helped by taking care of him. Beth told Zack that they would do something special together to celebrate when she was done with her exams, but Zack did not understand the concept of waiting for his mother's attention. Regardless, he did not complain much and behaved very well. It was as if he could sense that Beth needed him to be extra good this week while she prepared for and took her final exams.

Monday and Tuesday they had the final reviews. Then on Wednesday they had the Clinical Procedures and Anatomy & Physiology final exams, and on Thursday they had the Medical Terminology and Communications exams. Thursday after her Communications exam, Beth's classmates asked Beth and Jose if they wanted to go out to celebrate the end of the semester. Jose thought it was a great idea and wanted to go, but Beth was exhausted and wanted to go home and rest. Even though Beth insisted that Jose go, she was annoyed that he did not stay with her. She did not let him know that she was mad since she had insisted he go out. Instead, she went to bed early on Thursday night and slept most of the day Friday while Zack played on her bed with his toys.

Saturday Zack stayed with Maria while Beth went to the church to help Stacey and Gayle decorate for their wedding, which was the next day December 21, on the winter solstice. There were evergreens, holly, ivy, and mistletoe draped over the sanctuary and hall. There was an artificial Pine Mountain Superlog representing a Yule log covered with sprays of fir, evergreen holly, and ivy in a metal bowl waiting to be lit. They found deep green table clothes in the church linen closet that they ironed and placed on the tables. For a centerpiece, each table had a pot of ivy with sprigs of evergreen and holly stuck into the dirt. Green and red candlesticks in the church's silver candlestick holders were placed strategically on all of the tables and around the sanctuary. For party favors, there were evergreen votive candles and little green velvet bags filled with grain and corn. This represented the ancient tradition of sprinkling grain, corn, and ashes from the Yule log on the doorway of a home to prevent want and bring abundance, bounty, and fertility throughout the coming year. There was a Christmas tree in the center of the room, which was decorated with plastic fruit and nuts, strings of cranberries and popcorn, and silk flowers. They hung mistletoe above the doorways, and hung an especially long sprig over where Stacey and Gayle would exchange vows. Everything looked perfect.

Stacey and Gayle wanted Beth to go out to eat with them, but Beth looked forward to sleeping so that she would be rested for the next day's festivities. She was exhausted. Suddenly Stacey jumped up in surprise.

"Oh my God, I almost forgot the most important thing!"

Beth looked around the room. It looked complete.

"What did you forget? Everything looks perfect."

"Gayle, can you get the bag from the car?"

Gayle smiled knowingly and headed out.

"Yeah, I'll be right back. Don't go anywhere Beth!"

Gayle came back carrying a rather large Christmas gift bag and handed it to Beth.

"This is for you."

"For me? Why? You didn't have to get me anything."

"We wanted to get it for you, open it!"

Beth rummaged through the tissue paper and felt the soft feel of velvet. She pulled out a beautiful dark green velvet dress. It was very simple with long sleeves and a long skirt, but the scooped neck gave it an elegant look. She couldn't believe they got this for her.

"Oh thank you, it's beautiful!"

"It's our gift to you for being in our wedding. We thought the color would bring out the green in your eyes. But there's more. Look into the bag."

Beth reached into the bottom of the bag and pulled out a pair of green velvet shoes to match the dress.

"Do you like them?"

"Like them? I *love* them! They look like fancy dance slippers that a princess would wear to an elegant ball!"

They all laughed.

"Well, *you* can be a princess and wear them to *our* ball tomorrow!"

"Will you save me a dance?"

"Of course!"

When Beth got home she went to Maria's apartment to get Zack. She knocked hard, but it took a while for Maria to answer the door. The apartment was dark and Zack was not sleeping in his usual spot on the couch.

"Hi, sorry to wake you up. Is Zack sleeping in Vickie's bed?"

"Huh? No, he's been gone for hours."

A sudden panic ran through Beth's body.

"What do you mean? Where is he?" She was practically screaming.

"He's in his bed. Your boyfriend came by and brought him to your apartment. He said that he'd wait for you. I didn't think you'd mind, so I gave him your key. Is it okay that I did that?"

Beth felt relief that Jose was there with Zack, but what if it wasn't Jose? Had Maria ever met Jose? What if it was really Jeff? What if Jeff had been watching the apartment, saw Beth leave alone, came in and told Maria that he was Beth's boyfriend and then kidnapped Zack! Oh my God, Jeff kidnapped Zack! Her Zack was gone! She could feel her face turning white. Maria looked worried.

"I'm so sorry, did I do something wrong?"

"Oh, no. No, not at all. That's fine. It's better that he's sleeping in his own bed. Thanks. Thanks for watching him."

Beth was in a daze as she turned around and put her key into the doorknob. It seemed like the key would not fit, the knob would not turn and the door would not open fast enough. Finally it opened, and there was Jose sleeping on her couch. A waive of relief rushed through her body, she turned around and smiled at Maria who was still standing in the doorway of her apartment.

"It's okay, they're here. Thanks for watching Zack." She smiled again before entering her own apartment.

Beth peeked in at Zack who was sound asleep. He stirred a little, then rolled over. Beth went back into the living room and climbed onto the couch next to Jose. Her body molded into his, he was warm and strong. She hugged his chest and could feel his heart beating through his sweater. He unconsciously wrapped his arms around her, which made her feel safe. She did not want either of them to move, she wanted to stay exactly like this forever. Forever was cut short after about five minutes.

"Hey, when did you get home?"

Beth loved the way it sounded when he referred to her apartment as 'home'. It made it seem like he belonged there. She snuggled herself against him a little more, nuzzling her face against his chest. He tightened his arms around her. She forgot to answer him.

"Well now that you're home, why don't we go to bed? I hope it's okay that I came over. I got out of work early and couldn't call you since you don't have a phone. I figured it would be easier for me to stay over since we're going to the wedding tomorrow. We have to fix that, you know."

"Fix what?"

"The fact that you don't have a phone."

"Maybe Santa will bring me one."

"I thought you didn't believe in Santa."

"I don't."

Beth got off Jose and he followed her into the bedroom. She was about to get into bed, but he stopped her. He gently put his hands on her shoulders, standing her straight and still. He took a candle and some matches out of his bag, placed the candle on her bureau, lit it, and turned off the lights. He came back over to her and slowly began undressing her. She did not dare to move. He gently brushed his fingertips down the outside of each arm, down each finger, and back up the inside of each arm. His fingers barely touched her, yet she could feel every hair as it rose under his touch. He then gently traced along the sides of her chest, her waist, hips, outer thighs, knees, calves, in between each toe, back up her calves, inner thighs, spiraled along her stomach, to her belly button. He gently stuck his tongue into her belly button, came up to her breasts, and gently spiraled around each breast until he came to her nipples, gently sucking them. Beth's entire body started to tremble with the built up anticipation of him barely touching, yet paying detailed attention to every inch of her body. Her body was so weak that she felt like she was a rag doll ready to flop on the bed, but she stood perfectly still with her eyes closed waiting for whatever Jose would do next to her.

Jose folded back the comforter and guided Beth so that she was lying on the bed. He then took off his clothes and climbed under the covers next to her. Her body trembled under his hands as he firmly ran them along the same route that he gently traced while she was standing. His mouth followed his hands around her body, kissing, licking, and sucking every inch of flesh. He spent a lot of time at her feet, massaging her arches, ankles and calves while he sucked on each toe. When he made his way up her legs, licking long strokes up her inner thighs stopping just before he reached her crotch. Her body craved his tongue to continue to her crotch, she moaned and placed her hands on his head pushing it there. Instead, he lifted his head to her stomach where he licked small circles until he reached her breasts where he sucked and gently bit. She made small whimpering sounds that would have been screams of ecstasy if Zack were not in the next room. Jose silenced her by putting his mouth over hers and passionately kissing her. Her mouth craved him. Her entire body craved him. He was on top of her now. She reached her hands onto his butt and tried to lead him into her. He kept his body just above hers so that when she arched her pelvis up to reach him, he lifted himself just a little bit higher so that she could just feel the tip of his penis brushing against her. Her body was out of control. It was shaking like a drug addict in desperate need to have him enter into her. He pulled off her. She panicked until she saw that he was putting on a condom. He came back on top of her, only this time he let himself lunge down into her. She could not contain the scream that had built. Their bodies moved together in rhythm faster and faster until he exploded inside of her, releasing an orgasm for her that she had never experienced the like of before. Staying inside of her, they held each other tight and fell asleep connected.

Beth woke up before the sun rose and lay as still as possible so that she would not disturb Jose. Some how, during the night, she had shifted so that she was facing away from him. She could feel his naked body against her back and butt, and his arms and legs wrapped around her front. She held his hands and kissed them gently, very softly so that he would not wake up. The next thing she knew, her eyes were closed, she was laying on her back and she could feel Jose outlining her face with his finger. His finger traced her eyebrows, down her cheek to the tip of her jaw, around her lips and up her nose. She must have fallen back to sleep. She kept her eyes closed so that he would think she was still sleeping and would not stop.

After years of being told how horrible she was and being hurt, she never thought that she would be loved. She had become a pincushion that was constantly being poked with pinches, punches, harsh words, evil looks, insults and hostility. To be touched tenderly was something that she read about in romance novels. It was nothing more than a fantasy. She never expected that it happened in real life. Now, here she was, being loved. As Jose touched every part of her body with his love, it was as if he was blessing her and filling in and healing the millions of little punctures from the years of pain. He made her feel as if she actually deserved to be loved. She never wanted this feeling to go away. She understood the true meaning of Madonna's song, she was "like a virgin being touched for the very first time."

Even though the wedding was in the afternoon, Beth had a lot to do to be ready in time. She had to give Zack a bath, take a shower herself, and get both herself and Zack ready. Jose got dressed and was ready to go. He sat on the couch, bored since there was no studying, no TV to watch, no magazines, or papers to read. He went into Zack's room and played with him for a while. Finally he came out, put his coat on, and grabbed his keys.

"Hey Beth, I'm going to go out for a while. I'll get a paper or something. Just give me a call on my cell when you're ready. Do you need me to get you anything?"

"Don't be a jerk Jose. You know that I can't call you."

"Yeah, you're right, but Zack can. Can't you Zack?"

Zack stood in his doorway with a big smile on his face.

"Yup."

"What do you mean? What are you two up to?"

"Go in your room and call me Zack. But tell your mom a secret first, something that I wouldn't know."

Beth bent down so that Zack could whisper his secret in her ear. Beth looked mad at whatever Zack said, but Zack laughed. Then he went into his room and closed the door. Suddenly, Jose's phone rang.

"Hello? Oh, hi Zack. Long time no talk—yeah, I know. So, what's your secret? Oh, no. I'm not going to repeat that! Your mom will get mad at me!"

"What are you talking about? Who are you talking to?"

"I'm talking to Zack. He told me his secret."

"Yeah? What's his secret?"

"I can't repeat it."

"That's because you don't know it. This is just some joke you're playing on me."

"Okay if you insist, I'll tell his secret. Zack said that you shave your legs because they get hairy like a mama bear!"

Zack came running out of his room laughing. Beth grabbed him and started tickling him.

"I can't believe you told Jose that! You little monster!"

Zack shrieked and laughed more as Beth blew on his belly. Finally Beth stopped tickling him and held him on her lap, hugging him. She looked up at Jose.

"Oh I get it. You told Zack what to tell me ahead of time. I'm not stupid you know!"

"No, that's not it. The cell phone company has a new program. I can add an additional line for $10 a month. The phone comes with a rebate, so it ends up being free. Merry Christmas!"

"Oh Jose, I can't accept that."

"Please, it's for me. It's hard not being able to call you. Next semester it's going to be worse. We'll have the intern programs and might not get accepted into the same place. I won't be able to see you everyday like I do now. It only costs me $10 a month, that's not much. It's worth it to be able to call you and talk to you whenever I want. Besides, it will be safer. If your car breaks down, or anything, you can call for help."

"I can do that now on my phone that dials 911."

"Yeah, but with this you can call anyone. You can call me, your friends, or anyone from anywhere."

"Okay, okay, thank you."

"So, you'll accept it? Even though you said before that you wouldn't?"

"Yeah, I'll accept it."

Since the incident with the TV the week before, Beth felt as if she understood Jose in a different way. She saw his need to give to her as a form of proving his worth. Now that they had come together completely last night, she felt that she was open to him and did not have to be defensive about accepting gifts. She lifted Zack off her lap and went to Jose so that she could hug him and give him a kiss.

"Hey Zack, can you give the phone to your mom? I want to show her how it works."

"Sure."

Zack went into his room, returned with the phone, and handed it to Jose.

"See, you press this to make calls . . . I wrote your phone number on this little sticker so that you don't forget it . . . . . . Here is where you program your ring tone . . . This is the address book, see . . . . . . I already programmed my number into it so you just have to press this whenever you want to call me."

Beth sat silently as Jose showed her all of the options on the phone. She could feel tears welling up in her eyes. Not because she had a phone, although that was great, but because of how much Jose cared about her, loved her. How considerate and thoughtful he was. How he took care of her and kept her safe. Having a phone was secondary. It was something she had previously taken for granted and missed tremendously. She would be able to call Lisa, Stacey, and Gayle whenever she wanted. She thought about the folded piece of paper in her wallet with Sheila's phone number on it. Was she ready to call Sheila? She was still hurt that she had to find out about her leaving the hospital and having a boyfriend from Rosie. She also knew that Sheila could not call her and had given Lisa her phone number for Beth. Perhaps she would call Sheila after Christmas.

"Are you listening to me?"

"Yeah. I'm sorry, I was just thinking."

"Okay. Well, let me show you how to do this again . . ."

Beth knew she had to hurry to get ready for the wedding, but she did not want to interrupt Jose. He seemed so happy and proud. She tried to pay attention as he showed her how to get her voice mail, program phone numbers and all of the other features the phone offered. Eventually Jose was convinced that Beth knew how to use the phone and she was able to get ready for the wedding. The green velvet dress fit her perfectly, clinging to her body in all the right places. Her neck and chest were pale under the round dark green collar portraying simplicity and elegance. She wished her hair were longer so that she could wear it up in a French bun like she used to. Instead she blew dried and applied gel so that it spiked up on top and in front, and the sides went behind her ears. She carefully applied dark make-up to add color to her pale face. She let her pale complexion work to her advantage offsetting the deep green of her dress, her dark auburn hair, and her dark eye make up and lipstick. She looked in the mirror and actually liked what she saw. She pulled on her nylons and slipped into the green shoes. She felt ready and entered the living room. Both Jose and Zack looked up and stared in silence with big smiles on their faces.

"Well, why don't you geeks talk? What are you staring at?"

"Mommy, you look beautiful!"

Zack ran over and gave Beth a huge hug. Jose walked over to her, taking her hand in his.

"I feel like I'm taking a princess to a ball. What an honor this is!"

"Will you two stop it? You act like you never saw a woman in a dress before!"

"Well, I never saw a woman as beautiful as you. The brides are supposed to get all the attention at their wedding, no one is going to even notice them when they see you!"

"Yeah right, let's go."

Although Beth acted annoyed and indifferent, she was overjoyed that Jose thought she looked beautiful. She faintly heard Jeff's voice telling her how disgusting she was and that she did not deserve to be loved. She was able to block Jeff's voice out of her mind and instead focus on the way that Jose was looking at her. It made her feel sexy. It made her smile secretly and think, "Fuck you, Jeff. You're an asshole."

When they got to Jose's car there was a present in the back seat wrapped in silver paper.

"Hey Jose, what's that present for?"

"What do you think it's for? We're going to a wedding aren't we? We need a gift."

Beth was angry that she could not afford a present, and worried that her offer to baby sit Mia was insignificant.

"Jose, why did you do that? Will you stop buying things? I don't need your charity!"

"Beth, it's not even for you! It's for Stacey and Gail, from both of us."

"I already got them a present!"

"Yeah, well I didn't. I wanted to get them something. Why can't you let me have the satisfaction of giving them a present on their wedding day? If you don't want it to be from you then it will just be from me."

"What is it anyway?"

"It's just a crystal vase. I figured that's a pretty generic wedding gift."

"That's a nice wedding gift. They'll like it."

Beth gave Jose a forced smile and got in the car while Jose buckled Zack into the back seat. Her eyes were filling with tears that she did not want Jose to see. She thought of her wedding gifts, vases, dishes and the pretty things she left behind. She used to set the table with fancy china, silver, and crystal and put fresh flowers in Lenox vases. She had soft towels without holes, warm blankets, and fluffy comforters. Sheer lace curtains hung in the windows of her big, un-perfect house. She made sure that Jose was not looking when she carefully dabbed the corners of her eyes so she would not smear her makeup. She looked out the window, away from him while he drove to the wedding. She remembered going to weddings with Jeff and feeling like he wished that he could leave her at home. He probably would have if people had not expected her to come. No matter how nice her clothes, jewelry, and shoes were, she never looked right. Jeff made her feel that people would stare and make fun of her, that she would not fit in. Now she was sitting next to Jose who made her feel loved, and she was crying because he bought a wedding gift. They drove to the wedding in silence.

When they got to the church, Jose unbuckled Zack and got the present from the back seat. Zack reached up and held Jose's free hand before Beth had a chance to take it. She took Zack's other hand and the three of them walked together into the church, feeling quite like a family. However, not like the old family with Jeff where it looked perfect from afar as long as you did not get close enough to feel the tension. Beth went to look for Stacey and Gayle while Zack and Jose waited in the sanctuary. The entire church was festive and alive with the greens, berries, and dried fruit. The sunlight coming through the stained glass windows gave everything a magical tint. Gayle was in the main hall walking around the tables to make sure everything was in place. Stacey was in the kitchen basting the turkey and preparing the food. There were trays of sweet bread twisted into braids and baked to perfection; dishes of fruit cup were lined up on trays and covered with saran wrap; bowls of dried fruit and nuts were on the counter waiting to be put on the tables.

"Do you want me to put these out on the tables?"

"Oh, when did you get here?"

"We just got here. Jose and Zack are in the sanctuary."

"You look absolutely beautiful!" Stacey came over and gave Beth a hug and a kiss. "Today would never have happened if it wasn't for you."

"That's not true."

"Yes it is, and you know it."

"Okay, okay. But what about these bowls of fruit and nuts? Do you want me to put them on the table?"

"Sure, that would be great."

After Beth put out the bowls she lit the candles in the sanctuary. All the finishing touches were complete and they waited for the guests in the church office. Zack waited with them, Mia tried to lift herself up by holding onto the chairs. Jose sat in the sanctuary alone. Gayle and Stacey were dressed in complementing cranberry velvet and white lace dresses made out of the same materials but with different styles. They reminded Beth of a set of twins whose mother could not decide between two similar dresses, so she bought one for each of them. They each had a bouquet of orange and red flowers with evergreens, ivy, and berries. Mia was wearing a dress made of the same cranberry velvet.

"I know that a bride and groom aren't supposed to see each other before the wedding, but is it okay for two brides to see each other?" Beth asked.

"It better be or else we're in trouble!"

Gayle saved the mood, "I heard that if it is two brides then it is double good luck for them to see each other before the wedding."

"Thank God! Otherwise would we be destined for a shitty life full of misery?"

"How could there be any misery in the life that we're going to share together?"

"There's misery everywhere."

"How can you say that? Do you really think . . ."

Reverend Josh came in, cutting Gayle off.

"Okay, it's time to start. I'm going to enter now and you follow."

They all went to the back of the church and lined up, waiting for their turn to enter while the fiddle music played. Reverend Josh waited until the end of the song before entering and walking to the front of the church. There was a moment of silence before the fiddle music started again, this time joined by the flute and keyboard. Beth slowly walked down the aisle holding Mia and a bouquet of flowers; Zack followed with a pillow and the box with the rings on it; then Stacey and Gayle followed together holding hands. They all stood on the altar. Jose sat in front looking cute, smiling at Beth as if there was never an argument. Despite her attempts to be serious, she could not help but to smile back and would have laughed if Reverend Josh, did not distract her by starting his sermon

"Today is a special day for many reasons. For over thirty thousand years this day has been celebrated as the winter solstice. It's the shortest day of the year, which in turn leads to the return of the sun, longer days, spring, and new beginnings. Historically this time was filled with magic and hope for the coming harvest. The evergreens and holly were believed to have a magical life force since they are alive in the middle of winter when everything else is dead. As such, they were cherished and seen as a protector against negative forces. Today, we are surrounded by evergreens and holly to protect Stacey and Gayle as they start their life together. They are gathered under the mistletoe, which protects against illness and evil events, and brings the promise of love, marriage, and fertility. We have this evergreen tree, which is now widely known as a Christmas tree, decorated with dried fruits and nuts, which symbolize the return of summer's bounty. We have a wreath of holly and ivy, the wreath symbolizing the completion of a year and the start of a new cycle, the holly, and ivy representing the female and male protective elements. In the next room a Yule log burns, the fire representing the coming of heat and light.

"Stacey and Gayle chose this sacred day to create a union using all of these symbols as a representation of their life together. Out of the darkness, they are entering a life of enlightenment. They are beginning a new cycle not only in their lives, but in our society. Our society is leaving the old way of darkness through closed mindedness, and entering into a new cycle of enlightenment through acceptance. Despite the coldness and ignorance of prejudices and hate, a new era and life is emerging where people are allowed to love who they want, even if they are the same sex. Our ancestors had to overcome the threat of death from starvation, darkness, and cold; but were able to plant and sow seeds that were nourished with water and sun to provide a bountiful harvest, which allowed them to thrive. Stacey and Gayle will have different hardships than our ancestors, as their union will not be accepted by some. May they sow a different harvest nourished by love and support so that a new generation will thrive. As this sacred day brings the hope of renewed life through the coming of the light, spring and harvest; let this day be the beginning of a sacred life together for Gayle, Stacey and their child Mia.

"I bless this family as it starts a new life together. The fields of our ancestors needed a balance of rain and sun to nourish it and help it to thrive. In order for plants to produce a healthy harvest, they need attention and pruning to provide space and direction. So it is with this family. It will experience times of rain or sorrow and times of sunshine or happiness. It will need attention, yet each person will require her own personal space and guidance to have direction. Given this balance, may this marriage and family thrive in love."

After the service everyone went into the giant hall to eat the food and dance. This was the first time that Beth had been out having fun in many years. Zack ran around the room getting attention from everyone, being completely at home in this community. Beth was amazed at what an incredible dancer Jose was, bringing the passion of the night before onto the dance floor. She felt as if he was making love to her in front of all of these people without even touching her. For Beth this celebration represented the new beginnings that were manifesting in her life. She was now completely in her new life instead of trying to start it. She had friends, people who loved her, her own apartment and had just completed the most difficult semester of the nurses program. She felt complete.

Chapter 16

Beth arranged to meet Lisa at the Crisis Center on Monday morning to pick up the Christmas gifts, since there was no support group on Tuesday because of Christmas. Maria was working so Jose watched Zack. Even though Beth loved and trusted Jose, she felt nervous leaving Zack alone with him. She could not completely overcome her fear of men. She thought about her life and the absence of men in it, and knew it was good for Zack to spend time alone with Jose. She did not want the absence of a father to negatively affect Zack.

There was a very high energy as Beth walked down the hall to the Crisis Center waiting room. Everyone was laughing and seemed happy. No one noticed when she entered. She startled the woman behind the main desk when she asked if Lisa was there.

"Oh, hi Beth! Merry Christmas!"

"Merry Christmas. Is Lisa here?"

That was the first time this season that Beth had wished anyone a 'Merry Christmas'. At school everyone wished each other a nice 'break' and in the stores every one said 'Happy Holidays'. It made Beth feel happy inside to wish a 'Merry Christmas'.

"I think she stepped out for a minute. I know she's expecting you, so she should be back soon. Why don't you have a seat and wait?"

Beth sat in the rocking chair and watched everyone. What was usually an atmosphere filled with desperation and struggle, there was instead laughter and happiness. The spirit of Christmas was full and alive in this establishment. After about twenty minutes Lisa came through the front door.

"Oh Beth, you're here! Have you been waiting long?"

"No. I just got here. Merry Christmas!"

"Merry Christmas! You seem very relaxed. It's good to see you like this."

"Oh, it must be not having to worry about homework and exams. It's been nice just having fun and relaxing. I tried to sleep in today, but Zack was jumping on my bed to give me a 7:30 A.M. wake up call!"

"Yeah, well kids don't seem to understand the concept of sleeping in late. Just wait until he is a teenager, you won't be able to get him up!"

"Please, don't rush it. I love him as my little boy!"

"Yes, and little boys need Christmas presents from Santa. So, let's get some of Santa's helpers to help make Christmas for that little boy."

"We don't need any help. You and I can carry it out."

"No, we need help. Hey, Pam and Michelle! Can you help us bring Beth's stuff out to her car?"

"Sure," they both answered and started walking down the hall to one of the back rooms. Beth and Lisa followed them into a room where there were piles of trash bags with big name labels on them. There were four large trash bags with Beth's name on them.

"Okay, why don't we each take a bag?"

"Wait, there has to be a mistake, these can't all be for me. There's way too much stuff."

"Yeah, they're for you. There's stuff for you and Zack."

"For me too? I thought you were only getting stuff for Zack. I don't need anything."

"Everyone needs something at Christmas. Here, take this bag."

Beth took the bag and carried it out of the building, followed by Lisa and the other two women.

"There, that should give you and Zack a nice Christmas. Tell Zack that Santa said to be a good boy."

Beth grabbed Lisa and hugged her tight, trying not to cry.

"Thank you," she barely whispered into Lisa's ear.

"You're welcome. You deserve it. You're working really hard to get your life in order and deserve a little help from Santa Claus."

When Beth was alone in her car she let herself wail as loud as she could. She cried hysterically in the comfort of knowing that the car silenced her to the world. She cried not because she was sad, but because she was moved by Christmas. She felt first hand what the cliché's and Hallmark commercials capitalized on. To the majority of the population the hype about peace on earth and brotherly love was just a ploy to build up the holiday and create more sales. But today, Beth was a recipient of the goodness that humanity had to offer. She felt the magic and understood the message in 'A Miracle on 52nd Street' and the fact that there really is a Santa Clause. On the commercial level Santa is a fat man in a red suit riding in a sleigh pulled by nine reindeer on Christmas Eve bringing toys to children. That image representation puts Santa into a physical form making him easy to imagine. In reality, everyone who smiles at a stranger, wishes good will, spreads happiness by giving, or creates a festive atmosphere is Santa Claus. Santa Claus is a symbol that represents Saint Nicholas who gave to mankind. It is no coincidence that Christmas coincides with Jesus' birth, who also gave to mankind. Christmas represents the coming of light through the birth of a savior, which coexists with the coming of light through the winter solstice. It is not surprising that so many other great world religions also have major holidays with the same message this time of year.

Instead of experiencing Christmas as a season of stress at not being able to create the illusion of perfection, Beth felt the joy that is the cliché of Christmas. She had a pile of wrapped Christmas presents in the back seat and had no idea what was in them, nor did it matter. What did matter was that there would be a little boy on Christmas morning who would wake up to find that Santa Claus had come to his house. There would be a little boy who did not have to learn the hard way that Santa only comes to certain houses and that his was not one of them. There would be a little boy who brought joy into the world by being connected to all of the strangers who were Santa Claus to this house on Christmas this year. Did these Santa Clauses realize when they dropped a new toy into the box of presents for underprivileged children that they were actually being Santa Claus to their friends, neighbors, and coworkers? That even though their image of who the gift was going to may be someone far away and removed from them, it could actually be the child in the apartment above them, in the same class as their child in school or in the pew next to them in church?

Beth finally stopped crying and drove home in a daze. She felt as if everything was surreal as she drove past the decorations and people. She felt as if she was carrying a huge secret that for the first time in her life she actually understood what Christmas meant.

Beth and Zack went to Christmas Eve service with Stacey, Gayle, and Mia. Beth asked Jose to come, but he had promised his family that he would go to church with them. They went to the 4:30 children's service. It was jam packed with families, most of whom Beth had never seen before. Gayle laughed at the crowd.

"It is amazing how many people show up at church for Christmas and Easter, but are no where to be found the rest of the year."

They all laughed. Unfortunately they were not early enough to get a front pew, so had to sit towards the back where it was difficult to see. The service was designed to have audience participation for everyone who wanted to be part of the life size nativity scene. The story of Christmas was told while audience volunteers dressed and acted out the parts of the stars, animals, shepherds, angels, wise men and of course the holy family. Volunteers were called for each character to go in the back room and get on a costume. Zack almost jumped out of his seat when volunteers for the sheep were called and although there were many volunteers sitting closer, Reverend Josh spotted Zack and called him to be one of the sheep. Zack ran into the back room to put on the fuzzy white sheep costume and hat. Mia had the great honor of being the infamous baby Jesus.

After the service, the five of them went to Stacey and Gayle's apartment for dinner and to sing Christmas carols. It was a very relaxing evening and Beth felt the power and holiness of the holiday in a new way. This was the best Christmas that she ever had. She could not remember feeling such happiness and peace. Zack was sitting silently on the couch with a huge grin on his face and Beth knew that he felt the same way. She wondered what Jeff and Nancy were doing tonight. She wondered if Nancy was living with Jeff, if they were going to church or a party, if they were fighting or happy. Beth and Zack left early so that they would be sleeping when Santa came. Zack had no complaints about going straight to bed.

An ungodly screech jolted Beth awake. It was dark out and she was unsure if she had dreamt the scream. Her bedroom door suddenly swung open and Zack jumped onto her bed. That was it, something happened to Zack. She grabbed him and hugged him tight.

"It's okay, mommy's here. What happened? Are you okay?"

"Santa came!"

"Is that it? Is that why you screamed? Because Santa came?"

"Yeah, but you wouldn't believe it! There are piles of presents all around the tree. And stockings too, and candy canes!"

"That's great Zack, but it is still night. Santa wants us to stay asleep until the sun comes up."

"But that won't be for a long, long time!"

"Good, because mommy still needs a lot of sleep. Why don't you go back to bed until the sun wakes up?"

"I can't sleep."

"Okay, then just hug mommy and rest your eyes until the sun wakes up."

"Okay."

Opening the presents on Christmas morning was as much of a surprise for Beth as it was for Zack. All of the presents had already been wrapped and labeled by the Crisis Center, so all Beth had to do was place them under the tree. It did not take long for Zack to recognize his name on the labels. He quickly opened the presents to himself and then waited patiently while he watched Beth open hers. There was even a present for Zack's Christmas Bear, Monty. It was a book about a bear who wanted a boy for Christmas.

Zack looked at all of his gifts, not knowing what to play with first. There was a fire truck, little cars, art supplies, a nerf football, some picture books, new clothes and pajamas. Zack's favorite toy was a large pirate ship with pirate action figures, a parrot, and a treasure chest with real treasure. Beth's presents were a pair of jeans, two sweaters, pajamas, socks, a gift basket with bath supplies and a gold chain with a small gold angel on it. They each received a Christmas stocking filled with candy, small toys for Zack, and a brush and some perfume for Beth. Beth made mini-bagels and cream cheese for breakfast so that they could play with the pirate ship while they ate.

Jose broke their silent play by banging on the door, then stomping into the apartment carrying a huge wrapped box. The TV.

"Ho, ho, ho! Look what Santa brought to my house by accident! Wow! It looks like he came here too!"

"Yeah, Jose. Look at what Santa brought us! He brought a whole bunch of stuff because he knows that we were really good this year!"

Beth gave Zack a huge hug and kiss.

"Yeah Zackey, you sure were good this year. You're a really good boy."

"Let's open the present. Is it to all of us?"

"No, it's to you and your mommy. Santa asked me if I could bring it to you since it was getting heavy in his sleigh and he came to my house first."

"Oh boy! Let's open it!"

Zack ripped all of the paper off the box and started to jump up and down when he saw the TV.

"Look Mommy, it's our very own TV!"

"I have a few presents in the car from me to you guys. I'll be right back."

When Jose left the apartment Zack looked at Beth and asked, "What did we get Jose for Christmas Mommy?"

"Nothing Zack. I'm sorry. I forgot to get him something."

Beth thought of all the gifts Jose had given them and she suddenly felt like shit. The Halloween stuff, the wedding present, the phone, TV, and videos. How could she have forgotten to get him something? She suddenly did not want him to come back up the stairs. She just wanted to disappear. The yucky feeling in her stomach that had been gone for the past few days came back.

"I have a present for him. We made a special craft in school to give to someone that we love. I made mine for Jose."

Beth felt hurt and grateful at the same time. Why had he not made it for her?

"That's really special Zack. That will make Jose really happy."

"Yeah I know. Can we take the TV out of the box?"

"Yeah."

Beth ripped open the box and pulled out the styrofoam cube containing the TV.

"Where should we put it?"

"We have to put it across from the couch."

"We don't have a table."

"How about a chair?"

Beth took one of the kitchen chairs and placed it against the wall across from the couch. She plugged it in and turned it on, but none of the stations came in. They did not have cable. Zack's big eyes looked up at her without saying anything. Beth thought of the videos that Jose was getting out of the car.

"Look Zack, it plays videos. I bet we can get some out of the library."

"Okay."

Zack was obviously disappointed. He did not mention the fact that he would not be able to watch the TV shows that he usually watched at Maria's apartment. He was almost three and he was already accepting the hardships of life. If the deprivation of cable TV could be considered a hardship.

Jose came back carrying a pile of gifts. His smile faded when he saw the disappointed expressions on Beth and Zack's faces.

"What's going on in here? It's Christmas, you're supposed to be happy!"

Beth forced a smile.

"We are. It's just been a long day."

"It's not even ten in the morning yet."

"Yeah, well . . . nothing."

"Okay, let's just leave whatever's going on alone and change gears. I have some presents for you. Do you want to open them?"

Zack bounced back to his old self.

"Jose, I have a present for you! I want you to open my present first."

Zack ran into his room. The pang of hurt returned to Beth. Zack had not made her anything. She was being a complete ass whole for thinking like this and she knew it. She forced a smile and watched as Zack handed Jose a sloppily wrapped gift. Jose's dimples showed as he slowly unwrapped the present. Under the wrapping paper were layers of tissue paper, which eventually revealed a glass jar covered with little squares of colored tissue paper and a small picture of Zack. Beth thought of Zack's little hands dipping the pieces of tissue paper in glue and pressing them onto the glass jar and started to cry. She did not know why she cried, she just did. Both Zack and Jose looked at her, not knowing what to do.

"It's okay Mommy. Don't cry. I have something for you too."

She was not crying because Zack gave Jose the jar. She was crying because the jar was so beautiful and because she loved Zack so much. She did not understand the emotions that were coming out of her. She did not want Zack to think it was his fault she was crying. Jose was looking at her very confused. She wanted to say something to make him understand.

"I don't know why I'm crying. You must think I'm nuts because I cry all the time. This is my first Christmas on my own and it seems so *real*. Do you know what I mean? I used to work so hard on the holidays to make things the way they 'are supposed to be'. But now, I don't have to. Zack's present that he made at school is the best present here. I'm so happy. I don't know why I'm crying. It's like the happy emotions are too much for my body to hold so they're coming out through tears. I'm not making any sense am I?"

"I understand. You don't have to explain."

Jose put his arm around Beth and wiped her tears off her cheek with his other hand. Zack came running out of his room holding a little box wrapped in sparkly paper with a ribbon wrapped around it that had a large tag tied on it. He held it out to Beth.

"This is for you mommy."

Beth took the box and read the poem that was typed on the tag:

LOVE

This is a special gift
That you will never see.
The reason it's so special is
It's just for you from me.

Whenever you are lonely
Or even feeing blue,
You only have to hold this gift
And Know I think of you.

You never should unwrap it;
Please, leave the ribbon tied.
Just hold this box
Close to your heart:
It's filled with love inside.

Beth held the box close to her heart like the poem told her to do. She then pulled Zack close to her chest so that the box was squished between the two of them. She hugged him tight, kissed his head, and whispered in his ear.

"Thank you Zack. This is the best present I ever got in my whole life. I'll keep it forever and ever."

Zack squirmed away from her and ran back to the pirate ship. His energy level and lack of attention span were that of the majority of children on Christmas morning. He seemed satisfied that he gave Jose and Beth each something special. She was amazed that her little baby was very quickly becoming a wise child.

"Hey Beth."

"Yeah?"

"Why did you and Zack seem upset when I came in from getting the presents?"

"It was nothing."

"I want to know."

"There's no cable."

"Is that all?" Jose smiled widely, showing his dimples. "I can take care of that. Is there a cable cord anywhere in here?"

"Yeah, there's one on the wall behind the TV."

Jose found the cord and plugged it into the TV.

"It fits perfect."

"Yeah, but you need to subscribe to make it work."

"There are people in the building that subscribe. I bet the wire is active."

"No, you can't do that! It's stealing!"

"It's on anyway. It doesn't cost the company anything. How's that stealing?"

"All right, turn on the TV. If it works then I guess it's okay since it was there anyway."

"Wow Beth! Listen to you, what a rebel!"

Zack left his pirate ship to turn on the TV. There was a clear picture on the screen.

"We have TV!" Zack jumped up and down.

"Yeah, but there's no box. So it's limited on what stations you have. You can play movies on it too. See?"

Jose showed Zack how to play the movies. Beth took a shower and got ready so that they could go to Jose's family's house. She wore the velvet dress that she wore to the wedding. She was grateful that she had it since she wanted to look respectable to meet Jose's family. She was terrified that they would not like her since she was not Dominican. She looked in the mirror and as elegant as she looked, she felt that it would make her stand out too much. She went back into her room and changed into a skirt and sweater so that she would feel less self-conscious. She came out of her room.

"All right you guys, you ready to go?"

Both Zack and Jose looked up at Beth. Jose started to say something, but stopped himself. Zack spoke right up.

"But Mommy, why are you wearing that ugly skirt? Why did you take off the beautiful dress? The princess dress?"

"I figured that dress would be too fancy."

"But *I'm dressed fancy. You* should too. *It's not fair!*"

Zack stamped his foot down and scrunched up his face into a scowl. His nose was all wrinkly and his bottom lip pouted out. He was wearing the dress shirt, sweater vest and little kaki pants that he got for Christmas from 'Santa'. Despite his scowl he looked very handsome, very *fancy*. It made Beth feel like a hypocrite for having changed.

"You're right. I'll go change."

Zack smiled satisfied. Beth had just unintentionally reinforced the idea that having a tantrum would result in getting his own way. Jose sat silently on the sofa watching the entire scene. He also had a smug smile on his face and seemed to approve when Beth came back into the room wearing the dress. If it had been in her past life, she would have felt ashamed and degraded that she was forced to go and change. But in that life she would have changed because there was something wrong with what she was changing out of. In this life, she changed because there was something better that she was changing into. She felt happy that both Zack and Jose were impressed with the way she looked.

Jose pulled the car up in front of a large three family gray house. There were cars lined up in the driveway and down the street. Beth was honored that Jose invited her and Zack to his family's house for Christmas. It demonstrated to her that he was committed to her and thought seriously enough of their relationship to bring her home to meet his family. It scared her that the day he chose for her to meet his family was the most significant family day of the year. If she had met them on an ordinary day there could be questionable speculation about exactly what their relationship was. But for her to come to Christmas dinner stated that they were a couple and his family would judge her as such. Her first impression would have to be outstanding in order to be accepted. Beth thought that Jose was getting off easy as she had no one for him to meet and be approved by, and then she remembered Zack.

Beth held Zack's little hand as they walked up the steps to the front door. Jose had one arm around Beth's waist with his hand on her hip. He opened the door with his other hand and a gush of warmth, sounds, and aromas escaped, engulfing Beth's senses in a new sensation of experiencing Jose's culture. The music was a fast beat with drumming and Spanish singing. Her body automatically started to relax and sway to the rhythm of the music. She now understood why Jose's body seemed to constantly move and be part of his surroundings instead of being stiff like hers was. Looking around the room at the genuine smiles, Beth automatically felt accepted and her self-conscious nervousness about being here ceased. Jose's familiar smile that stood out elsewhere was at home here, where everyone possessed the same sincere openness. There was none of the awkwardness or stiffness that she usually felt when going to a new place where she did not know anyone. The aroma of spices and food cooking aroused Beth. They were not the traditional Christmas smells of Turkey and mashed potato, but more exotic smells that made her feel alive.

"It smells amazing in here. What's cooking?"

"All sorts of great stuff. Have you ever had Dominican food?"

"No."

"Well then, you're in for a treat."

A large woman came over and gave Jose a hug and kiss. She then hugged and kissed Beth.

"Welcome to our home! We're so happy to have you!"

"Thank you!"

"Beth, this is my mama Diana. Mama, meet Beth and her babe Zack."

Zack was hugging Beth's leg.

"Hello Zack. My grand babe will be happy to have another child to play with. His name is Babe Miguel. He's about your age. Let me go find him."

Jose led Beth into the room and introduced everyone. Beth hoped she would remember their names. Jose had already told her about everyone so she felt familiar with each person as she was introduced. Beth felt very conservative in comparison to these beautiful women who seemed so confident and sure of themselves. His younger sister Adia was sitting on her husband Miguel's lap. The two of them were so engrossed in each other that Beth was not sure they even knew anyone else was in the room. Beth felt pale and plain in comparison to Adia's dark olive skin and beautiful long, thick, curly black hair. There was a definite family resemblance between her and Jose. Miguel was in the service and had not seen Adia or their son since the day after Babe Miguel was born over three years ago. Adia was induced so that she would have the baby before Miguel was deployed to Iraq. Miguel was now home for Christmas week and then would be deployed back to Iraq for an unknown period of time. Babe Miguel was afraid of his father and would not come near him, but Miguel was so engrossed in Adia that he did not seem to mind his son's absence.

Jose introduced Beth to his younger brother Rofeal, Rofeal's girlfriend Daniela, best friend Pedro, and Pedro's sister Natalie. No one paid attention to the fact that Pedro would not stop staring at Adia and Miguel. Everyone in the room except for Miguel knew that Pedro and Adia were together while Miguel was gone. Now Pedro had to sit in the same room holding in his rage and jealousy as Adia and Miguel made love to each other with their eyes, unable to keep their hands off each other. As Jose explained it to Beth, Adia and Miguel had been in love since they were kids. When they were in high school Adia got pregnant, so they married. Miguel joined the Army since he saw no other way to support his new family.

When Miguel was away in the army, Adia was lonely and heart broken that he was gone. Suddenly she was home alone all day with a new baby and no husband. She cried everyday, convinced that Miguel would never come home and that she would not see him again. She was so sure that Miguel would be killed that she would not answer the phone and kept the lights off so that the military would think she was not home and would not knock on the door to give her the news that Miguel was dead. No one knew what to do to help her. That was the same time that Pedro started coming over the house more and more to hang out with Rofeal, but it soon became obvious that he was there to see Adia. Adia was scared and desperate, but Pedro was there to hold her and tell her everything was going to be okay. They soon became a couple. Despite how wrong Jose's family felt about Adia being with Pedro, they accepted it since it helped Adia to cope. They were relieved to see her emerging from her depression and getting back to herself. It was understood that Miguel would never know about this arrangement and that Pedro would stay away from Adia when Miguel came home. Although Jose said Pedro had no problem with this, Beth could tell that he was having some major difficulties with it now. He was sitting in the corner chair drinking a mixed drink like it was water. Beth could tell by his blood shot eyes that he had probably had quite a few already. She hoped he would be able to keep his part of the bargain.

Sitting around the kitchen table were Jose's mother's boyfriend Julio, Jose's grandmother Monica, and Monica's boyfriend Andi. They were talking to each other fast in Spanish and Beth had no idea what they were saying. She could not help noticing that they kept glancing up at her while they were talking. She wondered what there was to say about her that could take up so many words. They looked over at her and laughed again, but it was a happy laugh rather than the mocking laugh of someone who is making fun of you. Beth smiled back at them.

Jose led Beth into the kitchen where there were trays and pots filled with delicious smelling food.

"Hey Beth, have a yaniqueques."

Jose took a fried tortilla and put it into her mouth.

"Mmmm, it's good. What's that?"

There was a tray of cheese-filled pastries and avocado stuffed breads.

"Oh, these are really good. They are *bollitos de yucca* and *pan con aguacate*. You never had them before? Try them."

Everything was amazing. Beth was so used to eating quick or processed food, she was tempted to eat the entire plate of these delicious pastries and breads that obviously took hours to make. Her taste buds exploded with the flavors. Beth chewed very slowly so that the taste would last longer.

"Don't fill up yet, we still have the real food coming out! Do you want a drink? How about a glass of wine?"

"Sure. Thanks."

They went back into the living room with the young people. Rafeal was asking Miguel to tell them about what it was like in Iraq. Was it genuine interest, or an attempt to distract Miguel from Adia so that Pedro would not loose control? Adia was still sitting on Miguel's lap, hugging him. But at least Miguel was entertaining the group with his stories. Everyone seemed interested in what Miguel was saying except for Pedro who was staring at him with hate. If Miguel noticed, he did not show it.

As a child, Beth's uncle was always telling stories about when he was in World War II. Like her uncle, Beth was expecting Miguel to brag about his war stories of narrow escapes from death. Instead Miguel told how difficult and lonely war was. It made Beth feel sad listening to him. She was used to hearing the news stories about Iraq and the numbers of troops who were being shipped or died, but here was a first hand account of one of those troops telling about how much he missed home and family. Pedro shifted his gaze into his half-empty glass. Adia had her eyes closed with her head on Miguel's shoulder. Beth wondered what the two of them were thinking as Miguel told of his confusion about being in a place when he did not understand why he was there. He told about the conflicts he felt knowing that he had no right to be there, yet his desire to help the people. He told about the scared children who reminded him of his own little boy and how he gave them the candy and gifts that people from home sent him. In doing that he felt closer to his own son. He told about how he held pictures of Adia and Babe Miguel close to his chest when he tried to sleep at night. His comfort was picturing his family safe at home while he listened to the random bombs, judging by the vibrations how close they were to him. He told about the land mines that his troops would try to find and blow up so that innocent people would not get killed walking through them. It was a never-ending job as no matter how many bombs they set off, there were more buried when they woke up the next day. And then there were the car bombs. He did not want to talk about those as they meant sure death to many.

Finally he told of the journey home, how it was a surreal daze as he traveled from camps to airports via helicopter. Even when he was on the plane coming back to the States it felt like a dream, like he was not really going home and he was not really going to see his family. The first time he set foot back on U.S. soil (so to speak) was in the Dallas, TX airport. When he and his comrades walked up the ramp towards the door into the terminal he could hear clapping and cheering. He did not know what all of the commotion was, he thought maybe people were watching a sports event on TV. It was not until he entered the terminal and saw the people lined up that he realized they were clapping and cheering for him and his comrades, welcoming them home. It was then that he cried and knew that he was home.

Beth hugged Zack close. Everyone was silent and even Pedro temporarily lost the look of hate in his eyes. Despite the warmth of the room, Zack would not leave Beth. Babe Miguel was in the kitchen clinging to his grandmother. Both little boys were being very shy and holding onto what was familiar to them while surrounded by new experiences. Zack was introduced to a new culture and a room full of strangers. Miguel was introduced to his father.

Jose's mother, Diana, came into the living room to let everyone know that it was time to eat.

"Hey, it's Christmas, you should be happy. You're all young. You should be having fun! Come eat, celebrate!"

It was a relief to have the mood broken. Everyone followed Diana, shuffling into the dining room. Daniela and Natalie went into the kitchen to help bring out the food. Beth and Zack sat in the two seats next to Jose. Plates of food kept coming out until there was no more room on the table. Jose pointed to each dish and told Beth what it was. There was a soup like dish of beans and pork sausages (*habichuelas blancas y longaniza*), ripe plantains casserole (*pastelon de platanos amarillos*), boiled flour rolls (*bollitos de harira*), a large salad, rice and black beans (*moro de habichuelas*), stewed tripe (*mondongo*), marinated steak with fried onions (*bestec encebollado*), and fried chicken (*chicharron de pollo*). Everything looked and smelled amazing. Beth did not know what she wanted to try first. She decided to take a small taste of everything and then take larger portions of what she liked the best. Even that did not seem to work as she wanted more of everything. Luckily everyone sat around the table talking for a long time, giving her plenty of opportunity to continue adding food to her plate.

Everyone was enjoying the food and the conversation. Beth was used to much more formal Christmas dinners, but she liked the casualness and warmth of this one. She liked the fact that everyone was smiling, laughing, and talking at once. She did not understand most of what people were saying as the conversations were split between Spanish and English, but it did not matter. The atmosphere was happy, laid back and relaxing. It gave her a comfortable safe feeling, like this is what life was supposed to be about. A family and their friends laughing and eating together on Christmas day.

When everyone was done eating, Daniela, Natalie, Adia, and Diana cleared the table. Beth felt like she should be helping them, but Jose motioned for her to stay sitting. The women then served everyone coffee (*un cafecito*) and brought out dessert plates, forks and large trays with cakes on them. There was rich white three milk cake (*tres leches*), a special Dominican white cake with pineapple filling (*Bizcocho Dominicano*), and some sweet pastry filled with marmalade (*Empanadita dulces*). Beth ate so much at dinner that she thought she would not be able to have any dessert. However, looking at all of these amazing cakes and pastries she had to try each of them. They were all sweet, moist, and tasty. She could not remember the last time she had so much to eat, as she did not even eat this much at the two Thanksgiving dinners. She could not understand how Jose could be so fit when he was living in a house that had such an abundance of delicious foods. She did not know if she would be able to get up out of her seat any time tonight. Beth wondered if Jose thought that her scant supply of processed foods was pathetic.

Eventually everyone was done eating and slowly moved into the living room where the Christmas tree was. It was a beautifully decorated tree with hundreds of colored lights that reflected off the glass ornaments and generously applied tinsel. Zack had fallen asleep on Beth's lap while she sat contently watching everyone exchange presents. It had been such an exciting day for Zack that he was too exhausted to wonder if he was getting more presents. Unlike the food, the present opening was typical to what Beth was used to. There were gifts of clothes, jewelry, household items, books, calendars, and candles. Beth was caught off guard when Diana handed her a large box wrapped in shinny red paper. Beth could not find a nametag on it.

"Who's this for?"

"It's for you."

Beth was surprised as she had not expected anything and did not bring any gifts. She had an awkward feeling of unbalance since she was unable to reciprocate the giving. She looked desperately at Jose for help. He was smiling, his dimples showing, and nodded his head for her to open the gift. He took Zack off her lap and hugged him. The room was suddenly silent and Beth realized that she was the center of attention; everyone was looking at her with eager eyes. Beth carefully unwrapped the box so that she would not ruin the beautiful paper, then she removed the lid off the white cardboard box and pulled out what seemed like an endless amount of newspaper and tissue paper. Eventually she came to a large object wrapped and taped tight with bubble wrap. She could see bright green through the bubble wrap. Jose handed her a pair of scissors to cut the tape and unwrap the object. Beneath the bubble wrap was a beautiful ceramic doll that looked like it was made on a potter's wheel with details added onto it. She wore a wide rimmed green hat and long dress that had colorful flowers pained on them. The strangest thing about her was that she had no face. Well, she had a face that was painted light brown, but there were no features on it; no eyes, nose, mouth or hair.

Beth looked at Jose confused, "Why doesn't she have a face?"

"She represents the many faces of the Dominican people."

"What do you mean? What are the many faces of the Dominican people?"

"Before the Spanish invaded us in 1492 the Native Hispaniolans, the Tiano Indians, occupied the island. When the Spanish came they killed all male Tiano Indians and took the females for their slaves, thus insuring that all offspring from that point on were conceived by them. There were no more pure blood Tiano Indians, everyone from that point on was a new mix of Tiano and Spanish. To add to the genetic mixing pool, the Spanish started bringing African slaves to the Island in 1503. So the Domincans are one people who are many different colors and faces from a mixture of the Native Tiano Indians, Spanish and Africans. You will see blue, brown or black eyes; blond, brown, black, straight or curly hair; light, medium or dark skin; and many different features. This doll's face is left blank representing that the Domincans are many faces, but one people. We are not prejudiced or judgmental because of the color of your skin or how you look. We accept everyone as one, even if you have red hair, freckles, and green eyes!"

Beth blushed and laughed, knowing he was referring to her.

"Thank you, everyone. This is a wonderful gift."

She meant it too as she was not just receiving a doll, she was receiving acceptance. In giving her this doll Jose's family was accepting her despite the fact that she came from a different nationality and background. There was a time when she was a stranger to herself, a prisoner in her own life. She was increasingly finding herself in places that she wanted to be because she let her heart lead her to happiness. She was finding acceptance and community in places that she previously would have considered out of the norm, and it was wonderful.

Chapter 17

Beth was thoroughly enjoying her week off. She and Zack hung around the apartment relaxing; there were days that she did not even take a shower. Zack was perfectly content to watch movies and play with his new toys, especially his pirate ship. Beth was thinking more and more about the piece of paper that Lisa gave her with Sheila's phone number on it. She thought about acceptance, forgiveness and friendship, and how she missed Sheila enough to forgive her. Would Sheila forgive her if she found out about Jose from Rosie?

Beth got the piece of paper out of her wallet and dialed the number from her cell phone. The phone rang three times before a young girl picked it up. Beth was not expecting someone other than Sheila to answer.

"Hello?"

"Oh, hi. Is . . . um . . . Sheila there?"

"*Moooommmmm . . . telaphone!*"

Beth waited in silence for a while, thinking that she may have been forgotten.

"Hello?"

"Sheila? It's me, Beth."

"Beth? Oh my God! I can't believe it's you. I sound like such a jerk, I'm sorry. It's so good to hear from you! What's going on in your life?"

"I've been busy. I guess this is a time for changes. You know, the transition period between the old and new lives."

"Yeah, I know how that is."

"I have my own apartment and am in the nursing program at the community college. It's a one year condensed program so I don't have much time to do anything but study."

"That must be a lot of work."

"Yeah, well almost nothing else. I met someone in the program."

"Oh?"
"Yeah, he's a guy."
"A guy?"
"His name's Jose."
"Is it serious?"

Was it serious? Beth had never really considered this before. Then she thought about spending Christmas together and the night Jose spent at her apartment.

"Yeah, I would call it serious."
"Is he good to you?"

Beth thought about how patient Jose was when she was having hard times, and how great he was to Zack.

"Yeah, he's really good to me."
"Are you happy?"

Beth did not have to think before answering this question.

"Yeah, I'm really happy."

"That's good. You deserve it. There's a lot of changes in my life too. I met someone also. He was my doctor at the Jericho Rose Hospital."

Beth pretended she did not already know from Rosie about the extent the relationship had progressed to.

"The doctor, huh? See? I knew there was something going on between you two!"

"Yeah, you're always right. It was kind of weird at first because of the whole patient-doctor relationship thing. Even though you saw it, it took a while before we knew what was going on. Rob tried to hold it against me of course, saying that I was using Steve to make myself look good in court. But in reality even though Steve, that's his name, helped me in court, it was to my disadvantage that we were involved. We had to convince the judge that he was speaking in my favor because it was the truth, not because he was involved with me. He stood up for me and made me and the courts realize that I didn't try to commit suicide because I'm crazy, but because of the years of psychological abuse from Rob. Steve helped the courts to see that it's vital for both me and the kids that they stay alone with me regularly and see me for who I am, instead of who Rob convinced them that I am. Steve believes in me, which helps me to believe in myself."

"That's awesome. I'm so happy for you. How's everything going with the kids? Is it working out well with them staying with you?"

"Yeah, they stay here on Wednesday nights and every other weekend. We also go to family therapy together to rebuild our relationship. I know it sounds horrible, but attempting suicide actually helped me."

This was not the direction Beth wanted the conversation to go in.

"Sheila, we've been through this before. Attempting suicide was a horrible thing to do and not an effective way to get help. Please don't ever talk about it as a good thing again. I'm the one who had to walk in on you. Remember? What would have happened if we didn't find you? Your kids would have to go through life without you, knowing that you killed your self. Is that what you want for them?"

"I know. I'm sorry. I didn't mean it. Those were hard times; we all went in such different directions. I think about Monique a lot and how I almost ended up like her."

"Dead."

"Yeah, dead. But I didn't, thanks to you. I'm sorry you had to go through that, I'll never talk about it again."

"It's okay."

"No, it's not okay. Do you still see Stacey?"

"Yeah, I see her on Sundays. She got married last week."

"Oh? Who's the lucky guy?"

"The lucky woman is Gayle, she's really nice. She has a baby daughter named Mia and they're happy together."

"Can you really call that marriage?"

"It's legal in Massachusetts."

"Yeah, well what's legal isn't always what's right. Have you talked to Rosie lately?"

"I saw her at the Crisis Center Halloween party."

"Oh, then you don't know, she's in rehab. She OD'ed and almost didn't make it. Sounds like me, huh? She calls me a lot. I feel really bad for her, she has so much hurt inside of her but pretends it's not there and that everything is happy. But she can't hide from it, so she uses drugs to try to escape."

"It's her own fault. She could stop if she wanted to."

"It's not that easy. How can she stop when she's too afraid to face herself? It's her only place to hide."

"She has her children to think about. Where are they during all of this?"

"Guy's taking care of them. Her kids are the reason she's in rehab, she wants to get straight for them."

"I hope she can do it."

"I hope so too. Anyway, I should get going, the kids are here with me for Christmas vacation week, and I told them I'd bring them to the mall. But I'm really glad you called. Do you have a phone number and I can call you another time? Maybe we can get together or something?"

"Yeah, that would be great."

Beth gave Sheila her phone number, wondering if they would ever arrange to meet.

Beth looked in the cabinet to get something for dinner, and took out a box of pasta and a jar of sauce. The food she prepared always seemed so boring and plain. She thought about the amazing food at Jose's house and about the aromas that escaped from Maria's apartment, filling the entire building with a misty smell of garlic and spices. Thinking of Maria, she had not talked to her lately and wondered how she was doing and how her Christmas was. She decided to ask Maria if she would teach her how to cook the tomato sauce that caused the rest of the building to drool in envy.

Beth knocked and although Maria yelled that she would be right there, it took a long time for her to answer the door. When she finally opened the door, she looked horrible. She was in her bathrobe even though it was evening, her hair was a mess, she had no makeup on, her eyes were red, puffy, and almost swollen shut as if she had been crying.

"Oh my God, you look horrible! What happened? Where's Vickie? Is she okay?"

"Yeah she's okay, she's with Dominic. No one's hurt or anything. It's just that . . ."

Maria started wailing hysterically while they were standing in the hall. Beth hugged Maria until she could get herself slightly under control.

"I'm sorry. It's just that . . ."

Beth cut her off.

"Come into my apartment and tell me about it."

Beth led Maria into the living room. Zack looked up, but did not seem to think much about the two women and went back to his play. Beth brought Maria into the bedroom so they would have more privacy.

"All right, now tell me what's wrong."

"Oh Beth, it's horrible! Dominic is moving back to Italy and he wants to bring Vickie with him! He said that he can't bear to live in the States now that Josephine is dead and wants to go back home to his family. I don't know what to do! My entire life is living on the outside of his life with Vickie. I wouldn't be able to survive if I lost both of them! What would I have to live for?"

More suicide talk, Beth did not know if she was qualified for this. She decided she would have to take a harsh, authoritative approach to the situation.

"Okay Maria, stop this hysteria. First of all, Dominic is not taking Vickie anywhere. Second, we have to work on you getting your life back. You're young and beautiful, there's no reason for you to live in the shadow of someone else's life. Josephine is the one who's dead, not you. Understand?"

Maria looked at Beth in horror, but at least she stopped crying.

"How can you talk like that about my dead sister?"

"Because she's just that—D-E-A-D, *dead*. Get it? You're *alive!* Now start acting it. Face the facts: Dominic doesn't love you. He never did and he never will. So it sucks, big deal. But now you have to move on, let him go. Maybe it's good that he's moving to Italy, now you can get on with your life and not hold onto him. But Vickie, that's another story. She's not going anywhere, understand?"

Maria nodded her head "yes".

"All right, this is what we're going to do. First of all, you're going to make your own life. You're going to focus on a career, socialize, and get some hobbies. Second, you're going to create a relationship with Vickie that has nothing to do with Dominic. You're never going to ask her about him or what they do together. You're going to have a normal mother-daughter relationship. Third, you're going to let Dominic know that he can go back to Italy if he wants, but he can't take Vickie. There are laws about moving minor children out of the state, never mind about moving out of the country. Any questions?"

Maria shook her head "no."

"Good. The next step is to set goals for yourself. Do you have any dreams that you'd like to accomplish?"

"No, my only dream is to be with Dominic."

"Okay, well that's over. So now we have to make *new* dreams. What do you like to do?"

"Take care of Vickie."

"Yeah you're a great mother, but what are your personal interests?"

"I don't have any."

Beth thought about her original reason for going to Maria's apartment.

"What about cooking? The smells that come out of your apartment are amazing. That's the reason I went to your apartment in the first place, I wanted to see if you can teach me how to make your tomato sauce."

"Cooking isn't a hobby or interest. It's just what I do to get my mind off things."

"Isn't that the definition of a hobby? Have you thought about becoming a cook at a restaurant? I bet you would be able to get a job like that."

Beth snapped her finger.

"Do you think so? But I don't have any training or experience."

"Yes you do, it's just not formal. You should make a pot of your sauce and drop off samples at some local Italian restaurants. Actually, I have a better idea. How about if you teach me how to make your sauce before you become famous and it's a sacred, secret recipe! Once people taste what you can do, they'll be fighting to hire you!"

"Okay. Do you want to go shopping with me to get the ingredients?"

"Sounds good to me. How about going now?"

"Well it's too late to make the sauce tonight, but we can go shopping now and make it tomorrow. Is that okay?"

"Sure, I have no plans tomorrow. Let's go."

Zack reluctantly left his pirate ship to accompany Beth and Maria to the grocery store. Beth followed behind Maria, pushing the carriage and Zack up and down the aisles. Maria knew exactly where she was going and what she wanted. When Beth came to the grocery store she wandered around trying to find what was on sale so that she could get the most food with the least money. A fresh clove of garlic, a stock of celery, a large onion, a green pepper, a can of V8 Juice, a large package of ground hamburger, large cans of chopped tomatoes, tomato paste and tomato sauce. The total was $12.68. Beth thought the cashier made a mistake. She thought of the price she paid for the pre-made and processed food that she usually bought, compared to the large amount of sauce this would make. Never mind how much more tasty and healthy this would be.

The next morning Beth and Zack went to Maria's apartment after breakfast. Maria had just gotten up. Beth forgot that people without small children could sleep in the morning. She offered to come back later, but Maria insisted they come in while she changed. Zack was happy to watch the cable channels that they did not get. Maria started the preparations: she placed a gigantic pot on the stove, put the cutting board and knife on the table, and lined all the food they bought on the counter. She instructed Beth to peel the garlic clove, and to dice the onion, celery, and pepper. Maria filled the bottom of the pot with olive oil and set the temperature to medium. Every few minutes she wet her fingers and flicked the water into the oil until the oil sizzled when the water hit it. She then lowered the heat, pushed the cloves through the garlic press into the pot, and slowly added the diced vegetables. She stirred the vegetables until they were soft and then added the hamburger, rosemary, oregano, basil, and black pepper. Maria occasionally stirred the mixture on the stove while they talked.

"I thought about what you told me last night."

"And?"

"I think you're right, but I don't know how to do it. Make my own life, I mean. The plan that I had for my life is lost and I need to make a new plan, only I don't know how."

"I know how you feel. I had to rewrite my plan for different reasons. Life doesn't always go as expected, and plans often have to be rewritten. It's great when you have the opportunity to rewrite it before it's too late. Some people are too stuck in their lives to escape and start over."

"I love to cook. Do you really think I could get paid for what I love to do?"

"That should be the goal in everyone's life. I believe in you and that you can do it."

Maria handed Beth a manual can opener.

"Here, can you open the cans?"

Beth opened the cans and handed them one by one to Maria who carefully poured the contents into the pot while stirring slowly with her long wooden spoon. Maria turned the heat up and put the cover on the pot.

"I turn up the heat until it starts spitting, then I turn it down to medium low and let it simmer for a few hours. You just have to make sure that you keep stirring it so everything mixes together and doesn't burn."

"It already smells awesome, I'm getting hungry."

"Do you want some bread and cookies that I baked yesterday?"

Maria put a plastic container on the table that was filled with Italian sweet breads and cookies. Beth ate one of the cookies and was reminded of the delicious deserts at Jose's mother's house. The flavors and textures were different, but they both had the sensation of being baked with fresh ingredients, slowly and carefully.

"Maria, these are amazing! If you can't get a job as a cook, you'll be able to get one as a baker! I think your plan is already in the process from being a blueprint to becoming a reality!"

Maria had a huge smile on her face, it was the first time Beth had seen her sincerely happy. They went through the phone book and made a list of the restaurants that Maria would drop off a sample of sauce and cookies to. They then wrote letters telling who Maria was, and that she wanted a job.

The next day Beth and Zack drove Maria around to the list of restaurants to drop off the samples. When they were finally finished Maria flopped exhausted into the front seat, Zack was sleeping in the back.

"Well, that's it. Now it's just a matter of waiting and seeing if we get any response."

"No, we don't just wait! I never even took a marketing class and I know that you have to follow up on stuff! You're going to give them two days to try your food and think about how great it is. Then, you're going to call each restaurant and ask for a job."

"I have to call them all? What if no one wants to hire me?"

"Don't you mean how are you going to choose which one to work for? You're not going to stop until you go through the entire list. Then you're going to meet with the owner of each restaurant and see who gives you the best offer."

"Yeah right. I think you're getting a little carried away."

"No, I'm being realistic. I have no doubt that these restaurants are going fight over who'll hire you."

"I think I'll go home, say some 'Hail Mary's' and pray."

"God helps those who help themselves! Do you have any of the sauce left over? I'm starving."

"Yeah, I'll make some pasta to go with it."

The rest of the vacation week flew by; it was amazing how fast time went by when there was nothing to do. Jose came over for New Year's Eve to watch movies and count down the New Year. This was a big event for Beth as this was the beginning of the first year on her own, she had a feeling it was going to be a good year.

Chapter 18

Beth was excited about school starting again since they were doing the externship this semester. There were two classes that met on Tuesdays and Thursdays, Computer Keyboarding & Applications and Pharmacology; and they did the externship on Monday, Wednesday and a half-day on Fridays. On Friday afternoons they met as a group to discuss the externship and to pass in a report on what they had experienced that week. Beth was looking forward to putting everything they had learned to use. Her and Jose applied for the same location, but would not know where they were assigned until school started. Zack was also looking forward to going back to 'school' and kept asking to see his friends again.

Beth and Zack wore their new clothes on the first day of school. Beth remembered the excitement of going back to school when she was a child. Everyone had new clothes, toys, and stories about what they did during vacation. It was fun dropping Zack off and watching the kids eager to share their Christmas stories and presents. Beth went to the Computer Keyboarding & Applications class and looked around for Jose. Beth's classmates greeted her, but they were used to her keeping to herself and did not include her in their conversations. She waited for the class to begin.

The professor finally came in, handed out the syllabus, and reviewed what they were going to do this semester. Beth took two of everything since Jose did not arrive to class until it was half over. After class they stayed in their seats for an extra review to prepare for the externships. The professor gave each student a folder filled with the details of where they would start their externships the next day. Beth was doing hers at the local rehab center/residents' home, which had been her first choice. She leaned over to read where Jose would be going. He held up his paper for her to see and she beamed when she saw that they were going to the same place. He laughed quietly at her excitement. It was good to be back in school. There was a sense of excitement that reminded her of the innocence of her childhood.

It was scary for Beth to leave Zack at the college day care center while she went to the externship. This was the first time in his life that Beth was so far away from him for long periods of time. When they were at the college Beth knew that he was close by and she could go see him whenever she wanted. Now she would be far away from him and would not be able to check in on him or get to him quickly if anything happened. She tried to repress the panic she felt about what would happen if Jeff went to the day care center and took Zack. She would be too far away to rescue him. How would she be able to protect him? Luckily Zack would not know she was any farther away than she had always been, or that she was not there to keep him safe.

Beth walked back to her car after dropping Zack off. The panic got stronger as she got further away. She tried to do the breathing exercises that her therapist taught her. In—Out. It's ... Okay, In—Out. It's ... Okay. She continued the breathing exercises while she drove the few blocks to the rehab center. Jose's car was already in the parking lot. She parked a few spots away and walked into the front lobby. It was very elaborate and looked like a fancy hotel with bouquets of flower arrangements on highly polished wooden tables in between soft couches and stiff chairs.

The receptionist sat behind a large desk that looked like a wide preacher's pulpit. He must have been a college student as he was reading a textbook that was hidden on the lower part of the desk where the phone was. He wore a fake smile.

"Can I help you?"

"Yeah, I'm here to start my internship. I'm from the community college."

He squinted his long nose and looked down it at her even though she was standing above him.

"Yes, they're in orientation. It's the last room on the left down the hallway on your right."

"Am I late? Did they start yet?"

"How am I supposed to know? Go down and see for yourself!"

The long nose went back into the book. A sign she was dismissed.

Beth walked down the hall until she came to the last room on the left. It was quiet inside, a sign that they had not started yet. Jose smiled at her as she entered the room and took the empty seat next to him. There were five other people sitting at the tables waiting for the orientation to start. Two women were from their program, and there was another women and two men, none of whom seemed to know each other.

An old woman in a starched nurse's uniform finally entered the room. She scanned the room to determine what type of group she had to deal with.

"Ahh. Seven of you. We have a big group this time don't we."

She sounded like a wicked witch trying to decide the best way to cook them for dinner. Everyone sat silently, afraid to be her first victim. Her screechy voice continued.

"My name is Mrs. Homes and I expect to be addressed as such when spoken to. Everyone always comes in here thinking it's going to be fun and games, well think again. You're here to do the work that no one else wants to do. You're the lowest on the totem poles. You'll collect the charts, do the filing, serve the food, give the sponge baths, clean the messes in the bathroom, and run errands. So don't think this is going to be easy or rewarding in any way. You must be on time and complete what you're told to do immediately, without any complaints. You each get one white lab jacket to wear at all times. It's your responsibility to keep them clean and ironed. Are there any questions?"

No one dared to speak.

"All right, good then. I'll take attendance and give you your assignments. Let's see, there are three floors so I'll pair you off into three groups, each with a girl and boy. When I call out your name, raise your hand so that I can give you your nametag.

"Now to pair you up. Jose Perez and Jen White will be on floor two, Bill Clancy and Kim Jones will be on floor three, Dale Zimmerman and Gina Demonica will be on floor four.

"Mmmmm . . . that leaves Beth Parker."

Mrs. Homes stared at Beth as if she were a sore that had to be hidden somewhere. She glanced back and forth at Beth and Jose, her lips pressing together to form a tight smile. She noticed that they were together and smugly announced that Beth would be with Bill and Kim, seeming to purposely separate Beth from Jose. Jose smiled a sad smile that told Beth he was disappointed they would not be together.

"Okay, everyone get with their partner, take a lab coat, and proceed to the nurse's station on your assigned floor. The nurse's are waiting for you."

Beth introduced herself to Bill and Kim as they walked with the group to the elevators. The three of them got off on the second floor and walked the short distance to the nurse's station. They were warmly greeted by a heavyset woman with short hair and tight rows of curls lined along the top of her head. It reminded Beth of the hairstyles that were popular in the 80's. The woman's big smile and cheery personality was a relief after Mrs. Homes' militaristic approach.

"Oh good, my little group has arrived! I've been waiting for you. And there are three of you. I'm so lucky! My name is Carol LaFlem. You can call me Carol. Now, I have a nice daily schedule for you."

She handed each of them a piece of paper with a schedule and a map of the building, the second floor was detailed with the rooms numbered. She proceeded to review the schedule.

"We split up the rooms so that you do the same rooms everyday. The first thing you do each morning is get the breakfast trays from the kitchen, and deliver them to your patients. You have to make sure each patient gets the correct tray as some people are on special diets. You can help feed any of your patients who need help eating. After breakfast you collect their trays, record what they ate, and tidy up their rooms. The rest of the morning is used to help the patients with their social activities, going to their appointments, bathing and dressing them, and assisting with things such as collecting and filing the charts.

"Before you know it, it will be lunch time. Make sure you pay close attention and record accurately in their charts what they eat and their bodily releases." She smiled shyly as if she was embarrassed by the fact that the patient's pee and poop had do be recorded. "Some of the patients don't have many visitors and like it if you can spend time talking or helping them with their meals. Since there are three of you, you'll have extra time to spend with each patient. The care and happiness of the patients comes before anything, so always treat them with respect and honor their preference to either be left alone or enjoy your company.

"Any questions? No? Okay, then let me assign your rooms. There are eight rooms with two patients each when all the rooms are full. So, two of you will have five and one of you will have six patients. Your patients should be finishing up their breakfast, so I'll show you where the rolling carts are for you to collect the trays. The breakfast menus are on their trays, so it's easy to figure out what they ate and to mark it in their charts."

Beth pushed the large metal rolling cart down the hall, collected the breakfast trays, and met her five patients. She was surprised at how old and frail they all were. She smiled and introduced herself, but they were distant and barely acknowledged her. She pushed the cart full of half-empty plates and dirty trays to the kitchen where she unloaded them for the dishwasher. She then went back upstairs to see if any of her patients needed help going to the activities. Beth went from room to room asking if anyone wanted to go to *bingo*, but there was no response; it was as if she was talking to herself. The rest of the day was not much better. She enjoyed working with Carol, the other nurses, Bill and Kim; but the patients barely acknowledged her existence. She wondered if Jose was having better luck than her, but never got the opportunity to ask him, as she had to rush to pick up Zack on time.

Zack was happily playing with his friends when Beth got to the day care center. It was obvious that he had a much better day at school than she did at 'work'. He continued to play with his friends instead of running over to greet her like he usually did. Beth went over to see what occupied him so intently. He was playing with some small cars, driving them around in circles. Nothing out of the ordinary. She squatted down next to him, but he did not look up.

"What you playing with Zack?"

"Cars."

"Did you have a good day?"

"You didn't come."

"What do you mean? Of course I came. I'm here now."

"*No*! You were gone *all day*! You didn't come to play with me. I missed you!"

Beth did not know what to say. She never realized that the times during the day when she stopped into check on him were just as important to Zack as they were for her. She felt a sharp pang slash through the middle of her chest. This was a horrible ending to a horrible day and she was overwhelmed with guilt. She wanted to hug him, but was afraid he would push her away and she could not handle that. Zack continued driving the cars around in circles. After a long silence she finally spoke.

"I'm so sorry Zack. I had to go to a hospital today and take care of old, sick people. I couldn't leave them."

"But you're supposed to take care of me!"

"I know Zack, and I do take care of you. It's just that sometimes we have to do different things instead of being together all the time. Just like when you go places without me."

"Like when I went to the Christmas party?"

"Exactly like when you went to the Christmas party. Now that you're getting older, there will be times when we're away from each other and more days when I can't visit you. When you get bigger and go to real school mommies aren't allowed to visit except on special occasions. But that doesn't mean that I don't love you or will stop taking care of you. It just means that I'll have mommy things to do and you'll have little boy things to do. But I'll always be your mommy and you'll always be my little boy and we'll always love each other. I'll always keep you safe and I'll always be there for you."

"Do you promise?"

"Cross my heart and hope to die."

"Oh! Don't die!"

"Oh no, no. I won't *really* die! It's just an expression!"

Zack put down his car and gave Beth a big hug. Beth hugged him so tight back, she could feel him squirming to get free. She did not ever want to let him go. She just kept hugging him, trying not to cry.

Beth hoped Jose would come over tonight, as she did not want to be alone. She hated being alone when she felt sad; it just depressed her more. The air was freezing and she could not get her key to open the front door to the apartment building. The harder she tried, the more she could not get it to work. Zack pulled on her jacket.

"Do you want me to try, Mommy?"

Beth stopped and took a deep breath. She slowly took the key out of the keyhole, put it back in, and turned it. The door opened. Beth smiled down at Zack.

"Look, I did it!"

Beth felt proud of her small accomplishment. When the door opened, a gush of hot air and the smell of Maria's sauce nearly knocked Beth backward. The perfect way to make her feel better after such a horrible day. Maria opened her door when Beth and Zack reached the top of the stairs.

"I hoped I would hear you come home. I have good news, do you two want to come over for dinner and help me celebrate?"

What could be more perfect to help Beth feel better? Not only would she not have to cook, but she would be served by the best cook in town!

"That sounds absolutely wonderful! Let us take off our coats and we'll be right over."

When Beth and Zack came back to Maria's apartment Beth was impressed by its appearance. Where there were usually piles of old mail and clutter, there were instead small votive candles burning fragrantly. The table was set with three complete place settings of beautiful blue Italian chinaware. A bouquet of sunflowers was in a vase in the center of the table, giving the impression that the season was actually the peak of summer rather than the dead of winter. The apartment was neat and clean, looking as if the guest of honor would be a handsome GQ model instead of the single mother and her almost three-year-old son from across the hall.

"Oh my God, Maria, this is fabulous! I had no idea that these cookie-cutter apartments could look so elegant! I feel like I'm in a high class restaurant!"

"Well, I'm glad. Because that's precisely the image I was trying to create. Why don't you two sit on the couch while I bring you your drinks and appetizers."

Zack held on tight to Beth's hand as they sat politely on the couch. Zack was not used to being in a formal setting, even if it was just the apartment across the hall. Maria brought over a glass of red wine for Beth and a cup of grape juice for Zack. She placed a tray of cheese, meats, and small slices of fresh Italian bread on the coffee table in front of them. Although Beth had seen the coffee table many times before, she never noticed the intricate carving accented by gold leaf paint. Zack shyly took a piece of cheese and began to nibble it. Beth was not sure how much of his action was prompted by boldness and how much by the fact that he probably had not eaten in hours. Beth silently sipped her wine and let the affects of it slowly dissolve the stress of the day.

The first course consisted of a variety of appetizers placed in the middle of the table. There was brochette (thinly sliced French bread with fresh tomatoes and basil), tomato and mozzarella balls sprinkled with fresh basil, and fried calamari (octopus that is battered and deep-fried). Beth was full after trying a small portion of each dish. Her taste buds were in ecstasy as they savored the taste of fresh carefully prepared food, quite a change from the boxed and processed food they were used to. Beth ate very slowly as if eating this food was an experience, rather than just a source to sustain life. Between the wine and the food, Beth was feeling quite content.

"Now for the main course." Maria smiled as she got up from her chair and began transferring dishes from the oven onto the table. There was meat lasagna, sausages with tomato and peppers, and a bowl of linguine covered with Alfredo sauce.

"Oh my God, Maria! There's enough food here to feed a small village! Are you going to tell me the reason for all of this?"

"Yes. I'll make a toast before dinner. First and most importantly, let's toast to good friends."

They clanked their glasses together and sipped the wine.

"Second, I want to announce that I got *three* offers to work at some of the best restaurants in town. I was able to choose which one gave me the best offer. I'll be working as a chef's assistant at 'Pondevecio' restaurant downtown! I'm so excited! I can't believe I'll actually be getting paid for what I like to do! Not only that, but they're paying me quite well and with benefits! If things go well then I may actually be promoted to work as a fill-in chef! I can't believe this is happening, and it's all because of you. I don't know how to thank you. This is the best thing that's ever happened to me."

Beth went over and gave Maria a huge hug and kiss on the cheek.

"Oh Maria! I'm so happy for you! I knew you could do it. You just had to believe in yourself. Not to ruin the mood, but what about Dominic? Did you talk to him?"

"Yeah I did. He's not happy about it, but he agreed not to take Vickie with him. I think he's impressed that I got a job instead of falling apart. I think he was afraid to say no. I agreed to let her stay with him extra time until he leaves, which allows me to focus on my new job. I don't know what I'm going to do about working nights and leaving Vickie alone."

"Things will work out, don't worry now about what might or might not happen. Sometimes solutions present themselves when you don't expect them. Vickie could always come over and stay with me and Zack in the evenings. For now, let's celebrate your new job. Congratulations!"

Beth was so happy for Maria. She hoped she would be able to find the same happiness in her career.

With the rigid schedule at the nursing home, it was easy to adjust to a routine. Although her patients barely spoke to or acknowledged Beth, she was learning their individual preferences and personalities. Miss Lane and Tootsie shared a room that seemed like an imaginary line was drawn down the middle with each side reversed. Even their physical appearances were opposite, Miss Lane was a tiny black woman with tight white curls, Tootsie was a heavy white woman with tight black curls; Miss Lane had a heavy southern accent, Tootsie was pure Yankee. The imaginary line that separated the décor represented the personalities of the two women as well. Miss Lane's half of the room was very plain with the exception of a handmade quilt on her bed that had a variety of styles and fabrics which looked as if it was made by many people who added a little at a time over a long period. The few items on her dresser included an old clock and three photos in frames, an old photo of two little girls each holding up a huge crab, a wedding photo with the groom looking triumphant and the bride staring off as if she did not want to be there, and a more modern picture of a woman hugging a little girl. There were no signs of anyone ever visiting her. No leftover flowers, no cards, no small tokens or gifts.

Tootsie's half of the room was as full as Miss Lane's was empty. There were pictures of people doing various activities in frames of different sizes and styles crammed on the dresser. There were wedding pictures, formal family pictures, kids missing teeth in school pictures, snapshots taken at the beach, at picnics, dances, and numerous other activities. In between the photos were vases of flowers in various stages of wilting, knickknacks, and figurines of animals and people. The wall was covered with colorful cards and pictures drawn by children. There was so much stuff that it was impossible to notice any one thing. It was obvious by blur of colors, shapes, and textures that Tootsie received many visitors.

The two women in the next room, Claire and Barbara, were as alike as Miss Lane and Tootsie were different. It was impossible to differentiate their belongings. If the room was separated, Beth could not tell as there were identical objects and decorations on both sides. Each chair had a matching off-white slipcover with large pink flowers and mint green leaves, a pink frilly pillow and a crocheted afghan. The four pictures placed evenly around the room were in matching frames and had pictures of old fashioned scenes with people doing activities during each of the four seasons. The spring scene was of a young couple in love rowing a small boat on a pond. The summer scene was a family at the beach. The fall scene was a group of men on horseback out for a hunt. The winter scene was of a frozen pond in the center of town with people ice-skating on it. The bedside tables had matching lamps and the dressers had a series of figurines split between them. The only thing different was the arrangement of pictures on each dresser, which had different groups of people and styles of frames.

Beth's fifth and last patient was a man named Phillip who shared a room with one of Kim's patients, Ted. Phillip was a frail old man who was bald and very wrinkly. Although he had few belongings, his room definitely had a male aura. Just like every other patient, Phillip had a picture on his dresser. It was an antique picture of a beautiful woman on her wedding day, who Beth assumed was Phillip's wife.

As Beth got to know her patients she noticed individual differences. The obvious was the décor and pictures that gave Beth a small glimpse of their previous lives. The next indication was their food preferences. Claire and Barbara ordered the same things, like a couple of schoolgirls who called each other the night before to make sure there were wearing matching outfits. Miss Lane ordered the first option everyday as if she did not bother reading the menu, but just checked off the first box. There was no predicting what Tootsie was going to order, her choice in food was as inconsistent as the variety of her belongings. Phillip was a definite meat and potato type of guy. In addition to noticing a pattern in their menu choices, Beth also noticed a pattern in what and how much they actually ate. Phillip *never* ate his vegetables but faithfully ate his dessert. Although Claire and Barbara ordered the same menu, Claire ate more of the starchy foods and Barbara ate the salad and vegetables. Again, Tootsie was unpredictable. What she ate all of one day, she left on her plate another day. Miss Lane just picked at her food and barely ate any of it. At first Beth thought that since she did not pay attention to what she was ordering, Miss Lane got foods that she did not like by accident. But then Beth realized that Mrs. Lane did not eat hardly any food, regardless of what it was. This worried Beth and she let nurse Carol know of her concerns. Carol assured her that the doctors were already aware of the situation and were supplementing Miss Lane's diet with additional nutrients and vitamins intravenously. Carol suggested that Beth talk to Miss Lane while she ate her meals and encourage her to eat more. Carol also confirmed what Beth already suspected, that Miss Lane did not receive any visitors and the reason she was not eating might be because she was lonely. Beth thought of the people in the pictures on Miss Lane's dresser and wondered who they were and why they never visited. She thought about how difficult it must be for Miss Lane to see Tootsie's daily visitors, but having none herself. Beth hoped that she would not be abandoned and forgotten about when she was an old woman in a nursing home. Beth thought of Zack and smiled. Zack would never abandon her.

Beth had mistakenly thought that this semester would be easy since she had less studying to do as a result of the internship. Instead she was always exhausted, not having time to do anything but work, study, cook supper and then collapse until bedtime. Where Beth used to stay up studying long after Zack went to bed, she now went to bed shortly after him. Even though Jose worked at the same nursing home as her, they hardly ever saw each other. He would come over on weekends when he was not working and sometimes in the evening during the week. The majority of her energy went into work and it made her feel bad that she was not seeing her friends or doing much with Zack. Beth told herself that she would make it up by having a big party for his birthday in February. In the mean time she continued to focus on work.

As the days progressed, Beth did her duties quicker and more efficiently. This gave her more time to spend with the patients and get to know them on a deeper level than just analyzing what they were eating. Phillip told Beth stories about when he was a young man in the army, his twin brother who still visited him everyday, and how he and his brother had married twin sisters. He told Beth about his bride who recently died last year after they had been married for fifty-five years, and about the childless life that his brother, he and their wives spent together. Claire and Barbara explained to Beth that neither of them wanted to part with their belongings, so they decided to each contribute their favorite things from home and decorate the entire room together instead of each only having half the room. Although they had never met until they became roommates, they both felt as though they had finally found their kindred sister. Tootsie told Beth about her children, grand children, nieces, and nephews. All of whom visited on a regular basis. Most of all, Beth spent as much time as possible with Miss Lane as she was the one who seemed to be the most in need of company.

Miss Lane told Beth long stories about her childhood growing up in New Orleans. Back then she was called Laney, and she and her sister Claudia were inseparable. Beth thought of the old picture of the two little girls with crabs and imagined that must be Miss Lane and Claudia. Miss Lane told how they lived in the lower ninth ward in the same house that their father had grown up in. Years ago these were the houses that the slaves lived in and eventually their decedents were able to buy the houses, making it the first black owned neighborhood in the United States. The houses were owned outright and passed on from generation to generation. The neighborhoods were full of cousins and friends whose lives had been intermingled for generations. There was no crime because everyone watched out for each other. If a kid was doing something wrong, any adult would whap him and the kid's parent would be thankful. It was as if each kid had one-hundred pairs of eyes watching everything he did to be sure he behaved. The grandparents, parents, and kids all lived together. The grandparents took care of the kids when the parents were at work; the parents took care of the grandparents when they got old. No one was ever alone.

But boy would it get hot. On those sticky summer nights everyone swayed in the rocking chairs on their porches. There was always a banjo playing and the music would just move through your body as it echoed through the neighborhood. When it got really hot Laney and Claudia slept out on their porch, hanging sheets around them to limit the mosquitoes that according to Miss Lane were as large as hummingbirds. They stayed up all night giggling, listening to the music somewhere in the neighborhood and the bugs that gave their own concert.

Beth asked Miss Lane about Mardi Gras as her image of New Orleans was the partying that she saw on TV once a year. Miss Lane laughed and set Beth straight about the true meaning of Mardi Gras and the history of New Orleans. When the French invaded the new world, they sent the soldier's families too. This was different from the English who only sent the soldiers. By including the families, they needed to build towns, schools and start businesses to support the new community. This brought the culture and holidays of the French to New Orleans where they mixed with the traditions of the Black Slaves, and the Native Indians who helped them to survive in this new climate. These three cultures merged to form the very unique people of New Orleaniens. Samples of this unique culture are demonstrated in the jazz music that was invented in Jackson Park by the African slaves, and the food that is a mixture of French cuisine, African dishes, and native foods such as pecans and shrimp. Mardi Gras is a Christian religious holiday brought over from France celebrating the time before lent begins. The entire town is decorated for weeks before the holiday, similar to how the rest of the country decorates their homes for Christmas and other major holidays. The houses are covered with gold, purple, and green tinsel and beads, and Mardi Gras umbrellas and masks hang around and in the homes. Jazz music plays everywhere, bringing the holiday spirit into the soul of every person regardless of age.

The wild parades in the French Quarters get the most publicity, but the majority of Mardi Gras parades are family oriented. Each parade has a king and queen with a royal court, complete with a royal masked ball in the evening that is a very elegant and formal event. Miss Lane always dreamt of being the queen, or at least being on the court, but because of severe racism and segregation this was unheard of. However, she was able to participate in decorating the neighborhood float. If a family is lucky, they had a float that they decorate for the parade each year. Since her neighborhood was family, it was the neighborhood float. All of the neighborhood kids went to the other parades and collect as many beads, cups, candy, and toys as possible and then throw them off their float into the crowds of people who would yell, "Hey mista, throw me something!" In those days, the occupants of the float were masked and it was so wild that they tied themselves into the floats so that they would not fall out. Since only a few people could fit in the float, each house in the neighborhood took turns riding in the float. When it was not their turn, Miss Lane's father slept on the sidewalk the night before the parade guarding their viewing spot.

Each day Beth spent as much time as possible listening to Miss Lane's stories of New Orleans. The only problem was that because Miss Lane spent her mealtime telling stories, she was actually eating less instead of more. Beth was getting extremely worried that Miss Lane was loosing more weight and becoming frailer, But could not encourage her to eat. Beth reviewed the menu with her, but Miss Lane insisted it did not matter what Beth ordered for her, as the food was bland in comparison to what they ate in New Orleans. According to Miss Lane, her husband Stan made the best Gumbo in Louisiana. Beth was shocked that Miss Lane was married since she never mentioned her husband. Beth thought of the wedding picture and asked about him, but Miss Lane continued on about the food. Beth wondered if Miss Lane's husband had been abusive like Jeff, and that was why she did not want to talk about him. Beth continued listening about the gumbo, jambalaya, fried chicken, corn bread, sweet mashed potatoes ...

As Beth listened to Miss Lane talk about the feasts, she got an idea about how to get Miss Lane to eat. She decided to ask Maria if she could cook the foods that Miss Lane mentioned. Beth and Zack could bring Miss Lane the food during Saturday afternoon visiting hours. That way Miss Lane could have visitors and good food, and Zack could listen to all of the wonderful stories about New Orleans.

That evening when Beth got home, Maria had already left for work. Because of their different work schedules, they would not see each other until Saturday. Beth could not wait that long, so she set her alarm clock for midnight, sat in the hallway keeping her apartment door open incase Zack woke up, and waited for Maria to come home.

When Maria came home, Beth invited her in as she had something important to tell her. Of course Maria was worried and came in. Beth told Maria the entire story about Miss Lane and how she would not eat because she missed the home cooked foods of her childhood. Beth begged Maria to use her cooking talents to prepare a Louisiana style dinner for Miss Lane.

"Beth, I'd love to help, but I'm an Italian cook and know nothing about southern cuisine. I've never even eaten it before so wouldn't know what it's supposed to taste like. Can't you order out from a local restaurant and just bring it to her?"

"No. Although there seem to be restaurants from all over the world in this city, the Deep South failed to make its presence. Maybe there's still a grudge because we won the Civil War."

"Yeah right! That was how many years ago?"

"Long enough that you'd think people are over it."

"There are fast food fried chicken places with mashed potatoes, corn bread, and all that southern stuff. Why don't you get her some 'take-out' from one of those places?"

"That would be like getting Italian food from a fast food place instead of your restaurant. Is there any comparison?"

"I see the dilemma."

"Can't you just get some recipes from a cook book or something?"

"We could. But again, I don't know what it's supposed to taste like and wouldn't know if it came out right or not. I also don't know how complicated the recipes are or if I would have all of the ingredients."

"All right, so at least there's a 'maybe.' This is good. Here's my plan: I'll go to the library and get out a cookbook on New Orleans or Louisiana cooking. You can take a look at the recipes and see if you think you can make them. If you *can* make them then I'll go to the grocery store and get the ingredients. Then—Presto! We'll have a New Orleans style feast and Miss Lane will eat again! Thank you so much Maria, you're the greatest!"

Beth gave Maria a tight hug and kiss on the cheek. Maria actually blushed, not realizing that she had just involuntarily agreed to take part in this plan.

"You're welcome. The only reason I'm doing this is because if it wasn't for you then I would be in a massive state of depression right now instead of working as an assistant chef for one of the best restaurants in town!"

"Well, now it's your turn to help get Miss Lane out of *her* depression!"

"What goes around comes around, it's worth a try. But you have to work in the morning and need to go to bed. Good night Beth."

"Good night Maria. And, thanks."

Maria smiled at Beth and left.

Beth was sure that the public library would have a cookbook from New Orleans. However, with all of the budget cuts the library was only open minimal hours and was closed when Beth could go. Beth was concerned that the college library would only have academic books and not what she was looking for, but she picked up Zack and went anyway.

The reference librarian searched the computer and listed all the books that came up under New Orleans. There were many about the levies and hurricanes, and luckily a few about the cooking. Beth wrote down where they were and went to look for recipes. She was in luck! There were three cookbooks on New Orleans complete with Gumbo and Jambalaya recipes. She checked out the books, and left them on the floor in front of Maria's apartment door.

The next day there was a grocery list taped on Beth's apartment door with a note at the bottom stating that Maria had Monday off from work. Beth went to the grocery store on Sunday after dinner at Stacey and Gayle's house, and got everything on the list. It took her a while wandering around the grocery store, trying to find all of the ingredients. Rice, chicken breast, frozen shrimp, mixed peppers and okra, a large onion, carrots, celery, tomato paste, sausage, bullion, Jiffy cornbread mix, two quart freezer bags. Beth was worried that she would not have enough money; she used all of her food stamps plus $22.98 cash. Judging by the amount of food she hoped it would make enough to feed her and Zack all week, otherwise she did not know what they would eat.

Beth could not wait to get home from work on Monday. All day she kept smiling at Miss Lane in a way that made Miss Lane know that something was up. Beth checked with Nurse Carol who thought it was a great idea since anything to get Miss Lane to eat was worth a try! Even though she was being fed intravenously, Miss Lane continued to wither away and was looking like a frail baby doll. Beth was not sure how much longer it would be before she turned into a little black stick figure.

Beth smelled the aroma of southern cooking from the parking lot. The spicy smell stimulated and lured her quickly into the apartment building were she was overwhelmed with the gush of hot steam when she opened the front door. She could tell that Zack was also excited by the way he pulled her hand up the stairs. Zack walked right into Maria's apartment without even knocking.

"It smells awesome in here!"

"Do you think so? I did some improvising with the recipes, so I don't know if it will taste right. Do you want to try it and let me know what you think?"

The table was set for three people. Beth wondered why Vickie was not here since normally Vickie stayed with Maria on her days off. She considered if she would be imposing by asking where she was. Her curiosity won since she figured they were good enough friends to ask.

"Where's Vickie?"

"Oh, she's with Dominic. He's leaving for Italy on Sunday, so she's spending the week with him. I don't know what I'm going to do when he's gone."

"Maria, why are you talking like this again? It's been over a month since you started working and I thought you were doing well on your own. When are you going to realize that you don't need him and just go on with your own life?"

"No, not that. I mean that I don't know what Vickie will do while I'm at work."

"Oh, sorry. Silly me. I should have known.

"I'm home every evening. She can stay with me until bedtime, then just go across the hall to go to bed. At twelve and a half, she's old enough to be alone until you get home from work. We can even set up the baby monitor so that I can hear her and she can just call over to me if she needs anything."

"That would be great. I don't know where my life would be without you."

"We're all here to take care of each other. I can't wait to taste some old-fashioned Louisiana cooking!"

Maria scooped ladles of shrimp gumbo into the three bowls. It was absolutely delicious. Beth had never tasted anything like it.

"This is great, how did you make it?"

"Well, first I coated the chicken in cornstarch and browned it in olive oil, then removed the chicken and set it aside. I chopped up some carrots, celery, red, and green peppers, onion, and garlic and put it in the pot with the chicken drippings. I added some tomatoes paste, parley, bay leafs, chopped sausages, thyme, marjoram, basil, cayenne pepper and Worcestershire sauce. While this simmered, I cooked a pot of rice. When the vegetables were cooked I added the cans of chicken broth and let it simmer for an hour. I then added the frozen okra, the cooked chicken, shrimp, and rice and let the entire pot simmer a little longer. I let it sit to cool, and here it is! So you like it?"

"Like it? I *love* it! However, it sounds much too complicated for my boxed macaroni and cheese cooking abilities. I'll leave the cooking of good food to the expert. I'm the lucky one who gets to enjoy it! I'm totally amazed that you were able to make this when you've never even tasted it before. You're so talented!"

"Compliments like that will get you every where! Keep that up and you can come over every night for dinner!"

Beth put most of the gumbo and jambalaya in small zip-lock freezer bags and stuffed them into the freezer. The rest she put in two large containers in her refrigerator for them to eat during the week.

On Wednesday Beth scooped small portions of each into little empty margarine containers to take to Miss Lane for lunch. She dropped them off at the kitchen with instructions to give half to Miss Lane today, and half tomorrow. Beth could not wait to serve Miss Lane her native food.

Miss Lane beamed when Beth brought her the jambalaya, gumbo, and cornbread. Beth fed her small spoonfuls, and Miss Lane assured Beth that it was as good as her husband used to make. Although she ate much more than her usual portions, Beth was still disappointed with how little Miss Lane ate.

Beth brought Miss Lane containers of gumbo and jambalaya on Monday, Wednesday, and Fridays when she worked and on Saturdays when she and Zack visited. Zack grew very close to Miss Lane and brought her pictures and crafts that he made in school so that Miss Lane's half of the room was looking more and more like Tootsie's. Miss Lane became like a grandmother to Zack and he was excited to invite her to his birthday party. Miss Lane's eyes filled up with tears when she told him that she was too old and sick to come, but that she wanted to hear all about it afterwards.

Chapter 19

Zack's birthday was on February 14, Valentine's Day. Coincidently, it happened to fall on a Saturday this year. Although it was a little corny for a boy, Beth decided to add hearts to the Spiderman party theme. Zack insisted that he wanted *all* of his friends to come. That included Vickie and Maria; Jose and his sister and nephew; Stacey, Gayle and Mia; his "old family," meaning the people that they used to live with at the safe house which were Sheila, Rosie and her kids, and Lisa; and Zack's new school friends. Beth had no idea where she would fit all of these people since her apartment was too small and it would not be safe at the crisis center. Stacey suggested having the party at the church hall since members were allowed to rent it inexpensively. The large, easily accessible location was perfect and it was available on Saturday morning before visiting hours for Miss Lane. Maria offered to make a cake; Stacey, Gayle, Sheila, and Lisa all brought food and candy; and Jose helped her with the decorations and planning games for the kids. Everything seemed like it would work out fine.

Beth was extremely nervous as the day approached. She felt like she was anticipating a wedding rather than a child's birthday party. This was the first party that she was giving on her own, without basing every decision on how Jeff would react. This was also the first time she was entertaining all of her knew friends, the new community that she created. Everyone came and seemed to be having fun. It was more like an adult party, rather than a traditional child's party with just children and their mothers. It was a great mix of people. There were women, men, and children of different races, sexual orientation, and family types intermingling and having fun together. Beth sat for a moment and observed the happiness and activity in the room and she felt blessed that these were her friends and that this was her life. Jose came over, sat beside her, and held her hand. Zack, surrounded by his friends, was playing happily. Beth felt complete.

Zack told Miss Lane all about his party when they visited her that afternoon. The combination of the excitement and the sugar from the cake and candy made him full of energy and he could barely get his words out fast enough. Beth was happy that Miss Lane was eating the cake they brought her, and she tied a balloon onto Miss Lane's bed.

Beth was exhausted as they drove back to their apartment and she was looking forward to a quiet evening. Vickie was visiting her grandparents, so it would just be Beth, Zack, and Jose. Beth took a nap with Zack while they waited for Jose to come over, but when they woke up it was very dark out. It was eight o'clock and Jose should have been over hours ago. She checked her phone and there were thirteen missed calls from Jose. He had been trying to call, but she did not hear the phone. She was frantic that something bad happened to him, and instead of listening to the voice messages she immediately called him back. The phone kept ringing, and then went into his voice mail. She flipped her phone shut, then opened it back up and pressed 'redial'. This time he picked up.

"Hey."

"Jose? What happened? Are you okay?"

"Things are pretty bad. Did you get my messages? Where were you?"

"I was sleeping. I didn't get your message. What's wrong?"

"It's Miguel. They tried to reach us, but we were at the party."

"But Miguel was at the party too. What are you talking about?"

"Not baby Miguel ... big Miguel, Adia's husband. He's dead."

"Oh my God! What happened?"

"We don't know. They won't tell us anything. They said there has to be an investigation first. All we know is that he's dead."

"How's Adia?"

"How do you think? She's a mess. She feels guilty that she was at the party with Pedro while the news came that her husband was killed. She won't stop screaming, we can't calm her down."

"Do you want me to come over?"

"I would love to see you, I need you right now. But I think it's better that you stay there so I can support my family. I'll call you later, okay?"

"All right, I miss you. I'll be thinking of you."

"I miss you too. Happy Valentine's Day."

"Happy Valentine's Day."

"Oh, and Beth?"

"Yeah?"

"I love you."

"I love you too."

Beth snapped the phone shut. This was too much for her to process. Jose had never told her that he loved her before. She had been so busy planning for Zack's party that she had forgotten it was Valentine's Day. She wondered if Jose had planned anything for them for tonight. She suddenly thought of Jeff and their past Valentines Days, or lack of. She had grown accustomed to not expecting or giving anything on this day that Jeff considered "commercial nonsense," so it did not occur to her to do anything for Jose. It was a relief when Zack was born on this day so that she had a reason to celebrate with the rest of the world. She wondered if Jeff remembered that today was Zack's birthday, or if he was too busy with Nancy to think of him. Would they celebrate Valentines Day, or would it be "commercial nonsense" for her too? Beth felt like smacking herself for thinking about trivial things like how Jeff and Nancy were celebrating Valentine's Day, when Miguel was dead. Dead on Valentine's Day, on Zack's birthday. What a horrible day to die. Was there a good day to die? Did he actually die today? It suddenly occurred to her that it did not faze Jose that she missed his calls. If it had been Jeff, there would have been paranoid accusations. She did not know what to do, so she cried into the pillow so that she would not wake Zack up.

Beth asked Stacey and Gayle if they would take Zack to church so that she could be with Jose and his family. Beth had dealt with death before when her parents and grandparents died, but she had never experienced anything like this. Adia was hysterical as she was convinced that Miguel was killed as a punishment to her for being with Pedro. Jose's grandmother was sitting in the living room reciting the rosary in Spanish. Everyone else was arguing in Spanish, so Beth had no idea what they were saying. Only Pedro sat quietly, drinking away his shame. Jose wrapped his arms around Beth.

"You don't have to stay here, it's a disaster."

"Yeah, but I don't want to leave you. I want to be here for you."

"There's nothing you can do. I'm glad that you came, but I'll be okay. Why don't you go home for a while and I'll call you when things settle down. You can come back later with Zack, I think baby Miguel could use a friend."

"Are you sure?"

"Yeah."

"Okay."

Beth and Jose hugged for a long time before she left.

Beth was not sure where to go as she was not ready to face Zack at Stacey and Gayle's, but she did not want to be alone at home. She decided to visit Miss Lane.

Miss Lane was surprised to see Beth on a Sunday afternoon. She was alone since Tootsie was in the lounge area with her children and grandchildren where there was room for them all.

"Where's little Zack?"

"He's with my friends."

Beth started to cry.

"Oh honey, it's okay. You come sit over here on my bed and tell Miss Lane what's wrong."

"Something terrible happened. My boyfriend's brother-in-law was killed in Iraq. He was so young. And he had a little boy Zack's age."

"Death is never easy, especially when someone dies before his time. The thing about death is that you have to find a way to deal with it, to accept what you can't change. Different people have their ways of facing death. Some people try to act like they're not affected, that's no good because a person has to show his grief. Back home when people died we had 'funeral parades' that were like huge parties celebrating the person's life. First came the hearse with the casket, then came the brass band playing, followed by all of us poor souls who were left behind to mourn. The whole procession marched from the church to the graveyard wailing like they would wake the dead. There was music like you wouldn't believe, the horns would cry and mourn the person's passing like no human voice would be capable of. It's like the wailing of the horns pulled out the crying that's inside of a person, and the mourners would follow behind in harmony. There was a potluck feast afterwards with enough food to feed the entire town for a week. There was of course Jambalaya and Gumbo, and there was also fried chicken, sweet potato pies, pecan pies, ice cream, corn bread and much more. The music played and we ate and told our favorite stories about the person who had passed. Even the most hardened criminal would go out looking like a saint. Sometimes it went on for days."

"But Miss Lane, that's *horrible!* It's like you're happy the person died!"

"You're not getting what I'm saying honey. We weren't celebrating the person's *death*. We were celebrating his *life*. After all, when a person passes over to the other side it's what he did in his life that will make him missed in his death. So when a person dies, it's a celebration of a good life lived. The more the person was loved in life the greater the celebration will be."

"But Miguel was all alone over in Iraq when he died. We don't even know how it happened. All his family, friends and the people who loved him were here in the States and they're a mess. Everyone's fighting."

"If Miguel was loved by his folk back home, then he carried that love with him and touched people with it wherever he went. Even if no one was with him when he died, he wasn't alone. He had the love with him. Now Miss Tootsie over there—", Miss Lane waved to the empty bed, "she's lucky. She's ending her life surrounded by the people who love her. There's no better way to go. That doesn't mean that the people who aren't surrounded by their loved ones were any less loved during their lives. Look at me. I'm all alone in my death."

Beth was crying again.

"Miss Lane, don't talk like that. You're not dying."

"Don't be silly, child. Of course I'm dying. I'm getting close to it now. My loved one's spirits are here with me, beckoning me on. The only reason I haven't left yet is because of you and Zack listening to my stories. By me telling you the stories of my life, it's keeping the memories alive and a part of me will live on through you and little Zack. Thank you for that. It kept me from passing on without being forgotten. But even though my loved ones aren't here in person with me, just like that young man in Iraq didn't have his family with him when he passed, doesn't mean that I don't have their love. The most important thing in life, more than money, big houses, fancy cars, or important jobs, is to be surrounded by the people you love. All the other stuff comes and goes. Investments fail, houses burn, cars break, careers change. When that stuff's gone, there's emptiness. When the people you love aren't with you, you still carry their love inside. That love was inside of your friend when he died. That love is inside of me and I will carry it over to the other side.

"I'm glad you came so I can say bye to you. The spirits are calling me strong. I don't know how much longer I'll stay on this side. Thank you for bringing my loved ones back to me and letting me end my days with a new friend and good food. Take good care of that little boy of yours. Single mothers raised most of the great musicians in New Orleans. Being raised by a woman teaches them to be sensitive and see the love in life. Not that being raised by a man is bad, but they bring a different energy to the table. Either way is okay, so don't feel bad that you're doing it alone. Tell him that I said goodbye."

Beth held Miss Lane's bony hand up to her face and covered it with her tears. When Beth looked up, Miss Lane's eyes were closed and she had a peaceful look on her face. Miss Lane had passed.

It is said that when difficult times occur, they will either strengthen or destroy a relationship. Both Beth and Jose lost someone close to them in the same weekend. In addition to dealing with their own grief, they had to be there for each other. To Beth, Miss Lane had become like a surrogate mother to her and grandmother to Zack. Since Beth had no extended family, she chose to create her own through her friends, Jose, and people like Miss Lane. She had much loss in the past year, by leaving her old life behind to establish a new beginning for herself. She hoped this new life would be easier, but it already experienced significant loss and struggle. She remembered when her grandparents died and Jeff did not talk to her for two weeks, he was "giving her space so she could grieve." She felt empty and hurt, and needed someone to love her and carry her through the difficult time. Instead she was cast aside, alone in her hurt as if salt was being poured into her sores. Now she found herself hurt and vulnerable again, and was not sure if she would be able to survive if Jose let her down as Jeff had done. The act of existing and the job of surviving were difficult enough to accomplish, she did not know if she was strong enough to push forward through the hard times that are inevitable when one opens themselves up to others. Beth was not sure if she wanted to risk the hurt that came with loving someone. Feeling the loss of Miss Lane after knowing her for such a short time made Beth realize how vulnerable she was to being hurt by Jose. She knew he loved her and that they were happy together, but she had not thought further about their relationship. Where was the relationship going? Would she ever want to get married again? Technically, she was still married. If she did want to get married again, would Jose want to marry someone outside of his culture who had a kid?

Miss Lane always talked about how happy her life had been and Beth wished she could have an easy life like that. When Miss Lane died, she took with her the illusion of a happy life full of old time Jazz music, parties, and happy relationships. Beth wanted her life to be void of grief and suffering and instead be more like Miss Lane's. She wished that her life could be uncomplicated, that she would know what to do, and what the correct decisions were.

Beth could not bring herself to ask Jose what his long term plans were concerning her. Part of her was afraid to ask him because she was afraid he was planning to move on and leave her once they finished the program. Another part of her was afraid that he wanted to always be with her, she was not sure she was ready to make that commitment. Either answer was wrong, so she just pretended that everything was okay and let Jose assume her withdrawn behavior was part of the grieving process. Between school, work, and being there for his family, Jose was too busy to realize that Beth needed him more. There was not more of him to give.

Miss Lane's body was shipped to New Orleans to be buried with her family. After a long wait, Miguel's body was shipped back home to his family. Along with his body came news of how Miguel died. Miguel was patrolling and went to a suspicious looking car parked on the side of the road. As he opened the door to look inside, the car exploded. It was against their training to open doors of empty cars, but when the debris was cleared the body of a small child was discovered in the car. Those who witnessed it stated that Miguel was looking into the car window with a big smile on his face before opening the door. He must have seen the child and opened the door to help it. Maybe it reminded him of his own little boy back home, and his paternal instinct temporarily overtook the knowledge of what he learned in training. A small child had been sacrificed to lure Miguel into opening the door that would set off the bomb that killed him. Beth thought of Zack, baby Miguel, and all of the other children in her life. How could anyone deliberately sacrifice the life of a child for a cause? A pang of guilt briefly went through her chest when she thought of the life that she had prevented from being born. In her mind the two situations were not comparable as the cells that she aborted was not yet a child. Miguel's funeral was nothing like the "funeral parades" that Miss Lane told Beth about. In place of the Jazz music wailing through horns was the holy sound of organ music and the angelic voices of the choir. In place of a parade of musicians and mourners dancing their way from the church to the graveyard, was a funeral procession of a black hearse and limousine followed by many cars with their headlights on and little orange flags closed into their windows that read "funeral." In place of a party with Gumbo and Jambalaya was a reception with Dominican food. Instead of being a joyous occasion that celebrated Miguel's life, it was a time full of grief and sorrow that mourned his death. Beth hoped that Miss Lane's funeral was a celebration of her life like the ones she had described, instead of the mourning of a young life cut short like Miguel's.

Beth became increasingly aware of the love she had for Jose and the fact that she was losing the emotional struggle with herself trying to stay detached. Despite her efforts not to, Beth found herself becoming dependent on Jose during this period of grieving. She realized that in addition to not wanting to be alone, she needed Jose. She was tired of struggling and feeling that she had to create her life by herself. It was too hard. She wanted Jose to depend on and help her through the difficult times. She believed that loving Jose was worth the risk of getting hurt. Stronger than that, she did not think she had a choice as she totally and completely wanted to be with Jose. This realization scared her as she was becoming terrified of how she would survive if Jose left her, she could not handle another loss.

Beth found herself acting differently toward Jose. She got upset if he did not call her or if she did not see him enough, and would get suspicious if he talked about other women. She hated the way she was acting and tried to act as casual as possible around him so that he would not suspect how strong her feelings were. She was afraid that if Jose knew how she felt and did not feel the same way, then he would leave her.

Beth tried to divert her personal insecurities concerning Jose by focusing on Zack, school and work. It was not as easy since going to work was extremely difficult now that Miss Lane was gone. When Beth went into the room to take care of Tootsie, she would look sadly at the empty bed Miss Lane used to occupy. Miss Lane's belongings had been boxed up and put into the linen closet until they received instructions on what to do with them, reminding Beth of Miss Lane every time she opened the closet. Beth wondered if anyone would ever claim this box and why it was being abandoned. If it was not claimed in six months, then it would be donated to the local homeless shelter. Beth hoped that if the box was not claimed then she could keep some of the contents.

Beth was not prepared the morning she came into work and found Miss Lane's large cardboard box placed on the floor behind the desk at the nurse's station. Beth immediately confronted nurse Carol about why the box was moved. Nurse Carol excitedly informed Beth that Miss Lane's nephew had sent a certified letter naming him the executor of Miss Lane's estate and that he and his wife would be coming today to claim her belongings. The strangest part about it was that he had requested a meeting alone with Beth. Beth was terrified and filled with overwhelming mixed emotions. First she was angry and upset that Miss Lane's belongings were being taken away, then she was happy that Miss Lane's belongings were not abandoned and that family was coming for them, and finally she was afraid about why they wanted to meet with her.

The meeting was scheduled for two o'clock that afternoon. Beth was busy getting her work finished, but the entire day she was worried about the meeting and that she might be blamed for Miss Lane's death. Miss Lane never mentioned a nephew. She only talked about her parents, her sister Charlotte, and the neighborhood parties with her cousins, aunts, and uncles. Beth wondered if Miss Lane was ashamed of her nephew, and was afraid to meet him. She wanted to ask Jose if he would come with her, but did not see him the entire day.

Two o'clock finally came. Beth went into one of the downstairs meeting rooms with the big cardboard box and waited for Miss Lane's nephew and his wife. Beth had no idea what to expect and was caught off guard by the handsome, well-dressed man and beautiful woman who entered the room. The middle-aged man was wearing a tailored, tan, three-piece suit, was well shaven with short black hair graying around the sides, and his smile reminded her of Jose. The woman was wearing a bright red skirt and fitted suit jacket with a large matching hat. The pair looked as if they were wearing their Sunday best and going to Easter service. Beth sat in her chair, too surprised by this elegant couple to remember her manners and introduce herself. Luckily, they did not seem as impressed with her and broke the silence.

"Hello. My name is Thomas Lewis and this is my wife Holly. Are you Beth?"

"Oh, Yes. I'm sorry. My name is Beth Parker. It's very nice to meet you both."

Beth stood up and shook each of their hands.

"Thank you for meeting with us. You didn't have to, and it means a lot to us that you did. My aunt spoke so much about you. We felt that we needed to meet you."

"She did?"

"Yes. And we were told that you were with her when she died, is that true?"

"Yes, I'm sorry. There was nothing I could do to help her. I felt so horrible afterward, like maybe I could have done something to save her."

"Don't be silly, it was her time. It's hard that she was here all alone, away from family and all. I'm really glad that you were with her when she died. Was it peaceful?"

"Yes. She had just finished telling me about the funeral parades, and that her loved ones were calling for her. She seemed happy to go to them. How was her funeral? Did she have one of those big parades and parties that she told me about?"

"A funeral parade? No, things aren't the same since Katrina."

"Oh, but she wanted one so bad. She told me all about the parades and parties It all sounded so wonderful, growing up in New Orleans. She told me about the 'good ol' times' when everyone celebrated with the banquets of food, endless parades, dancing and music. What a wonderful life she had."

"Mmmm, that's interesting. I didn't realize she was still living in the past. Did she also tell you about the extreme heat and drinking? About how the combination of the two would cause fighting and riots, one of which killed her baby brother Jo Jo?"

"She had a brother?"

"Yeah, she had a brother. But when he was twenty-two he got in a fight during one of those parties and got stabbed. He died right there in the street with everyone dancing and partying around his dead body."

"That's horrible! Miss Lane only told me about her sister Charlotte, how close they were, how everyone thought they were twins and that it was like they had one soul in two bodies. Was Charlotte at Miss Lane's funeral?"

"Charlotte was my mother. She died about five years ago. Auntie Laney and my mother hadn't talked in over forty years. Not since my mother married Auntie Laney's childhood boyfriend, George, my father. Auntie Lane was so in love with him, they were engaged to get married."

"George? I thought Miss Lane's husband was Stan."

"He was, but she was in love with George. George was trying to save up money so he could prove himself worthy before they got married, but things didn't go as planned. A hot summer night, too much bourbon, mixed with wild dancing and a little teenage lust was the recipe that resulted in my conception. I don't think that either of them meant to do it, Charlotte and George both loved Laney too much to hurt her like that, or to care about each other in that way. Laney went onto the porch in the morning and found the two people she loved most, her sister and her fiancé, passed out and wrapped naked around each other. Auntie Laney freaked out, she went ballistic, attacked them both, throwing furniture everywhere. When my mother discovered that she was pregnant, George did his duty and married her even though he was in love with her sister. Auntie Laney vowed never to speak to either of them again. I think that she had her own private funeral for them."

Beth thought of Maria and her similar situation. Only this case, not only did Charlotte know that her husband was in love with her sister, but she had to go through life knowing she deceived her sister and destroyed their love.

"That's so sad. What happened to your parents and Miss Lane?"

"Well, my father became an attorney and moved up here in the north where he could pursue a career and eventually became a law professor at the university. They rationalized that it was a better carrier opportunity, but I'm sure it was to escape their past. My mother supported my father, but missed Laney horribly. I don't think either of my parents ever forgave themselves for what they did. They grew to love each other in a strange sort of way. I grew up listening to my mother tell stories about when her and Auntie Laney were children together, probably similar to the ones that my aunt told you. I used to hear my mother crying at night when my father was working late. My mother never went back to New Orleans, but she sent me to stay with my grandparents every summer to 'learn my culture.' I spent my summers with the family down there, much of which was with my little cousin Becka and her mother, my Auntie Laney."

"Miss Lane had a daughter? She never mentioned her, I wondered about her husband also."

Beth thought of the pictures that were on the dresser. There was the old picture of Miss Lane and Charlotte, the wedding picture, and the modern picture of a young woman with a little girl. The young woman must be Becka, but who was the little girl?

"So, she told you all about Charlotte and the old days but she never mentioned Becka?"

"No."

"I guess she was also hiding from the past. I suppose she never mentioned Emma either?"

"Who's Emma?"

"Emma was Becka's daughter, Auntie Laney's granddaughter."

"*Was?*"

"Mmmm, Aunt Lane was just added to the long list of deaths in my family caused by Katrina."

"By Katrina?"

"Yeah, by Hurricane Katrina."

"What do you mean? Miss Lane died of old age."

"Yeah, but she wasn't *that* old. In the past year she lost about a hundred and fifty pounds and aged about twenty years. Before Katrina hit, she was an overweight, outspoken, highly energetic 'big mama'!"

"I don't believe you. Miss Lane was frail and skinny. She barely spoke, she was quiet and shy."

"It's called depression."

"Tell me everything."

"Oh, how do I start? My aunt did end up getting married, and although she never stopped loving or missing my father and mother, she never spoke about either of them. I spent my summers playing at her house, but she never held it against me that I was the reason she lost her lover and sister. She actually favored me. Maybe she was holding onto the love she had for my parents through me.

"Her husband, my Uncle Stan, knew that he would never compare to George, but he didn't care. He loved Auntie Laney so much that it was enough just to have her, even if he knew that she didn't love him back. He worshiped the very ground she walked on. He was an amazing musician who could play the horn like you never heard; his suffering manifested into music. He spent his time playing his horn and drinking at the bars, parties, and parades, probably to escape the fact that his wife didn't love him. Those parade parties took away Auntie Laney's brother Jo Jo, sister Charlotte, love of her life George, and finally husband Stan. I don't know why she talked about those parades like they were something great, when they actually stole away every one she loved.

"Auntie Laney and Uncle Stan had a daughter, my cousin Becka. Auntie Laney poured all the love that was meant for my parents and that she refused to give Uncle Stan, into Becka. Her life revolved around Becka, who had the best of everything. Not only was she the princess of the family and neighborhood, but she was the little princess in the queen's court on the Mardi Gras floats. Becka married the high school quarter-back and they had a baby daughter Emma who was the most beautiful baby I ever saw. If it was possible to love a child more than Auntie Laney loved Becka, then she did with Emma who she cared for while Becka and her husband were at work. Auntie Laney couldn't stand to hear Emma cry, so she lay down and took naps with her so that she wouldn't be alone. Becka eventually ended up getting divorced, so Becka and Emma moved in with Auntie Laney. By this time, Uncle Stan died as all the drinking and late nights had worn down his body and he finally checked out.

"When the warnings came to evacuate because of Hurricane Katrina, everything was crazy. I was visiting in New Orleans, and insisted that Auntie Laney come north with me to my father's house. I had to physically drag her into the car, then drove up the coast for her to face my father. Emma was with her father and Becka couldn't get in touch with them. Becka refused to leave without Emma, so we left without them.

"After the storm was over, no one knew where anyone was or who was alive and who was dead. I drove with my father down to New Orleans to find everyone and to help where we could. Nothing could have prepared us for what we discovered. It was like a war zone with miles and miles of destruction. Everywhere we went, the houses had no windows, roofs, or walls. There were no people anywhere. At this point we didn't know if Becka had evacuated. We went to the neighborhood, but the houses were uninhabitable. We had no idea if Becka was dead inside of one of them, so we snuck around searching since we weren't supposed to be there. Eventually people spray painted messages on their houses so their neighbors and friends would know that they were alive somewhere. But at this time, there was nothing and nobody. There were holes that people chopped in the roofs to escape out of their attics and wait for help. It is customary to keep an axe in the attic for this reason. Once on the roofs, however, many people died of the heat and dehydration anyway. The rescue workers spray-painted large X's on the outside of the houses they inspected with codes and the number of corpses found in each house. Word slowly spread among the remaining occupants about who had evacuated or relocated, who had drowned, and who was still around. The people were living in horrific conditions. Everyone was taking care of each other, many people living in small unsanitary FEMA trailers, sometimes eight to ten people in one trailer the size of my living room back home. We questioned everyone about news of Becka, and finally were able to find out that she had evacuated to Houston, TX alone. At least she was alive.

"The next step was to find out where Emma was. We were hopeful that she and her father were able to evacuate. As a last attempt to find her we went to search Emma's father's house again. We had been there before, but it was so filled with water, destroyed furniture and belongings that we couldn't get in. The code on the outside of the house stated that the house had been searched and no bodies were found. In desperation, we decided to search one last time for clues about where they may have gone. This time, the water was gone and we were able to search the house. I will carry the image of what we found in my head forever. There was a horrific stench. We thought a dog or cat had gotten trapped in the house and died. However, when we followed the smell we found the bodies of Emma, her father, his wife, and their two children huddled together in the attic, rosary beads wrapped around the wife's fingers. They went up to the attic to escape the water, got trapped, and the heat baked them alive. For some reason their ax wasn't in the attic, and it cost them their lives. They were the first of Katrina's victims in our family.

"My father grabbed Emma's little dead body, hugged it, and screamed at the top of his lungs, refusing to let it go. I had to pry him away and force him out of the house, but not before he contracted a bacteria infection that eventually took his life. Another of Katrina's victims.

"My father and I went to Houston to find Becka and bring her home. She went berserk when she found out about little Emma and wouldn't come back to Massachusetts with us, she insisted on going to New Orleans where her baby was. Becka couldn't numb her pain with alcohol or antidepressants, so she took the bottle of pills with alcohol and that finally put an end to her pain. Another of Katrina's victims."

"But if Becka committed suicide, how was she a victim of Hurricane Katrina? She didn't die in the flood."

"No, but she died as a result of the damage caused by it. An estimated 1,464 people died in the hurricane and flood itself. However it is estimated that over five thousand people died as a result of it through related consequences such as crime, respiratory and other health issues, depression which led to drug and alcohol abuse and suicide, the list goes on and on. People are still dying today as a result of Katrina, such as my father and Aunt Lane."

"I'm sorry about your father."

"Thank you. My father and I came back to his home where Auntie Lane was. I don't know if the love they had as children was rekindled as they spent their days together, they may have confronted each other about the past, or just chosen to live together in silence. I'll never know. I left the two of them to sort out their past while I went back to New Orleans to do what I could to help. Since I'm a lawyer, I could represent people to protect their property and to get the funds from the government and insurance companies so they could rebuild.

"The trauma and devastation that Katrina left was bad enough, but the aftermath was just about as bad, if not worse. There is a people and a culture forgotten about and abandoned by its government and country. The media managed to convince the country that these were poor people who had nothing to lose and could easily be resituated in other places. It didn't mention that people lost everything that they had, and that these were working middle class professionals. They were teachers, lawyers, nurses, and accountants who owned their homes and paid taxes."

Beth was confused by what Thomas was saying. "But I did see a lot of media coverage about the devastation of Hurricane Katrina in New Orleans when it happened. I thought that everything was going well now."

"See, that's exactly what I'm talking about. When it happened, it was on the news all the time. However, it was also being portrayed that these people would be better off somewhere else and then it eventually stopped being covered. The American public has no idea the conditions that these people are still living in, or what they are dealing with. It's like a third world country right here in the United States with our own citizens.

"The public is aware of the lack of response to get help when the people of New Orleans were dying from the floods, what they don't know is that the floods weren't caused by the hurricane. The sun came out and it was a beautiful day after Katrina left New Orleans. People came out of their homes and were assessing the damage when they began to notice the water level increasing with salt water. The flood came after Katrina, the flood came when the levies broke."

"I thought the levies broke during Katrina, because of Katrina."

"Yeah, the levies broke during Katrina, but not necessarily because of Katrina. There is talk among the locals that many people heard a large bang, kind of like a dynamite blast, when the levies broke. Witnesses say that when the tide went out after the storm, there were holes where the levees had been that looked like blasts. It wouldn't be the first time that the levees had been blown up on purpose. It is well documented by the government that they blasted the levees in Caernarvon, LA with thirty tons of dynamite during the great Mississippi flood in 1927, and then they blasted the levees during Hurricane Betsey in 1965 so that they would prevent the floodwaters from overflowing and destroying New Orleans. So it's not unrealistic that if the witnesses are correct then the levees were indeed blasted during Hurricane Katrina in an attempt to prevent worse damage to the richer areas in the city of New Orleans."

"You're saying that the government is responsible for destroying the levees?"

"Does it surprise you that the government would choose to sacrifice some in an attempt to save others? I hate to disappoint you, but it's all about money and politics. Unfortunately, it's the poor and minorities that suffer the most from the decisions that are made to benefit the polls."

"But I thought the government was helping to rebuild New Orleans."

"How? Through giving the victim's money to rebuild their homes? The government money was used to rebuild the Superdome. In Mississippi each victim was given $150,000 through the 'Road to Home Grant' to rebuild their homes. In Louisiana there is a formula that uses the value of the home less the money received from the insurance companies to determine how much each citizen will receive. The average final result is a minimal amount that would be impossible to rebuild with."

"Then how is New Orleans being rebuilt?"

"Oh, that's a good question, most of the burden is put on the victims themselves. There are many volunteer organizations that help them, and their efforts have contributed to a large percentage of the progress. However, to get insurance reimbursement the work has to be done by a licensed company. Many contractors are taking advantage of the desperation by overcharging for their work. Another extremely important group that is contributing to the reconstruction of New Orleans is the illegal Mexican immigrants."

"What do you mean? How are the illegal immigrants contributing?"

"Well, think about it. They have the skills that are needed to rebuild and the desire to work. The contractors and citizens alike benefit from hiring the Mexican immigrants, and the immigrants benefit from the abundance of work. It's a win-win situation. If someone needs help with some work, then in the morning they go to an allotted spot and hold up the amount of fingers for how many workers they need for that day. They then choose the workers, bring them to the site and pay them each $100 cash at the end of the day."

"I never realized until recently how much our society depends on the work done by illegal immigrants."

"Yeah, they're the silent pillars of our society."

"I didn't know there is so much going on. No wonder you went back to New Orleans to help."

"Yeah. The only thing I regret is that while I was gone my father died. Also, by this time Aunt Lane had stopped eating, lost over hundred and fifty pounds, and was in a major depression. I had her admitted into this nursing home so that she would be cared for. That's where you met her. I'm thankful to you for being with her so that she wasn't alone when she died. Everyone else had already passed. I knew it was just a matter of time before she joined them. At least she had someone to care for her."

Beth was speechless. She had no idea that this kind old lady with the wonderful stories and deep wisdom hid such a horrible story. Her entire life was filled with hurt and deception, yet she chose to remember all of the good times, fun and love that she had in her life. It was amazing that Beth thought she knew Miss Lane so well, yet she actually knew nothing about her. Beth finally brought herself to speak.

"I am sorry for your losses, I had no idea any of this happened. I wish there was something I could do."

Thomas looked over at Holly who gave him a slight nod "yes". Thomas pulled a small package wrapped in newspaper out of his briefcase and handed it to Beth. Beth slowly unwrapped the paper and found a small sterling silver music box in it. When she opened the box the music played "Oh When the Saints Come Marching In." Beth tried to hand it back to Thomas, but he refused to take it.

"Oh no, this is for you. My father gave this to Aunt Lane when they were teenagers in love. Aunt Lane kept it hidden all these years. It was one of the few things that she took with her when she evacuated. Although Aunt Lane kept the box hidden, Becka told me that she used to hear Aunt Lane listening to it and crying late at night when she thought that no one could hear her. You can read the inscription on the bottom, 'To Laney, Love Forever George.' I found it packed in her suitcase. Please take it. I know that Aunt Lane would have wanted you to have it."

"Thank you. I'll cherish it always." Beth was crying as she closed the small box.

Chapter 20

Beth thought about how young and naive she had been when she married Jeff. She had no idea what love was or how much of life was outside the small world that occupied her entire existence. She was oblivious of the love and hurt that was occurring simultaneously as she lived her life and felt that her feelings were the only ones. She thought of all of the people who could not be with or lost the people they loved. Beth thought of Jose and how much she loved him and she realized that she did not want to lose him like Maria lost Dominic or like Miss Lane lost George.

It seemed the routine of work being integrated into the atmosphere of being a student took away the carefree aspect of school. Somehow the adult label that was associated with work replaced the child label associated with school. Beth and Jose still studied together, but not like they used to. They no longer spent hours alone at the library, using each other as pillows. The recent deaths that they were both mourning contributed to a more solemn aura between them.

Sometimes Jose stayed at Beth's apartment until very late into the night. Beth fell asleep wrapped in Jose's arms, but when the morning sun woke her up she found herself alone. When this happened there was an emptiness inside of her that missed him and wondered when he left. Other nights she lay awake with her head on his chest, afraid to fall asleep because she did not want to wake up and find him gone.

One night Beth was lying awake listening to Jose's heartbeat, feeling the pressure of his chest lifting her head up and down as he breathed. He thought that she was asleep and gently began shimmying himself out from underneath her. Beth felt a sudden panic, glad that she was awake and not wanting him to leave her. She held onto him tightly and he stayed a little bit longer.

March fifteenth marked the first anniversary of Beth leaving Jeff. It came and went again, almost unnoticed. Beth was feeling extremely anxious all day without knowing why. It was not until the end of the day when she was driving to pick up Zack that she realized it was one year ago today that she packed her bags and snuck out of the house on a cold spring morning. From that day on, she and Zack's lives would never be the same. She wondered who would be the first to pursue the divorce that had been filed almost a year ago. Would it be Jeff so that he could marry Nancy, or would it be her so that she could marry Jose? Were Jeff and Nancy still together? Would Jose ever want to marry her? Beth could not imagine that she would have the nerve to continue the proceedings, forcing herself to see Jeff again, unless it was so that she could marry Jose. Until then, she imagined that things would remain as they were. She preferred to not aggravate the situation and dreaded testifying at the eventual trial for the assault charges. The anniversary came and went like any other day with the exception that since Beth made it through an entire year, she was confident she would make it from this point on.

With spring came graduation. The early May flowers were in bloom marking new beginnings and hope. In addition to having a small ceremony for the members of the program, they would also participate in the college graduation ceremony. Beth was excited about being included in the college graduation even though she was only completing an assistant nursing program rather than receiving an associates degree. Jose's family was planning a party for Jose and Beth, including Beth's friends. Beth felt honored to be included, since she did not have a family of her own to celebrate with. Beth invited Maria, Vickie, Sheila and her boyfriend, Stacey, Gail, Mia, and Lisa. She contemplated on whether she wanted to invite Rosie and finally decided that she should.

The graduation and party were fun but sad. Beth was proud of her accomplishment, but was afraid of what would happen now that she finished. Would she be able to get a job? Would she still qualify for aid from the state once she started to work? Beth felt a small sense of comfort knowing Jeff would continue to provide health insurance for her and Zack, and the state would continue to attach Jeff's pay for child support. However, the childcare aid would most likely stop and she was not sure if she could afford childcare and fill in the gap between the child support, state assistance, and actual living expenses. She felt horrible thinking that it might be better to not work so that she could continue to get aid from the state, but she knew that was not an option. It was time for her to move on so the services could help someone else to become independent.

It was easier than expected to get a job, as the nursing home Beth did the internship at hired her. It was common for them to hire the interns since they had already seen how people worked. Beth chose to take the night shift from 11:00 P.M. to 7:00 A.M. since it paid more money and she could be home days with Zack. Beth and Maria worked out a schedule where Vickie came to Beth's house in the evenings until bedtime, and Zack would go to sleep in a porta-bed in Vickie's room when Beth left for work at 10:30 P.M. Vickie and Zack would be alone for an hour and a half until Maria came home from work at midnight. Since Vickie was old enough to baby sit and since they were both sleeping, neither Beth nor Maria were concerned about them being alone for this short time. Luckily Zack slept through the night until Beth came home at 7:30 A.M. Zack finished off the year at his "school" at the college and was then able to get accepted into summer day camp through the Crisis Center so that Beth could sleep days. Maria often brought home leftovers from work for Beth, Zack, and Vickie to have for dinner. It was a complicated schedule, but seemed to work well.

Beth did not question Jose when he picked up more hours bar tending instead of looking for a full time job. He eventually informed her that the reason he put off the job search was because he applied for a scholarship for Hispanics to get his bachelors degree in pre-med and eventually go to medical school. He had not told anyone he was applying so that if he did not get accepted then he could keep his disappointment private. He just received the acceptance letter that he got a full scholarship to the University of California and would be moving three thousand miles away in September.

Beth was completely devastated that her fears about him leaving her were confirmed. She was angry at herself for becoming attached and falling in love with Jose, and she was angry and hated Jose for being with her only to leave. She remembered him mentioning that he wanted to be a doctor someday, but she thought it was a "someday dream". She did not think it was today and he would leave her.

He tried to kiss her, but she pushed him away. She did not want him to touch her.

"Beth, please don't be angry. This doesn't mean that I don't love you."

"Fuck you! You're leaving me! You loved me, and now you're just walking away. Why did you even get involved with me if you knew you were going to leave?"

"I didn't know I was going to leave, and this doesn't mean it's over between us. I love you. I'll come home to visit, and will always be there for you."

"Are you saying that you want me to just sit here and wait for you while you're off living your life three-thousand miles away?"

"No Beth, absolutely not. I don't expect you to wait for me, but I also don't believe that it's over between us. I think if it's meant to be, then it will happen. We just have to live life and see where it leads. Maybe we'll be brought back together, but maybe not. If we're not, it doesn't mean the time we spent together wasn't real. I'll carry your love with me for the rest of my life, no matter what happens between us. I love you and that love will never stop, even if distance and life separate us."

"Fuck you, you're an ass-whole!! I hate you for leaving me! I wish I didn't love you."

Jose took his keys out of his pocket and twisted something off the key ring.

"I want you to have this."

Jose handed Beth a light blue stone embedded in silver, "It's called Larimar. It's the stone of the Dominican Republic and comes from the terrestrial crust, or the province of Barahona in the southwestern region of the country. When I miss home, I look into this stone and see the DR's beauty and pale blue oceans. I feel love and happiness knowing that although I'm far from the place I love, I always carry it in my heart.

"I want you to have this stone to know that even though I'll be very far away from you, I'll always carry you in my heart. I bought a necklace for you to wear this Larimar stone on so that you can always carry a piece of me with you. When you miss me or wish that I'm with you, just look into this stone and know that I love and am with you."

Beth wanted to hate him, to punch him and wish him dead. However, the pressure in her heart reached out to him and she found herself hugging and kissing him passionately instead.

"How will I survive without you?"

"You're a phoenix. You'll be more beautiful when I leave."

"What do you mean? How am I a phoenix?"

"As you know, a phoenix is a large mythological bird that lives for 1,100 years and then dies by burning down to ashes. It is reborn out of the ashes to a more glamorous, brilliant and powerful bird. It is beauty and strength that emerge from death and despair. You are a phoenix because when things are at their worst, you emerge more beautiful and powerful than ever. You take hardship and turn it into strength. That's why I love you so much."

With Jose gone, Beth began a new transition of complete independence. She never stopped loving Jose, but no longer had him to depend on. She had to learn to depend on herself for the first time in her life. Every decision she made, she made independently based on her own choices and desires. It gave her a sense of freedom that she did not know existed, as if she could accomplish anything.

The fact that her friends were creating the lives they wanted inspired her and added to her high expectations. Stacey and Gayle were happily raising Mia together. Beth remembered when Stacey was lonely and depressed, convinced that she would never be part of a family, or have a child. Now she was a mother and a wife, a member of a safe, loving family where she could learn to love herself.

Beth and Zack continued to go to church and spend their Sunday afternoons with Stacey, Gayle, and Mia.

Sheila was still dating her former doctor Steve, and was building a strong relationship with her children. After so many years of being degraded and emotionally tortured, she was still healing and was not completely stable. However, she was slowly moving in the right direction.

Beth was especially proud of Rosie who was making every attempt to stay clean and work with Guy to create a home for her children. Guy was proving himself to be everything that Rosie had always wanted from other men, but never got. Rosie had previously thought that by having a baby with a man she would be joining in a stronger union, but instead it pushed them away. Guy never gave Rosie a baby, but he did give her children a father. Where other men did not appreciate her, Guy got angry because she did not love herself enough to take care of herself and her children. He loved her enough to force her to come clean and make a family with him.

Maria was happily creating masterpieces in the kitchen of one of the city's most reputable restaurants. Vickie was thriving in the presence of her mother's confidence. Even Dominic was impressed with Maria's success and came back from Italy to attempt a new beginning. Now that Maria was becoming who she wanted to be, Dominic was falling in love with her individual qualities instead of seeing her as the shadow of Josephine. They were dating and slowly getting to know each other in a way that was never possible before.

Jose's mother Diana frequently invited Beth and Zack over to visit. Since Miguel died, Adia and Pedro got married and moved in together. Although the house always seemed full, Diana claimed that she was lonely and enjoyed Beth and Zack's company. Every one understood that Jose was studying hard and it was both expensive and time consuming to make the trip back to the east coast, but that did not make his absence any easier. Beth enjoyed spending time with Jose's family as she felt that being with them brought her closer to him.

Zack was no longer the baby who thought he was a big boy; he was growing into an actual big boy who was wise and outgoing. He was surrounded by so many people that loved him that Beth felt no loss about not have a biological extended family. Beth did not think Zack remembered Jeff or the abuse until one day when Zack was watching TV and Beth's worst fears came true.

"Hey Mommy, Daddy's on TV!"

Beth froze upon hearing these words and slowly went into the living room to find out what Zack meant. Sure enough, the five o'clock news headlines showed a mug shot of Jeff. The story stated that Jeff went to his girlfriend's work where she was a paralegal in a law office. Apparently they had been fighting because she wanted to break up with him, so he went to her place of employment and aggressively demanded that they talk. One of the attorneys in the office instructed him to leave, but the girlfriend (whose name was not being released) agreed to walk him to the lobby of the building. Shortly after the elevator door closed, there was a huge explosion. Further investigation confirmed that Jeff was wearing explosives attached to his body, which he activated in the elevator killing them both.

Beth thought immediately of Nancy, and knew she was the victim. Beth turned off the TV and hugged Zack tight as she cried. She was thankful that they were safe and knew that if she had not left, then she or Zack would have been Jeff's victim on the five o'clock news. Beth called Lisa to see if she could find out more information about the incident.

Two days later Lisa confirmed that Nancy was the victim and informed Beth that since her and Jeff were still married, all of the marital assets now belonged to Beth. That included the house, Jeff's retirement plan, and all their possessions. Beth vaguely remembered a life insurance policy that Jeff had taken out after Zack was born and wondered if it was still in force. She scrambled through her boxes to find the financial folders she had taken when she left Jeff, she was positive that one of them was labeled "life insurance."

Beth chose not to let anyone from her new life know about what happened with Jeff. She did not want people to know about her past or that her husband was capable of such a horrible act. She secretly took the blame, feeling it should have been her who was killed by Jeff. She felt guilty for keeping the abuse a secret from Nancy, wondering if Nancy would have gotten involved with Jeff if she had known the truth. Beth was too upset to be happy about the money she was receiving. She considered it "blood money," and did not feel she had a right to it since she had been separated from Jeff for almost two years. However guilty she felt, she was not stupid. She sold the house and everything in it, then set up a savings account with the proceeds from the house, the liquidation of Jeff's retirement account and investments, and the proceeds from the life insurance policy which had a death benefit of $500,000. The total amount of money in the account was over $800,000.

Beth was in shock about the entire situation and wanted to keep her new life as it was. She did not want to be treated differently, so for now she was the richest person living in a low-end housing project. She was happy she had the security of a substantial amount of money to provide for Zack.

News that Jose was coming home to visit for two weeks in June was a great diversion from the emotions Beth was feeling about Jeff and Nancy's death and inheriting such a large amount of money. Jose's visits always carried a strong array of mixed emotions. She was ecstatic to see him, but hesitant to give herself totally to him as she did not know where the future would lead.

Beth had not dated anyone else since Jose left, not because of a promised commitment to Jose, but because of a lack of desire to do so. She secretly wanted to date other people so she could escape from the hurt of having Jose leave her, however she could not bring herself to do it. Whenever she met someone who would be a good candidate to date she only saw their faults and how they did not compare to Jose. Instead of taking her mind off Jose, it made her miss him even more. So, she finally gave up on considering the possibility of dating. Beth did not know if Jose dated any one in California even though he said he was too busy studying to date. Beth did not know if it was true or if he did not want to hurt her since they both knew she would have no way of knowing. In accordance with their agreement, he was under no obligation not to date other women. Still, Beth hoped he was telling the truth as the thought of him with another woman made her want to throw up. Thinking of Adia and Pedro being together while Miguel was in Iraq did not give Beth confidence that fidelity existed.

Since she had no other choice, Beth lived her life and looked forward to the short and far between visits from Jose. She had a habit of stroking the cold blue stone that hung around her neck when she thought of him. When he came to visit and they were together, they laughed and made love as if they were never apart. Beth pretended everything was okay, and they enjoyed each other with the little time they had. Now that Jose was coming back for two weeks, Beth had something to focus her thoughts on and look forward to.

Beth insisted on being the one to pick up Jose from the airport. Zack stayed at Jose's mother's house where the entire family waited to greet Jose with a surprise welcome home party.

When Beth saw Jose walking out of the airport doors it was obvious that the stress from college was taking its toll on him. Although he was as beautiful as ever, there was a strain on his face and wrinkles where it had been smooth. The twinkle in his eyes was still there, but they looked tired and worn out. Beth had to catch her breath when she first saw him. The emotion that swelled up inside of her and the joy of seeing him made her forget to breathe. It only took a moment before they were tightly embraced, Jose rubbing his cheek against Beth's head of auburn hair. He was kissing and smelling her hair as he whispered in her ear.

"I missed you so much."

"I missed you too."

"I realized how much I need you."

"I know." Beth barely whispered her reply.

"I'm sorry to ask you this in the baggage claim area at an airport, but will you come back with me? I'm lost out there without you and I need you with me."

Beth was speechless. She never thought Jose would ask her to come to California with him, and up until recently she did not know if she would legally be able to move out of the state with Zack. Now that Jeff was dead, she could move anywhere she wanted and did not have to be afraid anymore. The fact that she was no longer in fear, or the realization that she was totally free to live her life without the shadow of Jeff following her for the rest of her life had not occurred to her before this moment. Jose did not know anything about that and misinterpreted her silence for rejection.

"It's okay if you don't want to come. I understand. It's very far away from home."

"No, no. It's not that. I *do* want to come! I always just wanted to be with you!"

"You do? Will you marry me too?"

"Yes . . . Yes, of course!"

"Yes? Are you sure?"

"It's the only thing I want."

"It's far away from your friends, and you won't know anyone. We'll be poor for a long time. I'll eventually be a doctor but won't be able to give you what you deserve since I won't make the income of a doctor. I want to help my people, so will probably always be poor."

"I know, I know. I don't care. I just want to be with you. I love you."

"I love you too."

They were both crying as they clung to each other, knowing they would never have to let each other go. Beth thought about the money in the bank and decided not to tell Jose about it yet. She knew she would tell him someday. She would have to when they got married. But for now, she kept it a secret.

Beth and Jose announced their engagement to Jose's family at the welcome home party. As was to be expected, everyone was overjoyed and eager to accept Beth and Zack into their family. Beth felt totally welcome and complete.

That night when Jose came to Beth's apartment he drove in her car, unable to leave in the middle of the night. Although Beth did not tell Jose about the money or the cause of death, she did tell him that Jeff died. She knew he needed to know that she was available to marry him both legally and in the eyes of God. If there ever was any guilt about making love when Beth was still married, there was none tonight. It had never been so tender and passionate, or their union so complete. Beth fell into a completely restful sleep where she dreamed again of a white light with the figure of a small child. Only this time, instead of a faceless figure, the form emerged from the light and her features were very clear. The young child was a baby girl with Jose's olive skin, big brown eyes and curls, and a childish feminine version of his features. She smiled at Beth reassuringly, somehow telepathically letting Beth know that her time was coming to return and be born into a loving family with happy parents. There was a feeling of peace and satisfaction on her small face as the light behind her grew fainter.

Beth opened her eyes and looked at Jose's sleeping face. The wrinkles that were there just this afternoon had disappeared. Beth felt at peace knowing that the baby who left her so long ago was waiting to come back to her, Zack, and Jose.

THE END

Edwards Brothers,Inc!
Thorofare, NJ 08086
01 December, 2010
BA2010335